Rob Thy
Neighbor

Rob Thy
Neighbor

A CHARLIE HENRY MYSTERY

DAVID THURLO

MINOTAUR BOOKS

NEW YORK

ROB THY NEIGHBOR. Copyright © 2016 by David Thurlo. All rights reserved. Printed in the United States of America. For information, address St. Martin's Press, 175 Fifth Avenue, New York, N.Y. 10010.

www.minotaurbooks.com

Designed by Omar Chapa

The Library of Congress Cataloging-in-Publication Data
is available upon request.

ISBN 978-1-250-07889-6 (hardcover)
ISBN 978-1-4668-9143-2 (e-book)

Our books may be purchased in bulk for promotional, educational, or business use. Please contact your local bookseller or the Macmillan Corporate and Premium Sales Department at 1-800-221-7945, extension 5442, or by e-mail at MacmillanSpecialMarkets@macmillan.com.

First Edition: August 2016

10 9 8 7 6 5 4 3 2 1

For Aimée

Acknowledgments

I'd like to thank Tom, Linda, Peter, Peggy, and many others in my extended family, plus all the friends and readers who have encouraged me to continue the work that Aimée and I began so many years ago. Your support has kept me going through some very dark moments, enabling me to smile once again.

I also want to acknowledge the contributions made by my agent, Peter Rubie, my wonderful editor, Hannah Braaten at St. Martin's Press, and the skills of a very talented copyeditor who helped smooth out the wrinkles in my storytelling.

Rob Thy
Neighbor

Chapter One

"I think those steaks are close to done, Charles," Gina suggested, nodding toward the gas grill with narrowed eyes.

"Huh?" Charlie replied, raising his voice to be heard over the loud audio from what sounded like a televised movie coming from the town house next door. It was a middle-class neighborhood with small yards, and the source of the noise was less than thirty feet away, across the narrow easement alley.

Nancy Medina, a tall blond APD police sergeant, and petite dark-haired Gina Sinclair's life partner, grimaced and glanced toward the four-foot fake adobe wall running along the property line. "I've never heard them crank up the sound like that before. Sam and Margaret are usually good neighbors."

Blue-eyed Gordon Sweeney, barely taller than Gina but as physically fit as a linebacker in his blue-and-orange Denver Broncos T-shirt and jeans, pushed back his chair from the round redwood picnic table and craned his neck to look over the wall. "Maybe they're having an argument."

Gina shrugged. "What about those steaks, Charlie?"

Charlie nodded. "They're done. Just the way we like them. Help me out here, Gordon." Charlie turned and looked toward the sand-beige stucco-walled house next door. Though that building was larger, the layout appeared to be similar to Gina and Nancy's place, and he could see into the kitchen through the window. "Damn, their entertainment system must be cranked up to ten."

Gordon grabbed a stoneware serving plate and held it out as Charlie stabbed each steak, then placed it atop the big dish. "Sounds like a Terminator movie," he said, nodding toward the wall. "Lots of explosions and gunfire. Definitely not a chick flick."

"The two steaks on top are the raw ones, right?" Gordon asked as he swung the plate around toward the table. Nancy moved the potato salad bowl aside, creating some space.

"Huh?" Charlie grinned, then nodded as Gina caught his attention. "Yeah, nice and juicy, made to order for the Hobbits."

"I consider us the connoisseurs, right, Gina?" Gordon said, taking his seat again beside Gina, a thirtyish attorney with short chocolate hair and delicate features. Today she was wearing a sleeveless top and linen slacks that accented her exotic looks.

Charlie, tall for a Navajo and clad in jeans and a UNM Lobos T-shirt, loved to give his old army special ops buddy and current business partner a hard time about his height. He glanced over at Nancy who, despite her tough job, had the stature and shape of a fashion model, further enhanced by the pale blue slacks and yellow polo shirt that fit her perfectly.

She scowled. "Careful with the trash talk, Charlie, or Gina will make you wash the dishes all by yourself."

Charlie sat down and, using the big fork, placed a steaming hot slab of prime beef onto each of their plates. "Then I'm shutting up and digging in."

Suddenly a woman screamed. The cry came from across the alley.

Nancy turned to look at Gina, who shook her head. "That wasn't the movie."

"Maybe we should go over there and check," Gordon concluded.

The slam of a door being thrown open, then running footsteps, caused them all to look toward the wall. The gate in the alley opened next.

Blam!

A bullet whined overhead. Charlie turned as the sound of broken glass indicated that one of the windows on the French doors behind him had been struck. He jumped up and raced to the wall as footsteps approached from across the alley.

Two arms came up onto the wall, one of them streaming with blood, just as a woman's head appeared. She was trying to climb over, terror in her eyes.

"What the hell?" Charlie yelled, reaching for the woman's upper arms.

"Help me!" she screamed, bleeding from a cut on her forehead.

Charlie lifted the injured woman up onto the wall, recognizing Margaret Randal, whom he'd met on a previous visit. Behind her, holding the open kitchen door of the Randal home, a young man wearing a blue hooded sweatshirt with a disheveled black knit cap in his hand was pointing a pistol in their direction. They were sitting ducks. "Shooter!" Charlie yelled.

The man with the gun hesitated. Charlie quickly yanked the woman over the wall just as the gun was fired. A chunk of the cinder-block wall broke off from the bullet strike, stinging his face and neck with rock-hard fragments. He let himself fall back, using his body weight to pull the woman down, out of the line of fire. Charlie landed on the thin grass, Margaret sprawled atop him.

He rolled over, holding on tightly to Mrs. Randal and covering her with his body. She looked up at him with frightened hazel eyes. "They're taking Sam. Three men . . ."

Gina dropped down on her knees beside Margaret. "I've got her, Charlie. Calling 911," she added, punching out the numbers on her cell phone.

He heard one of the French doors open as Nancy raced into the house, probably for her service weapon.

Charlie jumped to his feet and grabbed his steak knife. "Gordon!" he yelled, looking around, but his pal had already climbed over the wall. Charlie placed the handle of the steak knife in his teeth like some crazed movie pirate and leaped up and over the barrier, the palms of his hands providing all the grip he needed. He was in combat again.

He landed on the hard gravel in the alley with spring in his step. Ahead, beyond the open gate in the Randals' fence, he saw his blond Irish pal enter the back door of the town home, crouched low, knife in his right hand.

"Never take a knife to a gunfight," Charlie muttered to himself as he raced to join Gordon. Without any hesitation at all his buddy was about to take on maybe three armed men with a five-inch steak knife. They'd been in similar situations, but with much bigger knives—and body armor. If ever they needed their hand-to-hand combat skills, this was the time. Their close-quarters training would help even the odds—maybe.

Once inside the Randal house, Charlie realized that the interior wasn't the same as in Gina and Nancy's place. The layout was more traditional, and he was in the kitchen, separate from the living room and formal dining area. To his right was a hallway, leading into the interior, but it was perpendicular to his approach, and all he could see from this angle was the kitchen access.

The din coming from the TV in the next room was so loud he couldn't hear anything else, even the walls shook. A gun went off, the walls shook again, then there was a loud thud. Gordon came into view as he bounced off one side of the hall and staggered back. He leaped forward with a yell and disappeared back into the fray. Charlie ran to help.

Halfway down the fifteen-foot-long hall, his buddy was trading blows and kicks with a man a head taller. From the blue hoodie Charlie suspected it was the same guy who'd fired the gunshots earlier, but now he had the ski mask part of his cap in place. There was a pistol on the carpet behind the attacker, so Gordon had disarmed him. It was hand to hand, with flying feet included.

The shooter was better fighting with hands and feet than with a handgun, clearly, or Gordon would have taken him out by now. Or maybe Gordon had been hit. Charlie noted a steak knife on the carpet, out of reach.

Charlie was blocked off. He couldn't advance without getting in the way, and Gordon's opponent was using the narrow space very effectively. Behind the shooter in the living room Charlie could see a second attacker in a black hoodie and ski mask, trying to haul Sam off the carpet onto his feet. Randal, average height and weight, in his late fifties but fit, was putting up a fight despite having his hands taped together at the wrists. He was kicking and yelling, refusing to stand and even trying to head-butt his attacker.

"Help!" Sam's assailant yelled as his victim suddenly relaxed, falling away to the floor and evading grasping arms.

Immediately a third attacker in a long-sleeved gray sweatshirt and ski mask appeared from around the far corner of the hall, carrying a cloth grocery bag. He aimed a pistol toward Gordon.

Charlie threw his steak knife at the man's head, forcing the shooter to duck just as he fired. The bullet impacted the wall beside Gordon, who was already dodging away from his attackers. This gave the man engaging in the martial arts standoff with Gordon a chance to make a dive for the pistol on the carpet.

"Get back!" Charlie yelled, yanking a framed photo off the wall and throwing it at the attackers.

"Hit the floor, boys!" Gina yelled angrily from somewhere behind Charlie. As Charlie dove to the carpet he saw two pistols swinging around toward him.

Gina fired a shot, barely missing the perp trying to grab Sam. The bullet hit the big-screen TV, and suddenly the shattered machine was quiet, except for some electronic snaps and crackling sparks. She ducked back around the kitchen corner as the intruders fired two shots in her direction.

"Forget Randal, let's go!" one of the men shouted, firing another shot toward the kitchen. Charlie grabbed Gordon and yanked him out of the hall and around the corner just as the bullet flew by.

Charlie heard the door open in the living room and the sound of running footsteps. Jumping to his feet, he looked over at Gina, who was behind the kitchen island, pointing her SIG .380 toward the hall with shaking hands.

"Take it," she whispered, sliding the small pistol across the hard stone surface.

Charlie picked up the weapon. "They're outside!" Sam yelled from the living room.

"Where's Nancy?" Charlie asked, moving quickly, Gordon right behind him, steak knife back in hand.

"She circled the block and is coming around the front—I think!" Gina yelled back. "She needs help!"

Charlie reached the front door just as Sam scrambled to his feet. "Stay here," Charlie ordered, heading outside.

"Margaret?" Sam asked.

"Safe," Gordon answered as he ran past the man, just a few steps behind Charlie.

Charlie raced down the narrow sidewalk toward the street, looking for movement in both directions. Hearing running footsteps, he turned and saw Nancy coming around the corner about a hundred feet to his right, carrying her service weapon.

"There they are!" she yelled, pointing up the street.

Looking left past Gordon, who'd come up beside him now, Charlie saw a faded gray Chevy van parked across the street three houses down.

The masked driver stuck out his arm and fired two shots in their direction.

Gordon dove to the grass. Charlie dropped to one knee, raised his pistol, but spotted a jogger coming down the street just beyond the van. "Get off the street!" he warned as the van pulled out, accelerating with squealing tires. The runner swerved for the sidewalk, diving onto the grass beyond just as the van raced past. Gordon, who'd jumped up and was giving chase, stopped and checked out the jogger, helping the young woman to her feet.

Nancy lowered her weapon as the van reached the end of the block and skidded around the next corner, disappearing from sight. "Everyone here okay?" she yelled, jogging over to join him. "Gina? I heard gunshots coming from the house."

"We're fine, even Sam, I think," Charlie responded, thumbing

Gina's pistol on safety and slipping it inside his jeans pocket. "What about Margaret?"

"I called 911. A bullet sliced a groove down her forearm. I left her conscious and pressing a towel against the wound," Nancy answered. "Somebody needs to . . ."

"I'll take care of her," Gordon offered, jogging back to join them. "I'll go over the wall. It's quicker than circling the block." He turned and raced toward the Randals' open front door, where Gina now stood, looking out into the street.

"How's Sam?" Nancy asked as she and Charlie came up the sidewalk. "And you?" she added, giving Gina a quick hug.

"I'm still shaking," Gina replied.

They stepped into the living room, where Sam was down on his knees, unplugging the television cord from the wall socket despite the fact that his wrists were still taped together. He looked up. "It was still sparking, and the lights were flickering. I was afraid it might start a fire," he mumbled, then struggled to his feet. "Where's Margaret? Is she okay?"

"Gordon is going to take care of her until the EMTs arrive," Nancy explained, reaching over and touching his shoulder. "A bullet grazed her arm, and she's got a cut on her forehead."

"Help me get this tape off. She needs me." Sam's voice rose an octave.

"You have to stay here and tell the officers what happened," Nancy said, blocking his way. "Gina?"

"Yeah, I'll go help Gordon with the first aid," Gina offered. "But I'm going around the block instead of across the alley. That wall is a bitch to climb."

"I can toss you over, girl," Charlie offered with a grin, handing her the SIG before taking out his pocket knife to cut away the tape on Sam's hands. "You were a cheerleader in high school, remember, always at the top of the pyramid. Tumbling was one of your gigs."

"I'm retired now," she replied, checking to verify the pistol safety was on. "See you in a while," Gina added, then slipped by Sam and hurried out the front door.

A few minutes later, the EMTs' white and blue unit raced down the street past the Randal house, siren wailing, then turned the corner, circling around to Gina and Nancy's house.

"I've gotta be with Margaret," Sam insisted, standing to look out the window.

Nancy, who had a phone to her ear, shook her head and reached out, putting her hand on the man's shoulder again. "Only if you need the EMTs to check you out. Did they rough you up?"

He shook his head. "They just wrestled me to the carpet. I don't need a medic."

"Then let them take care of her. You'll have to wait until the officers have taken your statement anyway. Gordon and Gina have already stopped the bleeding, and Margaret is alert and talking to them. Here she is, talk to her yourself," she added, handing him the phone. Sam sat down again.

Nancy turned to Charlie. "You need to take Gina to the emergency room to be with Margaret so she'll see a friendly face and be able to feel safe again. Here's a squad car now, Sam." She nodded toward the window as a police cruiser pulled up.

"I'll take the shortcut across the alley," Charlie said, then turned to Sam. "Hang in there, okay?"

"Yeah. And thanks for all you did. You and . . . Gordon," Sam said, then turned away and spoke into the phone again. "I love you," he said to his wife, "and I'll be with you as soon as I can."

•   •   •

Gina looked up as Charlie dropped down off the wall onto her lawn. Margaret had been moved over into the shade beneath the roof overhang and had her head on a pillow taken from the sofa inside. The wound on her right forearm had been covered with a large first-aid-kit trauma pad, and Gina was using a cotton ball and antiseptic to clean up a small gouge in Margaret's forehead that was still bleeding.

Margaret had her eyes closed but held a cell phone to her ear.

"Got the bleeding on her arm under control," Gina whispered. "Gordon is—"

"Here with the medics," Gordon said, stepping out the open French door. "Watch the broken glass, people." He motioned toward Margaret with an outstretched hand, giving two EMTs in blue and white uniforms room to pass.

"Me too. Talk to you soon," Margaret said, then opened her eyes and handed the cell phone to Gina, who moved away so the medics could set down their cases of medical supplies and get to work.

Gina and Charlie stepped over to the picnic table, and she sat down, brushing away a fly from her cold steak. "Sorry about lunch," she said softly.

"Nobody can ever say you don't throw an exciting barbecue, cutie," Charlie replied with a grin, then looked down at the pistol sitting beside Gina's plate.

"You haven't called me cutie since high school, Charles," Gina said, rolling her eyes.

"Missed hearing it?"

"You still think I'm cute?"

"Naw. Now you're beautiful."

"You guys talking about me again?" Gordon said, coming over to the table.

They laughed; then Gina sighed and stood. "While the medics are getting Margaret ready to transport, can I get you guys to help me move the food back into the kitchen? No sense in creating a temptation for the neighborhood cats."

"Yeah, I say let them eat . . . mice?" Gordon said, grabbing two plates.

"Suppose the potato salad is still any good?" Charlie asked, looking at the big covered bowl.

"Who knows? Let's put it back in the refrigerator, then Google for advice on the way to the ER," Gina suggested. "But hurry. I told Margaret I'd stick with her at the hospital, and you two will need to get back here ASAP to talk to the detectives. They can get my statement later." Gina, as an attorney, was very familiar with law enforcement requirements during an investigation.

Charlie looked over at the EMTs, who'd already checked Margaret's vitals and applied more bandages and were waiting for an ambulance to transport their patient.

"Gordon, you got into action first and had already disarmed one of the bad guys by the time I arrived," Charlie suggested. "Why don't you stay here with Nancy and Sam and get the ball rolling with the cops? I'll take Gina to the hospital, then return to give my statement."

"Okay, guys, now that we have a plan, let's get this stuff inside before it starts to draw more than just flies," Gina said. "Oh, and Gordon, make sure to sign over my handgun to the crime scene techs. They'll probably need to keep it for a while. I'll leave it on the breakfast counter."

Five minutes later, Charlie and Gina were in his purple Dodge

Charger, driving southwest from Albuquerque's east side toward Saint Mark's Hospital, which was located downtown. The ambulance was already on the way, but there was no real emergency, so Charlie didn't push the speed.

After more than one experience as an armed civilian involved in a shooting, Charlie knew the procedure by now and was glad that it was Gina's pistol changing hands and not his own. Gina had fired her weapon, so the crime team would need to examine and process the handgun. Fortunately, he had his concealed carry permit and the Beretta 92 9 mm in the car at the moment. There was no reason to suspect he or Gina was in any danger, except for the fact that he and Margaret were the only witnesses who'd actually gotten a look at the shooter's face, and the bad guys were still on the loose.

"Hey, Gina, does Saint Mark's security know that Margaret can probably identify her shooter? He wasn't wearing his ski mask when he fired those shots," Charlie said as they stopped at a red light. "She should have protection."

"You're right. Margaret mentioned yanking away his cap. She also thinks she scratched his face, so they might be able to get DNA from beneath her nails. I passed that info along to Nancy over the phone, and she promised to give them a call. Did you hear if Sam also got a look at the perp?" Gina responded.

"No, but I sure did," Charlie said. "Dark-haired Anglo male in his late twenties, brown eyes, and a scar or mark above his left eyebrow. Maybe from that scratch. I could pick him out of a lineup."

"Well, two witnesses are better than one. You think that'll make you a target too?" Gina ventured.

"It depends on how worried this shooter is about getting

busted. If this wasn't his first crime, he might have a record," he answered. "And they were trying to hide their faces . . ."

"I hope whoever gets the case can track down these felons before they strike again. There have been several home invasion incidents the past few months. On the phone just now, Nancy said some have involved three perps, like today," Gina pointed out.

"Does she know who's working these cases?" Charlie asked, slowing to take the next corner. He could see the hospital now, standing fifteen stories high just off Central Avenue and nearly alongside the interstate just east of Albuquerque's Downtown district.

"Didn't have time to ask. You hoping it's Detective DuPree? He is a good cop, and he knows all of us."

Charlie shrugged. "That's for sure, but . . ."

"He might not be so happy to see you or Gordon again so soon. That what you're saying?" Gina couldn't help but smile as she looked over at him.

"Something like that. No, exactly like that." Charlie nodded. "We've got a history with that guy. Now, before we get to the ER, what else was Margaret able to tell you about the break-in before the medics took over?"

Chapter Two

Gina was used to cutting to the chase. "Margaret was in the kitchen, cleaning up after lunch, while Sam was putting a movie into the home theater system. Someone knocked at the front door, and Sam opened it up automatically. Margaret heard a scuffle and stepped into the hall to see what was going on. Three armed men with masks were manhandling Sam, and when they saw her, one of them pointed a gun and motioned for her to join them in the living room. Another turned up the TV sound, grabbed her purse off the bench in the entryway, and put it into one of those canvas grocery bags. Then he pushed her toward the bedroom, ordering her to fill the bag with her watch and jewelry."

"They were already wearing gloves, right?"

Gina nodded. "Yes, I asked her about that. She emptied her costume jewelry from one of those standing jewelry cabinets and put it in the bag. The robber then pushed her back into the living room, where one of the others grabbed the bag and added Sam's cell phone, wallet, and watch."

"What about their wedding rings? I noticed Margaret still had a big diamond on her ring finger," Charlie pointed out.

"Don't know. Maybe they didn't notice that or her earrings, which she was also still wearing. I'm sure the detectives will ask."

"So what about Sam?"

"They'd taped his wrists together by the time Margaret was led back into the living room. One of the robbers who'd been with Sam ordered the other two to take Sam to the van. Then he grabbed Margaret by the arm. When he started to push her into the bedroom again, Sam yelled and broke free for a second. Margaret screamed and grabbed at the guy's ski mask, scratching and trying to poke him in the eyes. The mask came off, apparently. She kicked him in the groin and ran through the kitchen and out the back door, heading for the back gate and the alley."

"That's when he started shooting," Charlie concluded.

Gina nodded. "Any more details than that, we'll find out later, I guess," she said, looking out the window toward the emergency room entrance as Charlie maneuvered the Dodge into the visitor lot. It was Sunday afternoon, and there were a few empty slots.

"I'll stay here so I can keep watch over Margaret. I doubt she'll be needing surgery, but I'm not a doctor, so I'll have to wait and see what they say. You have to go back to the crime scene to be interviewed by the investigating officers," Gina reminded Charlie, stepping up and out of the low-slung Charger.

"I'll walk you in," Charlie said, joining up with her as she came around to the front of the car. "How will you get home? Nancy?"

"Yeah, unless she's immediately assigned to the case. Right now she's working burglary out of downtown and is supposed to be off today, but that can change depending on department needs,"

Gina said, picking up the pace as they reached the wide sidewalk leading to the emergency entrance.

Saint Mark's was a massive dark red, almost purple brick and stone structure built in the late forties or early fifties. Charlie remembered it from his childhood, when his grandparents had been patients at the diabetes treatment center. An impressive structure to someone who'd never stood next to a building more than a few stories high while growing up on the Rez, Saint Mark's still looked the same in his eyes, at least from the outside.

A half hour later, Charlie walked up the sidewalk to the Randals' home, having parked at Nancy and Gina's and come around the end of the block. The street now had orange traffic cones restricting access. The RV-sized Albuquerque Police Department Crime Lab unit was parked at the curb along with three APD police cruisers and an unmarked detective vehicle with a code number Charlie recognized. He'd already learned, via a phone call from Nancy while en route, that Detective DuPree was the investigating officer.

He'd reached the yellow crime scene tape that further defined the area of focus when a familiar-looking uniformed officer came over to greet him.

"Mr. Henry, glad you're here. Looks like you've walked into another one." Officer Roseberg greeted him with a smile. "You fire any weapons this time?" The young, slender officer, who'd met Charlie during an investigation last year, held out his hand hesitantly.

"No such luck," Charlie replied, shaking his hand. Unlike many traditionalists in the tribe who didn't like touching strangers, Charlie now was a merchant, half owner of FOB Pawn, and every greeting or transaction began or ended with a handshake.

"Detective DuPree inside?" Charlie nodded toward the front door.

"He said to send you right in," Roseberg replied, holding up the yellow tape so Charlie could duck under.

"Thanks, I think," Charlie said, then strode up the narrow walkway. He recognized DuPree's monotone voice immediately, an affectation that Charlie suspected was meant to disarm his subjects, suggesting he was just going through the motions and not really paying attention.

Actually, DuPree was quite good at getting answers from the lower-IQ criminals who'd managed to get caught. Charlie's dad, Al senior, was a retired lawyer and tribal judge, and had advised his children many times in their youth not to be stupid enough to commit a crime.

"About time you showed up, Henry," came a familiar voice. The sandy-haired detective, about Charlie's height and weight but with a lower center of gravity, stepped out onto the covered porch, this time wearing a wrinkled cotton shirt and blue APD windbreaker instead of his checkered tan sports jacket. It was a hot summer.

"How's Mrs. Randal doing?" DuPree asked, holding out his hand for a quick shake.

"She got lucky with the bullet scratch and should recover completely, according to what I heard, except for a nice scar. The doctors want to keep her overnight," Charlie replied, following the detective into the living room and directing his last sentence to Sam Randal, who was seated on the sofa.

"Thank God!" Sam replied. "Gina was going to call and let me know."

"Gina thought she should wait until the interviews here were completed," Charlie explained, looking over at DuPree, who nodded, then at Gordon, who winked. His longtime friend and business partner was standing in the kitchen, coffee cup in hand, watching two of the crime scene team at work.

"I'll be going to Saint Mark's when I'm done here to get Mrs. Randal's statement, but right now I need to talk to you, Charlie, and Mr. Sweeney." DuPree paused, then turned to Sam. "Mr. Randal, I'm done with you for a moment, so I need you to step into the bedroom or maybe out back while I interview these witnesses. Just don't go off the property or talk to anyone other than my people. That includes using your phone. Once we're done here, you can go join your wife."

"I understand," Sam said, rising to his feet but wavering slightly.

DuPree reached out and steadied the man with a hand on his shoulder. "You sure you don't need to see a doctor, Mr. Randal?"

"Oh no! I'm still a little shaken up, that's all," the man said. "I'll be in the bedroom if you need me for anything."

Gordon came over, passing by Sam and giving him a nod.

DuPree motioned toward the sofa with a wave of his left hand. "Normally I'd separate you two, but you seem to feed on each other in a positive way, and by now I know I can trust you both. Take a seat and tell me what you heard, saw, and basically what happened this afternoon, starting with you, Sweeney. You were the first person to come upon the scene here, right?" DuPree asked, choosing the empty armchair for himself.

"Right, DuPree," Gordon answered, coffee cup in hand. "But Charlie was actually the first to get involved. How about we go back and forth with the sequence of events so it'll make sense, then you get into the specifics?"

"Whatever, but I'm going to write it up separately. You guys are pains in the ass, but at least you get the facts straight and pay attention to details," DuPree said, shaking his head. "You first, then, Charlie."

It took almost an hour before the interview concluded and Detective DuPree left for the hospital to speak to Margaret Randal. By then, Charlie had learned how Gordon had disarmed the perp who'd fired the shot that hit the woman, and his buddy's evaluation of the man's martial arts skills, which were, in Gordon's words, pretty damned good but not derived from military training. The implication was that the guy was probably their leader, and also a serious student of the discipline with at least a few years of experience in a martial arts program.

DuPree appeared to take that evaluation seriously and hoped it would lead to the narrowing of suspects. Another piece of good news was that Gordon heard a snap and moan when he first disarmed the shooter. There was a good chance that the man now had a broken or injured index finger on his right hand. If there was also DNA from the scratch, and it was on file, they might get enough evidence to make an arrest.

Important right away was the description Charlie was able to give from his quick look at the man after Margaret had pulled away his mask. Gordon, an excellent artist, quickly drew a pencil sketch based upon Charlie's observations, and DuPree took the drawing with him.

Just as DuPree was climbing into his unit, even better news arrived. One of the APD officers canvassing the neighborhood had discovered that the residents of the home where the bandits had parked the van had a security camera mounted on their porch.

DuPree now had potential video surveillance to add to Charlie's description. For once, the detective drove away with a smile on his face.

"Hope the surveillance images and Charlie's description lead to a suspect," Gordon said, standing in the kitchen with Charlie and Sam as the crime scene team packed up their gear, "and that DNA evidence will result in a conviction."

"The bastard needs to spend the rest of his life in prison," Sam declared. "He tried to kill my wife."

"Well, now that the cops have a better idea who to look for, that'll definitely speed up the process," Charlie replied, sipping from a bottle of water Sam had offered. "And that sketch you made was nearly perfect, Gordon."

"Nearly?"

"Too bad the crew already had their masks on when they showed up at your door, Sam. Your own camera collected really good images, but . . ."

"I never should have opened the door without checking through the peephole. But it's Sunday. Who invades someone's home on the weekend around lunchtime? I thought it was one of my neighbors," Sam responded. "We could have been killed."

"Sometimes, when you're supposed to be safe, at home, that's when you're most vulnerable," Gordon mumbled, now staring out the kitchen window.

Charlie looked over at his pal, shrugged, then turned back to Sam. "Well, Nancy's left for the hospital, and the crime scene people are probably close to done now, so I think it's time for me and Gordon to leave. You heading for the hospital too, Sam?"

"Yeah, but first I want to discuss something with you and

Gordon—once the police are finished." Sam nodded toward the living room.

Gordon turned to face Sam, then glanced over at Charlie, who shrugged. "Okay with me."

"Yeah," Gordon added. Then his stomach growled.

"In the meantime, how about I order us a pizza?" Sam suggested, smiling for the first time in hours. "Your cookout didn't exactly fill you up, did it?"

By the time the pizza arrived, the crime scene team was gone, along with the yellow tape that had blocked off the front of the house and a portion of the street. Sam hung up the phone, after calling to check on his wife, and sat down at the table where Charlie and Gordon were already helping themselves to the early dinner.

"How's she doing?" Charlie asked after taking a swallow of iced tea.

"She's asleep, according to Gina. She's been given something for the pain, along with antibiotics. When we're done here, I'll go see her," Sam added, his tired expression showing his age, which Charlie judged to be late fifties. Margaret was easily fifteen years younger and, according to Gina, had been Sam's office manager at his construction company when they'd married. Judging from the expensive furnishings, Sam's business was prospering.

"So, why did you want us to stick around, Sam?" Gordon asked. "If you wanted to thank us for helping out today, the pizza is enough."

Sam smiled, then sat back and thought about it a moment. "I can't help but wonder what they planned to do with me and Margaret. From what I've seen on the local news, at least with one of the most recent home invasions, the victim was kidnapped and dumped out in the desert to find his way back."

"That would give the remaining home invaders plenty of time to ransack the place," Charlie responded with a nod. "I've also seen those news reports, but if I recall, the victims have usually been elderly men or women living alone in upscale neighborhoods. I think this is the first time they've targeted a couple. Did you have any sense of their motives?"

"Well, when the screaming and shooting started, their plan, if they had one, quickly went to hell. I'm guessing they somehow found out where I lived and intended to hold me for ransom. My company has done very well—commercial construction and remodeling exclusively. There was a big article on me and the company in the business section of the local paper a few weeks ago."

"So why aren't you living in one of those McMansions along Rio Grande, or one of those gated communities up in the foothills?" Gordon asked.

"I've never been that image conscious. I prefer a low profile, if you know what I mean, where you won't set yourself up as a target. Our house, from the outside at least, is very middle-class, in a middle-class neighborhood. Until recently I drove a ten-year-old Chevy pickup. I have a two-year-old Camry now, and Margaret has a Honda Accord. We're not flashy people. Besides, living next to a police sergeant has made us feel very safe. Well, until now," Sam confessed.

"That proximity paid off today. You're here, and Margaret is safe and should recover completely, according to Gina," Charlie pointed out.

"Okay, let's get back to the issue. I'm guessing you want our advice on better ways of protecting you and your wife," Gordon said.

"In a way," Sam said, nodding. "I know from the news and talking with Nancy and Gina that you two have been involved in helping solve some criminal investigations, even though you're private citizens and business owners, not law enforcement. I also hear that you've both had extensive military experience and can take care of yourselves. Special forces, right?"

"Not *the* Special Forces, but yes, we've been involved in classified operations while in the Army," Charlie said. He didn't like talking about the special ops work he and Gordon had done in Iraq, then Afghanistan. Besides, it was all classified and often involved the snatching of high-value targets for CIA intelligence-gathering operations.

"Is someone connected to your business behind what happened today?" Gordon asked flat out. "Is that what you're thinking?"

Sam shrugged. "I can't rule that out. I do know that Detective DuPree and APD are anxious to track down the individuals who are carrying out these home invasions. The crimes really seem to make the news, particularly because they usually strike retired people alone, widows or widowers who live in wealthy neighborhoods. The fact that these crimes have been going on for several months now without any arrests makes it even worse. Law enforcement officers have been taking a lot of bad press, and they need a win."

"But you want us to find out if the three that broke in today and tried to kidnap you had other motives?" Charlie prodded. "Motives that don't fit the pattern."

"More than just robbing us and maybe stealing the vehicles, yes. I'd like you two to look into that, below the radar, I think is the proper wording here. I need you to protect Margaret, and me, and the best way of doing that is by being proactive—find the threat and take it out."

"Whoa, we're not hit men, and we're not going to do anything that breaks the law," Charlie responded, "even if we do take on this job."

Sam paused for a moment before answering. "No, no, I'm not asking for anything like that, not at all. But from what Nancy and Gina say, you two have excellent investigative and defensive skills that any law enforcement agency would welcome, and if attacked can defend yourself very effectively. Money is not an issue. I can pay you more than you'd ever get working for the police. Cash, even, if that's what you'd prefer."

Charlie looked over at Gordon. His expression was completely neutral, and to Charlie, that meant no. They'd worked together for so many years that much of their communication came in subtle expressions. "We have a business of our own to run, Sam."

"I also know how to run a business, and if I understand the situation, you have two very competent employees who can take up the slack if you have to be away for an hour or two at a time."

"We'll think about it," Gordon offered, looking over at the empty pizza box with sad eyes. "For now, though, didn't you want to visit your wife?"

"You're right. But I'm a little sore from getting roughed up by those punks. Would one of you drive me over? We'll take the Camry."

Charlie looked at Gordon, thinking that what Sam wanted

was a protective escort, not a chauffeur. "You drive, and I'll follow in my car. That way nobody will be stranded."

Sam nodded. "That'll work. If you guys don't mind. I'd really like to spend the night there with Margaret, but I'll need a way back home eventually, and if they let her come home tomorrow we'll be all set."

"Okay with me. Gordon?"

"Yeah, assuming you'll bring me back to Nancy and Gina's. My pickup's here, remember?"

"Then let's go. Okay if I make a quick change first?" Sam asked, heading for the bedroom.

Five minutes later, Charlie was in his Charger, sticking within the speed limit and following several car lengths behind the white Camry, heading west, retracing his earlier drive with Gina. Gordon, like Charlie, usually knew the quickest route anywhere in the urban area.

They'd arrived in Albuquerque fresh out of the service less than three years ago and had shared an apartment until going into a business partnership. They'd snatched up the north valley pawnshop, getting a bargain after the dirtbag owner had stopped paying the mortgage and dropped out of sight. By now they both knew their way around the city as if they'd grown up there.

Gordon was, after all, a child of the city. He'd been raised, roughly, in Denver, by a dysfunctional family in a run-down, violent neighborhood. By comparison, Charlie was the exception rather than the norm among Navajos—he'd grown up in Shiprock, on the Navajo Nation, but with professional parents and in a tribal-supplied house with all the modern conveniences, including running water, air-conditioning, and even a carport. His father was a retired judge with a law degree from UNM, and his mom had been a public school teacher for nearly three decades. Both lived their golden years—Mom called them silver—in their own home just off the Rez, east of Shiprock.

Still several blocks from the hospital, which stood lit up and imposing in the evening sky at this hour, Charlie was brought back down to earth when he was forced to stop as the traffic light suddenly turned from a quick yellow to red. Brakes squealed right behind him, and he clinched his grip on the steering wheel, hoping he wasn't about to be rear-ended.

The glare of headlights was harsh, and he reached up for the tab that would change the angle of the mirror and show a mere reflection rather than direct beams. The driver of the big SUV behind him was flipping him off. On a Friday or Saturday, this all too common gesture often resulted in angry words, a fistfight, or even gunplay. But this was Sunday, for God's sake, and he'd pretend he hadn't noticed.

Road rage was something to watch out for. Alert to the driver behind him, Charlie quickly realized the man behind the wheel wasn't alone—he was with two passengers. All three had on knit caps, and it was probably eighty degrees outside right now.

Somehow, these must be the home invaders again. But why? "Gotta warn Gordon!" Charlie mumbled as he groped for his cell phone. At least his pal and Sam were armed. Charlie had seen a handgun beneath the man's windbreaker after he'd changed clothes.

Suddenly the SUV whipped around him and raced through the intersection, barely missing a pickup entering from the right. The driver swerved and braked hard, almost T-boning the SUV.

A phone call would be a distraction at just the wrong time,

Charlie realized, if a drive-by was about to go down. He checked to see if he could run the light and saw the opportunity. Flooring the Dodge, he cleared the intersection and followed the SUV down the four-lane street, burning rubber and honking the horn in annoying cadence, knowing that would get everyone's attention.

Gordon had good instincts. He whipped the Camry to the right onto a two-lane side street just east of the hospital, trying to get out of the way. The SUV braked hard, following the Camry into the turn.

Charlie made up lost ground quickly, sliding through the corner with ease. Then he remembered this was a dead-end street with parking lots on either side. Gordon knew it too.

The Camry ahead slid around in a one-eighty, taking the width of the street for the maneuver, now facing the onrushing SUV head-on. The vehicle skidded to a stop, and the doors flew open on both sides of the big Chevy. Three masked men jumped out, guns in hand, and stood behind the opened doors, aiming at the Camry. Two were on the passenger side.

Charlie flipped on the emergency lights and hit the horn in one long, loud tone, then yanked the wheel to the left, going into a sideways slide that blocked the center of the street, trapping the SUV in the middle. He and Gordon were armed now; it was going to go down a little different this time. Hopefully Sam knew how to use his weapon, or at least how to stay behind cover.

Charlie reached for his Beretta, which was resting in a holster attached to the right side of the steering column below the dash, then swung open the door and crouched down beside the outside curve of the windshield, the engine block between him and the SUV. At the same time, as he'd done dozens of times over the past decade, he used his thumb to release the safety as he brought the weapon up, aiming automatically toward the closest target, two men by the passenger side door.

All three of the perps turned their heads at pretty much the same instant. There was a four-second pause as they pondered their situation.

"Lower your weapons!" he yelled. Too late. One of the men whirled around, a curse on his lips, and fired two quick shots. Charlie squeezed the trigger and put a 9 mm slug in the center of the idiot's chest.

Bullets began flying in his direction, and Charlie dropped below the engine block, moving quickly to the front bumper.

"They're getting away!" Gordon yelled as Charlie looked up, pistol first. The driver was racing toward the hospital about fifty yards to his left, and the second perp toward the big parking lot across the street.

"Call for help and stay with Sam," Charlie yelled. "I've got the driver." As he raced toward the fleeing figure, who'd already swerved away from the hospital's side entrance, Charlie heard his pal yell, "Copy."

A well-groomed lawn surrounded the front and sides of the big building, but the driver was now running toward the rear of the structure, where there was a basement-level emergency entrance and ambulance port. Next to it was a small parking lot Charlie knew was reserved for doctors and administrators. If the punk planned on taking a hostage, that was a good place to catch a member of the staff coming outside. Hopefully the gunshots would scare everybody off and they'd stay in the building.

The layout of the grounds forced the running man to move more to the right, and he reached the edge of the lawn, where there was a four-foot drop from a concrete retaining wall to the asphalt below. He came to a stop, turned to look back, then jumped down and dropped out of sight.

Suspecting an ambush, Charlie decided to hug the building and slip down to where the retaining wall connected with the structure. He came to the end, took a quick look, and saw the driver crouched low, running along the wall back toward the street. If he continued in that direction, he'd come out behind Gordon and the Camry.

"He's heading your way!" Charlie yelled, then flipped on the safety and jammed the Beretta in his belt before jumping down onto the driveway.

Hearing Charlie, the fleeing man cut to his left and moved away from the wall and among the high-end vehicles in the restricted lot. Again he dropped out of sight for a moment. Charlie stopped, watching for movement. The area was well lit and only about half full. After a few seconds Charlie saw a moving shadow. The man had made it through the lot and was now running up the alley north of the main building.

Charlie raced to cut him off but suddenly heard a voice to his left near the ambulance port. "Stop or I'll shoot."

A bad guy wouldn't have given him a warning, so Charlie complied. He turned toward the security guard, a man in his late forties crouched in a Weaver stance, revolver aimed right at him.

"I'm working with the police," Charlie offered the white lie, "and the man I'm chasing is one of the home invaders who shot a woman this afternoon."

"Or maybe you're the shooter," the guard responded. "Let me see your hands." His voice was a bit shaky.

"Okay. Just stay calm. Here are my hands," Charlie replied, working to keep his voice calm and unemotional despite the flow of adrenaline. He turned at the sound of sirens and saw the flashing lights of a police car coming up the main artery in front of the hospital. Facing the amped-up rent-a-cop, he was glad that the man didn't know he had the Beretta tucked into his belt at the middle of his back. Innocents had been shot for less.

Charlie's cell phone rang, and he suspected it was Gordon.

"Don't answer that," the man with the gun advised. "Keep your hands where they are."

"No problem," Charlie responded. "But as soon as you feel comfortable doing so, would you please use your radio and have security check on a patient, Margaret Randal, to make sure she's being protected. Once I lost sight of the man I was chasing, I have no idea where he went."

There were shouts over by the ambulance port, and the lights came on on one of the emergency vehicles as it pulled away from the unloading dock. The security guard turned his head only slightly, looking out of the corner of his eye—a sign of good instincts—and watched as the unit raced to the end of the driveway and onto the street beside the three vehicles still clustered there. It stopped, and there was the sound of voices.

"What the hell did you do?" the security guard asked, his voice now low and threatening. He took a step forward, then changed his mind. "Down on the ground! Face down!" he ordered. "And keep your hands away from your body!"

"Yes, sir," Charlie replied, then lowered himself to the ground. He wasn't saying any more. Once the guy saw the Beretta tucked into his belt, the tension was going to increase exponentially. No reason to freak the guy out by asking him to stay calm. Even some of the real cops nowadays had a tendency to start shooting once they saw a weapon.

Chapter Three

Charlie looked up as the steel door to the hospital's ten-by-ten "detention" room opened and Detective DuPree walked in. Windbreaker over one arm, the detective looked tired, from his matted, thinning hair down to his day-old beard. He smelled of coffee breath and cold sweat, but he didn't look pissed, at least not yet.

"According to Mr. Randal and your evil twin Sweeney, you broke up a carjacking and/or kidnapping attempt and only returned fire in self-defense. Now I want to hear it from your lips, Charlie," DuPree said, his voice low and clear. He held up a small recorder, and Charlie nodded.

"First of all, before I tell you what went down from my POV, I have a couple of questions," Charlie said, trying to suppress a yawn. It was almost 10:00 PM, and it had been a very long day.

"Is the person I shot, *after* he fired twice at me, the same man I saw during the home invasion at the Randals'?"

"He doesn't match the description you gave or the sketch Sweeney made from your feedback. And, unfortunately, the

Randals' neighbor's camera caught the perps already masked, so that won't help. So, no, it's almost certainly not the same guy. The man you shot died in the emergency room. The doctors weren't able to save him. He didn't have an injured trigger finger either, by the way. And let me guess what your other question might be. The answer is no, neither of the two men wearing ski masks who tried to hijack your pal and Mr. Randal have been located. Not yet. There are fifty officers out on the streets right now, searching. That it?"

"One more thing. Has the man I shot been identified? He have a family?"

"No, and we don't know. I have officers working on that right now. His fingerprints and photo are on their way to the crime lab. He wasn't carrying any ID."

"I feel for his loved ones, but I didn't have any options, Detective. It was self-defense."

"That's what Randal and Sweeney said," DuPree affirmed. "But let's go through this step by step and make it official. And hurry, this room smells like disinfectant. Unless, of course, you want to take this interview downtown to APD headquarters."

"No, let's get it done now. Downtown smells like jail."

A half hour later, still minus the Beretta taken by the crime unit, Charlie met Gordon, who was seated in a visitor waiting area at the end of the hall. Gordon looked up from his phone, touched the screen one more time, then slipped it into his pocket and stood. "Ready to go?"

Charlie nodded. "Definitely. DuPree reminded me not to leave the metro area, talk to the press, or shoot anyone else without checking with him first."

"Sounds like DuPree. It was self-defense, and the physical

evidence will back that up. Think the DA is going to press any charges?" Gordon asked, walking side by side with Charlie down the hall.

"Probably not. I just hope the dead guy didn't have a wife and kids. Regardless of what kind of person he was . . ." Charlie shook his head in disgust, knowing he'd have to get over this one as well.

"His family is probably better off without him."

Charlie shrugged. Gordon had lost his own father, and had never mentioned any of the details of the death during the years they'd known each other.

Nearly a minute went by as they waited at the elevators. Finally one stopped at their floor, and an older man in scrubs stepped out, pushing a stainless steel cart containing some electronic gear, then hurried away toward the nurses' station. Charlie and Gordon stepped into the elevator together. Now that they were alone again, Charlie spoke. "It seems trivial, but I have to ask. Did either of the bullets hit the Charger?" He pressed the button.

"You ready for this?" Gordon asked.

"You're shitting me. Really?"

"No, fortunately you're lucky. The shots were high and the slugs took off like wild geese, crossed Elfego Baca Avenue, then shattered a stained-glass window on the old Saint Mark's church," Gordon said, shaking his head. "The priest is mad as hell, and God is probably pissed."

Charlie laughed out loud, and Gordon joined in. Several seconds later, they stepped out of the elevator at the ground floor. "Thanks. I needed that," Charlie said. "Is Sam with Margaret right now?"

Gordon nodded. "He's up there now on the third floor. Gonna spend the night. And here are your keys."

"My car's been moved out of the street?"

"Yeah, one of the crime scene people moved it into the hospital lot after the parking areas had been searched for the third suspect. I should have gone after the passenger, you think?"

"Naw, protecting Sam was the right thing to do. If one of those two had circled back to the vehicles, Randal would have been a sitting duck."

"Sam was carrying, so he would have had a chance, at least. You know what, Charlie? I think this whole thing has been about Sam."

"Kidnapping, you mean, not robbery? It would explain their watching his house after the first attempt, then following the Camry and cutting you off. Yeah, it makes sense. It looks like the girls' neighbors are going to need some protection after all. I'm just not going to become someone's hit man. Like tonight, it'll only be in self-defense."

"Agreed. And if Sam has any other expectations, we can walk away."

They crossed the big lobby, nodded to a security guard inside the double doors, then stepped out onto the wide porch. Down the sidewalk ahead was the big hospital sign, surrounded by a flower bed, and beyond, the street.

"Got something for you, Charlie," Gordon said, handing him a piece of paper.

Charlie looked down at it as they passed under a lamp post. "A check for a thousand dollars?"

"Yeah. Your half of a retainer. I made the executive decision. We're now working for Sam Randal's company as independent contractors. Part-time security, part-time investigators, unless you want to back out. I got the feeling that you weren't going to take this physical attack on your body, much less your purple car, without some kind of retribution in mind."

"Damn straight. Besides, they shot at you, me, Gina's and Nancy's house, and their next-door neighbor, who is apparently a very nice, innocent woman."

Charlie ducked down below the earthen wall just before the second mortar round struck, shaking the earth and showering him with chunks of hardened clay and clouds of dust as shrapnel whistled overhead. The scent of charred wood and the crackling and crumbling of something heavy signaled to his brain that the flat-roofed stone-and-hardened-mud home on the other side of the wall had taken a direct hit. Anyone inside, Afghani family or the missing informant, was either dead already or in a world of hurt.

He heard footsteps, then swung around his M-4 as someone made contact with the wall just above his head. Looking up, he saw two bloody hands reaching over the edge. Charlie waited, heard a woman's cry that might have meant "Help," then stood, shouldering the M-4 by the sling. Suddenly he was face-to-face with a young Afghani woman. Her head was uncovered, her long black hair full of debris, and her pale green eyes wide with terror.

"Help!" she said, this time in English.

She tried to climb over, her arms on the wall, smeared with dirt and blood and what must have been ash. He reached over, picked the woman up beneath her arms, and pulled her up over the wall. Not knowing where she was hurt, or how badly, he sat her down on the ground. He started to look her over for injuries, starting with her head and upper torso, mindful not to touch her, which was definitely not acceptable in this corner of hell.

Still dazed, she gazed absently down the street. Two Afghani men, unarmed civilians possibly, began walking in their direction, shouting angrily. The woman quickly realized her situation, gathered up her shawl and covered her head, and scooted along the ground, moving away from him as she tried, unsuccessfully, to stand.

Charlie, in a crouch, backed away as well, looked down the street for Gordon, then saw several soldiers in his unit hurrying in his direction. He stood and turned to look at the woman, whose face was all but covered now. All he could see was her eyes, which were filled with tears. She knew he was still there but was afraid to look at him. Then he realized her eyes were blue, and the veil fell away. It was Margaret.

Charlie woke up with a start, shaking despite the July heat, then stared at the ceiling. Looking for a distraction, he noticed that the square shade on the overhead light was a little askew, probably the result of airflow from the ceiling duct when the air-conditioning kicked in. He turned and stared at the clock on the wall next, trying to think of anything but the dream.

The details, he knew, would fade after a while, at least from the nightmare, if he didn't review them again in his mind. As for what really happened five years ago, that was another matter entirely. He was stuck with that memory.

Charlie threw off the bedcover and sheet and sat up, swinging around and putting his feet on the floor. One day at a time, he reminded himself.

He arrived at FOB Pawn—FOB stood for Forward Operating Base, from their service days—at seven thirty the next morning, entering through the back entrance after a quick look at the back wall of the old brick building. There hadn't been any more spray-painting incidents since he and Gordon had "spoken" to the punks they'd caught tagging the walls. Charlie and his pal had reached an understanding with the neighborhood gangs over a year ago, and once the taggers learned of their connections on the street, the spray-painting had ended.

Gordon, who had an apartment walking distance from the shop, was already in the office. He sat on his side of the big desk, sipping freshly brewed coffee from their new K-cup machine as he gazed through the Plexiglas window into the shop. His pal had somehow discovered a pristine mug left by the previous owner that had the old business name—Three Balls Pawn—printed in bright red letters. Gordon had begun using it after "dropping" his Denver Broncos mug in frustration during a playoff loss.

They'd renamed the pawnshop despite the tongue-in-cheek historical reference. It also reminded them too much of the sleazeball former owner, who'd given them nothing but grief even after his early demise.

"Morning," Gordon mumbled, looking up from his mug. "You look like crap, Charlie. Nightmares back? Having to shoot someone, even in self-defense, is something that stays with you."

Charlie stepped over to the counter with the coffeemaker, picked up a packet of dark Italian roast, then slid his mug in position and began the brew, selecting the strongest setting. "Yeah. But it wasn't the shooting so much, it was that wall thing."

Gordon nodded. "And yesterday's events just brought it all back. PTSD is a bitch. Hey, helping that woman back in 'stan was the right thing to do, cultural taboo or not."

Both men turned to look at the LED monitor on the wall, having heard the sound of a key in the back-door lock. It was Jake Salazar, FOB employee and an ex-pro wrestler, who was in his early sixties. Jake was their senior employee in every possible way. The guy knew the pawnshop business after working for several years for the previous owner before being laid off. When Charlie and Gordon bought the shop, Jake agreed to come back and work for them. Of course he'd gotten a raise, but Jake was well worth the price.

"Hey, am I late?" Jake grinned, a standard comment made every time he came in and his bosses were already there. The rugged-looking Hispanic man, with cauliflower ears and a reconstructed nose from years in the ring or on the ropes, was a gentle giant if there ever was one, at least when their customers were civil and well behaved. He was honest, loyal, and reliable and could run the place with his eyes closed.

"Good morning, boss," Jake said to Charlie. "Other boss," he added, nodding at Gordon. "How'd your weekend go?"

"You read the paper today about that home invasion, the one where the woman got shot?" Gordon asked, waving his hand toward the newspaper on the desk.

"Yeah. Two of the neighbors jumped in and ran them off. Then later outside Saint Mark's, one of the lowlives got himself killed when they tried a replay with the husband of the gunshot victim." His voice trailed off at the end as he looked from Gordon to Charlie.

"What is it with you two? Every place you go, even here, the manure hits the fan. You're not just pawnshop owners, you're Wild West guardian angels."

"Saintly, we're not, but what can I say, Jake? We were having lunch with Nancy and Gina when someone started screaming. Next came a gunshot. The wounded woman ran out into the alley, then tried to climb over the wall into the girls' yard to escape the shooter. We helped. Sue us," Charlie suggested.

"And we were driving the husband to the hospital that evening when the trio tried to grab him a second time. You'd do the same, Jake," Gordon added. "Remember how you had our backs last year?"

"Okay, but I don't have a black cloud following me like you two, do I?" He looked up. "Never mind, now I need some heavy-duty coffee."

Charlie, who'd already brewed his cup, stepped back. "Go for it."

A few minutes later, on their second helping, all three looked at the monitor as Ruth's small sedan pulled up next to Jake's big black SUV and parked.

"Before Ruth comes in, just how much danger might be drifting into the shop from what went down yesterday?" Jake asked.

"It sucks that you have to ask that question," Gordon responded.

"But I see your point," Charlie said. "We think the target is probably Sam, the husband of the woman who was wounded. For some reason we still haven't determined, the bad guys want to snag him. They might try again."

"And you two are now involved, naturally," Jake said.

"Can't argue with that. My gut tells me they still want Sam," Gordon concluded, "but Charlie is the only person who can identify one of the bad guys."

Jake rolled his eyes, turning toward the door just as Ruth stepped in from the rear entrance. "So you've got a new crusade, right?"

"You know us too well, Jake," Gordon admitted.

"Who knows who too well?" Ruth's soft, gentle voice was such a contrast to what they'd been discussing. Even the woman herself was seemingly a contradiction at a small pawnshop on a side street in old Albuquerque's north valley. Ruth was average height, but that was the only thing average about her. She was smart, classy, and uniquely attractive. Her roots were from old East Coast upper-class money, and she'd had the finest upbringing. Her college education, with an MBA, could have landed her on Wall Street or with a Fortune 500 company.

In addition to all that, Ruth Adams—not her real name—was a single mother in the Witness Protection Program living under the radar. Her abusive ex-husband was in prison for a host of crimes, including insider trading, fraud, kidnapping, and murder. His sentence would keep him in prison until old age. Everyone in the room knew that, yet once before they'd all put themselves on the line to protect Ruth and her son. They'd do it again.

"It's not just because it's Monday, gentlemen," Ruth said. "Something has happened that maybe I should know about."

She looked at Charlie, who she knew was most vulnerable. He'd been attracted to her from the very beginning, as had most men who'd encountered the charismatic woman, and the feeling was mutual, though neither had ever acted upon that knowledge.

All eyes went to Charlie, and his face was getting warm. It was unlikely that his Navajo skin tones glowed red like an Anglo's, but he felt embarrassment all the same. "Okay, Ruth. I don't think there's any danger, but something unfortunate happened to Gordon and me yesterday that may result in the two of us having to go out from time to time. But I doubt you or Jake will be in any danger whatsoever."

"Unlike the last two occasions when you took on someone else's problems, like mine? Just who are you trying to save this time? Your sister, brother, parents, or a stranger again?" Ruth demanded, her voice calm, but firm nonetheless.

"Ever jump into a kidnapping during an afternoon cookout and end up having to skip the potato salad? Maybe you should read the lead story in the morning paper," Gordon suggested, a hint of mirth in his tone as he held up the *Albuquerque Journal*.

Chapter Four

It was 9:00 AM and they'd only been open an hour when Charlie got a text. He was standing behind the jewelry and small electronics case, having just locked up the display after adding two watches to the for-sale merchandise after the pawn agreement had expired. It was a concise message from Nancy, in APD Sergeant Medina mode, requesting he meet with her and Detective DuPree at APD headquarters for a follow-up interview at ten. The fact that Nancy had sent the message was significant. Maybe he'd gotten lucky and she was going to work the case.

Charlie looked around the shop. Jake was to his left, at the register closest to the front entrance, handling a transaction, and Ruth was back in the office, visible through the clear partition, working on the records. Their long-standing security procedures required the staff on hand to know where everyone else was, and, because he'd been transferring merchandise from that location to the display area, Charlie knew that Gordon was in the secure storage room, processing items that had been recently pawned and were not for sale yet.

"Going to see Gordon," Charlie announced to Jake, who nodded without looking up, continuing his current task. He entered the small hallway beside the office entrance just as Gordon came out of the steel door of the pawn storage room.

"That's all we can put out front today," Gordon announced, closing the door behind him. It locked automatically on the outside now and required a number code to gain access. "What's up?"

"DuPree wants me downtown to answer some questions, and the good news, maybe, is that Nancy sent the invitation," Charlie answered, stepping over close to the office entrance. Ruth looked up, smiled, and went back to her work.

"Think we're going to get lucky and DuPree has her assigned to the investigation?" Gordon speculated. "It would make our participation a lot easier, hopefully, being a step removed from DuPree himself."

"Just what I was thinking. If Jake and Ruth can handle business here, maybe you'd like to come along with me and we can have another talk with Sam. I'm not sold on the theory that this was just a home invasion gone wrong, especially after the second attack."

"If they'd wanted to get rid of a witness who could pick a bad guy out of a lineup, they would have gone after Margaret instead—and you," Gordon said.

"If you need to go somewhere, boys, Jake and I will be able to handle the shop. You might want to check with him, but I'm done here and can help out front," Ruth said, coming over to join them.

"Thanks, Ruth. We'll make sure to be back by noon, or at least one of us," Charlie answered, looking over at Gordon.

"Wanna take our own vehicles, just in case?" Gordon suggested.

•   •   •

Twenty minutes later, Charlie sat in a high-backed office chair in DuPree's cubicle at the main police station downtown on Roma Avenue, having stashed the Dodge in a nearby municipal parking structure. Gordon had elected to hang out at a downtown coffee shop rather than wait in the APD lobby.

Once done at the station, they were going to go over and meet Sam at Saint Mark's, hoping to find out who might have wanted to kidnap him. The obvious answer was ransom; Sam Randal was worth a lot of money. Then why not grab Margaret instead? She was smaller and might have been easier to handle. It would also be easier for Sam, as company owner, to round up the cash.

A civilian department staffer had escorted Charlie to the floor where DuPree and a dozen or more APD officers had their desks. Charlie, knowing the location of DuPree's cubicle, quickly crossed the big room.

The detective was away from his desk, another officer advised, but had asked him to take a seat and wait. A police sergeant Charlie had met during an incident a year ago happened to pass through the room and stopped to talk for a few moments. He'd just left when DuPree arrived, looking a little annoyed.

"Glad you could make it, Charlie," DuPree said, his frown fading to neutrality as he quickly shook hands, then took a seat behind his big metal desk. "I'd intended on having the surveillance images from across the street here for you to review in hope of finding any useful details, but there was a glitch and I couldn't access it from my terminal. Now I think it's been cleared up. Come on around here and have a look."

Charlie got out of his chair and stood beside the detective, looking over his shoulder at the computer monitor as DuPree entered the codes and a screen came up with the numbers and date that gave the time and location of the feed itself.

"This is only the portion of the feed for yesterday—Sunday—and I had a tech set it up so I could quickly access the moment when the perp van arrives. Here we go," DuPree added, his left hand on the computer mouse.

DuPree let the digital file run. The van arrived with three men faintly visible inside, all wearing black or blue ski masks. As the driver and another passenger in the rear seat climbed out the street side, the front passenger climbed out onto the sidewalk, facing the camera position.

DuPree cursed as they watched the man reach down and put his hand on a pistol stuck into his belt near his right rear pocket, then walk around the back of the van and join the men in the street. They all crossed the street, blocked from view by the van itself.

"I was hoping the camera had caught some details of the interior of the van," DuPree grumbled. "Something personal left behind."

Charlie shrugged. "Despite the mask, in my judgment, the front-seat passenger appears to be the same guy I saw unmasked. The upper torso and blue hoodie are a match, even the cuffs of his sleeves—and his weapon."

"You've got a good memory for detail, Charlie, and we're going to need that. Mrs. Randal wasn't able to give nearly as good a description, and wasn't convinced that the drawing Sweeney made based upon your memory helped all that much. She says that if we manage to locate a photo or an actual suspect, maybe it would help."

"What's the problem?" Charlie asked. "She was a lot closer to him than I was."

"Maybe she's blocking the image out of shock or fear. It happens sometimes. Perhaps it'll come back to her later. Unfortunately, eyewitnesses aren't always reliable. You may end up being the key to making the ID."

"What about his DNA? She scratched him, right? How about his skin or blood under her fingernails?"

"The techs got some blood and tissue, but they weren't able to take the samples until she was in the ER. There is some concern that they may have become contaminated. She grabbed her wound with that hand and mixed her blood and tissue with that of her attacker. That's something for the lab to sort out—if that's possible. The evidence is already in Santa Fe at the state crime lab. Wanna see the rest of the show?"

"Why not?"

The recording ran for almost five minutes, and during that time, there was no change in the scene except for the passage of a minivan. Then, suddenly, the three masked men ran up to the van and jumped inside. After the driver took a couple of shots in the direction of the Randal house, the vehicle disappeared from the field of view, replaced in a few seconds by Gordon, Nancy, weapon out, and Charlie, armed with Gina's .380.

"You know the rest. Now, tell me again, are you certain you could identify the shooter if you saw him again?"

"No doubt about it, Detective."

"Good."

"Can I ask you a few questions now, DuPree?" Charlie asked, noting that the detective's mood had begun to improve.

"Can't guarantee I'll be able to come up with an answer, but go ahead. And you can call me Wayne, Charlie," DuPree suggested, reaching across the desk, lifting off a folder that covered a name plate that read DETECTIVE W. DUPREE.

Charlie saw the opportunity to gather more information. "The man I shot and killed last night. Who is . . . was he?"

"His fingerprints were on file, and the deceased had a record of auto theft and burglary going back to high school. He's Anthony Donald Lorenzo, twenty-three years old, on probation and with a listed Rio Rancho apartment address. His mother and a younger sister currently reside in the Newark, New Jersey, area. They've been notified."

"And the man I saw, the Randal shooter?"

"Sergeant Medina is working on that right now downstairs, using the sketch you and Sweeney made. She's going to be assigned to me on the home invasions, including this case. I'm not sure the Randal incident is connected to the other crimes—there are as many differences as similarities—but until my captain tells me otherwise, it's my responsibility."

"You think the man I saw has worked with this guy before, and they have a history together?" Charlie asked.

"And maybe with the third perp? We have a better chance of getting all three once we get an ID on the guy who was unmasked. Punks who pull off these kinds of crimes usually have records and hang out with their crew. They're all pretty much losers and get caught, sooner or later," DuPree pointed out. "What else you want to know?"

"This has to do with something you've probably thought about already. What if this wasn't really a home invasion but a kidnapping attempt disguised as a strong-arm break-in. And it was directed toward Sam Randal, not his wife," Charlie suggested.

"Because they made a second move on him last night?" Du-Pree asked.

"Exactly. And if it hadn't been for Gordon and me jumping in the first time, they'd have hauled Sam away in that van."

"It fits. Kidnapping, for ransom, I suppose. Randal's construction company is doing quite well, according to my contacts in the local business community."

"You're already into this possibility, then?" Charlie concluded. DuPree was indeed smarter than he looked.

"Never rule out, or assume, when you need to determine the truth, Charlie."

"As with everything in life, Wayne. I should let you know that Sam Randal has hired Gordon and me to look after him and his wife, and at the same time help identify the attackers."

DuPree nodded. "I'm not surprised, considering his resources. Have you spoken to Randal yet about his personal or business enemies, those he knows about, at least? If we share information, we'll get to the bottom of this a lot quicker. Once I close a case it gives me more time to focus on the others. My captain is already breathing down my neck on these home invasion cases. And so on up the food chain to the mayor and city council."

Charlie thought about it a second. DuPree—make that Wayne—was right. With Nancy a close contact on the law enforcement side of this, they might be able to get to the suspects a lot faster. One down, two to go, and it would all be over. *Hopefully.*

"Sam is at the hospital with Margaret, and we need to keep both of them close if they are going to be protected, so that's where Gordon and I are going next. We hope to find out exactly why he's become a target. If they'd wanted him dead, it would have happened the moment he opened the door yesterday," Charlie said. "Maybe he's more likely to open up to us about it than to law enforcement—no offense—if it involves an iffy business deal, for instance."

"You've got a point."

They both turned as Sergeant Medina came into the room carrying a thick folder. Nancy was attractive and outgoing, but she was also smart and capable, having earned her rank quickly.

"Medina's got something," DuPree said as Nancy held up the folder, a grin on her face.

"We may have a winner, Detective," she said, handing the papers to DuPree. "Everything I've seen about this guy fits what we think we know. Hi, Charlie, glad you're here."

"Don't show the suspect's photo," DuPree warned. "Charlie needs to pick it from an array without any cues."

"Which is why I've selected three other photos with similar descriptions, Detective," Nancy replied without sarcasm. "That meets the legal requirements for a nonprejudicial photo array. Ready, Charlie?"

"Sure."

Nancy opened the folder and took out four color images, laying them out side by side on the desktop. The man in the second photo had a scar above his left eyebrow, but none of the others had such a mark.

"Take your time, Mr. Henry. Is the man you saw in the Randal home pointing a gun here?" DuPree asked, switching on a small digital recorder.

Charlie looked at the photos carefully, then pointed to the third image. "That's the guy, I'm positive. His hair is longer in the photo than when I saw him, and he has a scratch on his face now.

He's the person whose ski mask had apparently been pulled away at the Randal house. He was chasing Mrs. Randal and fired a weapon in her direction."

DuPree turned over the photo to read what was on the back. "Let the record show that Mr. Henry identified the photo of one Raymond Geiger, white male, age, umm, twenty-two in the photo, current address listed as Apartment 247, Sierra Avenue NW, Rio Rancho, New Mexico."

"That's it?" Charlie asked after DuPree stated the time and date, then switched off the recorder.

"Here is Geiger's file, which includes his arrests, convictions, and probation records," Nancy said, placing the folder in front of DuPree. "I took the liberty, assuming that Charlie could make the ID."

DuPree nodded. "So far, two of the crew are from Rio Rancho," he said, opening the file.

"I saw this Ray character in action. He's not nearly the martial arts equal of Gordon, but he has some serious hand-to-hand skills, even with an injured finger. Does he have martial arts training or a military record?" Charlie asked.

DuPree held up his hand as he read, then looked up after a moment. "No military record, but he owns and operates a martial arts school in Rio Rancho. The business name is Butkikin Dojo. What do you call those words that sound alike but have a different meaning?"

"Homophones, and don't ask why I know that," Nancy responded, daring them to comment.

"Clearly, Ray Geiger also has attitude," Charlie responded with a grin. "Mind if I ride along when you go to arrest him? That's where you're going next, right, Detective?"

Nancy looked at DuPree, who shrugged. "He's riding with you, Medina. And make Charlie stay in the vehicle. Geiger will recognize him. This might get tricky, and not just if Geiger resists arrest."

"Because?"

"Jurisdiction, Charlie," Nancy offered. "If we're in Rio Rancho, the actual takedown is the responsibility of the Rio Rancho department. Unless they have a warrant for him for crimes committed in Rio Rancho, however, they should be eager to turn him over to us."

"You could also use the state police, right?"

"Yeah, Charlie, but no sense in pissing off the RRPD," DuPree replied. "We still owe them after they looked after you and your brother last year."

Charlie nodded. "And it wasn't the first time I'd gotten their attention."

"That incident I choose not to remember," DuPree said, shaking his head. "Even if it helped them solve a murder."

Charlie's phone signaled a text message. He looked down. *I'm here. Much longer?* it said.

Soon Charlie texted Gordon back.

"I read Geiger's file, Detective," Nancy interjected, ignoring Charlie. "I also Googled him."

DuPree began sorting through papers. "And?"

"Geiger supposedly got his act together after his last arrest in New Jersey, turned his life around, and now promotes a martial arts program at his dojo in Rio Rancho for troubled youth. According to an upbeat article in the Rio Rancho newspaper, Ray's program helps redirect the energy of teens in a positive direction—keeps them out of further trouble," Nancy responded.

"And he's also training them to win their next fight," Charlie said.

"There's more," Nancy added. "Ray's got a family member living just a mile from his apartment, his father, Frank Geiger. Ray's mother divorced Frank when the boy was six. She remarried and now lives back east somewhere. What makes the father interesting is that Frank, in his early fifties, is a former NYPD detective who served seventeen years on the force," Nancy responded.

"Crap. The son is a young criminal from a broken home, and his old man is a divorced ex-cop who had problems controlling his own kid. Looks like Ray is back to his old tricks, this time in New Mexico. Just what we need," DuPree said.

"Yeah, more bad karma. You mind if Gordon comes along?" Charlie asked.

"Sweeney? Is he here too?" DuPree asked.

Charlie nodded and pointed down. "He just arrived."

"Hell no, I'm not having that wiseass around to square off with the suspect. I'm pushing policy letting you come along in the first place, Charlie," DuPree said. "And that's only to help us pick out the right guy," he added smugly.

"No prob. We planned on every contingency, so Gordon has his own vehicle. He can go ahead and make contact with the Randals at Saint Mark's. Maybe he can work on Sam and get him to open up about his enemies," Charlie said.

"You might want to get him started on that right away," DuPree suggested, standing, then retrieving his weapon from a desk drawer. "I plan to have Ray Geiger locked up by lunch."

Chapter Five

They met two Rio Rancho unmarked units in front of Butkikin Dojo, but the Rio Rancho detective who'd already taken a look discovered that the school was locked up and the lights were out. According to a sign in a window, the school didn't hold classes until midafternoon. They tried Ray's apartment next, but again, no one was around. Placing an officer to watch the building, Du-Pree decided to check with the father, Frank, who was supposedly unemployed. A quick drive-by along the street determined that Ray's registered vehicle, a red pickup, was in the elder Geiger's driveway, parked in front of a one-vehicle garage.

The boxy, two-story, flat-roofed rental house was in a relatively new development of maybe fifty densely packed units. Each dwelling had an attached garage and small backyard enclosed within a six-foot-high cedar fence. All the cookie-cutter structures, in southwest generic pueblo style with fake vigas, looked pretty much identical, even down to the same sandy yellow stucco walls and one tiny pine balcony extending out from an upstairs room.

As the two Rio Rancho detectives walked up to the gate that

led to the front entrance, the overhead garage door crept up with a faint rumble, revealing a large silver Chevy pickup taking up most of the interior. All the officers stopped in the driveway, hands moving to the butts of their handguns.

A tall, belly-heavy man in his late fifties wearing a sleeveless T-shirt was standing just behind the door in the center, holding a shovel at quarter arms. Nancy, standing beside DuPree, was the only officer in uniform, and the man in the garage focused his attention on her.

"What the hell does an Albuquerque cop want with me? You take the wrong turn on Highway 528, cutie?" The man leered, letting his eyes roam down Nancy's body.

The local detectives, who'd frozen at the sound of the garage door opening, had their weapons out now, pointed at the man. The garage had wooden shelves along both sides, constructed of unfinished two-by-fours and plywood. They held several cardboard boxes, with the labels of a moving company on the sides. Most were taped shut. Toward the front of the garage, against the wall of the house, was a long, heavy wood bench with a few hand and power tools in various locations, along with one-gallon paint cans and plastic containers.

"You Frank Geiger?" the senior officer demanded.

"Yeah, who are you?"

"Detective Larranaga, Rio Rancho police. Please set down the shovel, Mr. Geiger," the detective ordered, taking a quick glance into the interior of the red pickup in the driveway.

"Guess I'm busted, Officer," Frank replied sarcastically, revealing a significant limp as he stepped over and placed the shovel into the bed of the Chevy. "But the light at the corner was yellow, not red. I swear. Don't shoot."

"Lose the attitude, Geiger. Do you happen to know where your son, Ray, is right now?" DuPree demanded. "The red truck is registered to him."

"Who wants to know, fatty?"

Charlie, who'd exited Nancy's squad car unnoticed, fought hard not to smile. DuPree had lost some weight since they'd last met, but he still had a spare tire, though not as pronounced as Geiger's.

Finally Geiger noticed Charlie. "Ah, the Indians have arrived. Then you must be the cavalry, lady. Love your blue uniform, but where's your stallion?"

Nancy gave Geiger a cold "give me a reason" stare but held her tongue.

"I need to speak with your son, Raymond Geiger, in person." Larranaga demanded. "If I have to ask you again, I'm holding you for obstruction and we're going to the station." He brought out a set of handcuffs.

"No need, Detective. Hell, my boy's inside puking his guts out. We tossed back a few too many last night watching 'Backs baseball, and this morning he couldn't keep his breakfast down. What the hell is going on? Some kid at Bojo get kicked in the nuts and now his parents are claiming child abuse?"

"Geiger's stalling. Ray could be halfway down the alley by now," DuPree stepped toward the side of the garage, looking toward the rear of the house.

The RRPD detective shook his head, not taking his eyes off Geiger. "We know our business, DuPree. There's a uniform in the alley, covering the back of the residence."

"Yet you're giving the person you've come to arrest time to fetch a weapon or two and barricade the house," DuPree replied. "You wearing a vest, Officer Larranaga?"

Larranaga's face turned red. "*Detective* Larranaga. Screw this. Ray Geiger has earned some credit with this community, but you've got a point. The subject may now be armed and dangerous. If your son doesn't come outside and turn himself in right now, Geiger, I'm calling SWAT."

"SWAT? What the hell?" Frank yelled. "No, back off. I'll get Ray down here right now. He's unarmed, and I guarantee my boy is completely innocent of whatever trumped-up crap brought you here. My boy's made a big contribution to Rio Rancho. Ray serves as a positive role model to every tough kid in the community. If he got in a fight, he was jumped, and it was a hundred percent self-defense."

Geiger turned toward the door in the garage that led into the house. "Ray, come on down, the police want to talk to you," he shouted, stepping into the entrance.

"Hold on, I'm going to be right behind you," the detective announced. He nodded toward his partner. "Watch the front, Johnson."

"Don't go any further, Mr. Geiger," Larranaga ordered. "Stay on this side of the entrance. Is there anyone else in the house besides Ray? Tell me now," Larranaga insisted, unholstering his handgun and holding it down by his side.

"No, just Ray. And like I said, you don't need your weapon," Geiger insisted as he stepped back down into the garage, limping. "No reason to shoot anyone. My son is unarmed."

DuPree had flanked Geiger and the detective, reaching a position to back him up. He had his weapon out as well. Charlie looked over at Nancy, who also had her pistol out. She'd moved close to the corner of the garage so she could cover the other detective standing along the sidewalk leading to the main entrance in front, or turn to her left and back up DuPree.

Charlie, in the driveway, looked up at the window on the second floor, which was set back at least twenty-five feet from the garage roof. The window was open, and Ray Geiger was standing there, looking out. When Ray saw Charlie, he turned away and walked out of view.

"He's not puking somewhere. He's in a room above the garage, and the window's open," Charlie called out.

"Ray, dammit, come on down to the garage. The officers want to ask you some questions," Frank yelled through the now half-open door into the house.

"Did he have a weapon, Charlie?" DuPree asked, his eyes still focused on the open door.

"Didn't see one, Detective DuPree," he responded, still watching the window.

Less than twenty seconds later, Ray Geiger, looking tired, appeared at the door leading into the garage, wearing black sweats, running shoes, and a Yankees blue-and-white pinstriped jersey-style shirt. Frank stepped aside and motioned for Ray to enter the garage.

"See, my son is unarmed," Frank pointed out.

"Let me see your hands, Ray," DuPree demanded.

"You blind?" Ray drawled sarcastically, holding out his hands, palms up, and giving Nancy a broad smile. "But if your lady officer wants to search me . . ."

"Let me . . . please," Nancy replied, evil in her eyes. She reached into her pocket and pulled out a latex glove. "First for drugs. Drop trou and bend over, your hands on your knees, tough guy."

"Hey, you're supposed to start in front," Ray joked nervously. Nobody laughed.

"Hold out both hands, Ray Geiger, fingers extended," the Rio Rancho detective ordered. "Unless you want to submit to a cavity search in front of all these men." He looked over at Nancy, who now had the glove in place.

"This is bullshit," Ray grumbled, holding out both hands, still avoiding eye contact with Charlie. "I didn't do a damn thing."

Nancy brought out her cell phone and took a quick photo. "Right index finger is swelled up and discolored. Everyone see that?"

"Then I suggest extra care when placing the handcuffs. Someone might have broken his trigger finger," DuPree said, a smile on his face.

"What? I was injured last night breaking up a fight at the Outpost Bar. Two women, can you believe it?" Ray stepped back, looking over at his father.

"It's true!" Frank added quickly. "Find the women. They'll back us up."

"So, who put that day-old scratch on your face, Ray? Was that before or after the Diamondbacks game?" DuPree asked.

"Is my son under arrest? He's not saying another word, not until we talk to a lawyer," Frank argued. "Come on, son, we're going back inside."

"Don't move. Cuff the suspect, Johnson," Detective Larranaga said to his partner. "Gently, so there won't be any mistake about that injured finger. Send me that photo, Sergeant Medina."

"Already done. I've labeled it and forwarded a copy to your station and APD's crime lab as well," Nancy confirmed, watching Frank as he brought out a cell phone.

Ray started to fidget as the first cuff went into place. "Stand still, Ray," Frank ordered. "I want a video of this harassment for your lawyer."

Frank began a video recording with his cell phone as Ray was read his rights. Charlie noticed that the man was careful to capture the entire scene and everyone present, including Charlie, who was standing close to DuPree now. Within a few minutes, Ray, after being searched one more time for weapons and emptying his pockets, was placed in the rear seat of an unmarked police car. Once inside, he looked away, never directly at Charlie.

Ray's father was shaking, about to boil over by then, barely keeping his temper in check. DuPree approached him. "Mr. Geiger, did your son spend last night here?"

"You're not with the Rio Rancho force. Screw you and your questions," Frank sneered, clinching his fists. He turned his back on DuPree and stepped back into the garage.

"Please wait outside, Mr. Geiger," Larranaga ordered, coming up to stand beside DuPree. "I have jurisdiction here, and as a former police officer you already know about procedures and the rights of subjects taken into custody."

Frank took a deep breath, then spoke, his voice calm and controlled again. "I'm going to lock up my home and follow my son to the station. Ray has been contributing an essential service to the community, helping young people who'd gotten into trouble straighten out their lives. Once the local citizens learn how he's been falsely accused, my boy will be released. You can't order me around on my own property unless you have evidence of a crime or a warrant. And stay away from our vehicles. I saw you looking into Ray's truck."

"You might want to hold off making the self-fulfilling

prophecies, Mr. Geiger." The detective pointed toward a squad car coming up the street. "That would be the warrant—to search your residence and any vehicles present, including the red pickup, for weapons and other items that may be linked to one of several crimes committed in the past twenty-four hours. We are also looking for evidence and stolen items from previous crimes, including home invasions within the metro area. Remain on the property, within sight of an officer, but don't touch anything or interfere with this investigation unless you want to spend the rest of the day, or longer, at the station."

"I want to see the warrant before you pussies take another step," Frank warned.

"You getting this?" Larranaga glanced over at his partner, pointing to a lapel camera.

Detective Johnson nodded, grinning. "Since we arrived."

Geiger turned his back to them, mumbling under his breath.

"Think Geiger senior should be searched?" Nancy said, looking over at DuPree.

"I requested a weapons search that included all individuals present at the site," DuPree responded. "You volunteering?"

"Hell no. No gloves are thick enough to protect me from these assholes. That's their burden." She nodded toward the Rio Rancho detectives.

Charlie was close enough to Nancy and DuPree to hear their conversation, and knew he wasn't going to be allowed to be present during the search of the house. However, that would give him the opportunity to watch Frank, and maybe even ask a question or two. He didn't expect any answers, but how the volatile ex-cop reacted might give Charlie an idea just how much the father knew about what his son had been doing.

If Frank was aware of the home invasion and carjacking attempt last night, he might also know that some tall Indian was an eyewitness who could ID his son. It was natural for Frank to protect Ray—he was doing it already—but was he also involved at some level? Covering up a crime was illegal, and Frank, as a former cop, knew that.

Another squad car arrived with two more Rio Rancho officers, probably those who'd been covering the back of the property, and the detectives had a quick private conference before beginning their search. One patrolman was assigned to remain on watch in the garage while the other began a search, beginning with the two pickups.

As soon as the pickups were searched, Frank watched the officer who was poking through the boxes on the shelves and the tools stored in the garage, following him around. The second policeman, a huge black man with arms as big as thighs, came up immediately. "Please remain outside the garage, Mr. Geiger. I've been ordered to warn you once. Then, if you fail to cooperate, I'm to place you in the squad car. You've now received that warning."

Frank shrugged. "Good advice. The garage is starting to smell anyway."

The black officer laughed, and judging from Frank's expression, that wasn't the reaction he'd hoped to provoke. Geiger walked over to the drip line on the concrete, where the rain coming off the roof parapet stained the surface, and stood just inside the mark.

Charlie moved closer to Frank, who, like Ray, had made a point of not making eye contact. "Mr. Geiger, how often does Ray come over and spend the night? His own apartment is less than a mile from here."

Geiger didn't react. "Put things back where you found them,

Officer," he yelled to the cop searching among some hand tools. "Make sure those boxes are sealed again to keep the other roaches out."

Charlie persisted. "Frank, if you know about the crimes Ray committed, and that one of Ray's friends got himself killed while attempting to kidnap a man, you become an accessory to a serious felony. I've heard that ex-cops don't have a lot of friends in prison. And you are, what, fifty-five years old, with aggression issues and a bum leg? A ten-year sentence would keep you there until Social Security kicks in. Or do felons even qualify for Social Security?"

Frank thought about it for a moment, then finally looked directly at him. "Who the hell are you, Indian? Get off my property and go back to your frigging . . . casino. You're one of the kitchen help, right?"

Charlie had observed that some cops, especially ex-cops with intimidation issues, loved to provoke. Charlie ignored the cheap attempt at racism. "Ray has avoided looking at me because he knows who I am, and I think you do too. Not my name, but how Ray and I met," Charlie responded, watching his eyes.

There was a split-second reaction there, which told Charlie that Frank had been clued in to what Ray had done. Still, the ex-cop would probably be a tough nut to crack. As a trained, experienced police officer at one time, Frank knew the tactics and strategies used by law enforcement to get answers.

The question was, how good a cop had Frank been? How honest? His son certainly wasn't a very successful criminal, which might explain why the younger Geiger had tried to convince the public that he'd changed his character. At his young age, Ray had already been arrested and convicted twice, and now he had to play the falsely accused victim if he wanted to weasel out of the charges. Charlie wondered if now that he lived in New Mexico, the old three-strikes sentencing rules still applied. Or was there a three-strikes law anymore? It was doubtful, but he could ask Gina later.

Frank looked in his direction, more like *through* him, and for some reason Charlie had the chills. If Ray was a dangerous but incompetent criminal, or at least one stupid enough to get caught a third time, his father sent a more ominous vibe. Frank wasn't perfect in his attempts at deception, but he was, nevertheless, trying to play the cops. Chances were that the detectives searching Frank's home would find nothing that would help the case, and that the pistol, cap, and hoodie had been dumped hours ago. The same might be true of Ray's apartment, the obvious next stop on DuPree's list.

Immediately Charlie thought of the time and looked down at his watch. He'd better call Gordon. There was no way he'd make it back to FOB Pawn by lunch to relieve Ruth and Jake.

A few minutes later, he put away his phone and looked over at Frank. Though he'd been turned away during his conversation, Frank had closed the distance between them. Just what had the man heard, if anything?

Then a thought occurred to Charlie. Was Frank more than just Ray's father? Could he be the leader—the third home invader, still at large and unidentified? None of the men he saw had a limp, but could Frank be faking it now to throw them off?

Charlie didn't arrive at the pawnshop until two thirty. He walked into the office and found Gordon seated at the big desk, working at the computer terminal. Turning around, he stepped into the shop showroom and spotted Jake helping someone who was looking at watches, judging from where they were standing over the jewelry case. Ruth was farther up the counter, processing a recent transaction. They had installed a new printer that scanned and made copies of driver's licenses. These came from customers who were pawning items that needed to be recorded and later checked against stolen-property lists for local law enforcement.

Ruth looked over and smiled, a gesture he echoed back so easily it was almost embarrassing. She could weaken his knees with a glance, and he fought constantly not to come across as a complete idiot around her. No woman had ever made him feel the way Ruth did. One of these days . . .

"Welcome back, stranger," Jake said, breaking the daydream.

"Hey, Jake," he answered, focusing again on reality. Clearly they had things well in hand, so he returned to the office.

"How'd it go, Charlie, the arrest and all that?" Gordon asked, rolling back in his chair.

"Ray Geiger is the guy who shot at Margaret Randal, there's no doubt about that. I picked him out of a photo array, then confirmed it in person, though he avoided looking in my direction as much as possible. He's going to be transferred over to APD jurisdiction, then escorted downtown to APD headquarters so DuPree and Nancy can officially interview him."

"Did Geiger resist?"

"No, he was just a wiseass. The kid pushes the wrong buttons with cops. That makes me wonder just how well he gets along with his father, who makes Ray come across like Mother Teresa by comparison. It's clear that either Ray's good behavior has been an act, or for some reason he's been forced into breaking the law again. Maybe his dojo is failing and he needs the money."

"Maybe. Lots of small businesses fail within the first few years. You think there's enough evidence there to convict him?"

"Nancy and DuPree didn't find any physical evidence at any of the three locations they searched: the dojo, the apartment, and his dad's house. Oh, and the two pickups. I was surprised to learn, on the drive back, that Margaret wasn't able to pick Ray out of the same photo array I was shown. DuPree had another detective show her the photos this morning while he was in Rio Rancho, but she just couldn't make up her mind. DuPree's theory is that she's blocking it out, and that doesn't exactly cheer him up. How's she doing, anyway?" Charlie asked.

"From what I've heard, very well. No surgery was necessary, and the doctors have loaded her up with antibiotics to keep her wound from getting infected. She should be released either tonight or tomorrow morning. Sam is going to call once he gets word from the hospital on that," Gordon explained. "He has our cell numbers now."

"Good to hear."

"If Margaret wasn't able to ID the guy, what about the other details? Like his voice? She heard him speak, right?"

"Yeah, but from what I understand, that won't hold up in court on its own even if she recognized his voice, especially when she couldn't pick out his photo. It's just not enough," Charlie responded.

"Did Ray have the scratch and a broken trigger finger?" Gordon asked.

Charlie nodded, reaching over to the shelf for his coffee mug. "The scratch, yes, and his index finger was swollen—hopefully broken. Ray said he was injured breaking up a fight outside a bar between two women, and his dad backed him up."

"So that will have to be followed up on, and even if they can't get any witnesses, the reasonable doubt is still there. But I find that particular alibi hard to believe. Even after I messed up his finger, the guy I fought with in the hall was still too quick for a couple of women to manhandle, unless they were trained professionals, or just lucky," Gordon said. "Unless Ray was staggering drunk."

"I see your point. I suppose that DuPree or Nancy is going to check out the story. Unless you wanna give it a shot."

"A shot, maybe single malt? Good idea. Any idea where this alleged confrontation took place?" Gordon asked, a grin on his face now.

"Sure do. It's called the Outpost Bar, and I know a charming little guy who's great at getting the ladies to talk."

"Little? I prefer compact," Gordon replied. "No, robust."

"How do you know I was talking about you?"

"You said charming. Who else could it be?"

"Got me there," Charlie said. "In the meantime, why don't we give Jake and Ruth some help out front? Traffic should be picking up soon from those customers dropping in on the way home from work."

Charlie stood, but Gordon shook his head. "Finish your coffee first. It could be a long night, and we've already had a long couple of days."

Chapter Six

The Outpost Bar was at the eastern end of a single structure mini-mall off Rio Rancho's busy Southern Boulevard. In the unit just west of the bar was a pet-grooming shop, followed by a payday loan establishment and a nail salon. The anchor business taking up the entire western half of the building was an Albertsons grocery.

Gordon was driving his four-year-old oversized pickup, which fit right in with the half dozen or so similar vehicles and a couple of SUVs more or less grouped outside the tavern. This side of the big asphalt parking lot was mostly empty, with almost all the other vehicles lined up in front of the Albertsons. At 6:00 PM, even with the summer sun still bright in the sky, these were the only two businesses still open.

"So, is this a cowboy bar, a blue-collar bar, a sports bar, or what?" Gordon asked as they climbed out of the big pickup. "Just what kind of outpost are they talking about? I can't tell from the generic sign."

"Maybe it's just a bar, and the Outpost name comes from the fact that it's at the end of the structure," Charlie replied, looking at the customer vehicles as they walked across the lot. "The stickers and window decals cover all the bases—the cartoon Chevy guy peeing on the Ford, the I'M A HORSE OWNER AND I VOTE on the bumper, the U.S. Marines decal on the rear window. There are a couple of gun racks, but no guns, just a fishing rod."

"So, no chick cars."

"There are women Marines, and this is New Mexico. As for horse owners, half of the women riders drive pickups and tote their own bales of hay," Charlie pointed out. "And a lot of them drink beer."

"Okay, but Rio Rancho itself isn't much of a cowboy town, despite the name. Closest thing to cowboy territory is along the river in the village of Corrales—minus the bicycle crowd in spandex—or north or south out of Albuquerque in the country."

"Yeah, but there's only one bar in Corrales. A cowgirl has got to go somewhere for a cold beer and a pickup line," Charlie commented as they stopped on the sidewalk in front of the entrance. "Besides, it's still early. It's probably mostly people who just got off work or are retired. Those patrons out to party won't show until dark."

He turned and looked toward the other businesses along the length of the big one-story building. "There are surveillance cameras, bro. One by the title loan store, and another just this side of the Albertsons. And check out the one at the corner." He pointed to the top of the covered roof at the eastern corner of the bar.

"Think they'd catch any activity out here, like a fight in the parking lot or along the sidewalk?" Gordon asked. "There are plenty of light poles, so even at night . . ."

"Well, if we can't find any human witnesses to this alleged fight, maybe we can convince someone to let us take a peek at their video. It's worth a shot," Charlie added, "even if we end up having to get it with a court order from RRPD. Only problem is, I don't know when this took place, only sometime during a twenty-four-hour time span, more likely when the bar was open."

"Hey, we don't think it even happened, right?" Gordon pointed out. "What we're looking for is the lack of evidence, which, when you think about it, doesn't help as much as it should. Let's grab a late-afternoon brew and strike up a conversation with the bartender."

He reached for the brass handle on the big wooden door and pulled. Unfortunately, just then someone was coming out. The man, wearing a ball cap and sunglasses, collided with Gordon, knocking him back.

Charlie was able to grab Gordon and keep him from falling to the sidewalk. The man coming out wasn't as lucky, however. Somehow he caught himself with outstretched hands, barely avoiding a face plant. The man cursed and scrambled to his feet.

"Hey, buddy, you okay?" Gordon asked, reaching out to help him. The guy turned away, nodding his head, and limped toward the parked vehicles. He jumped into a silver pickup, then raced away across the lot. Quickly he pulled out into traffic and drove away.

"No comment, no excuse me, no hey, you made me fall, wanna fight? What's his deal?"

Charlie shook his head, entering the pickup's license plate's letters and numbers into his phone. "Gordon. That was Frank Geiger, Ray's father. He didn't want me to realize who he was. And with the limp, that means he wasn't faking it."

"Double strange. Are you sure?"

"Pretty much. That silver pickup is identical to the one parked in Geiger's garage. I can ask Nancy to verify if it belongs to the guy. Let's go inside. I have a good idea what he was doing here, so follow my lead with the questions."

"I see where you're going with this. Besides, now I'm suddenly thirsty."

The bar was generic, just like the sign, but based upon the images of soldiers, sailors, and airmen that covered the back wall, it catered to military veterans and their friends and families. Rio Rancho was a relatively new, politically conservative community, and the home of many seniors. At the moment, the almost exclusively male clientele in the room was older-model retirees.

As they took seats at the bar, they looked around casually. There was no waitress, just the bartenders—a balding man in his fifties and his helper. The young man appeared, based upon facial features, to be the bartender's son.

"You two young men looking for a cold draft on a hot afternoon," the senior barkeep asked as he came over, "or maybe something with a little more bite?" He motioned toward the counter behind the bar, which contained a bottle of almost every brand of hard liquor Charlie had ever seen.

"Scotch ale for me," Gordon responded immediately.

"Same here. Hey, we just ran into Frank Geiger. Doesn't his son own that martial arts school off of Southern? Something dojo?" Charlie added, reaching for his wallet.

"Oh, yeah, Frank," the man replied, sliding the first tall glass over to Charlie.

"Looked like he was in a hurry. What's he up to now?" Charlie asked offhandedly, taking out a twenty. "For both of us," he added.

Gordon took the second beer. "Thanks, pal!" he said to Charlie.

The bartender was on automatic, taking the twenty, placing it on the register below the bar counter, then handing back the change.

Charlie slid back the ten. "We'll have a refill in a while. So what was bugging Frank today? He looked all pumped up."

"Oh, he was asking me if I'd heard about his son, Ray, getting caught between two hostile mamas out in the parking lot Saturday night. Said Ray had messed up his finger when one of the gals hit him with her tote bag. Musta had a brick inside, he said."

"Girl fight, huh? Anyone call the cops?" Gordon asked casually after taking a sip of his beer. "I worry about Ray. Heard he had a few run-ins when he was a kid back east."

"Yeah. Nobody called any cops Saturday night around here, but Frank was looking for witnesses in case one of the women decided to press charges or sue his kid's ass. It was the first I heard of it myself, and I was here until closing time. I'd have seen and maybe heard if the cops had shown up," he said.

"Women, they sure know how to push our buttons," Gordon responded.

The man behind the bar nodded. "Got that right. So how do you two know Ray?"

Gordon took a long sip before answering. "Martial arts is one of my passions."

"Yeah, Ray has some skills, so I heard. That martial arts school helps keep kids busy and out of trouble. Teaches them discipline. You a teacher or a student?"

"A little of both, beginning with Boys Club back in the city.

Growing up, I had to learn to take care of myself on the streets,"
Gordon admitted.

"Survival of the fittest. I hear you," the bartender replied.

"Hey, bro, let's park it at a table so I can lean back and stretch
my legs. I've been running around town all day," Charlie suggested
to Gordon, pointing at an empty table right by the entrance. Then
he turned to the bartender. "My dad would love this place. He was
a Marine."

"You serve? You look familiar," the bartender added, bringing
over a basket of chips and salsa.

"Army. Four deployments," Charlie responded, not wanting to
mention the times his face had been in the local paper or on
TV since he'd come home to New Mexico.

"Thanks for your service, soldier," the bartender added, extending his hand. "The next beer is on the house. I'm Donnie."

"Charlie. This is Gordon. We served in the same unit."

Donnie shook Gordon's hand next. "Being a little guy, guess
you had to learn how to kick ass."

Gordon shrugged.

"You have no idea," Charlie said.

After a while, Charlie remembered to call Nancy. Several minutes
later he got a text confirming that the silver pickup belonged to
Frank Geiger.

"You ready for another beer?" Charlie suggested, showing Gordon the news.

Gordon shook his head. "Naw, I'm driving. Let's kick back a
little longer, finish the chips and salsa. Then we can hunt down
some pizza or burgers."

"Good idea. What's the news on Margaret and Sam?" Charlie

asked, looking around the bar, noting that the place was starting to fill up now. Donnie had turned on the big-screen TV on the far wall, and a pregame show was gathering the attention of the old-timers.

"Margaret's getting released sometime this evening, about nine or so. Sam wants us around but said he'd give us a call ahead of time."

"Okay with me."

Several minutes later, chips and salsa gone, the guys stood and stepped away from the table.

"Hey, Charlie, I still owe you guys a beer," Donnie reminded them from behind the bar.

"Aw, we gotta run. We'll take you up on it next time," Charlie replied. "Have a good one."

"You too, soldier."

They stepped out onto the sidewalk, immediately feeling the wave of heat still drifting off the parking lot, but it was nothing compared to what he'd experienced overseas or even on the Rez growing up. Still, it brought sweat to the brow within the seconds it took them to walk over to Gordon's pickup. There were more cars in the lot now, though the truck was still sitting alone, with no vehicles adjacent at the moment. The closest car was an unoccupied, generic-looking faded silver sedan a hundred or so feet away.

Gordon thumbed the key fob, and both door locks on his truck clicked open. "Think Frank Geiger is going to worry about you now?"

"No doubt. I'm the only witness who can swear that his son was one of the three—and the guy who shot at Margaret. Nancy said Frank had been at the Rio Rancho station on Southern until

Ray was transferred to APD downtown. He didn't beat us to the bar by much."

"A few minutes earlier and we'd have met up with him inside," Gordon said, climbing behind the wheel. "Spinning Ray's alibi for the broken finger."

"Yeah. Frank is a streetwise cop, well, former cop, so he knows how to muddy the water. That alibi was probably his idea in the first place," Charlie pointed out as he fastened his seat belt and lowered the sun visor on his side. "I just hope DuPree and Nancy can gather up something else to help make the case. I'd hate to have the conviction depend on me pointing out Ray in court. If this goes to trial, the defense attorney is going to come at me with both barrels."

Charlie turned his head, hearing a strange scraping noise coming from below the truck as they started moving. "What was that?"

Gordon quickly put on the brakes, coming to a stop maybe fifty feet from the parking-lot exit into the main street. "There's a low rumble, like sounds of something dragging underneath the truck. Think it's on your side." He looked over at Charlie.

"It's probably just a tumbleweed, but it deserves a look," Charlie suggested, unfastening his seat belt.

"I don't trust Frank," Charlie added, "and he knows why we went to that particular bar. He may have come back and tampered with something underneath. We were inside long enough, he had time."

Gordon turned off the ignition and grabbed the keys. They both got out quickly, closed their doors to make room, then crouched down onto their knees, looking beneath the pickup.

"There, a plastic trash bag attached to the frame on this side of the engine mounts," Charlie observed. He lowered himself onto the asphalt and gazed underneath. "It's been hooked by a wire. I think I can reach it."

"Watch out for the glass," Gordon warned. "Someone broke a beer bottle or two."

"I hear you." Charlie rolled onto his side, inched beneath the pickup about a foot farther, and reached up and pulled the wire loose. Then he crawled and slid back out from underneath, pulling the trash bag out with him.

He stood, holding the bag, which probably weighed a pound or less. "Feels like trash inside, appropriately enough. That was put up there while we were in the bar," Charlie said, taking a quick glance around, seeing no one in the lot. "But why such a juvenile—" He didn't finish the thought, distracted by the sudden noise of an accelerating engine and the squeal of tires on asphalt.

Charlie turned around, letting go of the bag. The silver-gray sedan was racing right at him, tires smoking in a blue cloud as the vehicle rapidly accelerated. The pickup door was shut, and he was trapped, standing in the open. Heart pounding, he dropped and rolled beneath the pickup, feeling the rush of wind a few seconds later as the car raced past. There was a thud, the pickup trembled, then the car whipped out into the street. He heard something bouncing across the asphalt, then roll to a stop.

Charlie rolled out from beneath the truck, looking down, and saw that the car had broken off the passenger-side mirror. That was what he'd heard rolling away.

"You okay?" Gordon yelled from the other side of the pickup.

"Hell yeah! Let's get that bastard!" Charlie reached for the door handle.

By the time he was inside, Gordon already had the truck in

gear. Cursing, they had to wait for a passing car, but the pause gave Charlie a chance to fasten his seat belt.

Gordon drove off the curb, turning hard right at the same time. The big pickup bounced like a bucking bronco, but Gordon maintained control and held the vehicle in the lane as he pressed down on the gas pedal.

"Grab your Beretta," Gordon yelled, focusing on traffic, but Charlie was already on it. He opened the glove compartment and brought out his backup 9 mm weapon, identical to the one currently in the hands of the crime lab. He'd left it in the vehicle before entering the bar. They both had concealed carry permits, but no one was allowed to consume alcohol in a bar or tavern if armed.

"Was it Frank?" Gordon asked, weaving past slower-moving vehicles as he doubled the speed limit. The sun had fallen low in the sky, though, and they were heading up Southern Boulevard, right into the western horizon. Eyes still forward, Gordon reached over to the center console and grabbed his sunglasses by feel.

"Didn't see the face, too much glare off the windshield, but who else knew we were here?" Charlie said, trying to look ahead for Gordon. He tapped his shirt pocket and brought out his sunglasses. "Damn. I cracked a lens."

"You sure that's all? The car went flying by."

Charlie felt down his right leg, finding a damp spot on his pants about halfway up his thigh. "I must have rolled over some glass. I'm leaking blood."

"A little or a lot?"

"Not much. I'm starting to feel it now, and I think it's just a puncture, not a scrape. Good news is that it missed my junk. It'll wait until after we catch up to the bastard."

"*If* we catch up. I just lost sight of him," Gordon grumbled, having to brake suddenly to avoid rear-ending an old pickup hauling construction-site trash.

"Next street, I think he turned right," Charlie exclaimed, looking across the parking lot of another strip mall ahead of a Walmart superstore on the next block. The faded silver sedan was heading north now.

The light turned red, and both lanes ahead were blocked by traffic.

"Hang on!" Gordon yelled, gunning the engine and hopping up the curb onto the parking lot. "Watch for people and cars, I'm cutting across!"

Ten seconds later, they raced out of the parking lot in the direction the sedan had gone, but by then it had disappeared up the street. "I'll check left, you check right," Gordon suggested, keeping the pickup within the speed limit now. They cruised north for another half mile; then Gordon pulled off the street and backed into a parking slot in front of a convenience store so they could observe passing traffic.

"Maybe he'll double back?" Charlie asked.

"Naw, we lost him. We've gotta call the cops," Gordon reminded him.

"Probably should have done that sooner."

"We were kinda busy. Too bad we had to leave our pistols in the truck when we went into the bar."

"Yeah. If we'd have had weapons in our hands I might have forced him to swerve away," Charlie mumbled, entering 911 on his phone display.

"Or you'd still be standing there, and he'd have had the extra second or two he needed to bounce you off his windshield like a bug. How bad are you cut, anyway?" Gordon asked, looking at the bloody spot.

"Not enough to slow me down. I think the bleeding's stopped." He felt around the spot and found an object imbedded in his skin. "Definitely feels like a piece of glass, or maybe a sharp rock. Not a nail or piece of metal."

"Don't cut your finger trying to dig it out. Leave it there to plug the wound. You're gonna need a medic and some antibiotics, Charlie."

Charlie whistled low.

"What?" Gordon asked.

"There are tire tread marks on the cuff of my right pant leg. Talk about close."

Charlie and Gordon arrived back at the parking lot in front of the Outpost five minutes later. A police car was already there, parked in front of the bar, emergency lights flashing in the twilight. Several onlookers were on the sidewalk, including the bartender, Donnie, all kept there by one of two Rio Rancho patrolmen. A second officer, powerful flashlight in hand, was searching the surface of the parking lot itself.

Gordon parked next to the police car, and he and Charlie climbed out of the truck, identifying themselves to the officer. The sound of more sirens seemed to come from three directions, but the boxy EMT vehicle pulled in first.

"Prepare to be pantsed, Chuck," Gordon joked.

"Crap. That hasn't happened since elementary school," Charlie replied. "It took three guys."

"Stay positive. Maybe one of the medics is a woman. It only takes one of them."

Chapter Seven

When Charlie eased back out of the EMT van, minus his right pant leg chopped off almost to his Hanes, his entire leg smelled of antiseptic. There was one large bandage in place where a quarter-sized chunk of beer bottle had been removed, and three smaller ones from lesser pieces of glass. He was also scuffed up with minor road rash in several spots, including his elbows and left shoulder, but looking back it was a miracle he hadn't been struck by the car.

Gordon was a hundred feet away, close to the street curb, apparently describing the series of events to Detective Johnson, one of the detectives who'd arrested Ray Geiger that morning. It seemed like years ago now. A crime scene van was parked south of the incident scene, and large floodlights illuminated the area where Gordon's pickup had been when the shooting started, enabling a detailed search of the lot.

Charlie hadn't walked twenty feet in that direction before Detective DuPree saw him on the move and approached.

"Damn, Charlie, now the bad guys are throwing cars at you.

Sweeney claims there are even tire tracks on your pants," the detective said. "Shake your hand for luck?"

"Yours or mine?" Charlie responded, grinning slightly. "It was half luck, half American Ninja Warrior. If I hadn't had those couple of seconds to drop and roll under the truck, I'd have been thrown halfway across the parking lot."

Then Charlie thought of something. "Did anyone check for paint scrapes on the side mirror knocked off Gordon's pickup?"

"Yeah, your pal thought of that right away. The finish was faded silver or gray from what he thinks was a VW Passat. He picked out the VW based upon photo comparisons he was shown. There were a few paint stripes on the mirror, and Sweeny thought it was from the original finish, not primer, so the lab people might be able to identify the manufacturer. Can you confirm the make and model of the car?" DuPree asked.

"Not enough to verify the ID. It was an older model, and I don't remember any corporate letter in the center of the grille, like an *H, T,* or *VW.* I was out of the country for years, though, and I'm less familiar with auto makes and models," Charlie explained. "From the engine noise it was at least a V-6, however, and I got the impression that the grille was a rounded rectangular shape."

"That fits with a Passat, which comes with higher-performance options, and backs up Sweeney's observations. What about the vehicle plates? Sweeney would only say that the yellow color matches NM tags."

"I couldn't make out a number or letter, but I agree that the plates were New Mexico yellow," Charlie said, nodding.

"Maybe we'll get lucky with the paint job," DuPree said. "But narrowing down the driver might be a little easier. Your pal thinks it could have been Frank Geiger. Sweeney bumped into a guy with a bad leg coming out of the bar over there not too long before you were ambushed. Says you recognized the guy."

"That last part is certainly true. The driver could have been Frank, though I didn't really get a good look at his face. There was some glare on the windshield, and all I could see was a cap and sunglasses."

DuPree nodded.

Detective Johnson, the plainclothes officer who'd been talking to Gordon, came up just then. He nodded to DuPree, then formally introduced himself to Charlie.

"Mr. Sweeney speculated that the man who almost ran you down might have been Frank Geiger. Can you confirm that?" Johnson asked.

"Not visually, but based upon the timing and the fact that he knew who and where I was, it's likely. This was a deliberate hit, not a random attack, and he and his son are the only two people I know of who might want to kill me—at the moment."

"I appreciate your honesty, but what about the friends and relatives of Anthony Lorenzo, the man you shot last night in the hospital area during the carjacking attempt?" Johnson inquired. "Or maybe the third perp? Could it have been someone else following you around who's not associated with previous events, or maybe a proprietor from the bar? The perp wasn't in a silver pickup, it was a faded silver-gray sedan, probably a VW or Toyota, and the license plate was yellow, in-state tags. Is that correct?"

"Where is all this going?" DuPree asked the detective. "Frank Geiger is at the top of my list."

"Then you'd better get out your eraser, DuPree. I just got word that until a few minutes ago, Frank Geiger was at the Rio Rancho Department of Public Safety, about a mile up the street. According to the duty officer and staff at that location, Geiger has been there for almost an hour, filling out forms and requests for copies of arrest records and transfer papers on Ray. There are surveillance cameras that will back that up. Geiger's Chevy pickup is in their lot."

"Then Frank Geiger couldn't have been the driver," Charlie acknowledged. He turned to DuPree. "You know what that means?"

"Yeah, Charlie. Geiger must have set up the hit on his way to the station. He has an airtight alibi for that time interval."

"You certain that Frank Geiger was the man who came out of the bar and bumped into Mr. Sweeney?" Johnson asked.

"I'm sure, limp and everything. Like the detective said, Geiger must have headed straight to the station. It would have been tight, but certainly possible, assuming the guy in the car was already in this area or within a half hour. He probably lives in Rio Rancho or in Corrales, or maybe north Albuquerque, even."

"Rio Rancho makes sense. The dead carjacker was from this community, so my theory is the guy who tried to run you down was the third perp, the one that got away. He couldn't have been Ray Geiger, who's already locked up," Johnson surmised. "And now, Detective DuPree, it looks like we're still working a case that overlaps. Just when you thought it was all yours."

"So we team up. There is a joint agency procedure already in place, thankfully," DuPree responded. "Agreed?" he added, holding out his hand.

"Agreed," Johnson replied with a firm shake. Then he turned to Charlie. "What were you and your friend Sweeney doing at the Outpost Bar?"

Charlie suspected the detective already knew, or had an idea, as did DuPree. "Mr. Sweeney broke, or at least badly injured, the trigger finger of the person who shot Mrs. Randal on Sunday after-noon during the home invasion. That person is Ray Geiger, who claimed earlier today to have injured that finger outside this bar while breaking up a fight between two women."

"So you decided to check up on his story?" Johnson responded, looking over at DuPree.

"I'd asked Detective Larranaga to follow up on that, but apparently he hasn't got around to it yet," DuPree said.

"All of our detectives are carrying a heavy load, but I can't speak to the issue," Johnson replied. "I'll handle it from here."

"Charlie, tell me what you and Sweeney learned in the bar. It won't be admissible in court, but it might save us some time," DuPree insisted. "And after you fill us in, I want you and Sweeney to leave the criminal investigation to law enforcement professionals."

"Of course, Detective DuPree," Charlie lied. As always, when he was committed to someone, in this case protecting the Randals, his friends, and himself, he was going to be on the offense. The concept of defense was a tactic he only employed after forcing his enemies to attack. He would, of course, try to avoid breaking any major laws.

By then, Gordon had come over and heard DuPree's warning. Trying to look sincere, he listened while Charlie described their visit to the bar and what Donnie, the bartender, had told them. Gordon confirmed the narrative.

Johnson promised to follow up checking the alibi and agreed to search the surveillance cameras outside some of the businesses for any evidence that might prove useful. He told them to remain on the scene, then excused himself and walked over to talk to the bartender.

While they were waiting for permission to leave, Charlie got a call from Sam Randal, who was waiting with Margaret while her release papers were being prepared. Nancy, off duty, had joined them at Saint Mark's, then followed Sam and Margaret home. Nancy had agreed to watch their house the rest of the evening.

Finally, around eleven, Charlie and Gordon pulled up at the curb across the street from the Randal home. They chose to split up the rest of the night, one of them watching the house while the other slept next door, on Nancy and Gina's sofa.

Charlie, too hyped up to sleep, took the first watch, remaining in Gordon's pickup. He hadn't wanted to take the extra time needed to get his own vehicle, which was still at his house. Selecting a spot along the curb a few houses down the street from the Randal property, he was in position to watch the front entrance without being obvious.

Charlie adjusted the driver's seat to accommodate his six-foot-plus frame, tilted the back just a little, and adjusted the mirrors in order to spot anyone coming up from behind. Then he used a wet sponge, bottled water, and paper towels he'd gotten from Gina to clean the leather upholstery on the passenger side where he'd left blood earlier. It didn't take long because most of the blood had soaked into his pants leg, which had been cut away by the EMT. He felt kind of odd still wearing half shorts, half pants, but it wasn't cold at all, and the bandages on the gouges and scrapes would have rubbed his pant leg—if he'd still had one.

Once he was settled, his Beretta resting on the console beside the stick shift, Charlie checked his e-mail. There was nothing but spam. The Doppler radar on his KOB weather app showed nothing but clear skies ahead, so it was going to be a cloudless night. The closest streetlight was at the end of the block, but the moon was up and bright, and once in a while he'd spot a small bat flashing through the glow, snagging an insect. Used to being awake and alert at night after so many years deployed or in training, he was at ease. Gordon was going to relieve him at 2:30 AM.

Around midnight, a car full of teenagers approached, the sound system of their low-slung Nissan shaking the truck with the boom-boom of profanity-enhanced rap. Charlie nodded to the driver, who, surprisingly, nodded back. After the kids tossed a few beer bottles out onto the lawn on Charlie's side of the street a few houses down, the car continued around the corner. Anyone sleeping along the block was probably awake now.

Sure enough, Charlie saw movement around the living room window of the Randal house. He and Gordon had already warned the Randals to stay away from anywhere they could be seen from outside, especially when their lights were on. At least Sam, or whoever it was, hadn't turned on the lights.

Ten seconds later, his phone rang. "Everything okay?" Sam asked in a sleepy voice.

"Just teenagers out partying, Sam. Get some rest," Charlie responded.

His watch continued, and only one marginally suspicious vehicle came by, a van with tinted windows. There was no way Charlie could see the driver, but he was on the same side of the street as the Randal house, and noted that no windows were rolled down in the passing vehicle. No one but a complete idiot would try shooting through a closed window that close to their face. If it was a recon, it was a one-time event, and for all he knew, it was just a burglar sizing up the neighborhood for tomorrow morning's break-ins. He couldn't get a good look at the license plate; it was either worn thin or coated with dried mud—an old tactic among criminals, he'd heard.

Most burglaries in this part of the country took place during daylight hours when people were at work. However, recently, in this area burglars had begun to encounter armed homeowners, and at least two perps had been shot. So many burglaries were committed by drug addicts that Charlie doubted this would slow the crime rate by much. At least the home invaders that had hit the Randals hadn't been high enough to go completely psycho on them.

After a couple of hours, he thought about playing some music, then decided it was better to listen to the night. Although he mostly heard crickets, it was important not to miss the sound of a kicked-in door, breaking glass, or even a scream. He was on a mission, after all, even if there were no insurgents or terrorists sneaking through the neighborhood. He had to stay smart.

Hours later, lying on the comfortable leather sofa in Nancy and Gina's open-space living area, he looked through the windows of the French doors that led to the patio and beyond. They'd decided not to close the curtains so it would be easier to watch the back of the Randal residence in case someone tried to sneak in through the alley. Nancy or Gina had placed clear packing tape over the eye-level bullet hole. At least it was safety glass and hadn't really shattered or splintered. A glazier was supposed to be coming by sometime in the afternoon to replace the pane. Gina had already patched the hole in the wall after the crime tech had removed the bullet.

Charlie didn't know if he wanted to sleep or not, with the nightmares likely again, but he was bone tired. He closed his eyes just for a moment, then awoke in broad daylight.

"Morning," Nancy whispered from her stool beside the breakfast bar. She was wearing her dark blue APD uniform, working days with DuPree, so her shift would be coming up before too long.

Checking the clock above the sink, Charlie noted it was nearly seven.

"Care for some oatmeal and blueberries? I made enough for four," Nancy offered. "There's also coffee. K-cups, pick your favorite."

"Where's Gordon?" Charlie said, swinging his legs around and sitting up.

"He's out on the patio, finishing his brew while watching the Randal house. He ate a half hour ago when he came in."

"I'll pass on the oatmeal, but can I grab a cup of coffee? I need to hurry home, take a shower, then put on some decent clothes."

She looked him over, then grinned. "You remind me of a kid who got into the first aid kit on Halloween."

"Hey, my sister did something like that once. She wasted a whole box of Band-Aids, playing nurse to me after I'd gone into Mom's roses trying to retrieve a baseball. Damned thorns are lethal. But first, let me see if Gordon is willing to loan me his truck for an hour."

"Why? That no-right-pant-leg style makes you look . . . well, maybe it makes other people look. Stare, actually," Nancy joked. "Is there such a thing as a half-flasher?"

Gina, who didn't have to be at her law office until nine, gave Charlie a ride to his home. Later, he met Gordon, who'd gone by his own apartment, just before eight. Jake had come in a bit earlier and was eating a breakfast burrito out front by the register.

They sat silently at their desks, half asleep as they drank coffee. Then Charlie's cell phone rang.

"That's early," Gordon said, standing to get a good look at Charlie over the desk computer monitor.

"It's Nancy," Charlie muttered, touching the display. "Can I put you on speaker?" he asked, touching the symbol anyway.

"Who's with you?" Nancy responded, her words clipped.

"Just Gordon."

"Okay. I've got some news you two need to hear. Ray Geiger made bail."

"That's not good. Where are you?" Gordon asked, stepping around beside Charlie.

"Watching the street and the Randal house from my APD unit," Nancy responded. "I'm on duty, and I'm going to visit the Randals and give them the news. Apparently, DuPree wasn't told that Ray had been released until an hour ago."

"So Ray could be anywhere right now?" Charlie asked.

"Not really. Despite Ray's clean record in NM and his martial arts for youth program, the DA managed to talk the judge into requiring an ankle monitor due to the violent nature of the charges, the joint agencies involved, and other factors. Ray is allowed to move freely within the community but is required to notify the station if he wants to leave Rio Rancho city limits. He's at his father's house right now."

"So he and Frank are basically free to come and go?" Charlie concluded.

"Yeah, but there's some good news. Although the tracker has unlimited range, RRPD is going to put a tail on Ray, plus keep Frank Geiger's residence under surveillance 24/7. If either Geiger gets a visitor, the surveillance team will know," Nancy added. "Supposedly."

"What about phone calls?" Gordon asked. "Internet?"

"Not in the terms of release. Unless there is probable cause that either of the Geigers is communicating with that third suspect and an additional warrant is issued, we won't know. Nobody is listening in."

"Until it's too late," Charlie grumbled. "Where is NSA when you need them? You think Frank might try to do something else? I don't think he's the third guy because of the limp, but . . ."

"Maybe he's the fourth, the planner, the guy behind the scenes," Gordon ventured. "Or he was waiting in the back of the van during the home invasion and was never seen."

"Which is why DuPree wants me to help protect the Randals until we get a better handle on exactly what's going on. He can't rule out this crew's participation in the other home invasions. There's also the likelihood that the hospital attack was an indirect attempt to get rid of one eyewitness," Nancy said.

"Snag Sam in order to silence Margaret?" Gordon asked.

"Hoping that my quick look wouldn't be enough on its own—if she refused to make an ID while her husband was held hostage. That seems a bit too complicated from a group of thugs just strong-arming people in their homes," Charlie pointed out. "And at the time, they didn't know Margaret wasn't going to identify Ray. Do they know that now? I'm not clear on police procedures. Nancy?"

"If this goes beyond a grand jury, the defense will be told. Until then, the Randals are still considered witnesses that might be targeted."

"So what are Ray's options on this?" Gordon asked.

"If the DNA trace from beneath Margaret's fingernails from the scratch on Ray's face isn't conclusive in itself, juries tend to go with eyewitness testimony and whatever other strong evidence is presented. Geiger's attorney may argue that the dead perp, Anthony Lorenzo, was the shooter at the Randals' house, not Ray. You're the only solid eyewitness, Charlie," Nancy explained. "It may all hinge on you, especially if no other evidence, like the gun, is produced."

Charlie nodded. "That establishes a motive for the attempt on my life yesterday. My money is still on Ray's associates or someone Frank called in to do the deed. Ex-cops might know the names of criminals they crossed paths with who are willing to earn a little extra money."

"Frank could still contact the guy who tried to run you down and request a do-over. The guy has to be someone who lives or hangs out within fifteen or so minutes of that location," Gordon said.

"Or even closer. It took a few minutes to hook up the distraction under your truck," Charlie reminded him. "Unless Frank did that himself."

"Okay, guys, it sounds like Frank might be the key to this," Nancy interrupted. "Rio Rancho cops agreed to notify us if Frank leaves his house, but don't have enough officers to follow him, so—"

"Don't say it," Gordon responded quickly, nodding to Charlie. "Just keep an eye on the Randals."

"Nancy. Tell Gina to watch her back," Charlie added. "She's part of this too, and if the men think they might be able to get some leverage that'll help sour the case . . ."

"Already done. I've gotta go now. There's a man here to replace the windows and I want to make sure he's legit. You guys be careful," Nancy added. "Oh, and for what it's worth, Detective Du-Pree asked me to remind you two not to do anything that might hurt the prosecution when this goes to trial. Neither one of you is a cop."

"No problem. You know us, Sergeant Medina," Gordon replied indignantly.

Nancy mumbled something, then ended the call.

"What did she call us? Smart assets?" Gordon grinned, looking up as Ruth came in the back door from the alley.

"Good morning, gentlemen," Ruth announced with a smile. "What's new?"

Chapter Eight

Charlie and Gordon sat at a Starbucks in the same shopping center as a Lowe's Home Center and Albertsons grocery in Rio Rancho, having arrived there about fifteen minutes after three. It wasn't likely that Ray would have wanted a police car parked outside his dojo during business hours, so they'd assumed that he wouldn't be present when his martial arts school opened at three thirty for afternoon and evening classes. An ankle monitor would have also raised some hard-to-explain questions, or maybe not, depending on how many troubled teens were in a particular class. It might have even upped his street cred.

Frank Geiger, however, could show up to continue managing operations, though, according to the Web site, he wasn't a regular instructor except for a personal defense class he sometimes offered to seniors. Charlie had guessed that Frank might be there today, and if he was, it might be a good way for Geiger to make contact with the remaining member of the criminal trio without undue suspicion.

Nancy promised to notify them any time Frank left his residence, with or without his son, via the Rio Rancho officers watching the senior Geiger's home, where Ray was staying at the moment.

Charlie was reading an article on ankle bracelets on his smartphone when the text tone sounded. Gordon, drinking a double espresso while staring out the window, turned his head. "Nancy?"

Charlie nodded, reading the text. "Frank just drove off, alone, in his silver pickup headed toward Southern."

"If he's coming to open Butkikin Dojo, he should be here in less than ten minutes. If he's going out for groceries or anywhere else, we've guessed wrong. But the timing is right. First class begins at three thirty," Gordon said, looking at his watch.

Charlie smiled. "Somebody could already be there to open up. I'd imagine one of the other teachers also has a key to the doors."

"It's what we do," Gordon said, then took a big sip of coffee. "I wonder what it's like running a martial arts school?"

"You would do all right. You already know martial arts, even the vocabulary. Bet you could have taken out that guy in the hall in a hurry if there hadn't been two guns waving in your direction."

Gordon grinned. "Bit of a distraction, all right. Even Bruce Lee would have had trouble blocking a bullet. But you showed up, and you kick ass along with the best."

"When I have to." Charlie stood. "Let's get into a better position to watch the dojo and see some faces. If Frank shows up, I'm betting he parks in the front beneath a light pole. This is New Mexico, where newer-model pickups often end up in Old Mexico."

"Yeah. I wonder if we really made a dent in that." Gordon recalled the strange turn of events last year with a gleam in his eyes. They'd helped, indirectly, in bringing down one of New Mexico's biggest auto theft rings.

It took less than two minutes for Charlie to cross the parking area and position the Charger directly across from the cleaners. From there, they could watch the front of the dojo, which was the next leased unit. All the businesses were constructed with a row of large windows along the side of the building facing the parking lot.

On the dojo glass were posters of students in white martial arts uniforms going through drills and mock combat. These were interspaced with photos of the black-uniformed teachers in action poses, along with a poster-sized copy of a newspaper feature on the school. School hours and the times of the various youth, adult, and senior classes were also posted.

The spacious parking lot itself was typical of those in New Mexico, where land was cheaper and a majority of the driving-age citizens had access to one or more personal vehicles. Metro public transit was limited to a couple of cab lines, city and retirement home busses, and the Rail Runner train. That service carried commuters on a single north-south route that extended from Santa Fe down the Rio Grande Valley to the community of Belen, less than forty miles south of Albuquerque. Rio Rancho, the smaller city to the northwest of Albuquerque, lay several miles west of the closest passenger terminal.

They were parked barely fifty feet away from the entrance, and Charlie was adjusting the rearview mirror and side mirrors to watch the front, when Gordon spoke. "Here comes a silver Chevy pickup, man at the wheel."

They kept watch out of the corner of their eye, seemingly busy with their phones as the pickup parked beneath the closest light pole to the dojo. A man wearing slacks and a black sweatshirt with the school logo climbed out, took a quick glance around the lot, and strolled toward the entrance with a pronounced limp.

"Just as predicted," Gordon gloated. "It's Frank, right? All I got before was a chest in my face and a view of his backside."

"It's him. Notice the trained-police-officer scan of the environment, instead of the head-down cell phone fixation most people have these days. He isn't even carrying the beloved device in his hand, or texting," Charlie said.

Gordon chuckled, still gazing at his phone, which at the moment was on the main screen. "Old man just isn't clued into the tech world, is he?"

"Says the guy who sleeps with his phone."

"Hey, she loves me."

His smartphone still at read angle, Charlie watched as Frank unlocked and opened the door, then stepped inside and turned the sign inside from CLOSED to OPEN.

"Think he noticed us?" Gordon asked.

"Yeah, but did he recognize who we are?" Charlie adjusted the bill on his baseball cap, which was bumping into his sunglasses.

Gordon had on a thin hoodie, despite the hot afternoon sun, and, unlike yesterday, no sunglasses.

"He got a long look at me the other day when Ray was arrested. We were kept outside together. I should have added a fake beard."

"You'd have a better disguise with a unicorn horn. Navajos can't grow beards."

"Hey, scraggly ones I can manage. Like a sixties' hippie."

"We weren't even around in the sixties, dude."

"That expression sure was." Charlie sighed, finally setting

down his cell phone. "So, we wait and take photos of any adults or older teens that show up."

"Those on my side I get, those on your side are yours, Charlie. Once it gets dark, we're screwed. The flash gives it away. I should have brought my old-school camera, the one that just takes photos."

"No worry, we should still have enough light at closing time if these parking-lot lamps give off any glow at all."

Gordon groaned. "We gonna stay that long?"

"Maybe. If we hope to catch Frank meeting up with someone, this could be the ticket. The shooter or third man in the crew could come in as a student or visitor and not stand out, and even if they look like hoods, remember that this dojo professes to help youthful offenders. Frank isn't going to use his regular phone, and they may have already gotten rid of any burners, if they carried any at all. None were found on the body or in the van."

"Frank would know we know that, wouldn't he?" Gordon argued.

"Worst-case scenario, we waste our time playing with our phones."

"Ah, that's a good point," Gordon responded. "How much time does Frank have to get Ray out of hot water? Ray is out of action with that ankle bracelet. It's up to Frank and the third guy to take care of things. If I was that guy I'd be in Colorado or Wyoming by now."

"Gordon, you'd never run out on your team."

"But if I was that guy, I wouldn't be the loyal, dedicated, highly capable Gordon Sweeney. I'd be Punk Number Three, John Q. Loser, the inferior marksman."

Charlie reached for the dashboard media system. "Music?"

"Yeah. Let's save our phone batteries for photos."

• • •

Charlie and Gordon kept watch, taking photos of adults and older teens that matched the physical descriptions as they arrived or left the dojo. They took a dinner break in the middle of the second tier of classes, returning to their stakeout not long after. About ten minutes after nine, when it appeared that the last student had left, Frank and two of his instructors, in black martial arts uniforms, came out and walked directly toward the Charger. All three were carrying fighting sticks.

"What's with the clubs?" Charlie said, watching the men approaching. He saw no need to reach for his Beretta.

"Those are bastons or mutons, sometimes used in Arnis, a Filipino martial art," Gordon responded. "Too short for stickball, great for defense or attack in the hands of a master. One of the earliest martial arts weapons was a wooden staff."

"Not knowing the history, I would have guessed it'd be a rock," Charlie commented. "Looks like we're about to be intimidated." He reached for the door handle.

"Watch out, Charlie. They always go for the biggest target first."

"Tell me about it."

Gordon sighed, stepping out the passenger side, glancing around the basically empty half of the parking lot. "At least we don't have an audience—yet."

"Mr. Geiger, do your son's students know Ray is out on bail wearing an ankle monitor after being arrested for a half-dozen violent crimes, including kidnapping and attempted murder?" Charlie asked as the three men approached.

"Frank told you about that, right?" Gordon announced to the instructors. "You sensei have no problem with standing on the wrong side of the law?"

The two men looked at each other, then Frank.

"So Frank fed you some BS about us?" Gordon added. "No surprise."

"My son is innocent. He was set up because he got into some trouble in his teens," Frank argued. "And you two are trying to scare off the staff and students. Get the hell out of here."

Charlie shook his head. "Ray's been arrested a dozen times and convicted twice for crimes beginning when he was in his teens, Frank. Add to that a home invasion, robbery, assault, attempted murder, kidnapping, and more. He'll be your age or older when he finally gets out of prison. Man up to the truth about your son," Charlie responded, pushing the envelope just a little more.

"He's already out on bail. You're just here to piss me off, Indian," Frank replied.

"Clearly, it's working. So call the cops and report us. Just know, if you decide to start a fight, Ray's going to have two of his instructors out of commission and have to cancel most of the classes," Gordon replied. "You're going to need the school's income for his defense attorney when he goes to trial."

The smaller of the two instructors, still a few inches taller than Gordon, laughed. "Cocky, aren't you? You wanna take this inside and show me what you've got—besides trash talk?"

"Anytime, anyplace, shorty," Gordon replied.

"Maybe we *should* settle this indoors," Charlie suggested, noting that a grocery store employee who was gathering shopping carts from the parking lot had stopped and was watching them. If the cops came by, it might end up actually helping Ray's case and hurt his own testimony as an eyewitness. He and Gordon intended to do what it took to ID the other perps, but not in public. "You don't want to hurt your rep, do you, Frank?"

"You looking for an excuse to walk away now, Indian?" Frank sneered.

Charlie laughed. If Geiger only knew who'd actually be able to walk away once Gordon got his hands and feet on them. "Lead the way, grasshopper," he teased, bowing.

Less than a minute later, they entered the large training space of the dojo, where most of the tile floor was covered with blue vinyl exercise mats. The back wall, except for a door leading into a hallway that probably contained an office and dressing rooms, was lined with full-length mirrors. Their presence created the look of a much larger workout space.

When they'd entered, one of the instructors turned on two of the four rows of recessed overhead lights, then Frank locked the door, leaving the keys in the mechanism. Whatever happened in the dojo stayed in the dojo.

Now they stood in the middle of the room atop the largest mat. The surface was firm and offered good footing.

Charlie shook his head, not taking his eye off the larger instructor, who'd been sizing him up. "Boys. You might want to put down your sticks and walk away while you still can. Let Ray and his pop fight their own battles."

"Listen to the man," Gordon added.

"Come on, shorty," the guy snarled. "Make your move," he insisted, taking a stance.

"You might want to borrow your friend's baston, kohai," Gordon said, using the term for a less experienced student. "You're going to need both weapons."

The guy paused, apparently realizing that Gordon might not be such an easy target after all.

Charlie watched their eyes, checking for any signal or glance that would send a warning. Frank had been closing the distance and was the immediate threat at the moment. Charlie glanced down and saw that he was clutching a roll of coins in his left hand. A hard ex-cop fought old-school dirty, especially one who had a bad leg.

Charlie sideslipped Frank's sudden attempt at a sucker punch. The jab grazed his cheek, but the move left Frank open to a counterpunch, which caught the older man in the nose just as he was shifting his weight forward. Blood erupted from Frank's nose and splattered the vinyl.

Frank staggered back, instinctively kicking out, anticipating that Charlie would move in quickly to finish him off. Charlie, instead, had maintained his balance and a defensive stance, anticipating an immediate strike from his second opponent, the taller instructor.

It was the right move. The man rushed in, aiming a blow with his baston at Charlie's shoulder. Charlie had already closed the gap, and the attacker found himself too close to be effective. He struck Charlie with his wrist instead, which must have hurt. The impact caused him to lose his grip on the weapon, which bounced off Charlie's back onto the floor.

Charlie, in his face now, caught the man off balance, hammering him with an elbow on the side of his head. The man staggered, bumping into Frank, who was trying to close in again, and they both stumbled.

Gordon's opponent had attacked an instant later than Frank, swiveling at the hip and attacking Charlie's pal with a powerful rear kick, the sliding step providing maximum extension of his right foot. The attack was designed to strike up high, aimed at Gordon's throat.

But Gordon was quicker, having reacted instinctively to the move. He'd stepped inside the kick, using his side to block the man's leg, then pinned it to his left side with his arm. He twisted the leg around and forward, turning his attacker away and exposing his backside and groin. Instead of taking him out right then with a kick to the balls, Gordon kicked him in the butt and knocked him to his knees. The baston flew out of his hand and bounced across the mats onto the hard tile close to the wall.

Frank, bleeding at the nose and enraged now, rushed in on Charlie, faked a left jab, then threw a hard right. Charlie wasn't in the mood for a street fight. He ducked left and punched Frank in the ribs. Frank gasped, staggered to the side, then reached down to his waist.

"No gun there anymore, Frank. You're not a cop. Calm down before you go too far," Charlie yelled, trying to reason with the guy.

The tall instructor came forward with a karate move next, striking out with the sides of his hands, feints with his knees, then a kick to Charlie's thigh. Charlie blocked the strikes with his forearms and hands, keeping his hands up, stepping back slowly, encouraging his attacker to move in. The next time his opponent threw a left jab, Charlie blocked it with his right palm, bringing around a left roundhouse and putting his body into the blow. The man's right was up, but the force of the punch knocked away his hand, and Charlie caught the man fully in the cheek. He spun around, spitting up blood, then came up in defensive mode, his eyes wide with surprise, and maybe some fear.

"Walk away, guys," Gordon warned. "You're outmanned and you know it. And Frank, you need to go to Urgent Care. Your nose looks like raw liver."

Charlie glanced behind him, noting that the grocery clerk he'd seen earlier was on the sidewalk outside, face to the window, trying to see what they were doing. "It's only a matter of time before that kid brings up his cell phone and calls the cops. Why don't you boys calm down, clean up, then go home before you get us all arrested? Once this dojo is in the news and the bad press comes down, you can kiss your jobs good-bye," he told the two instructors. "And how about you, Frank? How is losing Ray's business gonna help keep him out of prison?"

"Stay out of this, bastards. I'm not done with you," Frank warned, holding a handkerchief to his bloodied face.

"We're not done until Ray and his third partner are serving time, Geiger. Keep it up and you're going to be sharing his cell," Charlie added.

"Satisfying workout, sifu," Gordon announced cheerfully, looking at the battered instructors, who were also wiping away blood. "But remember this: To subdue the enemy without fighting is the greatest skill."

Charlie looked over at him. "*Now* you tell them?"

Gordon shrugged. Gordon turned the key in the lock, and they stepped out of the dojo, greeting the curious grocery store employee with a cheerful "good evening." Without a backward glance, they walked across the lot to the Dodge.

A few minutes later, as they drove east down Twentieth, a squad car raced by, emergency lights and siren wailing. Gordon looked back in the side mirror. "Is that for us?"

"Not unless the kid actually made the call. I doubt Frank is eager to turn us in at the moment. Bad press for a martial arts school, when the butt kicking was done by two rookie pawnshop owners," Charlie said.

"We may not get a visit from the cops, but Frank isn't going to let this slide," Gordon reminded him. "There was hate in his eyes. He would have used a gun if he'd been packing."

"I know, and he's a sneaky bastard who'll take the cheap shot," Charlie observed. "He's going to strike back, so be ready, anytime, anyplace. We're targets now, maybe more so than the Randals."

"Good for them. We can handle ourselves."

"God's ears," Charlie said, nodding.

"From your lips to . . ." Gordon grinned. "Where have I heard that before?"

Chapter Nine

Charlie lay there in bed, looking up at the ceiling. He'd stayed up late, watched Stephen Colbert, then finally decided he might be able to doze off. But it hadn't happened. He turned over and glanced at the clock, the only light source in an otherwise pitch-black bedroom. It was 1:30 AM, and he just couldn't stop thinking about Frank Geiger, the blood on the dojo mats, the struggle in the Randal house, the shooting in the street, chasing the guy who got away, the Afghani woman, and so on, all of it endlessly recycling in his head.

"Crap!" he grumbled, throwing off the top sheet and swinging his legs around to the floor. Maybe he'd try some of that herbal tea Ruth had given him and find something to read. The TV or computer screen only kept him awake, something about the blue light and body chemistry, he'd heard. Maybe he should have skipped *The Late Show*, or perhaps, more to the point, stop getting into fights and dangerous situations. That was supposed to have ended when he didn't re-up.

He put on the teakettle, found the box of tea bags and a mug, and staggered into the living room to check out the bookcase. He'd grown up with books—his dad was a lawyer and then a judge, and his mom a public school teacher—but all those years deployed overseas had kept him from buying any hardcover anything.

Instead he'd traded around his paperbacks, once read. While growing up, he'd read a lot of military history, especially World War II stories of combat. Nowadays he'd lost interest, having seen the reality of war firsthand.

He looked across his meager collection and picked up a small book Jake had given him for Christmas, titled *The Darwin Awards*. Gordon already had dibs on the book when he was finished.

About forty minutes later, the tea kicked in, Charlie found himself too bleary-eyed to read, and he wandered back to bed. He fell asleep quickly, then began to dream.

It was the Afghan woman again at the wall, bloody and begging for his help to pull her over the wall to safety. He hesitated, somehow knowing it was all going to go wrong, but she continued to scream, and this time he saw it wasn't the Afghan woman after all, it was Gina. He grabbed her up, lifting her over and into his arms. She pushed him away, turned, and screamed at an Afghani man who was pointing an AK at them.

Charlie reached down for his M-4, which was leaning against the wall. A gunshot went off—and he woke up.

It was his cell phone. Grumbling, he looked over at the clock and realized it was after seven. As he picked up the phone, he saw it was Nancy calling. Had something happened to Gina?

"You just wake up?" Nancy said immediately.

"Yeah. Thanks, I'm running late. Something wrong?"

"No. What about you? Get hurt last night?" Nancy asked pointedly. "Maybe in a fight?"

"Oh, you heard?"

"I can put two and two and you and Gordon together and come up with the right answer, Charlie. Detective DuPree called me ten minutes ago and reported that Frank Geiger had come home around midnight last night with his face all bandaged up. I'm guessing he didn't slip in the shower."

Charlie thought about the wording for a moment. "Were any police reports filed?"

"Why do you ask?"

"You first, Nancy. Or is it Sergeant Medina at the moment?"

"Nancy, right now. But if you try and bullshit me . . ."

"Okay. If you have to know, Geiger the elder and two martial arts instructors roughed us up in that dojo of Ray's last night."

"Roughed you and Gordon up? And there were just three of them? Liar."

"Okay, they tried to rough us up."

"What were you doing there, exactly?"

"We were watching to see if Frank was going to make contact with the third man in Ray's crew. We were fishing for visuals on possible suspects."

"There's some logic in that, but DuPree thinks Frank would use a burn phone instead of a face-to-face," Nancy pointed out.

"That occurred to me too, until I realized that at least one of the crew, the guy I shot, didn't even have a phone, and none were found in the van they left behind or on the street," Charlie said.

"Maybe Ray or the other guy who got away took the extra phone?"

"Naw, you carry your own phone. It would have been in his pocket. Hey, if Frank was advising Ray on his criminal activities, he'd want his son to avoid any obvious mistakes, like using cell phones," Charlie said. "Even burner phones can be traced some-what by proximity to cell towers, right?"

"Okay, Frank is a professional cop advising amateur crooks. Getting back to the reason I called. Was it you or Gordon who smashed Frank in the face?"

"It wasn't Gordon, and there wouldn't have been any trouble at all if they hadn't come out to confront us. Geiger threw the first punch—a cheap shot that he ended up paying for, well, out of the nose. The two instructors jumped in about that time but got a beatdown lite from us. We knew that both were under pressure from their boss's dad to work us over. No sense in sending them to the hospital. We barely left a mark on them."

"Beatdown lite. Never heard that one before."

"I'm creative?" Charlie suggested. "So now what?"

"Sam Randal is going back to running his company this morn-ing. There is an armed security guard on the premises. Margaret is staying with Gina, who's working at home today, and I'm going to keep calling back and checking. I told them to contact you or Gordon if needed."

"Okay, then. You're working with Wayne."

"Wayne, as in Wayne DuPree? Did I miss something, or do you two have a bromance going on all of a sudden? Nobody calls him Wayne and lives to tell about it." Nancy sounded surprised.

"I have enough sense not to use his first name in public, girl. I think he's hoping I'm less likely to keep things from him if we're kinda buds," Charlie joked.

"Like that's going to happen."

"What direction will the investigation take today, Nancy? Any clues?"

"I'm running down names of anyone who knows Ray or the

late Anthony Lorenzo, hoping to find the third suspect and/or the guy who tried to kill you outside that bar. DuPree is going to see if there are any connections between Ray and the previous home invasions, showing his photo to previous victims, checking on Ray's alibis on the other attacks, similar MOs, stuff like that," she explained. "As for anyone who might have it in for Randal's company, we still don't have any names to run through the system. I've got to go, Charlie, but you stay in touch, and you and Gordon don't do anything stupid."

"Hey, you know us."

"Exactly. Later." Nancy ended the call.

It was midafternoon at the pawnshop when Nancy called again, catching Charlie in the midst of helping a customer eager to sell some old sixties-era board games. Charlie suggested that Nancy speak with Gordon instead, who was in the secure room placing new pawn in storage.

When Charlie was done with the transaction, having accepted a fair offer for the Avalon Hill strategy games, he looked around the display area. Jake was an aisle over, helping a man select an old TV and digital converter, and Ruth was assisting a young couple looking at engagement rings. He excused himself as he passed by Ruth, and was at the end of the counter when Gordon came into view around the far corner.

Gordon nodded to him, then went into the office. Charlie followed.

"Nancy has some interesting news, or maybe the lack of news," Gordon said, selecting a K-cup of his favorite coffee for the brewer.

"Ray and the dead guy had no criminal friends or outside contacts?" Charlie inquired skeptically.

"Not that. According to DuPree, neither Ray nor Tony Lorenzo could have been on scene for all of the previous home invasions. Lorenzo couldn't have been involved in at least one of the incidents because on that occasion he was working a temp construction job in Rio Rancho, and Ray was working at the dojo with a construction crew at the time of the previous attacks, either teaching a class or doing some remodeling of the facility. That means that the attack on the Randal home was probably Ray's first home invasion—at least the first that was reported," Gordon added. "It's possible the gang behind this has more than three members, of course, and they trade off on their hits to provide alibi material."

"I get that. But again, why did they pick the Randals?" Charlie wondered aloud. "I think I recall DuPree mentioning that he believed that the previous victims had been identified as easy marks, mostly older females. And they were targeted on weekdays after neighbors had gone to work. Neither Sam nor Margaret is old or fragile, and they were both at home. On a Sunday."

"Why don't we talk to Sam? If there is no personal motive that links him to Ray Geiger or Tony Lorenzo, then Sam may have made a business-related associate into an enemy. What if Ray and his crew were just hired to do the job? The Randals were being robbed, sure, but the bad guys wanted to take Sam with them. Maybe there's a big safe at his office, or they intended on dragging him to an ATM and making him empty out his account," Gordon suggested. "Or what if they wanted a hostage so they could convince Margaret to do that in exchange for Sam?"

Charlie looked at his watch. "Unless he took off early, we can still catch Sam at work. Let's see if Ruth and Jake can close up today."

●   ●   ●

Firm Foundation, Randal's construction company, had its office and warehouse just at the northern margins of Albuquerque's east side. Dozens of large and small metal warehouses lined the interstate here, which were now flanked to the east and south with new housing developments and infrastructure as the city had expanded over the past few decades. Farther north, development virtually ended at pueblo tribal boundaries, except for the casinos, but there was still acreage available in what was zoned as industrial turf.

Gordon, driving his pickup, turned off the road onto the paved street, which was lined with a dozen or so businesses on either side. A few vehicles were heading in the opposite direction, most likely workers coming off shift and heading home.

It was just a little after 5:00 PM, but the sun was still high in the sky and the temperature topping off in the upper eighties. Cumulonimbus clouds were building atop the Sandia Mountains farther east, but there were no anvil tops yet. It was unlikely to rain here until evening, if at all. The summer monsoon was off schedule, and the humidity was in the teens.

About a quarter mile down August Avenue was the large tan metal structure that comprised Firm Foundation's main warehouse and garage, according to the two-foot-high lettering on the side of the building. A smaller metal structure, similar in size and shape to one of the portable buildings that dotted local public school campuses, was set up just inside the main gate of the barbed-wire-topped chain-link fence.

There were two parking areas, one presumably for employees, which contained a variety of private vehicles, and another with a collection of company pickups and flatbeds, two cranes, a big fork lift, and an eighteen-wheeler and trailer.

Gordon slowed and entered the gate of the compound, then parked against one of the concrete barriers along the wall of the smaller structure, beside Sam's white Camry. A metal sign identified this building as the office.

They climbed out of Gordon's pickup, and Charlie looked toward the warehouse, which had a long sliding door that was wide open. From this angle he could see pallets of construction materials such as rebar, sheet metal ducting, heating or cooling systems, and bags of plaster or concrete. At least a half-dozen men in work clothes and hard hats were visible moving around inside, finishing their final tasks of the day. He could hear laughter, loud voices, and country-western music from someone's portable player.

A security guard wearing a cap and a gray uniform, sidearm at his hip, came out of the office and walked down the graveled path toward them. He was carrying a small coil of heavy-gauge wire and pliers. "Can I help you with something, gentlemen?"

"I'm Charlie Henry, and this is Gordon Sweeney. We're doing some work for Sam Randal. He's expecting us," Charlie added, not knowing how much information Sam had shared with his people.

"Mr. Henry and Mr. Sweeney, glad to meet you, and thanks for looking out for the boss," the guard replied. "I'm Pat. I've been working the day shift here for three years. "

Charlie took a close look at the guard. He was in his early fifties, with confident posture and sharp eyes. "You spend any time in the military, Pat?"

"Twenty years in the Air Force, most of it working base security in Spain—AP," he added, indicating the Air Police. "It's a lot quieter here, though I still get to use my Spanish."

Gordon chuckled. "Nobody causing any trouble, then?"

"None at all, except for a hole someone cut in the fence over there last night." He pointed to a spot a hundred or so feet away, about halfway between the two buildings and even with the parking lot where the company vehicles were parked.

"Did they get inside the property and maybe tamper with the vehicles? That's some expensive-looking equipment over there," Charlie observed, looking at the closest vehicle, a big crane mounted on a truck. He wondered if the earlier attackers might have started targeting Sam's business in retaliation for Sunday's fiasco—or last night's fight.

"Naw, the opening isn't big enough for anyone to squeeze through. They didn't leave anything on the ground, not even tracks. Nothing was broken either, just the vandalism with the fence itself. I'm going to wire it up before I leave. Then someone will weld on a patch tomorrow morning."

"Can't see it from here," Charlie observed. "Is it at the bottom?"

"You'd expect that if someone was thinking about crawling underneath. Going over this fence and having to deal with the barbed wire would take some effort—not something your basic thief would attempt. But no, it's only about eight inches square, waist high, and the kid or whoever took the wire with him. At least I can't find it anywhere. Doesn't make sense, nothing bigger than a cat could squeeze through. Dumb-ass vandalism," Pat pointed out.

"Maybe it was taken as proof that he'd done the deed, like a middle school dare. When did you notice the hole?" Gordon asked, looking down the fence line.

"Ralph, who has the night shift, discovered it around daybreak. He figures it must have happened when he was using the facilities in the warehouse. Otherwise he would have seen the punk."

"Think Ralph scared him off?" Charlie asked.

"He'd already split by then," the security guard answered. "If the goal was just to cut out a square of fence, the job was done in a hurry."

Charlie nodded. "Doesn't sound like it's related to recent events, but let's take a look before we talk to Sam," he suggested. "There must be some logical reason for this. Why didn't they do it way over there, across the compound, far from the road, where nobody driving by would be likely to spot them?"

"With all that's been happening lately, I've begun to expect the unexpected," Gordon said.

As they were walking toward the spot, Charlie caught up to Pat. "How tight a fit is that gate when it's closed?" He turned and looked at the gate, about a hundred feet away.

"Nobody could squeeze through, if that's what you're wondering." the guard responded. "You'd need to cut through a hardened steel lock or pole vault over the top. There is always an employee on-site, and we have cameras that cover the interior, two aimed at the gate."

"Has security around here always been this tight?" Charlie asked as they approached the fence.

"Yes, it has. The only loss we've ever had at Firm Foundation was a month ago when someone broke into Sam—Mr. Randal's company pickup at a work site."

Charlie looked over at Gordon, noting his sudden attention. "What was taken?"

"Nothing that could be determined. All the tools, radio, registration, and work gear were still there."

"How'd the perp break in?" Gordon asked.

"Jimmied the lock, apparently. The only reason Mr. Randal

knew there was a break-in was when he sent the job foreman to the pickup for some blueprints he'd left on the seat. The glove compartment contents were on the floorboard and seat cushions," Pat explained.

"That sounds like a pro," Gordon pointed out. "I used to . . . well, I know how easy it is to use a slim jim to get inside an older model vehicle."

"Yeah, that's what I figured went down. When I was an AP, I rescued dozens of airmen and staff who'd locked their keys in their vehicles. Just slide that sheet of metal down the window and unhook the door latch."

By then, they'd reached the fence and could see the hole in the chain links.

Gordon felt the edge of the cut wire. "Good-quality bolt cutters. This took less than a minute to do."

"Odd," Charlie said, pointing to the soft ground outside the fence line. "Footprints have been smoothed out, all the way to the street. Would a kid think of that?"

"No evidence except for tool marks left behind," Gordon said, staring at the empty lot across the road. "And no camera coverage from an adjacent building. This area of the city is pretty much deserted at night, I suppose."

"Except for on-site security," Pat reminded them. "And there's no through traffic coming from the east. August Avenue dead-ends two blocks further up the street."

"Well, we'd better go connect with Sam," Charlie said, turning to look back toward the office. "There he is now."

"Guys!" Sam yelled, standing on the concrete porch and waving in their direction. "There's a problem! Get over here!"

"Now what?" Pat mumbled.

Suddenly there was the enormous boom of a heavy-caliber rifle. A second later there was a roaring whoosh and a wave of heat coming from behind. Out of the corner of his eye, Charlie saw that the big cylindrical fuel tank on the crane had burst into flames.

Chapter Ten

"Down!" Charlie shouted as the air behind them erupted into a ball of fire and flying metal. "Someone call 911!"

"Sniper!" Gordon added through the roar. "He's using HEIAP rounds."

Charlie rolled away from the crane, which was already billowing a cloud of acrid black smoke, then turned around, staring out across the street as he brought out the Beretta from the holster beneath his jacket. No conventional cover was safe when under attack by high-explosive, incendiary armor-piercing ammunition. They had to take out the shooter—fast. He looked for someone with an oversized rifle among the warehouses, vehicles, and storage compartments on both sides of July Street.

"Check out the white van to the left of the green building in the alley," Gordon shouted, his pistol out as well.

Charlie saw an old van about a hundred yards distant, positioned in a narrow gap between adjacent two-story warehouses. The vehicle was facing away from them. One of the van's rear doors was open, the shaded interior too dark to see the contents. The sniper's position was possibly in the bed of the van.

A second shot rang out, the large projectile whistling overhead with a sharp crack, exceeding the speed of sound.

"A clean miss this time. Smoke hiding the target," Charlie yelled, coughing as the cloud began to spread in their direction. "I saw the muzzle flash. He's shooting from inside the van. Must be a fifty cal."

"No use returning fire, bro, shooting through a chain-link fence with our weapons," Gordon replied. "We're screwed."

"Give me some suppressing fire anyway, make him worry. Keep moving so he can't get a clear shot. He's got a very narrow field of fire inside that van, so I'm going to flank him to the west," Charlie called. He jumped to his feet and ran to his right toward the gate. "And keep Sam out of sight!"

His urban combat training took over now. The office building would screen him for a few moments, and he should be able to cross the street unseen, assuming there was only one shooter. If he kept moving, using the buildings across the street as cover, it would be hard for anyone with a heavy sniper rifle to track him, especially up close. He also was praying that the weapon was bolt action rather than semiauto, giving him a couple of seconds between shots, at least, if and when the shooter changed positions. Up close, his short weapon could be brought to target faster if the guy stuck to his sniper rifle. All he needed was a clear shot.

Charlie was across the street within seconds. He raced down the far side of the second building over, guessing that the shooter would expect an approach from the closest building. He couldn't go left through the gap where the sniper was located without crossing the field of fire. The desert ground was flat and dry here, bare except for a few tumbleweeds, the usual blown trash and papers, and knee-high tufts of buffalo grass and other clumps of weeds. The only concealment was the sides of sheet metal buildings, and the biggest risk was being caught running alongside this wall before he reached the corner.

He'd already heard Gordon provide at least three shots covering fire, and one return shot came from the .50 cal rifle somewhere ahead and to his left. The weapon had a muzzle brake, undoubtedly, but the sound echoed between the walls of these buildings like thunder. The shooter, inside the metal van, would have gone deaf by now if he wasn't wearing ear protection.

Once he reached the side of the building, Charlie raced forward with his weapon aimed ahead. He was ready to shoot anybody waving a firearm. Hopefully no innocent bystander would pick this moment to step out in front of him.

In the distance, Charlie could hear the wail of sirens. The shooter had to make his next move before reinforcements arrived, not knowing if it was the fire department or the police.

Charlie reached the far corner of the building. The van was two buildings to his left, and if the street layout was the same here, the road dead-ended to the east. The shooter would have to drive past here.

Charlie took a quick glance to the left. The van was pulling out from between the two buildings, about a hundred feet away. He ducked back, trying to decide how long to wait before confronting the driver.

Then he realized there were two men standing in front of an open bay door across the street from where he was, watching the van. If he waited any longer, they'd be in his line of fire. He came around the corner, crouched low, pistol extended, and saw the van—heading the other way! He fired one round into the driver's-side rear door of the vehicle, hoping for a lucky shot.

The Chevy van raced maybe a hundred feet, swerved around the black and yellow dead-end barrier, then churned up huge rooster tails as it proceeded across the dirt field, fishtailing wildly.

Beyond lay the western edge of a mobile home park, with streets that would lead into Albuquerque's eastern and southern neighborhoods. He lowered his pistol and placed it in his holster. Then he heard voices.

"What the hell is going on? You a cop?" One of the men, a mechanic, based upon his overalls, yelled at him.

Then there was a loud pop from behind him. Charlie turned and saw the truck crane burning fiercely over in the Firm Foundation compound. Three men were spraying fire extinguishers at the conflagration, but something new had exploded, maybe a tire, and they'd need help. Loud horns honking distracted his attention, and he saw a fire truck racing up August Avenue. Maybe they'd be able to save something, or at least confine the fire to the crane.

Turning back, he noted the van had cleared the field and entered the mobile home park. He grabbed his cell phone and was looking down at it when it rang. "Charlie, let's get this one," came Gordon's voice.

A familiar horn sounded, and he looked west toward the frontage road. Gordon was racing toward him in the pickup. Charlie stuck the phone in his pocket, ran across the street, and waited for his pal to slow enough for him to jump in.

Charlie leaped up into the pickup, quickly fastening his shoulder strap and seat belt. "Let's roll!"

"Straight ahead, across the field? I see dust," Gordon said.

"Yeah! Follow the tracks into the trailer court." He pointed. "I hit the van, but it hasn't slowed him down."

As Gordon bounced the big pickup across the open ground, Charlie tried to focus on the GPS on the dashboard. "There are two main roads leading south out of the neighborhood. Take the first one. It leads all the way to Alameda Avenue."

Gordon had to slow down to a crawl for a woman and three kids who'd come out into the street. "A white van just come through here?" he yelled out the window.

"Moron nearly hit my daughter," the woman yelled. "He didn't have a license plate, just one of those dealer tags. Gillis Motors."

"Call 911," Gordon yelled back, speeding up only to the posted limit until clear of the neighborhood. Then he floored it again.

"The van is probably headed south on . . . East Sunset. Dealer tags for Gillis Motors," Charlie said into his phone, searching ahead and down side streets as they passed them by.

"Nancy, DuPree?" Gordon asked, his eyes on the road.

"No, APD Dispatch. They're sending more units to the area," Charlie replied. "I'm staying on the line in case we get lucky."

They hurried south, reaching Alameda Boulevard, which was crowded with after-work traffic this time of day. "East or west?" Gordon asked.

"Hell, he could be anywhere," Charlie admitted. "Your call."

"Hundreds of vehicles on the road. Let APD look for him." Gordon turned west, heading down toward the valley. "We lost another one, Charlie. Might as well circle back to check on the damage. I made Sam get back inside and stay low."

Charlie nodded to his buddy.

"No sign of him, ma'am," Charlie told the dispatcher still on the line. "We'll call if we spot the van, which also has a bullet hole in the rear door, driver's side. Good luck with the search."

They returned to the Firm Foundation compound, visible a mile away from the slowly dissipating cloud of black smoke still lingering overhead. There were a half-dozen fire trucks and emergency vehicles, their flashing lights illuminating the air above in an early evening glow rivaling the sunset.

A uniformed officer stopped Gordon at the wide-open gates, but Pat, the security guard, was standing nearby and asked the officer to let them in. They were directed to the opposite side of the big enclosure, and it took a while to cross the grounds with so much activity going on.

Charlie looked at the damage to the crane, which stood alone now, the adjacent vehicles having been moved a safe distance away. The fuel tank attached beneath the deck of the rear crane unit had blown open like a shredded beer can. White foam covered what must have been a burning pool of diesel fuel on the ground. Flames had apparently spread to the portable crane's Kenworth cab just forward of the fuel supply and enveloped the interior, which had a nasty burned-rubber-and-plastic smell. Three firemen were cooling off the toasted metal with a fine spray, though it was clear that the fire was out.

Charlie looked around the compound and saw Sam standing next to a squad car and talking to a police sergeant, judging from his stripes. He and Gordon came up, and the officer instantly noted the handguns at their waists before looking up at their faces. "Now I know where I've seen you two before," the sergeant said.

Charlie recognized the officer from last year, when armed robbers had shot up the pawnshop.

"Dispatch says APD officers are searching for the shooter. We lost sight of him once he reached Alameda Boulevard," Charlie offered. "He's armed with a high-caliber rifle, maybe more."

"So there *was* a sniper?" Sam asked. "What happened, Charlie? Gordon ordered me into the office before he took off to help you out."

Charlie nodded toward the buildings across the street. "The shooter was positioned in the back of a white van parked over there between the green building and the one on the left, lined up perfectly to shoot through the hole he cut in the fence. He was using incendiary ammo, almost certainly from a fifty-cal rifle. The bullet penetrated and ignited the fuel tank."

The officer nodded. "I've seen those in gun shops, on the police range, and in civilian competition. Big suckers, distinctive blast, awesome firepower."

"It could have been worse, I suppose. There wasn't much fuel in the tank. The crane had barely made it back from a work site," Sam replied. "Still, the vehicle is probably a total loss."

"Now we know why the hole was cut in the fence," Charlie pointed out. "The shooter was concerned that a wire might deflect the round. Probably wouldn't have made much difference with a projectile that massive, at this range."

"Still, a hell of a shot," Pat declared.

"Guy knew what he was doing. This was well planned," the sergeant concluded.

"The hole was cut sometime last night. Considering the trajectory, the fuel tank must have been the target all along," the security guard observed. "But the crane could have been moved anytime during the day. So why wait until late afternoon to take the shot?"

"Scare tactic. Intimidation? Whoever did this wanted a witness," Charlie decided. "Maybe his intention was to wait until someone came to repair the fence."

Sam nodded. "Guys, that's what I was trying to warn you about when the manure hit the fan. I'd just gotten a call from someone—don't know who—and he said that something was about to go down."

Charlie and Gordon exchanged looks. "What exactly did he say?"

"His exact words, as best as I can remember, were 'Now you're going to pay for what happened to my friend. Look outside.' It was a private caller, no number or ID, and when I tried to respond, he'd already disconnected. I stepped outside to warn you."

"And that was his signal to start shooting," Gordon added. "The sniper was the caller, and he had eyes on us the entire time."

"Exactly. Thank God this was an attempt to hurt the business, not kill anyone, at least not yet. All the heavy equipment and structures are insured, but that crane is worth north of 200K—used. My rates are going to skyrocket now."

"We need to come up with some answers that'll lead to a suspect," Charlie declared. Something strange was going on, and every day the situation seemed to be getting worse.

"I wish I could come up with a better idea of possible motives," Sam said, his words directed at those seated around his massive quarter-sawn oak kitchen table. Margaret was seated next to him, DuPree and Nancy opposite the Randals, and Charlie and Gordon at the ends of the table.

"All I can think of is the time I had to stop using Eldon Electrics as a subcontractor after Jim Eldon and I disagreed on a business issue," Sam explained, looking over to his wife for confirmation. "That was over a year ago."

Margaret nodded.

"How did Eldon respond to that, losing the jobs?" Gordon asked.

"Jim was pissed, but I never heard from him after that," Sam answered, glancing at Margaret again. "I don't think he was the caller, either. I know his voice."

"What about Hank and Carlito?" Margaret suggested softly, looking down at her tightly clenched hands.

"I forgot about those two," Sam observed. "And I suppose the guy on the phone could have been Hank, though I can't be one hundred percent sure. I caught him and Carlito stealing from a work site after hours about two months ago. They'd unhooked a couple of appliances that had just been installed and were loading them into their truck."

"You turn them in?" Charlie asked, glad to hear more names.

"Not at first. They made excuses, then agreed to hook everything back up if I just let them quit instead of firing them. It wasn't until I discovered them breaking into the warehouse a few days later with copies of their old keys that I called the police," Sam explained. "I dropped the charges after the investigating officers couldn't get any more evidence against them. I haven't seen or heard from them since."

"These are people that might provide some answers. I'll need the full names of those two thieves, Mr. Randal," DuPree said, sliding a notebook and pen over to Sam. "Text me anything else you have on them once you can access your records."

Sam nodded.

"So that's it? Sam can't come up with any more possible

enemies, and you don't work for the company anymore, is that right, Mrs. Randal?" Charlie asked.

"Please call me Margaret. There are times when I put in some hours at the office. If Tanya calls in sick, I go in and handle the clerical work, answer the phone, and do some of the account-ing," she explained. Charlie assumed she was referring to the young woman he had seen talking to officers earlier in the after-noon. "And I also help out when there's a business crunch."

"I suppose this has been asked before, but have either of you had any dealings with Ray or Frank Geiger, in business or otherwise?" Gordon asked.

"I've never met nor spoke to either man that I recall," Sam replied immediately, sliding the notebook with the former em-ployees' names back to the detective. "I can't even guess at what connection they might have to me or the business,"

"Same with me," Margaret added.

Charlie noticed that she'd been looking down at the table or across the kitchen whenever she made a comment. He was no psy-chologist, but the lack of eye contact from the moment they'd sat down bothered him. Margaret's voice had sounded strained after her husband mentioned Jim Eldon, the electrical contractor. Was she lying about something, afraid of being targeted, or was he just misreading her because she was still upset? The fact that he was now the only eyewitness able to testify put him on the spot, of course, but he was used to being a target. Still, her body language bothered him a little.

"Detective, have you found any connections between the pre-vious home invasions and what happened here on Sunday?" Margaret asked, turning to DuPree and changing the subject. "You think it might be the same people committing the attacks, right?"

"We haven't conclusively linked any individuals to the other crimes, unfortunately, though we're unable to rule out Ray Geiger's involvement. Geiger runs his martial arts school during afternoons and evenings, and none of the home invasion incidents were night attacks. We can't prove he wasn't involved, is what I'm saying," DuPree clarified.

"Or that he *was* involved," Charlie countered.

"That's the problem," DuPree responded. "Anthony Lorenzo, the attacker that got himself killed, had an alibi for at least one of the other attacks, at least according to those we were able to interview. We don't know yet if Lorenzo ever visited the martial arts school either. Those students who sign up for classes have to leave their names and contact information, and sign a release, but according to Detectives Larranaga and Johnson, they didn't find Lorenzo listed in the school records."

"If this is connected to previous attacks, there must be a fourth individual involved," Nancy speculated. "That's assuming that the man who tried to kill Charlie in the parking lot, threatened Sam this afternoon, then shot up the crane is not the remaining attacker who first struck here on Sunday."

"The current staff at Ray's martial arts school has also been cleared. The two male instructors have day jobs and were with their families on Sunday, and there's a female instructor, who wasn't involved in the rumble in the parking lot." DuPree looked at both Charlie and Gordon disapprovingly. "She had the day off, apparently. Anyway, she's a UNM student who does not, even remotely, fit any of the descriptions given by any of the victims." There's also a former woman instructor who quit or was let go that the detectives have not yet interviewed. She left the school a few months ago."

"So, we're back to the theory that our home was first targeted for robbery, then that night the same people tried to kidnap me. I wonder if that was done in an attempt to persuade Margaret not to identify the guy she unmasked, not knowing she couldn't anyway. And when they saw Charlie, they tried to shoot him for the same reason," Sam concluded, his voice shaky. "The attempt to run him down could have simply been retaliation for the loss of their criminal partner. And we know that couldn't have been either of the Geigers."

Charlie shook his head, saw Gordon's doubt as well, then turned to look at DuPree.

"That's too complicated for home invasion thugs, and I don't see Ray Geiger as any genius. I don't think we're getting the whole picture here," DuPree responded. "They wanted to grab you, Sam, during the initial attack—then later. Kidnapping you was part of the plan all along. What happened this afternoon may have been retaliation for Lorenzo's death, but why not take a shot at Sam when he came outside, or Charlie at the fence?"

Charlie found himself in agreement and nodded. "I don't think we've identified the leader of this conspiracy either."

"You thinking Frank Geiger, Charlie?" Nancy observed.

"He has police procedural knowledge, and the training needed to know what kind of evidence to avoid leaving behind. If that's true, he's also got his kid involved, despite the public image of Ray's rehabilitation," Charlie answered.

"What about that third guy?" Gordon offered. "I agree with Sam that he could have been the guy trying to kill us, well, Charlie, outside the Outpost. He could also be the same guy who shot up the crane."

"Which means he's skilled with a powerful rifle. Whoever he

is, I think he's someone who lives in the Rio Rancho area and has met up with Ray Geiger and Tony Lorenzo," Nancy said.

"Have the Rio Rancho police been any help with that at all, Detective?" Margaret asked DuPree.

"They're supposedly trying to learn who Ray and Tony hung out with, but they haven't even been able to link up those two, much less the third guy," DuPree admitted. "As far as that list of martial arts students, they have a lot of names to run down."

"But don't any of the local cops know Frank?" Charlie interjected. "From what I've learned about police officers from my father, and more recently around here, retired cops often know and associate with current members of law enforcement. People they've worked with, sometimes, like a brotherhood."

"Yeah, my dad is an example of that," DuPree admitted. His father was a former deputy sheriff in the county and was well known among the older generation in Albuquerque's north valley, where FOB Pawn was located.

"You think any of Frank's possible contacts in the RR department might compromise the case, or be providing Ray's old man with information that shouldn't be shared?" Charlie asked.

DuPree shrugged. "I hope not. I'm having enough trouble being kept up to date as it is. Until we get some new leads concerning the person or persons still out there on the streets, including following up on the names you've provided, you two need to be very careful."

"Margaret and I are thinking about moving out of the house until it's clear we're no longer in any danger," Sam announced.

"That could create some new problems. Either way, you'll need security. You still going to work, Sam?"

"I'll be safe there."

"You're still going to need protection away from the office, especially out on the road. That pistol over on the counter won't be enough," DuPree warned. He looked over at Charlie. "You taking part in this?"

"I sure am. Gordon too."

DuPree sighed. "Okay, tell me the bad news first."

"The tick-tock from that damn clock is going to keep me awake all night!" Gordon whispered, rolling over onto his side.

"Says a guy who could sleep through an artillery barrage or spread eagle on the deck of a chopper cruising so low it raises dust," Charlie replied, looking up at the canopy of the enormous king-sized bed with bleary eyes. "Now I remember why I left the Army—so I'd never have to sleep in the same quarters as you again."

"The Randals have a wonderful-looking sofa in the front room, bro," Gordon mumbled.

"So take a hike and a pillow. That couch is too short for me, but . . ."

"Damn, I hate it when you're right," Gordon replied, sitting up on his side of the bed.

"Deal with it. We're probably a lot more comfortable than the Randals. They're on Nancy and Gina's sofa bed in the study right now," Charlie reminded him, "and neither of us has ever spent the night in a house this plush before."

"I have, but I'm not saying with whom," Gordon chuckled, getting to his feet.

"How much sleep did you get?"

Gordon picked up his pillow, handgun, and flashlight, then walked to the bedroom door. "Sleep?" He chuckled. "See you in the morning, roomie, sooner if someone tries to sneak inside."

"Maybe we'll get a break and the guy will make a move tonight."

"Never thought I'd be looking forward to something like that."

Charlie woke up at six, heard running water in the bathroom, and decided it was Gordon, not a filthy burglar. He went into the kitchen and, after successfully finding the necessary items, started the coffee. The house phone rang, and Charlie picked up the receiver in the kitchen.

"This is Sam. I'm coming across the alley, so don't shoot me, okay?"

Charlie laughed. "Thanks for letting me know."

The bathroom door opened. "That the phone?" Gordon asked.

"Sam's coming over."

"Copy that. I'm out of the shower now, and getting dressed. Do I smell coffee?"

Chapter Eleven

Charlie and Gordon arrived at FOB Pawn a little after opening time, 8 AM. Jake was already there, booting up the computer network. When Charlie entered the office, Jake shook his head. "I heard on the news about that fire at the construction company. Isn't the owner the same guy you've saved, what, twice now?"

Charlie nodded. "What exactly did you hear on the news?" He was curious, recalling that DuPree wanted to keep certain details from the public. Knowing that someone was out there willing and able to set vehicles and industrial equipment on fire from a distance would only generate fear, and there was already a history of individuals in the metro area running around at night in residential areas igniting parked vehicles.

"A man driving a white van set a portable crane on fire but got away before police arrived. The fire marshal and city detectives are investigating what was clearly vandalism. Something like that," Jake explained. "They didn't say how the fire was set."

Jake looked over at Gordon, who'd just locked the alley door behind him, then shook his head. "More to it than that, right?

Were you two there, by any chance? I know you're looking after Randal and his wife."

"Yes to all of that, Jake. We tried to catch up to the guy, but he had too much of a lead and we lost him in afternoon traffic," Charlie responded.

"Are the Randals still in danger? Any idea what the motive could be besides money? I understand the guy owns a construction company."

Gordon shook his head. "Cops are still trying to figure that out. How's business been here the past two days? You and Ruth have any problems with customers? Troublemakers?"

"Not at all, just the usual haggling with people who want more money for their pawn or outright sale. We had a couple of youngsters with their older-model smartphones who ended up walking out claiming they could get more at the flea market. But hey, that's nothing new," Jake added. "We're also careful not to buy anything that might be stolen, after last year's problem."

"Well, we'll be here as much of the day as possible to give you two some relief. Gordon and I are trying to figure out our next move, and Sam Randal is adding another security guard to his staff so we won't have to be there at his company location. He still wants an escort going to and fro, however, so Gordon and I will be leaving a little early," Charlie said.

They'd decided to vary the routine. Margaret was going to go with Sam to work some days, and when Gina could work at home, Margaret would be sticking with her, where she'd be more comfortable. To anyone watching the house, they meant to create the impression Mrs. Randal was still at home. Gina, of course, was armed, and she was also well trained in martial arts. She'd had self-defense instruction while in law school, knowing that lawyers often ended up in the middle of disputes.

At five in the afternoon Charlie headed home, hoping to grab a quick dinner, shower, and change of clothes before meeting Gordon at Nancy and Gina's. Nancy had given Sam a ride to his business that morning, and Gordon was providing a lift home. The girls were getting paid from the money Sam had used to hire Charlie and Gordon; they'd already worked that out.

Charlie was only about a mile east of the shop, taking his normal route home up Comanche Boulevard, when he noticed a silver pickup following him. Shrugging it off as nothing—there were hundreds of silver pickups in the city—he kept driving. A few miles farther up the road he made the right turn onto Robertson, his neighborhood street, which accessed a quiet residential area and was no thoroughfare.

A few blocks south of Comanche he checked the mirror and noticed a silver pickup. It looked like the same Chevy he'd seen before, so he decided to check it out. At the next intersection he turned right, drove to the end of the block, then made another right turn back north. He'd circle the block.

The silver pickup didn't follow. It kept on going up Robertson, out of view. He was being careful, that was all, he told himself. A few minutes later, though, as he approached the block where his small house stood, he saw the same Chevy parked right across the street. As he slowed to turn into the driveway, he saw the face of the man behind the wheel of the pickup, bandage on his nose and all. Frank Geiger, the mangy bastard, didn't even bother to look over.

Thumbing the button on the garage remote, Charlie waited

for the overhead door to open, then pulled the Charger into the single-car garage. Frank obviously was starting out the evening with mind games, so Charlie wasn't going to take the bait. Whoever was supposed to be watching the Geiger house had dropped the ball. Whenever Frank left the house, he was supposed to be informed. After the martial arts workout, Charlie knew to look over his shoulder. The Army had trained him to be the predator, not the prey.

Charlie walked into the house through the garage, checking carefully to make sure nobody had broken in since he'd been here last—more than twenty-four hours ago. He couldn't be certain, of course. Frank had been a cop, and no doubt had picked up some skills regarding entering and exiting a locked building without leaving obvious signs. Cops didn't always break in with a hearty kick or a battering ram if they knew how to pick a lock.

The first thing he usually did when coming home for the day was to check the mailbox on the porch. He walked outside, not looking at Geiger, who was still sitting in his pickup, pretending to be staring down the street. Charlie picked out the electric bill, an ad for a dish TV provider, and a grocery flyer, then went back inside, locking the door behind him. No sense in making an illegal entry too easy.

He decided not to turn on the TV and listen to the news, instead going to the fridge to pick out a frozen dinner. Then his cell phone rang. Bringing it out, he looked down and saw it was Nancy.

"Hey, Charlie, you at home?"

"Just got here. I'm going to grab something to eat, then come over."

"Okay, Gina and I are both home now. I thought you should know that Frank Geiger left his residence about an hour ago. He hasn't returned, according to the patrolman on surveillance. Sorry for the delay, I was just notified. Rio Rancho is dragging their feet when it comes to communications regarding the Geigers."

"Thanks, but I already know where he is," Charlie said, looking out at the pickup, in plain view from the window over the kitchen table.

"Where'd you spot him?" Nancy asked, her voice taking on an edge. "You haven't been watching his house, have you?"

"No, it's the other way around. He's parked across the street on Robertson."

Several seconds went by before she answered. "He might be armed. I found out he has a concealed carry permit. He also may be in violation of the court order warning him not to approach your residence or business."

"I doubt he'll stick around much longer. He's game playing, and I'm doing the same, like I don't know he's there. If he's hoping to psych me out, he's going to lose," Charlie replied.

"Yeah, I know. Just don't get complacent. The guy has issues beyond the obvious. I got word from DuPree that Frank Geiger didn't exactly retire. He was forced out of the NYPD after an IA investigation. He was allowed to resign instead of facing charges, which explains how he was able to obtain a concealed carry permit in New Mexico."

"What did he do that got him unhired?" Charlie asked.

"Don't know, except for the mention that it was a suspected criminal matter, and a deal was made through the lawyers. DuPree is trying to get the details but says they might not be available. Personnel matters and crap like that. Don't want to hurt the department's reputation by putting this out in front of the public."

"Sounds like the same kind of PR issue APD has been facing

recently. Do you think it had something to do with Ray, his criminal offspring?"

"That's a possibility, I guess. What's Frank doing now, by the way?" Nancy asked. "Think I should drop by?"

"No. If he was going to make a move, he wouldn't have telegraphed it like this. It's just the old 'I know where you live' routine."

"Okay. One last thought. If he follows when you leave, let me know, and I'll have an officer pull him over for trying to tamper with a witness," Nancy said, then ended the call.

A few minutes later, Frank climbed out of the truck, crossed the street, and walked down the sidewalk past the house. He crossed back over a few houses down, returned to his pickup, and drove off.

Charlie watched the ritual from his kitchen table while dining on a microwaved pizza. Once he was done, he turned on the TV, left the living room light and porch light on, then drove over to Nancy and Gina's. Later, he or Gordon would be sleeping at the Randals'. Sam and Margaret, would do what they'd done the night before, crash with Nancy and Gina after going across the alley and climbing over the back wall. They had a stepladder now to put in place when needed.

Gordon lost the coin toss, which meant Charlie could spend the night at his own place. Around nine thirty, returning home, he eased down Robertson Avenue, taking it slow and wondering where Frank Geiger was at the moment. A block from his house, something already looked odd at the place. Instead of continuing down the street, he turned at the next intersection, taking a closer look during the turn. Down the block he could see that his blue recycle bin was tipped over in the middle of the driveway instead of sitting beside the garage wall. The few mashed-up plastic and cardboard containers that had been inside were now scattered across the concrete drive. It was probably just a youthful prank—kids were out for the summer—but after Frank's visit he knew to be careful.

His quick glance confirmed that the porch light was still on and the doors—front entrance and garage—appeared to be closed, so it was just petty mischief so far. He'd already heard, while at the girls' place, that Frank Geiger had returned home. It was doubtful Frank had enough time to hang around this area waiting for Charlie to leave, return to overturn the recyle bin, then make the twenty-to-thirty-minute drive all the way to Rio Rancho. Maybe this was just a coincidence.

Only Charlie had never been fond of coincidences. He slowed to a crawl and continued to ponder the situation. The normal re-action to discovering upended trash in your driveway—trash that had to be removed to gain access to your garage—would be to get out of your vehicle and go pick it up, then move the bin back to its place. If you were somewhat paranoid, however, you'd be very careful to examine the trash first for something disgusting. If you'd been deployed in the military or trained in explosives ordnance, you might also suspect an IED.

Charlie was all of the above. He had to assume the worst. If the sniper was after him now, there was no way an ordinary wind-shield or car body could protect him from a .50 caliber bullet. Only the engine block would help, and that would just slow the projec-tile down and trash the engine for good.

He picked up speed, at the same time reaching down for the Beretta in its holster attached to the steering column below the dash. Placing the weapon within reach on the empty passenger seat, he half-circled the block, passing through the intersection with Robertson farther south, looking toward his house now from the opposite direction.

There was no white van anywhere, but there was a dark sedan parked along the curb toward the end of the block, one he'd never noticed on the street before. He passed by close enough to see that someone was sitting behind the wheel, looking up the street toward his house. Charlie drove three more blocks, then turned onto the main avenue bordering the neighborhood. Once he was out of sight, he raced one street down, made a right turn, then headed back into the neighborhood, intending to come up behind the sedan this time.

Before he reached the final turn, however, he decided on a change in tactics. Instead of arriving in his Charger, he parked along the curb of the intersecting street, got out with his pistol, then walked up the alley behind the houses on Robertson Avenue, carrying the weapon casually down at his side by his knee, safety on and finger off the trigger. Most of the residents had chain-link fences along the alley in their backyards; a few had low cinder-block walls. He'd have cover until the last minute if he'd made the right move.

Of course, he might *just* be paranoid, and then the worst-case scenario would be frightening neighbors as he hopped their fence or wall and slipped alongside their garage while passing through. He knew most of them on sight, however, and might not get shot, at least right away. This was New Mexico, and a high percentage of the citizens owned at least one firearm. He'd have to be stealthy. At least nobody kept their dogs outside at night on this block, and the cats weren't overly aggressive.

The sedan had been parked three houses down, so he'd be

passing between the Miller home and the home where Joe, the auto mechanic with the stringy beard, lived with his squeaky-voiced wife, Sherry. Hopefully Joe wasn't in his garage working on that old yellow Corvette at this hour.

He reached the spot he'd been looking for, tucked the Beretta in the holster, then eased over the four-foot cinder-block wall. How many times had he climbed over a wall lately?

The sedan was still there, with the driver visible in the front. The passenger-side window was all the way down. Charlie stopped by the front of Joe's garage and listened, watching the car, which was parked just within sight at the end of Joe's property line, defined by a small flower patch. It was at least a hundred feet away, and in the dark all he could see was the driver, wearing a cap, looking in the direction of his house.

The person looked down at something on the other seat, then back up. It occurred to Charlie that if the person was armed, weapon placed upon the passenger seat, he'd have to get out and shoot across the hood, or scoot over and fire out the passenger window.

The guy was probably right-handed, Charlie recalled, if it was the same shooter. At that range he wouldn't be packing a .45 handgun—too far away—or the bulky .50 cal Barrett—too close. A more sensible weapon would be an AR-style carbine, basically a "civilian" assault rifle that fired semiauto. Of course, a traditional hunting carbine would do as well.

As Charlie watched, he noted the person would often look at the side mirrors, checking to see if anyone was approaching on foot from behind. It was a warm summer night, a good time for children or adults to go for evening walks. His choice of approach, from the house side, was a good one.

Still not seeing a weapon, Charlie waited for just the right moment. He waited until the person in the car looked into the rear
view mirror, checking his six. Then Charlie walked as quickly and
quietly as he could manage down the driveway toward the street.
He had his pistol ready, safety off now, and would approach from
over the man's left shoulder—nearly the middle of the street. The
car's engine was running; he could hear it now. Charlie could also
read the New Mexico license plate, mentally recording the letters
and numbers despite a guess that the tag had been stolen.

He was closing in, less than twenty feet away, when suddenly
headlights came from behind him. Was it a trap? The driver approaching honked loudly, and Charlie was forced to step toward
the right-hand curb. He lowered his weapon hand down along his
pant leg, hoping the oncoming driver wouldn't notice the pistol.

The guy ahead in the sedan turned around just then and raised
up over the seat back for a look around, exposing the long barrel
of a carbine he was holding—and his face. The headlights revealed
a young man in his twenties with pale, delicate features, dark hair
and eyes, and a tattoo all over his neck, like a net or web.

The car coming up from behind screeched to a halt right beside Charlie. "He's got a gun!" a young voice shouted, pointing
right at him. The car's engine roared, and from the squealing tires
and weaving flashing headlight beams, Charlie knew the driver
coming up from behind had thrown the car into reverse.

Charlie had been made. It was time to get off the street before the tattooed man could start shooting. He raced to the right
and leaped over a low hedge along the sidewalk, trying to break
his fall with one hand and still not lose his weapon.

The barrel of the Beretta struck the lawn as he landed, and
the pistol bounced out of his hand, sliding across the low-cut grass,

out of reach. He got lucky. The sound of burning rubber told him the driver had decided to flee instead of shooting it out.

Charlie rose to his knees and grabbed the Beretta. There was a clump of turf stuck against the muzzle. He cleared the barrel, then jumped up. There was no chance of hitting the guy now, and no real reason to shoot anyway, so he slipped on the safety and jammed the pistol into his belt.

Charlie watched as the fleeing vehicle turned left at the end of the second block and disappeared, blocked by the houses. Turning around, he saw the car that had given him away idling in the middle of the street, headlights illuminating him. He waved for the car to approach. "Screw you," came a youngster's shout, and the car swerved and headed down a side street.

Charlie walked down the sidewalk toward his house, then heard a familiar voice and stopped.

"Charlie, you okay?"

It was Madeline Greene, the university student with the blue-streaked hair who lived across the street. She was standing on her parents' front porch, looking out from behind a big support post.

"Yes, Maddie, I'm fine. I think it was a burglar staking out my house," Charlie lied. "Call the police, will you?"

"Okay. Let me get my phone," Madeline said, then stepped back inside.

Other porch lights started coming on, and he could see faces at windows. Bringing out his own phone to call DuPree, he wondered what might have happened if he hadn't been on his guard. This was probably the same guy who'd tried to run over him outside the bar, and the recycle bin had been tipped over to lure him into the open for a clear shot. But now Charlie knew what he looked like. The next time they met, Charlie was going to end it.

•   •   •

He was finally alone again and at home. Gordon and the girls were on higher alert now, and DuPree had been briefed, having decided to leave the on-site questions and description to the detectives on duty. This had been a different vehicle and weapon, so there was no real evidence that this was the same sniper that had set the crane on fire at the Firm Foundation compound. The carbine he'd seen, at least the barrel, had been much smaller than a .50 cal, with a blade front sight. He'd guessed that it was a Ruger. Still, DuPree insisted on talking with Charlie the next morning.

But Charlie wasn't sleepy at all. He was still so pumped that his hands were shaking as he drank decaf, sitting in the dark at his kitchen table. If he was able to sleep at all, he knew the dreams he'd have wouldn't include the scent and taste of cinnamon buns and Navajo tacos, or a family picnic down in the bosque.

Memories of combat and the losses he'd seen and experienced had never been painted over by drugs or alcohol. He hadn't hidden from the trauma and had worked on his PTSD symptoms time and time again, talking and sharing with friends and family, especially Gordon. He'd been told that these symptoms were all part of a disconnect between combat and the rest of his life, so maybe having a friend like Gordon, who'd walked the walk with him, was one of the ways of coping.

Navajo traditionalists, including a *hataalii*—a medicine man his father knew—had suggested conducting a four-day Sing called the Enemy Way to eliminate the evil presence that was torturing him from within, interfering with his assimilation back into society. But Charlie, having lived so much of his life without following the old cultural beliefs, believed it would be hypocritical of him now to attend such a ceremony. He hadn't said so, however, not wanting to offend, and instead had put it off time after time. No one had pressed him on it; the need and belief that the Sing would heal had to come from within himself.

Charlie coped as best he could, keeping busy and trying to have his mind occupied with other things, but it was late at night, when he was alone with his thoughts, that his memories bothered him the most. He'd never take it out on anyone else, that was one battle he'd already won, but he wondered if he'd ever be able to win the war. At least it was better now than before, and he refused to feel sorry for himself.

He took a final sip of coffee. Perhaps another of the unread books on his shelves would make him sleepy—maybe a mystery or thriller this time. No matter what, unless he got some rest, he wouldn't be any good to anyone, and right now, he had taken on the responsibility for looking after the Randals—and putting a stop to whoever was trying to end his life.

Charlie slept soundly when he finally hit the sack, and when he woke at six thirty he couldn't remember dreaming at all. His luck was still holding. Around seven fifteen, as he pulled out of the driveway, he wondered if he should take extra measures to protect the house from an intruder. The building was a rental—owned by his cousin Nestor, who now lived in Santa Fe—but maybe he should add extra locks and an alarm or surveillance system. He wasn't so much worried about his stuff. After so many years in the military, on the move, he didn't own that much anyway except for the Dodge and half of the pawnshop. Both were insured. Unfortunately, he was a target again now, and there were many ways to make that house a death trap.

Chapter Twelve

"Are you sure, Charlie, that you haven't made enemies not connected to what happened to the Randals?" Detective DuPree asked. "At least one of them with a neck tattoo?" He'd been with Charlie and Gordon for a half hour now, in their small office at FOB Pawn.

"Can't think of any, offhand," Charlie replied, "and I would have remembered that face and tattoo. I've seen a lot of ink in this business, but not that particular combination. Most of the people we deal with here either walk away satisfied with their transaction or take off when we can't agree on a price or the terms and conditions of a pawn. You already know about my past issues with gang members and those people I've helped put in jail. They're still put away, right?"

DuPree nodded. "The key players, at least. I had to ask, if only to rule it out. The timing of the moves against you clearly indicates a connection with more current events."

"What about the third home invader?" Gordon asked. "The one that got away—so far, at least."

"Or the friends and family of the man I shot?" Charlie added, not wanting to voice Anthony Lorenzo's name aloud. He'd heard it too much already. Despite his reluctance to take part in an Enemy Way healing, as a Navajo he'd been raised to respect the traditional customs of his tribal ancestors. These included not naming or calling attention to the dead, or to their chindi, the evil in everyone that remained after death. While he didn't believe in ghosts, he'd been haunted by the death of others too many times not to recognize their influence on the living, spiritual or otherwise.

"Lorenzo was estranged from his own relatives, including his single-parent mother and siblings," DuPree began. "The biological father is in a Texas prison for robbery and manslaughter, serving fifteen years. The deceased had two older brothers, both now working as roughnecks for a drilling company operating in the Permian Basin of West Texas. Their criminal records only include a couple of bar fights, and I've seen their photos. No visible tats, and the descriptions don't match. The man's body was shipped to the mother, who apparently lives in Midland."

"Any local friends? He certainly knew Ray Geiger and the third fugitive," Gordon asked.

"The deceased didn't attend school here. At least there's no record of it in the public systems. He dropped out of high school at seventeen, moved to Rio Rancho at eighteen, then worked construction for various subcontractors. I was able to get a warrant, through a Sandoval County judge, and scored a list of all the individuals who were officially enrolled students or employees of Ray's martial arts school, but there were no hits or connections to Mr. Lorenzo. We have names, addresses, ages, and a few more details on the employees. Sergeant Medina has a copy and is probing for possible suspects among the fifty or so that fit within the profile we have right now." DuPree shook his head. "It's a work in progress."

"Any hits on the guy last night?"

"I had people do a quick search in the photo databases, looking for everyone who had a web type of tattoo on their necks, the real distinguishing feature you could provide. There are several, but none of those with the right ink seemed like a match—wrong age, wrong weight, or wrong sex. You can come downtown and look at what we have, or I'll have images sent to your phone."

"Do that. What about the car?" Charlie asked.

"I have people checking surveillance cameras in the vicinity. The license plate was stolen from an employee's van parked at the Cottonwood Mall on the west side."

"Not far from Rio Rancho, home of the Geigers—and the dead guy," Charlie reminded them.

"Their law enforcement people are being briefed every shift. Supposedly, the Geigers were both at the old man's place during that time," DuPree said, then shrugged. "They're also looking for the subject's car."

"What we have now is several incidents but very little to go on, except for Ray Geiger, the dead guy, and that face you saw last night," Gordon observed. "What about your house, Charlie? The bad guys know where you live. What if they decide to try again?"

"My next-door neighbors are going to keep an eye on the place for me, and Maddie, who lives across the street, is a part-time student at UNM and is at home most of the time. If anyone sees a vehicle or person who doesn't belong in the 'hood, they'll call APD. They also have my cell number," Charlie added.

DuPree stood. "That'll help. I've got to get going. There's a lot of legwork to do before we get any more names or suspects—other than Ray and the spiderweb man."

"What about those names Sam gave you, the employees who'd tried to steal from the work site?" Gordon asked.

"They've kept a clean record, and both work at a south Albuquerque Home Depot in the building materials department, one of them as a driver. I'm having some local officers check on their off-the-job activities," DuPree responded.

"And that electrician, Eldon?" Charlie asked.

"Haven't been able to catch up with him. I left a message on his cell phone, but he's apparently a one-man operation with no current business address. If I don't get a call back, I'll have an officer stop by his house," DuPree said.

"He live in Rio Rancho, by any chance?" Gordon questioned.

"Naw, someplace on Albuquerque's east side, near the fairgrounds. Don't track him down, guys, not yet. He's a long shot anyway."

"Okay, but I've noticed that Mrs. Randal reacts every time his name comes up, so there might be a personal connection," Charlie decided to point out.

"Personal how, Charlie?" Gordon asked. "Like something going on between Margaret and Eldon?"

"Yeah, maybe. To me, it seemed like she got nervous talking about him," Charlie said. "But it was just a feeling I had."

"I'll make sure I check up on the guy, then," DuPree responded. "We've got to cover all the bases."

"Sounds reasonable. Can we get a copy of the list of students and employees at Ray's dojo?" Charlie asked.

"I'd e-mail you one, but that would show up in the system and create some privacy issues. However, I can print out a hard copy for you. Nobody needs to know, okay?" DuPree replied.

"Not a word," Gordon responded. "Trust us."

DuPree laughed. "Yeah. You fellows still watching out for the Randals?"

Charlie nodded. "Along with Gina and Sergeant Medina, when she's off duty. It doesn't look like the bad guys are through yet, at least with Sam. We also want to make sure Margaret isn't attacked."

Gordon nodded in agreement. "Threaten her and they'd have leverage over Sam, for money or whatever they want."

Charlie looked at his watch. "That's my cue. I've got to go relieve Gina, who's looking after Margaret. Gina's got some business at the courthouse downtown."

Margaret Randal was a short, attractive redhead with a great smile and just enough freckles to enhance her wholesome country-girl look. She was a few years older than Charlie but much younger than Sam. Charlie wondered, sitting across the kitchen table from her while they ate cold ham sandwiches and fruit salad, what had attracted her to Randal. He was old enough to be a father figure, and certainly very successful, so maybe economic security had also been an issue.

Charlie just didn't know the woman well enough to discern her motives, and certainly it wasn't his right to judge. But now was the first time they'd really been alone. It might be a good opportunity to see what she thought and knew about her husband that hadn't been spoken when Sam was around.

Charlie knew he'd have to be subtle. Margaret had confidence, brains, and ambition, though she didn't seem to be in the same league as Gina or Nancy—or Ruth. He also didn't want to be charmed and misled.

"I can't thank you enough for all you've done for me, for us, Charlie. If you hadn't pulled me over that wall, I might be dead right now. I finally feel safe, well, more safe. I wish Sam would just stay home until all this has ended. Jeff, the foreman, can keep things going. But that company is Sam's career, and as long as he knows I'm being protected, he's going to be there handling the business.

"Can I pour you some more iced tea?" she added, reaching for the silver carafe with her left hand. Her right forearm was still bandaged from the bullet wound.

Her grip on the carafe was shaky, so he stood and grabbed it with both hands. "I've got it. You're right-handed?"

Margaret nodded. "And clumsy with my left. Thanks."

Charlie poured the tea, then sat back down. "I understand you were working at Firm Foundation when Sam bought the company."

"I was *the* office staff. When Bobby Jackson, the owner, decided to retire and sell out, I thought—there goes my job. The new guy will bring in his own people. But Sam was new to the industry. He chose to keep all of the employees so the transition would be as smooth as possible. He's great at managing the money and handling the clients, but he hadn't worked in the construction industry and had a lot to learn about landing contracts. Jeff was very helpful when it came to day-to-day operations."

"How about you? How did you end up working there?"

"My dad was born here in the city, took up carpentry and worked construction. He eventually earned a senior position at one of Albuquerque's biggest residential developers. I took business classes in high school, distributive education stuff, and accounting at the technical vocational school here. In the summer, I worked as an intern, pretty much for my dad."

"You followed in your family footsteps, then."

"More like my dad's. My mom was a housekeeper, raised my three brothers and me, and by the time my father died I was already on my own. He'd retired years earlier, but I had a good résumé and had already landed a job at Firm Foundation. I'd been there two years when Sam bought the company. We fell in love, got married, then we decided maybe I should only work when needed. We plan to have children pretty soon, while we still can."

"You've got time. You're almost retired from the business world and only what, thirty-four years old?"

Margaret laughed. "A kind guess. I'm thirty-six. I'm now officially an independent contractor. I help out at Firm Foundation when Tanya is on vacation or ill, or on special occasions. I work maybe twenty days a year, mostly during tax time."

"So what's the deal with Sam? He's not from around here, I assume, but what lured him to New Mexico and Albuquerque?"

"He's a self-made man from Connecticut with no business training except in high school and the school of hard knocks. After his parents died in a traffic accident, Sam started working for a small insurance company as a courier, learning all he could around the office. He took community college business courses, worked his way up in the company, earned an associate's degree and got into sales, and made so much on commissions over the years that he was able to buy out the elderly owner. The business flourished; he invested wisely and was smart enough to sell out just before the big recession. Prices were low here in New Mexico with the economy in a downturn, and he got a good deal with Firm

Foundation because Mr. Jackson was anxious to sell. With no siblings or family ties, he says it was the right move, especially because he met me," Margaret said with a smile.

"Sam seems to have prospered," Charlie noted. "Why live in this modest neighborhood when you could buy a big house in the foothills, along Rio Grande Boulevard, or near the old country club?"

"Sam's a great businessman, but he's very low-profile, down-to-earth. Humble, I'd say, despite being an only child. Maybe it's because of his childhood, but he doesn't flash around his wealth, like some people do who are newly rich. He was really annoyed when the business edition of the *Albuquerque Journal* did a story about his success with Firm Foundation. Not that he doesn't deserve it. Sam shuns publicity, and his donations to charity are always done anonymously."

"You two seem very close. Does the business require Sam to be out of town a lot?"

"No, he's a homebody. Sam sends Jeff on any required business trips. Anytime Sam leaves the city we're together, and it's always on vacation, never business. I want for nothing, and we've driven all around the country. He's afraid of flying. Neither of us has any desire for the fancy stuff, like a Mercedes, a swimming pool, or a housekeeper. I was raised in what used to be considered a middle-class family, and I've never associated with what my mom called the upper crust. Sam pays his employees well, and Jeff Candelaria has been foreman since before Sam took over the company. I'm the only person with the company who no longer works full-time. Except those two who got fired, of course."

"And Jim Eldon, the electrical contractor," Charlie suggested softly.

Margaret's face flushed for a moment, and she avoided eye contact. After a brief pause, she spoke. "Mr. Eldon wasn't really with the company, he was subcontracting. I don't know the details about why Sam decided not to hire him anymore, and Sam hasn't talked about it. I think it might have just been a personality conflict," she added.

It sounded like a lie, but Charlie decided not to press the issue, starting to think this was unrelated to what was going on now. "Sounds like you know the firm and his work as much as anyone. The detective has asked you this already, but now that you've had time to think about it, have you been able to come up with any idea why your home was targeted, then Sam and the business?"

"No, and we've gone back and forth about this, searching for answers. We still can't believe this could have anything to do with his business dealings or personal life, yet clearly, there's someone out there who wants to do him harm."

"Sam's only been here in the city for a few years, right? What about his past, before he came to New Mexico? He ever talk about that?"

"No, he says that it was so boring it would put me to sleep. Lower-class childhood, and after high school, nothing but insurance policies and claims and sales, learning how to run a business. Nose to the grindstone. Sam always put his work first until he met me."

"How about his personal life? His past. Old enemies, girlfriends, stuff like that?"

Margaret laughed. "Before we got married, he told me all about his old girlfriends, and gave me the chance to do the same. Clearing the air, he said. Once we both had our say, he wanted us to never speak of it again. The past was done and gone, and all we needed to think about was now, and toward the future. He'd already thrown out his old photos, and I offered to do the same. He said to keep my family photos, but definitely not those of my old boyfriends. He's the jealous type, if you hadn't already noticed."

Charlie said nothing, wondering just how many boyfriends Margaret had had in her life. Perhaps Jim Eldon had been one of them, and Sam had found out. She was definitely appealing— looks, personality, the whole nine yards.

"Hey, don't give me that look. I grew up with very strong, conservative values, and that was a long time ago," Margaret protested, her face turning almost as red as her hair.

"None of my business," Charlie replied hastily, feeling his own face starting to flush.

"Let me clear the table."

Charlie's cell phone, in his shirt pocket, began to ring. He brought it out and checked the caller. It was Madeline Greene, his neighbor from across the street.

"Hi, Maddie, what's up?" he asked, hoping it was good news for a change.

"Hi, Charlie. Did you call for a plumber this morning? There's a white van with a West Mesa Plumbing sign parked in front of your driveway."

"No, I didn't. What is the plumber doing? Is he checking the water meter at the sidewalk?"

"Nope. I can't see much, but I think they went inside your house. Over the top of the van I can tell that the garage door is open."

"They? How many?" Charlie knew something was up. Nestor insisted that Charlie always handle things like this.

"Two men, wearing caps and white jumpsuits, or whatever men call them. I can't see them right now, so they must be inside, or out in the backyard," Maddie responded, her voice raised an octave. "Want me to take a closer look?"

"No! Stay home and away from the window, Maddie. Lock your doors, call the police, and report a burglary. Remind them that this was the location of a suspicious incident just last night."

"Okay."

"I'll be there as soon as I can, Maddie. Stay safe," Charlie added, turning toward Margaret, wondering if this was just a diversion to lure him away.

"You think this is a trick?" Margaret asked. "I heard most of that."

"I can't leave you here alone. The police will handle it."

"No. Let's mess up the burglars' plans. I'm going with you," Margaret said, reaching for her purse and phone, both on a nearby serving table.

"You sure?" Charlie said, reaching for his light windbreaker, which would help conceal the Beretta at his belt.

"Let's go. On the way I'll call Gordon and Nancy," Margaret said, bringing out her keys. "I'll set the house alarm on the way out."

Charlie tried to reconnect with Madeline on the way but couldn't get through. APD Dispatch probably had insisted she stay on the line until a patrol car arrived. He was a lot closer to his house coming from the Randals' rather than the shop down in the valley, and it would take less than ten minutes to get there. He knew that was like forever to a burglar, so he'd be way too late. Local response time supposedly averaged less than four minutes to have an officer on the scene, depending on the locale and time of day. Maybe they'd get lucky.

"We're almost there. When we arrive, stay in the car with the doors locked. I'll leave the engine running and the air conditioner on," Charlie told Margaret as he turned onto his street. "If you feel threatened in any way, honk the horn and yell as loud as you can."

"Of course. And don't worry about me. I have a revolver in my purse and Nancy showed me how to use it," she replied, her voice taut. "I'm never going to be taken by surprise again."

He'd come the quickest way, approaching from the south, and as he drove up the street he could see a white and blue APD cruiser parked a few houses down. He couldn't see any officers, but Madeline, in cutoff jeans and sweatshirt, was standing on her porch, phone in hand.

She saw him and waved, then stepped off the porch and walked halfway across the lawn toward the street.

"Pretty girl, even with that streak in her hair," Margaret commented as he pulled over to the curb. "You ever ask her out?"

Charlie laughed. "She's smart, good-looking, and way too young for me, Margaret."

"Age doesn't have to be a barrier, Charlie," Margaret responded.

Charlie nodded, still wondering exactly what the attraction was that had brought Margaret and much-older Sam together. From a man's point of view, he could see why anyone would have been attracted to the woman beside him. But Sam? Guess you had to be a woman.

Charlie climbed out. "I'm going to check it out. Remember—"

"I'll stay here," Margaret completed the thought. "Be careful."

Charlie nodded, then crossed the street and met Madeline as she reached the sidewalk.

"Hi again, Charlie. The plumbers closed the garage door and took off just a few minutes before Officer Wilson arrived. I told him all I knew, and then he made a radio call to the station, I guess. Right now he's looking around back. He told me to stay here," Madeline said. "I took some video as they were driving away, and the officer copied it into his cell phone."

"Thanks so much for keeping an eye on the place and calling the police. Did you notice if they took anything?" he asked, looking back across the street.

"When they came back outside, they loaded two big toolboxes into the van before they climbed in and drove away," Maddie replied. "And, oh, they were wearing gloves, which I thought was odd, considering it's already in the eighties outside."

"Be sure to mention that to the police. Maddie, you going to stick around for a while?"

"Sure, what do you need?"

"There's a woman in my car—Margaret—that I'm trying to keep safe and out of public view right now. If anyone takes an interest in her, give me a call?"

"Sure will. Is she the victim of that home invasion?" Madeline asked.

Charlie nodded. "But let's keep that to ourselves."

"Gotcha."

"There he is," Charlie said, seeing the uniformed cop coming around the corner of the garage. Charlie waved, stepping out into the street.

"I'm Charlie Henry, sir. I'm renting that house. And I have a concealed carry permit," he pointed out, lifting his windbreaker so the officer could see he was armed.

Tall and fit-looking, Officer Wilson seemed familiar, but Charlie didn't recall why. Over the past few years, since acquiring the pawnshop, he'd seen his share of law enforcement people—and they him. The good news was that he'd made more friends than enemies.

Wilson relaxed slightly, smiled, then spoke. "I was told this was your residence, Mr. Henry. Your name has come up several times lately during shift briefings. I'm Officer Wilson, and I worked with Sergeant Medina in vice a few years ago. Let's take a look inside. Stay behind me, please."

"Did you find how they got inside, or if they vandalized anything, Officer?" Charlie asked, following the man toward the house.

"I haven't been able to make that determination yet from the exterior. All the windows are closed, the front and back doors are still locked, as is the garage, and there's no sign of forced entry. Your neighbor, Miss Greene, with the blue hair and Daisy Dukes, advised me that these plumbers, or whoever they are, had the garage door open for a while. Are you missing your garage remote, sir?"

The gadget was kept in his glove compartment, out of view, and he'd checked during the drive over. He glanced back at the Charger, and Margaret waved at him.

"No, and there was no sign the garage door was tampered with?"

"I didn't see any physical damage," Wilson responded. "An experienced burglar, however, may have several remotes, trying them out to see if one is coded to your frequency. Burglars have been known to drive through residential areas during the day, operating remotes, watching to see if any overhead doors start to open. Especially in older neighborhoods."

"Trial and error?"

"Exactly. But there's an even lower-tech way to defeat the mechanism itself and gain access. A long wire with a hook can be used to release the locking mechanism on the inside of older-model doors, the one at the top. After that, the door is raised manually. Usually a small mirror attached to another stiff wire is slipped beneath the door, which has been pushed up a few inches with a wooden wedge. That mirror helps the burglar position the hook. Let me take a look around the bottom of the garage door before we go inside."

"I'll get the remote from my car," Charlie suggested.

A minute later, he joined the officer, who was crouched in front of the overhead door at the midpoint, where it made contact with the concrete driveway.

"I think that's what went down," Officer Wilson announced, bringing out a cell phone and taking a photo. "There are some recent scrapes on the door and the concrete where the mirror was slid beneath the rubber weather seal. I also found marks where the wire and hook were inserted. Before they exited, the intruders must have reset the lock mechanism device to try and conceal their means of entry."

"Hopefully nothing inside has been trashed. Can I open the garage now?"

Wilson nodded.

Charlie touched the remote. The door came up, rumbling a bit as the long screw mechanism spun, raising the heavy door. It was old and noisy, but it still worked, and Nestor could see no reason to replace something that was still safe and functional.

"Clearly, then, they reset the mechanism," Wilson confirmed.

"They probably pushed the inside button to close the door, then ducked out before it came all the way down. Take a look around the garage and see if anything is missing or has been disturbed. Protocol keeps me from calling in the techs on minor incidents, so we'll need to find something else wrong before I make that request. Miss Greene says she watched the two men leave and they weren't carrying away anything except for toolboxes. You missing any?"

Charlie shook his head. "No, my only toolbox is the blue one on the counter over there."

"Okay. Do you have guns, jewelry, or electronic devices small enough to fit in a couple of toolboxes?"

Charlie nodded. "A couple of handguns, plus some jewelry, like watches, cufflinks, and a few rings. Also some turquoise items. Lately, I've been the target, not my stuff," he reminded the policeman. "I doubt whoever came in here today was out to rob me—which makes me wonder exactly what went on inside. I don't see anything in the garage missing, or even disturbed."

"No gas leak I can detect either, or accelerants like gasoline. But I need you to check inside the house. Try to avoid touching anything unnecessarily," Officer Wilson said, walking over to inspect the door leading into the house from the garage. On the back wall of the garage was a second door leading out back, the big barrel bolt still in place. "None of the doors appear to be damaged or tampered with, and the door leading out back is still locked on the inside." He reached for the doorknob. "This one is also locked."

"Odd. I always lock the door with the dead bolt, not the lock in the knob," Charlie said. "The dead bolt requires a key both inside and out. They must have turned the button on the knob, then shut the door behind them as they came from the kitchen into the garage. But how did they get in? All the windows are kept locked."

Wilson looked at the doorknob. "This is decades old. They probably bumped the mechanism using a blank key and a rubber hammer, basically taking it apart. Then, once inside, they put it back in place."

Charlie nodded. "I saw that done on TV. Makes sense, especially if they also know how to open the garage door with a cheat."

"So they got inside the house, but put everything back to normal, then locked up as they left?" Wilson asked. "Why make everything look untouched?"

An alarm went off inside Charlie's head, and for a few seconds he was back in Iraq, breaking into a house or business. Quickly his buried training and survival instincts rose to the surface. At least twice lately someone had tried to kill him.

"Because they were setting up a booby trap," he mumbled.

Chapter Thirteen

"Huh?" Wilson took a step back. "Maybe the bomb squad should check it out."

"I've encountered IEDs before, Officer. Let me take a quick look—visual only. Just don't touch anything, okay?"

Instead of inserting the key in the doorknob, Charlie put his key ring back into his pocket and began to examine the narrow space between the door and jamb, beginning around the lock mechanisms. The house and attached garage were forty-plus years old, and the doors and jambs had many years of wear and abuse, which left gaps, especially in places where small drafts weren't so noticeable, like the kitchen.

"There's a flashlight among the hand tools on the counter," Charlie said, examining the door carefully.

Wilson handed it to him within seconds. "You know what you're doing?"

"I've had some ordnance training," Charlie replied, still looking for anything that didn't look right. He switched on the flashlight and took a closer look at something that had already caught his eye. "There's a thin wire bridging the gap between the door and jamb—on the inside, in the kitchen. Reminds me of a clothespin bomb from that old sixties-era anarchist's guide."

"Pardon?"

"Book belonged to my dad. Don't ask. With the device I have in mind, a clothespin is part of the trigger. A piece of wood is connected to a wire fastened to the door trim. This wood is inserted between the jaws of the clothespin attached to the door, and prevents two wired metal contacts on the clothespin jaws from touching. These contacts are connected, one each, to terminals of a battery. Opening the door yanks on the wire and pulls out the wood, closing the jaws on the clothespin and completing a circuit. Juice from the activated battery sets off an electrical detonator and the explosives. Low tech, no cell phone required."

"I get it." Wilson nodded, taking another step back. "This is definitely a job for the bomb squad."

"Let's make sure first. No sense in calling in a false alarm," Charlie said. "Whoever did this had to exit the house, but not through this door. We can get in the same way."

"Miss Greene said they were around back before they closed the garage door. Maybe they made their final exit by crawling out a window along the back of the house facing the alley? When I took a quick check before, the three windows in the back were closed, but I didn't check to see if they were locked. I was looking for broken glass or an open window."

"I'm not going to open the front door either. They may have set a similar trap there," Charlie speculated. "The garage door leading out back looks fine, and I couldn't have entered the garage through it anyway because of the barrel lock on the inside. We can go out back through it."

A minute later, they found a set of shoe prints below one of the bedroom windows. "This one has been forced open, probably with a big screwdriver," Charlie said, "and the screen has been removed." He took a careful look, just in case, then slid it open and pulled himself up, over the windowsill, and onto the bedroom floor. This was the second, unused bedroom and contained only a small desk, chair, and several storage bins. The window screen, damaged from a quick removal, had been leaned against the interior wall.

Officer Wilson followed him in, taking more time, having to avoid catching the gear attached to his Sam Browne web belt on the window frame. Charlie thought about giving the guy a hand but decided the officer might be too proud to accept help. He was as tall as Charlie, and once inside had no problem dropping down to the carpeted floor.

Charlie led the way into the living room, then stopped and pointed toward the front entrance. A wire was wrapped around the interior doorknob, passed through a loop screwed into the wooden baseboard, and was attached to the pin of a hand grenade duct-taped to the wooden floor.

"Shit. Now a grenade?" Officer Wilson exclaimed.

Charlie laughed. "You recording this on your lapel camera, Officer?"

Wilson chuckled nervously, then reached up to his camera controls. "Now I am. Watch your step, Mr. Henry."

Charlie looked up at the kitchen light fixture; he didn't see anything else out of place, like a bulb filled with gasoline, so he switched on the light. Across the room a few feet from the door leading into the garage was a big pipe bomb, a lantern battery, and wires leading to, as he'd already guessed, a wooden clothespin glued to the door, with another wired piece of wood inserted between the jaws. It was anchored to the door trim by wire and a screw eye.

"There it is. Simple and by the book," Charlie announced. "I can disarm everything with a pair of wire cutters or the scissors I have in a drawer over there, or just remove one of the wires from a battery terminal."

"No, let's wait for the bomb squad. That's their responsibility. I'll take photos and send them to the unit." He brought out a cell phone. "We safe to use a phone in here?" he added, looking around for a possible third bomb.

"Sure, as long as someone doesn't try to force one of the doors. Just don't touch anything." Charlie was pretty certain there were no more bombs. He was never supposed to survive getting this far into the house.

Wilson glanced around, clearly not at ease. "I'll take the photos, then we go back outside—through the bedroom window."

Charlie shrugged. After encountering booby-trapped weapons, antitank mines, and IEDs constructed from artillery shells, he wasn't particularly worried. "No prob."

Once the bomb squad and their containment vessel arrived— basically a blast-suppressing armored sphere on a trailer towed by a pickup—a tech entered the house through the bedroom window while everyone else watched from a block away. By then there were at least two dozen residents, three camera crews, and several passersby lined up waiting for something to happen—or not. All the houses on the block had been evacuated, and Charlie had joined Margaret, moving the Charger farther down the street but still close enough to watch. In his mind, this was still all connected to the original attack on the Randals, and there seemed to be no end to the drama. He needed to keep her safe.

Five minutes after he'd entered, the APD tech came out the front door and gingerly placed the grenade into an armored box, then signaled for his partner, who was wearing a heavy protective suit, to enter through the front door and remove the pipe bomb. Once that was done, they carried the armored box holding the two explosives to the containment vessel and placed it inside.

A K-9 officer and a bomb-sniffing dog then swept the house and garage. The team worked quickly and was out in a few minutes with an all-clear report.

Charlie stood beside his Dodge while Margaret remained inside, the windows rolled down now and the engine turned off. The temperature was still rising outside, and the crowd was beginning to disperse when a familiar-looking unmarked police car came up the street and pulled alongside him.

"You okay, Charlie?" Detective DuPree asked, looking out the driver's window. Then he noticed that it was Margaret in the car. "What's Mrs. Randal doing here?"

Charlie quickly explained, then added, "I think the officer in charge of the scene wants me to see if anything is missing from my house or has been added. I'm going to bring Margaret inside with me, okay?"

"Anything beats sitting inside this car on a hot summer day," she said. "And I feel safer with Charlie around," she admitted to the detective. "He did have that young woman across the street watching me when he was inside, so I was never alone."

DuPree nodded. "We still want you to keep out of sight, however, Mrs. Randal. Charlie, go ahead and pull into your garage, then close the overhead door. I want you," he added, turning to Margaret, "to enter the house out of view."

Charlie agreed. He'd been the target of a potential sniper here last night, and even if Margaret wasn't an intended victim at the moment, he wasn't about to risk putting her into the line of fire. Charlie still didn't know exactly why Mrs. Randal hadn't been able to identify Ray Geiger, when she was the one who pulled away his mask. At this point, Charlie was the only person who could, or would, point a finger at Ray as one of the home invaders. Of course, there were two more reasons for him being a target now. He'd killed Anthony Lorenzo and could also identify the man with the spiderweb tattoo.

DuPree waited with Margaret at the small kitchen table while Charlie took a quick look around the house. Nothing had been disturbed. His backup .380 was still in its hiding place, fastened via Velcro to the bottom of a wastebasket, and his ammo supply and extra clips were in the nightstand. He had very little jewelry, and all of it was still there. The cardboard box in the spare bedroom closet with his computer disks and personal tax papers was closed, rubber band holding the flaps in place. His laptop had apparently remained untouched as well.

He came back into the kitchen, where his two "guests" were finishing the Cokes he'd offered. "Nothing taken, nothing added that I was able to detect. Madeline Greene, the young woman across the street, said the plumbers were here only a few minutes after she contacted me. Exactly how long they were inside isn't known because she didn't really notice them at first. They must have carried the bomb materials in those toolboxes, set up the devices, then climbed out the back window and left through the garage," Charlie surmised. "They didn't want my stuff, they wanted to get rid of me, or at least put me in intensive care."

"I got that from Officer Wilson and his sergeant, who also interviewed Ms. Greene. She had to leave for a college class, but I have her phone number and she has mine," DuPree said.

"I've requested an ATL—attempt to locate," he explained to Margaret, "on the van for all local agencies, and APD officers are checking surveillance cameras in the area," DuPree continued. "The plates were stolen, and the company listed on the van's sign insists they don't own the vehicle. These perps were very careful, even keeping their faces hidden by ball caps and sunglasses. All Ms. Greene could provide was an approximate height and weight. She speculated that there was a third individual, a driver, because she never saw anyone enter or exit from the driver's side. She never saw him or her, however, and the driver may have entered from the passenger side and been one of the two plumbers."

"Any theories on who these fake plumbers were?" Charlie asked. "Someone connected to the other incidents, I suppose. Kill the eyewitness, or revenge for the death of their friend, maybe, like with the crane?"

"Both? In this case, though, we can again rule out the presence of Ray Geiger and his father. Frank is at the dojo, and Ray's monitor shows he's still at his dad's place. Unfortunately, you've made yourself a dangerous enemy, Charlie," DuPree added. "He's not giving up, either, that's my guess. You might want to find another place to stay for a while."

"Maybe there are two groups of attackers out there, one who's trying to kill me, and another just out to hurt Sam Randal. If it was the same guy who tried to run me over, then why didn't he take a shot at me with that fifty-cal rifle the other day when I was standing beside the fence? Even with the chance that the fence might deflect the projectile a few inches, I still think he had a better chance killing me with an armor-piercing bullet than with that car," Charlie pointed out.

"You have a point, but you can't afford to take any chances," DuPree warned. "Today, two people tried to blow you up."

"Nobody is going to run me off," Charlie argued. "Gordon and I are taking turns protecting Margaret and Sam—when he's at home—but I'll take my chances. I know how to look out for myself."

"Are you sure, Charlie?" Margaret asked. "We can pay for other accommodations as long as this lasts."

"Thanks, but I prefer to handle things my own way. Right now, though, Margaret, I think you might want to go back home, where it's safe and a lot more comfortable. Sam will be coming home from work in a while," Charlie added, "and Gina and Nancy will be right next door."

Charlie turned to DuPree. "Are we done here?"

The rest of the day was easy. Charlie had been relieved by Gina when she got off work, so he'd gone back to work at the shop and sent Jake and Ruth home. He and Gordon had handled the customers, completed the remaining paperwork of the day, and swept the floors, then closed up. After that, they'd stopped at a WisePies for pizza and iced tea while Charlie described today's potentially deadly incident.

Still in limbo, waiting for news, the name of the guy with the tattoo, or any other evidence they could actually pursue, they'd decided to call it a day. Gordon had elected to protect the Randals again, wanting to give Charlie a little more rest and the chance to unwind.

It had been a long twenty-four hours with little sleep, and Charlie's system had reverted to civilian time, so he was already drowsy by the ten o'clock news on Channel 7. He was reaching for the remote when he discovered that the lead stories concerned the Albuquerque residential bomb threat and an armed stalker in the same neighborhood. These acts were increasing police patrols in his area of the city.

He sat back on the sofa, wondering just how much of his privacy was going up in smoke tonight—if there was any left at all.

Fortunately, both stories were sketchy on details. First, there was a short, vague report of an armed stalker in a stolen sedan watching a resident's home, including generic shots of the neighborhood. According to the reporter, police were asking that the teenaged eyewitnesses who'd left the scene step up, contact the authorities, and assist in providing evidence. A possible motive and the name of the intended victim were being withheld from the public in order to project the individual's safety, according to the reporter.

The bomb threat coverage provided more visuals and shots of the bomb squad in action, but at least no cameras had been directed at him, only at the police, and he had avoided an interview. Charlie's name wasn't given, but mention was made that he was a decorated veteran from a prominent Navajo family. The conclusion by the reporter was that this was an apparent follow-up attempt on the same individual.

"The same individual is sleepy," Charlie mumbled to the screen, but by then, the news reader had already moved to the summer drought story. He touched the remote, turning off the TV, and stood up from the couch, looking over at his half-full plastic water bottle. He'd just cap the thing and put it back in the fridge. Passing back through the living room after shutting off the kitchen light, he picked up his Beretta from the sofa arm and walked down the hall into the back of the house.

It was still hot outside but down to seventy-five in the house, so he decided not to turn on the swamp cooler. A quick shower would help, though.

He continued into the bedroom, flipped on the lamp atop the nightstand, and then placed the handgun on the bed. Three minutes later, stripped down, he stepped into the shower. The warm water was soothing on his aching muscles and the various cuts and bruises.

Ten minutes later, Charlie sat on the bed. Yawning, he realized just how much his years in the military still shaped his habits. Even though he'd stayed in the shower longer than usual, he still bathed in a hurry. He quickly added triple-antibiotic salve and a stick-on bandage to the biggest gouge. He was healing well.

At least in those locations where it was actually safe to sleep undressed, he usually slept in lightweight pajama bottoms and sometimes, in cooler weather, an old T-shirt. He'd also learned to have a pair of moccasins or boots within reach.

The shower had bumped up the humidity in the bedroom, and it felt a little swampy at the moment, an uncomfortable environment for a child of the desert. Maybe he should open the window to let in some fresh air, then read a little.

Moccasins on, he walked around the foot of the bed to the window, parted the curtains in the center, and unlatched the catch. As he slid open the window, he heard what sounded like a car engine. *What was a vehicle doing coming up the alley this time of night?*

Charlie took a quick look and spotted a pickup just beyond the low chain-link fence. Realizing he was in a vulnerable position, he moved away from the window and stretched across the bed, reaching to turn off the lamp on the nightstand. No time to present a silhouette.

"Hey, Charlie!" an unfamiliar male voice called out as he strained to touch the switch.

The booming crack of gunshots erupted, and the window exploded with flying glass as bullets dug into the wall across the room and above the foot of the bed.

Chapter Fourteen

Flat on the bed now and with his night vision still impaired, Charlie groped for his pistol, found it, and then rolled off the mattress onto the floor. The wall thudded from the impact of slugs on the stucco—so many coming at once that there had to be at least two shooters. Most were hitting waist high or lower now. No time to hang around.

Staying as low as possible, Charlie crawled out into the hall mostly on his belly, more snake than human, while considering his options. There was no way he was going to be able to slip out the back door of the house to take these people head-on; he'd be in full view—with no cover. Firing out another back window was also too risky.

There was a brief pause, then more shooting. Clearly this was no gangbanger drive-by. Unlike last night, this time there was more than one shooter, and they had reloaded. Their attempt to blow him up had failed, so this time they were sticking around long enough to finally take him out.

Wary of a secondary ambush, a tactic he would have employed

with enough troopers, he reached the front door, threw it open, then ducked low, looking around the doorjamb for a shooter in case they had the balls to send a third guy to assault the house from the opposite direction. The front yard was clear and the street empty, so he raced to the corner of the house opposite the garage, noting that the shooting had stopped. If they had run out of ammo, they would have fled, so he deduced that they were reloading with a third or fourth magazine, or watching, trying to decide what to do next.

He inched along the wall, flattened, then saw the pickup idling there, headlights still off. The glow from the moon and nearby interior lights revealed a shooter in the back bed, rifle or carbine up, probably waiting to see if he was still alive and able to fight back. The driver was holding a pistol—there was no long barrel visible. Clearly they weren't motivated enough to assault the house, or they would have done it already.

Only a few more seconds went by before both shooters began firing again, slowly and methodically this time, aiming low, selecting the back door and the bathroom and second-bedroom windows.

Charlie took careful aim and fired four shots at the figure crouched in the back bed, then shifted aim quickly and placed two rounds into the driver's door. The driver yelled, more of a scream, actually, and the vehicle lurched forward. Charlie hugged the wall and fired three more rounds into the pickup cab as it accelerated to his left, weaving back and forth, churning up gravel and dust from the unpaved alley. He tracked the vehicle, knowing he still had several rounds, but decided to hold off because the field of fire now included two houses and a neighbor's garage.

He jumped to his feet and ran into the backyard. "Call the

police!" he yelled at the top of his lungs. "Men with guns in a pickup!" he added, reaching the four-foot-high wire fence at the alley. The pickup was now at the end of the block, and chasing after it on foot was pointless. He hurried over to the back door, which was full of holes. It was locked. Dumb. Without the key, he had to race around front. Entering the house, he stumbled around in the dark, trying to grab the house phone with shaking hands.

He took a deep breath, then dialed Gordon's number. His buddy might also be a target; it had happened before. Then he realized the phone was dead.

The telephone line and switches were mounted on the back wall of the house and had probably been put out of action by a bullet strike. Charlie walked into the bedroom, his moccasins crunching broken window glass, and flipped on the light switch. The overhead light came on, and he looked down at the night-stand. The lamp had been shattered, but his cell phone was still there, thankfully intact.

He stepped out into the hall, touching the screen for Gordon's number. Once it started to ring, he surveyed the hall. No bullet strikes here—no, just one, but it was nowhere near close enough to have damaged the gas heater or the pipes. He couldn't smell gas either, which was a good sign.

Gordon spoke as Charlie continued walking toward the living room. "Hey, what's going on, Charlie?"

Charlie set his pistol down on the sofa, then walked over toward the front door, which was still open. "You okay? Everything quiet at the Randals'?"

"So far, except for your phone call waking me up. Why?"

"Watch for a possible attack. I just got hit."

"Hit? As in shot?"

"No! Just shot at. Gunfire. A lot, maybe fifty rounds. One of the shooters had a rifle or carbine with a high-capacity magazine. The back walls of the house are like Swiss cheese. But I'm fine, and hopefully none of the neighbors were hit by strays. I yelled for someone to call the cops."

Charlie heard a siren. "Sounds like they're on their way."

"They know your address by heart," Gordon replied. "Stay safe."

"Thanks. Looks like I'm going to need a place to stay tonight. My house, well, Nestor's house, is shot to hell."

"What doesn't kill you makes you stronger, Chuck."

"I need a bed, Gordon, not a life coach."

"Right. You can stay at my apartment, or use the sofa at the Randals'," Gordon said. "I'm going to let Nancy know what's going on. Then I'll take a look around outside. Call you back in five."

Charlie woke up, remembered where he was, and looked up from the Randals' soft leather sofa to see Gordon in the kitchen area, sitting with Sam and Margaret at the dining table. He glanced down at his wrist watch. It was 8:30 AM.

He'd slept inside a folded blanket with a velvet sofa pillow beneath his head, so he just swung around to a seated position. He was still in slacks and a T-shirt, so there was no reason not to stand up and search for his socks and shoes. "Who's minding the shop?" he asked.

All three at the table looked over at the same time.

"Jake and Ruth. I'm planning on going down in a few minutes, but there's some news you'll want to hear," Gordon replied.

"They caught the shooters?"

"No, but they found the pickup," Gordon said, "and there was blood on the driver's seat. You hit at least one of the attackers."

"Thought so. Have they named a possible suspect?" Charlie added, putting on his socks. He knew from experience there was more.

"Not yet. But late yesterday afternoon, the Geigers were able to convince a judge to give Ray a little more freedom. Both father and son had alibis for the time those fake plumbers were at your house," Gordon explained.

"They could have hired that out, or maybe put the third perp up to it," Charlie replied, shrugging on his shirt, which had been draped over the back of the sofa. "The fact that no shots were fired into the garage makes me think the plumbers were also the shooters and knew where my bedroom was located. But having the Geigers get another break is troubling."

"Well, the judge bought their lawyer's argument. Ray still has to wear the ankle bracelet, but he's free to come and go within Bernalillo and Sandoval Counties as long as he stays away from Sam and Margaret. Firm Foundation and this neighborhood are also off-limits."

"And Frank?" Charlie asked, slipping into his cowhide Western boots.

"He's been told not to communicate with any potential witnesses, including the Randals, Nancy and Gina, and either one of us. Otherwise, he's free to roam. RRPD pulled the officers they had on stakeout."

"If you want to back out of this, Charlie, I understand," Sam said. "You and Gordon have become targets from the moment you jumped in, and now it's clear someone is out to kill you for what you've seen and done. You also have a business to run. I can relate to that."

Charlie looked over at Gordon, easily reading his expression. "No thanks, Sam, we're going to stick this out. We keep making little dents in the case, and it won't be long before we either catch those still out there or point them out to the cops. I can identify another one of the suspects, remember."

"But there are at least two of these dangerous men out there, and they keep coming up with weapons and explosives. They also know where we live and work and have attacked our business," Margaret argued, reaching out and putting her hand over Sam's. She looked up at her husband, and he shook his head slightly.

"There were three at first, then two, now three again, at least, adding a new guy to replace the dead man—if we still include Ray. The Geigers have to know the others, and most likely are in contact with at least one of them. Once we get the name of that third stooge from the attack on you here, the rest should come together," Gordon said. "It might well be the guy with the spiderweb tattoo, which at least gives us a face to try and identify. Most of the brass found in the alley came from a .223 rifle or carbine— maybe the same weapon Charlie saw before."

"Sam, are you going into work today?" Charlie asked, wondering if he and Gordon might be able to squeeze in some detective legwork before Cousin Nestor arrived from Santa Fe this afternoon to deal with the insurance and repairs on the shattered rental house. When Charlie had checked the mail at his house yesterday, the list of dojo students and former employees DuPree had promised was there. Looking over it late last night, he'd noticed something interesting. Now he had a plan.

Sam stood. "Yes, but I was hoping you or Gordon could escort Margaret and me over to my office first. There's a lot of paperwork to do, and my better half here has volunteered to help me out. I'll have security on site, and it'll free you two to do some work on my, well, our behalf."

"Just what I was thinking," Charlie responded. "Let me have a few minutes to get ready, and we'll get started."

"So this Lori Hanson was one of the sensei at Ray's dojo until a month ago?" Gordon asked, looking over the list of students and employees Detective DuPree had unofficially provided.

"Yeah, and I'm thinking because she agreed to meet and talk to us, she might be in the mood to give us some details not provided to the Rio Rancho cops, assuming they've even interviewed her at this point," Charlie responded. "She mentioned being contacted by the cops, but didn't say anything else about it."

"You're hoping she knows something about the dead guy, or the mysterious third member of the crew—web-tattoo man?" Gordon suggested. "And because she no longer works for Ray, she has no reason to try and protect her job. We might just get a lead here, pal, something she hasn't told the cops."

"I'm counting on you to pour on the charm, Gordo. What is it with you and the women, anyway? I've never seen anything like it."

"Hell if I know, I'm not even tall. Good-looking, yes. Charming, okay. But not a towering example of man flesh."

"You forgot modest."

"Clearly. Sometimes I need to hold something back."

Charlie laughed as he turned into the Starbucks lot off of Highway 528 and eased into one of the slots beside a well-used Jeep with a canvas top. There was a line of cars in the drive-up lane, and four tables on a patio, but they'd agreed to meet inside.

"Suppose she's here yet?" Charlie asked, looking around at the cars parked in the slots to the east. There was a Jeep, one of those smaller Humvee models, a Honda Civic, and a slick-looking restored Camino with a custom metal cover over the bed.

"Honda or primo Camino?" Charlie added.

"Easy. The lady kicks butt but doesn't make a lot of money. I say the Jeep," Gordon responded. "See that pink ribbon sticker on the bumper?"

"Probably right," Charlie said. "Let's find out," he added, stepping out of the Charger.

Through the big glass windows beginning waist high, Charlie had already spotted a petite blonde in her twenties sitting alone by the time they reached the door. She smiled and waved with her tall container of coffee.

"Charlie?" she asked.

"Yes, Ms. Hanson, and this is Gordon, my partner."

"Well, hi, Gordon," she said, holding out a well-developed arm to shake his hand as they approached the small table. "Sit down and join me. And call me Lori. You're really good-looking guys. How long have you two been a couple, may I ask?"

Charlie and Gordon both laughed. "We're not even close to gay, Lori. No offense to anyone. Charlie is my *business* partner," Gordon responded, now red-faced as he took the seat next to the athletic-looking woman. "We co-own the FOB Pawn shop in the north valley."

Lori laughed. "My bad. And, for future reference, I'm not gay or married either," she said, winking at Charlie, who was still standing. "I'm just a physical fitness addict who loves helping young women learn how to defend themselves."

"Um, before I sit, can I get you anything, Lori? Another coffee? Muffin?" Charlie offered.

"Coffee, no, blueberry muffin, yes. I skipped breakfast after my morning run, and I'm starving."

Charlie stepped to the counter and ordered, noting that Lori and Gordon were already engaged in conversation. The woman, attractive with a broad face and bright blue eyes, was dressed in jogging pants, running shoes, and a short-sleeved athletic jersey that reminded him of a women's soccer top. Lori was outgoing and confident.

There were no customers in line except at the drive-up, and he soon had coffee for himself and Gordon, plus three blueberry muffins. Charlie sat down after handing out the food and joined in the conversation.

"You mind repeating why you left Butkikin Dojo?" Gordon asked, then took a sip of coffee.

Lori laughed. "Everyone just calls it Bojo. I don't mind talking about it at all. Like I was telling Gordon, I eventually had it up to here when the boys and men wouldn't stop hitting on me or making comments heavy with sexual innuendo. They'd say things like wanting to take me on, if I liked it rough, or worse. It was always between classes. I hardly ever got any out-of-line BS from the so-called bad kids, the ones who'd been busted or were on probation. Most of those guys and gals are dead serious about developing their skills and improving their focus and fitness, or they wouldn't have been there. They also knew they were being watched, not only by the instructors but by their parole officers or social workers. Most of the crap came from the older high school boys and community college jocks."

"What about the other sensei?" Charlie asked. "Didn't they back you up?"

"When they were around, mostly. But they didn't want to lose any students—they're paid a percentage of each student's fees. If they heard, they'd laugh it off like the troublemakers were just trying to be funny, or shake their heads as a warning. On the other hand, they didn't let anyone bother the female students. They all knew that Ray needed the clients, and if word got out that girls were being harassed, he could lose a third of his business overnight and they'd be out of a job."

"What about Ray?"

"He was pretty serious about it all. He tried to talk me out of it when he heard I was thinking of quitting. It worked the first time."

"What finally happened that set you off?" Charlie asked.

"A couple of Ray's buddies, who'd come to see him but never taken a class, kept making comments, licking their lips. Finally they asked me to come with them after class and party. When one of them asked me my favorite position, I kicked him in the balls. He got up, pissed as hell, but one of the other instructors stepped in."

"What happened next?"

"I found Ray and told him that if his friend Tony showed up at the dojo while I was there, or if I saw his face again anywhere else, I was quitting."

"Tony. Anthony Lorenzo?" Gordon asked.

"That's him. When Ray tried to defend the guy, saying Tony was probably just high, I told him I was done with Bojo and handed over my ID badge. Mail me my check, I said. Ray didn't try to stop me, so I walked out. Now I teach self-defense classes at the community college, and nobody gives me any shit. Some of my students have left Bojo and followed me there, and it pleases the hell out of me."

"You said a couple of Ray's buddies. Who was the other guy?" Charlie inquired.

"They just called him BJ, and I never asked what that stood for," Lori replied with a shrug. "He wasn't really much of a problem. Around me he sometimes added some lame follow-up to Tony's crude comments, but BJ never initiated anything on his own."

"Can you give us a physical description? What kind of car did he drive? Anything that'll help," Gordon asked.

"Does this have something to do with Tony's death and why the cops want to talk to me? I thought that might have been him that got shot during the carjacking attempt I heard about downtown. Then I found out that Ray had been arrested for the same crimes. Should I even be talking to you about this?" Lori asked, suddenly uncertain.

"Did you also hear on the news about the people that broke up the home invasion, and later the carjacking—which was really a kidnapping attempt? Tony shot at them that night, which got him killed. He was accompanied by Ray, and maybe BJ," Gordon responded.

Lori thought about it for a moment. "Ah, then you must be the two neighbors who saved the couple in the house."

"Exactly. Ray and the other two got away, though Ray was later identified and arrested, and Tony was killed in that carjacking attempt. Since then, someone has been trying to kill Charlie because he's the only one who saw Ray's face during the home invasion," Gordon pointed out.

"Then why haven't the cops talked to me about this yet?" Lori asked.

"Hell if I know. They say they're overworked, and truth is, they do have a couple hundred students and instructors to interview.

They may have put you further down the list because you no longer work there," Charlie suggested.

"So, now we're getting to the reason we needed to talk to you, Lori. Can you tell us all you can about any of Ray's other pals, starting with BJ?" Gordon asked softly. "Charlie's life is on the line. Yesterday they rigged bombs in his home, and last night they shot up his place, barely missing him. He can't stay there anymore as long as the remaining members of Ray's crew are gunning for him."

"I'll tell you everything I can, guys."

Charlie brought out a pen and a small notebook. "I was hoping you'd help us out. Describe BJ."

"The guy is tall and slender, with a narrow face and pale features, like a vampire," Lori began.

"Dark hair, dark eyes, maybe?" Charlie asked immediately, suddenly very hopeful.

"Yeah. Kinda Goth, and with a lot of tattoos on his arms. He usually dressed in black or dark brown. A leather vest, sometimes. His latest tat was a big spiderweb around his upper chest and neck. What, you know the guy?" Lori asked.

Charlie nodded. "I think I saw him the other night, though we weren't formally introduced. You sure you never heard his full name?"

"Not that I recall. Maybe someone else at Bojo knows what it stands for."

"That's something we can pass along," Gordon suggested. "What else you got?"

Lori leaned back in her chair and took a final sip of coffee. "That's all I can remember, guys, but if you give me your number, Gordon, I'll call if I think of anything else that might help."

Charlie slid the notebook over to Gordon, who ripped out a blank page, then wrote down his name and number, plus the one for FOB Pawn. He slipped that paper over to Lori, who looked at it closely.

"Where have I seen that name before—FOB Pawn?"

"It's been in the local papers, on the Net, and on TV news. We had an attempted robbery at the shop last year, among other things," Gordon explained.

Again Lori thought a moment before speaking. "Yeah. I remember because that led to another incident down in the Corrales bosque, south of Rio Rancho. Nobody screws with you two and gets away with it. You two are vets, right? Seen some combat?"

Gordon and Charlie exchanged a quick glance, then nodded, but didn't pursue the subject.

"Anyway, thanks for your help, Lori. I have one more question, if you don't mind," Charlie said. "What do you think of Ray's dad, Frank? You met him, right?"

"Yeah, Frank helped me with some of the larger classes once in a while, though his bad leg prevented him from demonstrating the kicks. The guy gives me the creeps. He treats all of the instructors respectfully but gives his son a hard time when no students are around. Frank's always leaning on Ray, criticizing nearly everything. Frank is a bully, a petty tyrant. I'm surprised at Ray, actually, getting involved in these crimes. I never thought he'd do anything that would get him busted again. Every day, at the beginning and end of a lesson, he had something to say to the students about consequences and being responsible for their actions. He had me convinced he was really going straight," Lori said. "He played me, and everyone else, I guess."

Charlie nodded. "Do you think Frank might get violent?"

"Definitely. From the vibes I got, he must have been a hard-ass cop back in New York. I'd hate getting on his bad side. If you ask me, the NYPD is better off without officers like him. I'm glad he retired early," Lori added.

Charlie shrugged. Obviously she didn't know why Geiger had left the force.

"Lori, you've been such a great help to us. Can I get you something else to eat or drink? Maybe some coffee for the road?" Gordon asked.

"No thanks, Gordon. I've got a class coming up in an hour and I need to stay light on my feet." Lori looked down at her cell phone. "It's time I get going, as a matter of fact. But it's been nice meeting you two. Like I said, if I think of anything else, I'll call."

She stood, and Gordon stood as well, stepping out away from the table to let her pass.

Five minutes later, Charlie crossed the Alameda Bridge heading east, as Gordon read through Lori's description. "Pretty detailed, even the spiderweb tattoo on his neck, which she said was new. If BJ has a record, and his photo was taken before the tat was added, that may explain why there wasn't an immediate hit. I think it's especially interesting that she mentions BJ having an accent, like Ray and Frank. She said that it sounded like her idea of a New York/New Jersey blue-collar accent," Gordon said. "If there is such a thing."

"Well, around here, that does suggest Rio Rancho, though I'm sure if you took a survey, there are a bunch of former easterners scattered around the metro area and all kinds of accents. But it gives us a starting place—and initials, hopefully, unless BJ is just a nickname. You think you could work up a sketch based upon her description?'" Charlie asked.

"Yeah, a generic one, at least, and I think I should do two, one without the tat. Lori might be willing to look it over and correct any details," Gordon suggested. "Should we pass this along to the Rio Rancho cops, or sit on it?"

"Let's give it to our detective, along with whatever sketches you can come up with, Gordon. DuPree's worked with us on this from the beginning."

"You suppose he'll be disappointed that the RR cops don't already have this information?" Gordon asked.

"More like pissed," Charlie observed. "They should have already interviewed Lori. Until just a few weeks ago, she was in a position to see who Ray hung around with, at least at Bojo. I wonder if they really are swamped with investigations, or if the cops up there are taking their time for other reasons. Frank was an ex-cop and may have had contacts within the department before all this went down, maybe even made some friends. You suppose someone on the force could be looking out for one of their own—kind of?"

"Not unless he has a real friend on the force, and I didn't get that feeling from the detectives we've run into. Bad cops reflect on all of them. Still, it's something DuPree needs to work on. The detectives might just resent our gathering information that they should have uncovered on their own."

"You're probably right. Let's get to the shop, and you can work up sketches while I help out Jake and Ruth," Charlie suggested, turning south down Albuquerque's Fourth Street. "They can take their first coffee break a little early this morning."

"Sounds good. I'll also enter what Lori gave us into the computer so we can send it as a file to DuPree. And Nancy too?" Gordon offered.

Charlie nodded as they stopped at a red light about a mile north of FOB Pawn. "Just send DuPree's first."

The sound of a siren caught Charlie's attention, and he checked the rearview mirror. He eased to the right and quickly slowed to a stop along the curb just as an APD police cruiser roared past at high speed. He started to move back out into the lane, then heard another siren and stopped again. This time it was a fire department EMT vehicle.

This time he waited.

"Must be a traffic accident," Gordon commented. "Don't hear any more."

Just then, Charlie's cell phone rang. He brought the device out of his shirt pocket and looked at the display. "It's the shop," he announced, activating the speaker, then setting the device on the console.

Charlie recognized Jake's voice instantly.

"Boss, it's Jake. Get over here as soon as you can. I just found a body in the alley."

In spite of the message, Jake's voice was almost normal. The guy was good at keeping his cool. He'd seen worse.

Chapter Fifteen

"You and Ruth okay?" Charlie asked immediately.

"Yes. I called the police just a minute ago, and I already hear sirens. I'm going back out into the alley to meet them."

"Ask Ruth to stay inside the shop. We're just a few blocks away ourselves."

"Jake, before you go! This is Gordon. Is the dead man . . . How old is he?"

Charlie knew instantly that Gordon was trying to rule out Sam.

"Young man, maybe twenty-five. He'd been shot in the torso, I think," Jake responded quietly. "And maybe the head."

"Does he have a spiderweb tattoo on his neck?" Charlie asked.

"How'd you know, boss?"

Charlie looked over at Gordon, who nodded. "BJ."

"Brice Lester Jorpeland is BJ's legal name," DuPree announced, nodding toward the crime scene tech, who was placing the contents of the victim's pockets into an evidence pouch. Charlie had confirmed that this was the man in the sedan, armed with a carbine, who'd been outside his house the other night.

"No wonder he preferred BJ," Gordon commented, looking down the alley, which was mostly blocked, with the ambulance closest to the street and the crime scene van farther inside, opposite the green-painted trash bin. Jake's and Ruth's vehicles were next to the building in their regular slots. The body had been removed from the trash bin and was now in a zipped-up body bag on a lightweight gurney.

Two unlucky techs were beginning the examination of the contents of the trash bin, first handing out the black plastic trash bags that had been dumped by the pawnshop. Fortunately, unless something had been added by an outsider, most of the trash was just junk that couldn't be sold or recycled.

"Getting to the point, Charlie, you think you might have been responsible for the victim's torso wound during that incident at your house?" DuPree asked.

"Based upon the trajectory, yes. If he was the driver of that pickup, one or more of the bullets I fired through the driver's door would have struck him around that level. The victim had a bandage on that wound, is that right?" Charlie asked, looking toward the body bag.

DuPree nodded. "He might have been able to drive the pickup a little farther, and it would explain the blood found in the interior of the recovered vehicle. Until we get a match with the blood, though, we won't know for sure if he'd been in the vehicle cab."

"Could he have been the guy shooting from the pickup bed?" Gordon asked. "He was the guy with the carbine the night before."

"I doubt it. There was no blood back there. Just a lot of sand and some plastic fibers," DuPree said. "The lab techs believe the shooter probably lined that side of the pickup bed with some sand-bags for protection. Then they were dumped later. The other shooter, or shooters if there were more than two, could be any-where now. The medical investigator said there's no exit wound from the chest trauma, so the bullet is still in there."

DuPree looked over toward the crime scene van, where the investigator had gone to work on his report.

"You've got my Beretta already, and I'm betting any recovered slug will match what I fired the other night. But I didn't shoot the guy in the back of the head—that's the work of someone else, not me," Charlie stated.

"Looks like this guy was finished off by whoever was with him, then dumped here last night or early this morning to point the finger at Charlie," Gordon said. "Which means that there are more than the three original perps involved. That the way you see it, Detective?"

"Yeah. Crap. I'd hoped to have all this wrapped up today after you sent me the physical description and those sketches."

"How close did I get?" Gordon asked.

"Not bad, especially with the tattoo on the neck. I'm eager to see if BJ had a criminal record prior to getting that prominent tat-too, and what kind of background he has in common with the other dead guy and Ray Geiger," DuPree responded.

"Detective?" one of the crime scene techs called out from the trash bin. "There's nothing else in here except an empty six-pack and some miniatures. Want us to bag and tag them for possible prints?"

"Yeah, get it all," DuPree responded. Then he turned back to Charlie and Gordon. "Good work with that Lori girl. I've already passed along what she gave you to the detectives at Rio Rancho.

They didn't offer any excuses, but promised to pick up the pace and follow up on BJ's associates with another interview of Ray Geiger."

"So they still don't have anything new?" Charlie asked.

"Not according to Detective Johnson. Just denials from Ray's attorney that his client was involved. The fact that the detectives haven't been able to corroborate his Outpost Bar alibi doesn't seem to bother him. He still claims that the scratch came from one of those women."

"What about Charlie's ID of Ray at the scene?" Gordon asked.

"I'm betting that if this goes to trial, the defense attorney is going to claim you were too far away, and things were happening too fast for Charlie to be certain. That, and the fact that Margaret Randal can't make the ID even though she was right next to him, could do some damage. Add to that his father's claim that Ray was at his house during the invasion."

"Mothers and fathers always lie to protect their kids, even when they commit the crime right in front of them. What about DNA?" Gordon asked. "Margaret scratched the guy, and they sent nail scrapings to the state lab in Santa Fe."

"No results yet. This isn't TV. In real life these tests can take weeks, especially here in New Mexico," DuPree reminded them. "The state lab is always behind schedule."

"So unless we can get something else solid against Ray, he has a chance of walking. That's it?"

"We'll get more. But Charlie, you need to continue to watch your back. And pick up your original weapon. It's in my vehicle in the cardboard box. The lab people are done with it for now. Also, don't stay in the same place two nights in a row, watch for a tail, and be unpredictable," DuPree advised. "Instead of Sam

Randal, it looks like the crew has settled on *you* as the target, at least for the moment. Which makes me even more certain that Ray Geiger is guilty. Why else go after the only eyewitness?"

"Ray, and maybe his dad, obviously have someone else working on their behalf trying to take Charlie out," Gordon concluded. "Does that mean you think the Randals are going to be safe now?"

Charlie shook his head. "They attacked his business, so we can't risk it. I'm still not sure that we know why the Randals were targeted, or why they tried to kidnap Sam—twice. My being able to pick Ray out of a photo array is just a complication. I'm not part of the original motive, I'm just the most dangerous liability to them."

"Good point. With you, however, it might be more a revenge motive for the shooting outside the hospital, which also serves the Geigers. I'm going to go into the Randals' backgrounds and Sam's business and personal relationships. Part of the picture is still missing," DuPree observed.

"Anything else on Eldon, that electrical contractor he cut ties with?" Charlie asked.

"Nothing yet. Officers can't get anyone to answer the door, and all my calls have gone straight to voice mail."

"Maybe the guy was a friend and Mrs. Randal feels awkward discussing it," Charlie pointed out, recalling his earlier conversation. "It's worth pursuing a little more."

DuPree nodded. "You're right about that."

"We'll do what we can in the meantime," Gordon said.

DuPree groaned. "Just stay away from the Geigers. Can you do that?"

"For now. But we're going to be working around them just a

little," Charlie answered, not mentioning the idea he had in mind at the moment.

An hour later, having sent Ruth and Jake to an early lunch, Charlie looked over into the office where Gordon was seated and caught his eye. There were two customers in the shop at the time, looking through sale items on the Cool Shelf, the area with various used fans and room air conditioners.

Gordon came out of the office and walked over to the front register where he was standing. "What's up?"

"I was wondering if you'd give Lori Hansen a call, tell her about BJ, and thank her again for her help. Pour on the charm, then ask if there are any others at Bojo who engaged in conversation with any of our suspects, Ray and the two dead guys. We know there is at least one more still out there," Charlie noted.

"Yeah, maybe she can think of someone, or lead us to someone else who might know—other than those sensei who helped Frank test the durability of the floor mats."

Charlie grinned.

"Whatever. I'll give her a call," Gordon replied. "Wave if things start to get busy out here. Just the two at the moment?" He looked up at one of the big surveillance mirrors to verify. It gave him an idea. "I'll do that now."

Gordon went back to the office and got on the phone. About ten minutes later, he came out into the shop again and gave Charlie the thumbs-up sign. "I asked her about surveillance cameras at the dojo," he said. "There aren't any, but one of the neighboring businesses might have them. She's friendly with most of the people who work around there, so she's going to check.

She's free until seven tonight. I told her we'd come get her as soon as Ruth and Jake were back from lunch to take over here."

"We should have thought of that before," Charlie said. "Or the police should have, anyway."

"Better late than never," Gordon said. At that moment, the customers at the Cool Shelf announced they were ready to make a purchase, so Charlie went over to wait on them.

By the time they'd completed the transaction, Jake and Ruth were back. Charlie and Gordon let them know where they were going and headed out to pick up Lori at her apartment.

When they arrived at the Rio Rancho shopping center where Bojo was located, they parked in front of the supermarket, farther down, hoping that the Dodge would blend in. Dodge Chargers weren't rare, but Charlie's was purple and relatively distinctive.

Luckily, just a few minutes after they arrived, Lori's friend Rachel, who worked solo at the dry cleaners next to the dojo, was able to help them out. She agreed to let them copy the surveillance DVDs so they could survey them elsewhere. While Charlie copied the disks onto a portable machine, Gordon and the two women remained in the customer area of the business, talking about Bojo and those individuals they remember seeing that fit the right adult age group.

Though there were only a few disks to copy, which covered just the past month, there were three sets, one for the two front cameras, one for the interior, and a third for the camera covering the back exterior of the building, which included the rear door and a loading dock.

"I'm done here," Charlie announced, coming out of the office, a partitioned area located in the back room, which contained mostly large rails on a conveyer system, long sorting tables, and a few laundry bins.

"Great, and thanks, Rachel," Gordon said to the tall, slender black woman who managed the place. Though she'd never had any problems with students at the dojo, like Lori, Rachel had been harassed by BJ and Tony Lorenzo and hated it. The punks had followed Lori into the dry cleaners once, and the women had some difficulty getting rid of them.

"I hope this helps track down the animals responsible for the attacks," Rachel replied, moving away from the window, where she'd been watching the parking lot. "I can't recall anyone else in particular who might be connected to BJ and Tony, and I still have a hard time believing Ray is involved. Of all my neighbors here, he's been the most respectful. But if you know for sure it was him, Charlie, you've gotta do the right thing and send him back to jail."

"Lori said that none of the kids who've had problems with the law have ever caused any problems for her. How about you?" Charlie asked Rachel as he looked out the big picture window toward the parking lot. Bojo students were beginning to arrive, dressed in their white uniforms.

"I've been asked out a few times, but always very politely, and by older students who came in alone. BJ and Tony came around together, feeding off of each other's comments," Rachel admitted. "They eased up when I showed them my boyfriend, though." She pointed to a photo on the wall of a tall, broad-shouldered Marine in full dress uniform with a row of campaign and other decorations. "Joe is currently deployed on the *America,* an amphibious assault ship. He's the only man in my life."

"Oorah," Gordon exclaimed. "May he come home safe."

"Speaking of safe, guys, there are several kids hanging around Charlie's Dodge. From here, they look like some of the crew Ray has been trying to set straight," Lori interjected. "I know some of those kids, and they've never been any trouble, at least here. But with Ray's current situation . . ."

"Looks like they're loyal to the man, either way," Charlie concluded. "Let's go see what they want, Gordo."

Gordon nodded, then looked over at Lori.

"I'm going with you boys. There must be ten of them. You might need some backup if they step over the line," Lori added, then turned to Rachel. "Thanks for your help, girl. We'll let you know if the visuals lead the police to a suspect."

"I can lock up and follow you down," Rachel offered.

"Not necessary. Stay here and take care of your business. You don't need to make an enemy of Ray and his pop," Gordon replied.

"I'll keep watch, and if it gets ugly or I see a gun I'm calling the police," Rachel said. "You two guys stay out of trouble. Lori here knows how to take care of herself."

Charlie nodded, wondering if they'd made the right decision, leaving their concealed carry weapons in the car. "Of course."

Chapter Sixteen

The moment they stepped out of the dry cleaners, several sets of eyes turned in their direction and conversations ended. There were two teenaged girls among the ten or so people standing on the sidewalk in the shade, and none of the school's students looked to be over twenty years old. At least three of them were as tall as Charlie, however, and even the girls were Gordon's size.

"A word of advice," Lori whispered as they walked together down the sidewalk toward the gathering. "Try not to do anything that's going to get these people in more trouble with the law."

"All we want to do is nail the bad guys," Charlie replied. "But clearly these people are here for a reason."

Gordon nodded. "And we're always reasonable."

As they approached the loose gathering, Charlie brought out his car keys slowly and in clear view, not wanting to send the signal that he was arming himself with a knife or gun. They were all young people who'd supposedly been in trouble and, with that, probably some fights. Self-preservation required a certain level of profiling. He knew none of these people, but teens with an unpleasant history were often reactionary, paranoid, and prone to sudden violence.

He had no death wish, nor did he want to injure anyone, which was likely to happen if he or Gordon was attacked. With so many potential opponents, they couldn't afford to hold back. These kids didn't understand who they were dealing with.

All he wanted to do was to be able to drive away with his friends and have the opportunity to find out whoever was messing with the Randals and trying to kill him. Though he doubted anyone here was behind what had happened, they were inadvertently supporting Ray's criminal behavior, and Charlie didn't believe he'd be able to change any minds about that. He'd remain stable and provoke as little as possible. Despite his pal's love of combat, he doubted that Gordon would push anyone into a brawl either, and he'd have to take it on faith that none of this crowd was packing heat.

"Hey, people, glad to see everyone is still working out at Bojo. I miss you guys," Lori began immediately.

Charlie smiled. Smart girl.

"You too, Lori, but did you know you're hanging around with a guy who's trying to send Ray back to jail?" asked one of the oldest of the group, a husky fireplug of a guy almost as tall as Charlie.

To not speak now would show weakness, something he dare not do with these people, who were used to taking aggressive positions when confronted. But maybe he could lead everyone in a different direction. "I'm Charlie, the man you're probably here to see. Do you have any fathers, brothers, or sisters who've served in the military? Afghanistan, Iraq, maybe?"

He noticed a few nods. "I served four tours, the last two in Afghanistan. I saw friends get wounded, blown to pieces and killed, but I lived through that hell and came back without a scratch, at least one that shows on the outside. Now, here at home, in the past week, somebody has tried to kill me three times. *Three.* Two drive-bys, plus a pipe bomb planted in my kitchen. You may have seen some of that on the news. That's me they're talking about. That's gone down *because* I stepped up and helped keep three guys with guns from kidnapping a man from his home—after they chased down and shot his wife."

Nobody had a quick response, so he kept going. "I didn't serve my country to come back here and get blown away, not on the street or in my own home. If Ray Geiger did the deed he's been arrested for, that's between him, God, and a judge and jury. When it goes to trial, you go sit in the courtroom and have his back if you want. Look me in the face and know that I'm telling the truth. Just don't screw up your own life by trying to mess with mine. So if you've got something to say, say it now."

"Ray says he didn't do it, and we believe him," one of the girls shouted out.

"And if you say it was him, you're lying," another young man said, stepping up closer to Charlie.

"You weren't there, Fabio. It's okay to believe in your sensei. Ray has helped all of you," Lori said. "But he's also made mistakes in the past. What will serve him best right now is letting the jury sort it out. Don't do anything that's going to come back on him— or his school, or his father."

"His old man sucks," someone over by the sidewalk mumbled. "But I know Ray didn't do any of that shit."

"Then show Ray he's worth something to you, and that he's making a difference in your lives. Stick with your martial arts training. Stay out of trouble. Don't screw up," Lori called out loudly.

"He's probably in there now, wondering where the hell you are." She looked down at her cell phone. "You're late. Get to class, people!"

They began to move away, giving Charlie a parting mad-dog glare, then looked away and picked up the pace. Within thirty seconds they'd all entered the dojo.

Gordon, who'd taken a casual stroll around the Charger, joined Charlie and Lori, who were still watching the door of the martial arts studio.

"So, did they key my car?" Charlie asked.

"Not much. Don't worry, I know a guy," Gordon replied.

"I'm calling this a win, boys," Lori said. "You guys have some good personal skills. Now, can we get out of here?" she added as Charlie pressed the key fob, unlocking the doors. "I feel like I'm in hostile territory."

After taking Lori back to her apartment, the guys returned to the shop, planning to watch the surveillance footage whenever they could get free. Today, Margaret was at Firm Foundation working with Sam, so hopefully, they could make some progress in identifying whoever was still trying to kill Charlie. Maybe DuPree and Nancy would learn something as well.

Charlie was out front, positioning watches and turquoise jewelry in their Plexiglas display cases, when his cell phone rang. It was Gina, calling from her own cell.

"Hey, Gina, what's up?" He could hear what sounded like traffic in the background. "You having car trouble?"

"No, Charlie, I'm actually out in front of the courthouse. Lately somebody has been following me every time I leave my office, especially when I'm going back and forth between there and the jails or court. I think it's only when I'm on foot. If they've been watching the house or following me in the car, I haven't been able to pick up on it yet."

"Crap. I'm guessing you've actually laid eyes on the person, right? Any idea who it might be?"

"No," she replied. "I keep seeing what looks like a man, or at least someone without curves, about five foot eight, slender, usually wearing a light hoodie and black baseball cap. He has on dark loafers or those low-cut canvas-style shoes some of the skaters wear. Oh, and cheap sunglasses."

"Dresses young. I hope he's frying in the heat. You get a hair color? No beard or mustache?" Charlie pressed.

"My impression is that the person, probably a man based upon his stride, has brown hair, not black. There's no beard, but the guy has a big 35 mm style camera with a telephoto lens. I've seen him taking pictures of me."

"You're a beautiful woman."

"Don't be creepy, Charles."

"I'm considering every angle. You think it might be someone from one of your cases? Maybe a guy working for an opposition lawyer, or someone who came out on the losing side in a lawsuit?" It was a logical question he had to ask. Often, many thousands of dollars in judgments or settlements resulted from her work, and lawyers couldn't help but make enemies.

"I guess so, but why keep following me? I'm not meeting with any secret witnesses or conducting any business out of the ordinary. Everything I do is in private or open court," she responded. "It's getting kind of scary though."

"You still carrying that .380?"

"Everywhere it's legal, of course. Could this be someone

connected to the Randals? One of Ray Geiger's crew, maybe? There's one or more that's still out there." Her voice was subdued, almost a whisper.

"Unless you've coincidentally picked up a stalker."

"You trying to cheer me up?"

"How long have you noticed this person on your trail?"

"Just the last two days, though it could be longer, I suppose. I'm always on alert, you know that. I do most of my out-of-office work downtown in court or the county government offices, and the streets are filled with people who are dealing with the system. Two big jails, law enforcement buildings, courthouses, street people, associates of criminals. I walk among them nearly every day."

"Okay, then the first thing we need to do is corner the guy. Then we learn the motive, if there is one. What happens if you move in his direction and try to get a closer look?"

"I've tried to be very subtle about it, not letting him know I've spotted him. Still, he backs off and slips away. The guy is always watching and anticipating what I'm about to do. The only times I've ever got more than a glance is when I catch his reflection in a window. Last time I did that, though, I think he caught on and disappeared. Usually when I'm downtown it's during business hours, and there are a lot of people on the streets. It's easy for him to blend in. He's changed his look since last time, but only with the color of his outfit, like different-color jeans or hoodie. Or his cap. But it's the same guy."

"Is he watching you now?"

There was a pause, then she answered. "I'm standing close to the curb at the intersection right now, and I took a three-sixty look around. I don't see him at the moment, but he was across the street when I left the building. That's what finally motivated me to call you."

"You tell Nancy about this yet?"

"You crazy? She'd go postal and start gunning for the guy. You know how protective she is, and she needs to stay focused on dealing with her current assignment, which is running down whoever's after you and Sam Randal. Her work with DuPree in the violent crimes division could be a real career boost. She needs to worry about the investigation, not me."

"Like I don't care what happens to you?"

"No, it's because I know you do that I called. You're not a cop, and because of that, you can think and work outside the box—and the rules. You could have been a top-notch FBI agent or cop if you'd gone in that direction. How about helping me out?"

"Of course. But what will Nancy say?"

"I'll deal with that when it happens, and don't you say a word that'll get back to her. Meanwhile, just so you know, if this guy makes any move toward me I'm going to put him in the hospital," Gina affirmed.

Charlie knew that Gina had been trained in Krav Maga, the Israeli military fighting system, while attending law school at Rutgers, and that she and Nancy worked out together. Nancy had mentioned more than once that her personal defense skills far exceeded what she'd learned at the police academy after only a few workouts with Gina.

But hand-to-hand training wouldn't keep someone from being ambushed, shot at, run over, or poisoned, so it always made sense to be proactive. Gina was doing the right thing, asking for backup.

"Where are you going next?" Charlie asked, a plan forming in his head.

"Back to my office for maybe an hour, then home. Nancy and I are going grocery shopping as soon as she's off duty, assuming something doesn't come up."

"Okay. Follow your routine. Just don't go into any confined spaces or a parking garage where you might walk into a trap. I'm going to come down to your office and keep watch on the building. Once I'm in position, I'll call and let you know. What I'd like you to do then is walk back to the county courthouse via your normal route, then pass through the lobby and security station. Once you're cleared, get out of sight for a while. Maybe go to one of the waiting areas outside a courtroom and stay there for about fifteen minutes. I'll be in the area, out on the streets, trying to spot your stalker. Don't look around for me, just stay normal, especially when you come back outside. If I spot the guy, I'll call and give you instructions on what to do, if the situation allows. Unless I tell you otherwise, return to your office, get in your car, and go home. Got that?"

"Okay, but I have to leave my handgun in my office. I can't take it into the courthouse."

"Yeah, but I'll be close by."

"Shouldn't I call if I spot him?"

"No, that might just scare him away. He's been very careful up till now. You can take calls that come in that won't distract you, but don't make any outgoing calls unless you're confronted. Trust me, I'll be in the area, watching, and I know how to blend in," Charlie affirmed.

"Okay. I'll see you . . . when I see you, I guess. Be careful, Charles."

Charlie placed the phone in his pocket and looked around the shop. Three people had come into the place while he was talking to Gina. Jake was up front and already talking to two of them. Ruth was somewhere in the back, but she could cover the front register if he asked. He'd take the opportunity to tell Gordon what was going on with Gina, come up with a disguise, then head downtown.

Driving Gordon's borrowed truck, he circled the block where Gina's law office was located and quickly spotted the likely stalker sitting on a wooden bench, looking toward the seven-story building.

The guy was seated in front of a motor vehicle office just west of where two street vendors were pitching costume jewelry and hot dogs to passersby. He was fiddling with a big camera and was wearing a gray sweatshirt-style hoodie and a brown ball cap. It was hot downtown at the moment, and his head was uncovered except for the cap and sunglasses, revealing short, medium brown hair. From his clothing, posture, and size, Charlie judged that the man was probably late teens to midtwenties, just the right age for Ray's crew and most of his older students.

Charlie parked in the multilevel public garage a block north of the courthouse, adjusted his tie, grabbed his briefcase, and then stepped down out of the pickup onto level 4 of the relatively cool, shaded concrete parking structure. Once he was out of the structure, he'd be just another suit on his way to a business meeting, or to do whatever the hell those white-collar people did from nine to five. The advantage of wearing the expensive, almost new gray suit liberated from the clothing rack in FOB Pawn was that it concealed the pistol tucked in the holster back on his hip.

He'd had to wear his black boots, but fortunately they weren't considered too much of a break in corporate protocol here in the Southwest. He doubted the stalker would know the difference, however, if he was the kind of punk who hung around with Ray Geiger.

Gina's shadow might not be connected to the Randal situation at all. He could be associated with some legal hassle regarding her law firm, or even be a sick puppy who just happened to discover and become obsessed with the woman. It was difficult for anyone not to notice Gina Sinclair whenever she was out in public.

Stepping into the shade granted by the recessed doorway of an upscale clothing store, Charlie brought out his phone and called Gina. "I'm in position now, watching the person I believe is the subject. Come down and walk to the courthouse, as planned. Don't go too fast, just hurry a little like you forgot something and need to get it done before you can call it a day. And don't look around for the guy. He's wearing a gray hoodie and a brown cap. Whatever you do, if he comes into your field of view, avoid eye contact."

"Got it." Gina's voice, normally soft and a little high pitched, was low and firm—the one she reserved for strictly business.

A couple of minutes went by before Gina, dressed in a dark brown suit with a light blue scarf, stepped out of the building and came down the steps to the ground-level sidewalk. She was carrying a small leather briefcase, a fixture of her profession, at least in his limited understanding of lawyerness.

He turned away to watch Camera Guy. From this point on, Charlie needed to ignore Gina and focus on the target—and at the same time not get made. Fortunately, there were a half-dozen or more suits walking briskly along the same sidewalk, none of them standing out in any way, at least to him. Charlie had considered disguising himself as a street person, but in this particular downtown location there was often a cop or two coming or going, and he'd decided that it might make him a subject of attention and avoidance at the same time. So far, he'd made the right decisions.

Camera Guy had noted Gina's presence from the moment she came out of the building, and now he was watching her through the camera lens, which also concealed his face. Knowing the direction Gina would be taking, Charlie moved down the sidewalk on his side of the street to take a new position. He watched the guy, who was now on his feet, out of the corner of his eye. As he'd warned Gina, it was safer not to look directly at the subject. The rule applied equally around the world, whether you were hunting your prey in Afghanistan or Albuquerque.

He waited, and when Gina continued on toward the end of the block, the target followed, casually, looking from side to side occasionally as if studying the architecture of the multistory buildings. His gaze always returned to Gina, however, and though Charlie was very careful, Camera Guy never looked back. His focus was clearly on Gina and what she was doing.

Once she went inside the courthouse lobby, lining up behind a few other suits at the mandatory security check point and awaiting the x-raying of her briefcase, her stalker stopped across the avenue, sat down on one of the steps leading up to the building, and began fiddling with his camera.

Charlie stopped, turned around, and quickly circled the block, coming around the building and waiting in the shade. He brought out his cell phone, noting that Camera Guy had also shifted his position and was now across the street, still technically on courthouse grounds but seated on a low, decorative concrete wall. Behind him was a small basement diner incorporated into the courthouse structure that served mostly county employees and others who had business there—like juries. It was a good place to watch for Gina, then follow, regardless of what direction she took.

Charlie continued walking east past the courthouse. Once out of sight of Camera Guy, he crossed over to the same side of the street as the courthouse, then came up to the eastern corner of the municipal building and sat down on a bench, cell phone out and to his ear. He couldn't see the target, who was around the corner maybe a hundred feet away, but he would spot Gina as she left the building and came to the crosswalk at the intersection. To return to her office, she'd cross the street, heading north. Charlie decided to speed things up a bit and called Gina.

"Hey, girl. Let's make it happen. Head back to your office, the usual route. After you cross the street and get down the block about halfway, I'll call you with some instructions."

"So he's back?"

"Yup, and I'm going to nail him. Depending on how this goes down, I may end up contacting DuPree. Just keep your distance and do exactly what I say. Unless I tell you otherwise, once you get to your office, lock the door and wait for my next call. It may be a while, but be patient. If anyone else shows up and you feel threatened, start screaming and call 911."

"Got it. I'm on the sixth floor, so it may be a couple of minutes before I leave the courthouse. Be careful, Charlie."

Shortly thereafter, still pretending to be studying his cell phone, Charlie watched as Gina walked across the inlaid stone of the courthouse grounds to the corner, the intersection of Lomas and Fourth Street. She waited, along with several other people, for the light to change, then crossed Lomas to the north.

By then, her tail had stepped away from the wall and was walking quickly toward the street corner. He wouldn't make this light—it was already too late—but clearly he wanted to cross on the next cycle. Charlie waited. He'd catch the one after that. With the layout of the route back imprinted in his brain now, he had a plan.

As expected, Camera Guy followed Gina from about fifty feet back, maintaining his distance and pausing to look at the buildings, camera in hand. Time to make a move, Charlie decided, touching the phone display and sending the call.

"Gina. Slow down to just below normal. Once you get to the next corner, instead of crossing the street, turn to your west, continue down the sidewalk until you reach the alley, then quickly jaywalk across the street."

"Heading north again?"

"Copy. Um, exactly. You'll notice me coming up the alley in your direction. Once I'm almost at the end, cross the street, but don't look at me after that. Just turn east and quickly walk down the sidewalk to the next corner. Head north again, for your office. And don't get run over or look back. Clear?"

"I think I see what you're doing here."

"Good. Wish me luck!"

"Luck. Bye." She ended the call.

He turned around and raced back toward the courthouse, turned west at the corner, then ran in that direction to the alley. Now all he had to do was sprint the entire block and come out ahead of the target before he could turn the corner. Even if he did, however, the guy should be close enough to grab.

Several people watched, curious, as he ran past them, but he smiled and nodded, muttering "I'm late" every time he passed someone. Reaching the alley, he cursed the weight of the boots and the fact that he was carrying a briefcase. Halfway up the alley, at full sprint, he also cursed the tie and the sports jacket. He slowed once he spotted Gina standing there on the sidewalk, having just crossed the street. At the end of the alley, he took a quick peek around the corner. No sign of Camera Guy. Good! He'd counted on the guy not wanting to look around the corner immediately, in case Gina had noticed him and stopped just out of sight. The guy had been careful so far not to get too close.

Charlie hurried up to the northeast corner of the building as quickly and quietly as possible, then set the briefcase down against the wall, out of the way. Now he waited. If he could only keep from breathing so loudly after the race up the alley, he had a chance to nail the guy.

He watched as Gina walked up the sidewalk, turned the corner, and disappeared to the north. Listening, he heard a click. Less than ten agonizing seconds went by; then the man stepped into view, heading in Gina's direction.

The guy flinched as Charlie suddenly appeared at his side.

Chapter Seventeen

"Gotcha!" Charlie gasped, still a little out of breath as he yanked the guy around and shoved his back against the building wall.

"What the hell? Hey, let me go!" the young man yelled, his voice cracking.

Charlie had his left hand on the guy's throat, thumb at the Adam's apple. His right arm was cocked, ready to punch, if necessary.

"Not until we have a talk, kid. Why have you been following that woman?" Charlie demanded, anger in his voice. The poor kid was barely out of his teens, probably about to pee his pants, if he hadn't already.

"What? No, let me go. Or I'll . . ." His voice squeaked as he struggled for air.

"What, call the cops? I am the cops," Charlie lied, pulling back his jacket to show the authentic-looking badge taken from the pawnshop display case. "What's your name, kid, and why have you been stalking that woman? You know she's a lawyer, right?"

Charlie almost felt sorry for the kid, who was either a great actor or clearly out of his element. He loosed his grip on the punk's throat so the guy could still breathe, and, seeing the guy's camera about to fall to the sidewalk, he reached down and grabbed it.

"You just a pervert, or what? What am I going to find on your camera?" Charlie insisted.

"Don't arrest me, Officer. Just take a look at the photos. They're just of that lawyer, Gina Sinclair, and she's fully dressed, out in public. Really. I'm a freelance photographer doing a job for my client. Look for yourself."

"First, kid, what's your name, and how old are you?" Charlie asked, easing his grip but not removing his hold.

"Nineteen. Well, almost. My name is Eric Sharp. I'm a journalism major at CNM. Here's my wallet," the kid answered, his tone shifting from frightened to confident as he reached for his back pocket.

Charlie fell for it—almost.

A knife suddenly appeared in Eric's left hand. "For Tony!" he snarled. His arm whipped around, stabbing at Charlie's gut.

Charlie's training had already kicked in. The blade encountered the camera instead of his stomach. The deflected knife bounced off, slicing Charlie's finger and ripping at his jacket and shirt. The camera fell to the sidewalk.

With his bloody right hand Charlie grabbed the kid's wrist, bending it out and away, slamming his attacker's hand into the wall with a soft crunch. Eric cursed in pain, but the scream was cut short as Charlie tightened his squeeze on the kid's throat with his left hand, then shoved the back of his head into the side of the building. Again there was the dull thump of flesh and bone striking brick.

The knife fell to the sidewalk with a clank.

Eric tried to kick, but Charlie was so close there was no force to the blow, just pressure. Charlie kneed the guy in his groin, then let him go suddenly and jumped back. The kid collapsed with an agonized gasp, then a yelp as his knees cracked on the sidewalk.

Charlie kicked the knife off the sidewalk into the gutter. "Face down, flat on the sidewalk, dumb-ass, or I'll bounce you off the wall again!" he ordered. The guy struggled for a few more seconds, then gave up when Charlie pushed his face into the concrete.

Realizing that someone was standing at the corner, Charlie looked over his shoulder and saw two girls in their teens standing there, cell phones up, clearly recording the action. That gave him an idea.

"Did you get the part where he stabbed me with the knife?" Charlie placed his bloody right hand on the scrape across his stomach, adding more color to what he knew was a minor wound.

The young, skinny teen with multicolored hair and a tight, shiny gray dress six inches above her knobby knees nodded, the pink phone still up. She was staring at his bloody shirt, which was important to his new plan.

"We all did, Charlie," Gina yelled, running across the street toward him. "I called 911."

Both girls looked around, then turned and directed their phones toward her.

"They're on their way," Gina announced, her voice shaky as she got down on her knees beside Charlie, fear in her eyes. She reached into her purse and brought out a canister of pepper spray.

Charlie wanted to cuss out Gina for not sticking with the plan, but now he could use that to his advantage. He turned his head so only she could see his face and winked. "I'm okay," he mouthed.

Her mouth fell open just for a few seconds before she whispered, "You bastard," then put the spray back into her purse.

"Call Detective DuPree," he said, then groaned, playing it up for the teens. His knees still in the middle of the kid's back, he turned to address the second girl, who'd stepped closer, her eyes focused on the fresh blood at his stomach. "You need to stand clear," he whispered hoarsely. "I'm cut real bad, and if he tries to get away . . ."

Charlie collapsed onto the kid, pinning him to the sidewalk, his left hand cutting off the guy's ability to speak. At the same time, he was trying to look seriously wounded. "Play along," he whispered to Gina.

Gina stared at him angrily for a few more seconds, then finally relented. "Don't you die on me, Charlie," she moaned, clinging onto his arm tightly. "Help is on the way."

The girl lowered her phone and turned to her friend. "Let's get out of here," she whispered.

They disappeared around the corner of the building just as Charlie heard the pulse of a siren, that brief tone a cop usually gives when signaling someone to pull over. Out of the corner of his eye he saw a police car coming up the street from the west.

"Don't let the cop run over the knife," he told Gina.

Eric, or whoever the hell he was, started struggling again, but now Charlie didn't have to fake dying anymore. He twisted both the guy's arms up and across his back at a painful angle, and the guy stopped jerking around. "Stay still or I'll break it," Charlie ordered as Gina stood up and stepped to the curb, holding her palm up, then pointed to the knife in the street.

The car stopped at the curb on the opposite side of the alley, and the APD cop climbed out. Charlie recognized the short, slender officer instantly. It was Jan or Janet something, the young officer who'd been first on the scene a couple of years ago when he and Gordon had been ambushed. Hopefully, she'd remember him as well.

If Charlie knew anything about the current generation, those teenaged girls were already uploading what they'd just seen onto the Internet. To misquote Mark Twain, hopefully the news of his death would also be exaggerated, and some of the heat would be off.

It would be nice to think that Eric was the last perp out to get him, but experience had taught him never to jump to any conclusions. He was convinced now that Gina had just been the bait to lure him out into the open, where he'd be vulnerable. This slippery kid had set him up and almost succeeded, but now, if he was thought to be dead or hospitalized, it might take some of the pressure off. Maybe he could operate under the radar for a day or two.

"Mr. Henry," the officer addressed Charlie as she approached, hand on her holstered handgun. Then she looked at Gina. "You called to report an assault, Counselor?" she added.

Charlie noted the officer's name tag. Her last name was Martinez. "This guy sliced me with his knife. It's over there, just off the curb," Charlie announced, pointing toward the spot.

A second APD unit suddenly came around the far corner, stopping with a screech, blocking the street, and Eric turned his head to look. He saw Officer Martinez for the first time. "Oh shit," he mumbled.

"You know this dipstick?" Charlie asked, moving aside and giving the officer room to handcuff the guy's hands behind his back.

"His name is Ted McConnell, and he gets off hurting people. Served time for manslaughter right out of high school. Isn't that right, Ted?" Officer Martinez asked, snapping the cuffs into place on the man's wrists.

"Mr. Henry. You're bleeding. Stay still!" the officer exclaimed, finally seeing the wet crimson smear on his shirt.

A black police officer with a shaved head—a sergeant, judging from his stripes—came up quickly. "What's the situation, Martinez?" he asked, looking at the suspect, then Charlie. "Damn, you get cut up, sir?" he asked.

"Not too bad," Charlie replied, rising to full height as he looked at his hand first, then his stomach. Blood was still flowing, but at a low volume. "But my suit is pretty well trashed."

"Sergeant. Can you control the suspect while I get my first aid kit?" Martinez asked.

"Go ahead," the sergeant replied.

"I've already called for the EMTs," Gina announced, coming closer and putting her hand on Charlie's shoulder. "We need to stop the bleeding and get you checked out."

More sirens sounded in the distance as the sergeant hauled McConnell to his feet, then made him hug the wall while he searched for other weapons.

Charlie walked out the hospital's emergency entrance, slipped past a parked ambulance, and jumped into Jake's black SUV.

"How you doing, Doctor?" Gordon asked, noting Charlie's dark blue scrubs and fake hospital staff ID as he gingerly fastened his shoulder belt and stretched out with a groan.

"The slice on my gut wasn't much more than a deep scratch, but it stings every time I twist or turn. I can't feel my finger at all, though." Charlie held up his right hand, the middle finger bandaged with gauze and a lot of tape.

"Right back at you," Gordon responded, flashing his own middle finger at Charlie as he pulled away into the wide passage leading toward the street.

"At least it's not my trigger finger."

"So you didn't need any stitches?"

"No, the knife blade was sharp but didn't go too deep. I'm glad the guy's camera was hefty enough to deflect it. If I hadn't had the camera to block the jab, I'd have probably bled out on the sidewalk," Charlie admitted. "The kid played me for a sucker from the very beginning."

"Good old survival instincts come in handy sometimes—that and a lot of training."

"Yeah. I remember when I found out that a standard ballistic vest would stop a pistol bullet but not a sharp knife," Charlie said.

"Important detail to know, considering most of our missions were hands-on," Gordon said. "Maybe you should learn from your ancestors and take up a bow and arrows."

The skills he'd acquired during four deployments had probably kept him alive today, Charlie knew. He thought back to their missions in Iraq, and later in Afghanistan. These operations were usually intelligence assignments, where they identified and grabbed insurgents for interrogation. This was work that usually required them to hand over their prisoners for processing while they were still capable of speech. There had been several incidents involving hand-to-hand combat, and not every potential resource had survived the takedown.

"I'll have to top off the gas tank and thank Jake for the use of his vehicle this afternoon. There's no way we can ensure we won't be spotted if we keep driving around in my purple Charger or your pickup," Charlie said. "You already have a rental for me, right?"

Gordon nodded. "Once I know we're not being followed by someone who doesn't believe you're still in the hospital, we'll meet up with Detective DuPree and Nancy."

"Somewhere out of sight, I hope."

"Yeah, the third floor of a downtown parking garage, west of the train station. The van is already there."

"Generic white?"

"No, I managed to track down one that's a faded blue. Won't stick out so much at night, in case we decide to stake out somebody's place."

"Disguised as shop owners."

Gordon chuckled, pulling off the street into a minimall. Instead of coming to a stop, he circled around the end building, then entered the alley and headed in the opposite direction. "Gotta lose the tail."

"I didn't spot anyone."

"Just making sure."

Five minutes later, Gordon parked in a space beside Detective DuPree's unmarked sedan, nodding to the detective as they came to a halt. Nancy, in uniform, walked over to join them. When they'd come into view, she'd been standing several feet away, apparently looking at the city streets over the wall of the open structure.

Gordon stepped out immediately, but Charlie took his time. If pushed, he could move quickly enough, but right now he was taking it easy.

Nancy was first to meet him, and she gave him a gentle hug. "Thanks for looking out for Gina," she whispered. "You got lucky, though. McConnell is a crafty little bastard, so I've been told."

Just then, DuPree walked up, stopped, and shook his head. "If there's really a God up there, Charlie, he or she has been working overtime looking out for you. Still, you're pressing your luck, which is why I need you to disappear for a while. The DA is going to depend on you when Ray Geiger's case comes to trial, and I've been advised to keep you safe."

"Advised?" Gordon asked, coming around to join them.

"Okay, ordered, whatever," DuPree said with a shrug. "Hell, Charlie, you've been kicked, punched, stabbed, and shot at this week."

"Don't I know it? All that's left is getting run over, though not for lack of trying."

"How about a vicious animal attack?" Gordon suggested, straight-faced.

"Make it a rattlesnake—poison. Two at once," Charlie responded.

"Let's get serious, guys," Nancy said. "According to what Gina told me on the phone, we have one solid motive for today's attack—Tony Lorenzo's death. Uh, sorry, Charlie, I've been forgetting lately. It's okay to say his name out loud, isn't it?"

She was referring to the traditional Navajo reluctance to speak of the dead by name.

"Yeah, no problem. Once they've been dead three days, it's safe," Charlie replied.

Gordon looked at him with raised eyebrows. Charlie shook his head slightly.

"Anyway, you and Ms. Sinclair both heard McConnell yell the guy's name as he attacked you with the knife," DuPree summarized. "That suggests the motive was revenge on you, not the Randals, and implies that the guy knew the deceased. He couldn't have been the third attacker. They're all accounted for."

Charlie nodded. "That's the way I see it. Which begs the question, just what was the connection between the dead guys and McConnell? How did they know each other? Were they doing these home invasions together—including BJ? And where did they meet? Jail, Walmart, or the Cattlemen's Club?"

DuPree shrugged. "We're looking into that now, not only within the area but also through NCIC—the National Crime Information Center. If we can find a connection leading back to Ray or Frank Geiger, either back east or here, we might be able to close the circle on this business, and the Randals will be able to relax a little."

"God's ears," Gordon added.

"You people still looking out for those two?" DuPree asked Charlie.

"We have coverage at night, and the Randals usually sleep at Gina and Nancy's place," Charlie replied. "Sam hired extra security at work, and today Margaret is with him at the company location. We've been working to identify whoever else is still involved with what's been going on—starting from the first incident. The Geigers, I believe, are the key to all this, but the motive still isn't clear."

"We got copies of camera surveillance from the dry cleaners near the dojo, and from viewing the feed I've already spotted the two dead guys entering or leaving the school," Gordon explained, bringing Charlie up to date. "If the Rio Rancho cops working the case still haven't obtained the video assets yet, you might want to make that suggestion."

Charlie looked over at Gordon. "Let's get together and see if Ted McConnell shows up in the images, partner, now that we know to look for him."

"Or anyone else within the age group not suited out for martial arts," Nancy added. "And will you send copies of the images to my private e-mail address? It won't be admissible at this stage, not until it comes directly from the business owner, but that can come later. That okay, Detective?" she asked DuPree.

"Whatever it takes. Let's just make sure we don't do anything that will hurt this case when it goes to court," DuPree replied.

Charlie looked at Gordon, then at Nancy, who nodded imperceptibly.

"Sure," he answered, nudging Gordon.

"Gotcha," Gordon said hastily.

"Yeah, right. Just stay out of trouble, guys," DuPree said.

Twenty minutes later, Charlie and Gordon arrived at a motel that was easy walking distance from a tribal casino outside Bernalillo, a small town several miles north of Rio Rancho. Gordon pulled up and parked beside the motel office next to an older-model blue van with tinted windows.

"That'll be your ride for a while, Charlie," Gordon announced, handing him a set of keys. "The rental papers are in the glove box."

"What about my Charger?" Charlie asked, not wanting his car to become a target.

"Jake will keep it in his garage," Gordon answered. "This place is enough out of the way that you should be able to keep a low profile but still be within twenty minutes or so of the shop. And you have three routes going back and forth from the city."

"Good choice. And with so many Indians, who's going to notice one more hanging around here, even a taller, less chesty Navajo? I guess I'll have to go sign in and show a credit card to get my room key."

"Yeah. I'll stop by your house and pick up a suitcase of clothes and toiletries so you can get out of that grimy suit. Well, what's left of it."

"Good. And thanks for bringing this sweatshirt. If the person at the motel desk saw me in my bloody shirt and jacket, they'd call the cops for sure."

"How's the finger?"

"EMT did a great job. She said it didn't need any stitches."

"Did she kiss it and make it better?" Gordon teased.

"Of course. Now let's get moving. Going over those surveillance DVDs together will take some time. If it's okay with you, once I get to my room, I can start viewing them while you go get my stuff."

Gordon nodded, reaching for the door handle. "Let's get you set up with the player and disks in your motel room. Then I'll be on my way."

Chapter Eighteen

Charlie decided to clean up and take a nap instead of viewing the surveillance disks. When Gordon returned, he was refreshed and ready to get to work. Gordon had already been through the disks on his own, so he handled the controls, fast-forwarding through the hours when there were few or no human images to examine.

Charlie took notes, recording dates and times when someone who didn't seem to fit the look of a student entered or left the dojo. They ignored, for the present, anyone who was clearly an adult accompanying a child. When they came upon BJ or Tony, they stopped and viewed the scene again.

Soon Charlie spotted Ted McConnell. His image had jumped out because of his characteristic cap and hoodie. He'd come to the dojo twice, both times within a few days of the first home invasion and while Tony was also there, though they hadn't arrived together. Immediately, Charlie and Gordon had additional, coincidental evidence that connected Tony and Ted to Ray.

"That pretty much nails it for Ted's involvement in one or

more of the incidents," Gordon pointed out. "Any chance he could have been the one who tried to run you down outside the bar?"

"Don't think so. Ted has a smaller build than the guy in the Passat. At least, that's my impression, though I only caught a quick glance of the upper body. I suppose he could have been the guy who shot up Sam Randal's crane, though I can't see a knife guy using that much firepower, or even having access and training to use it. As for the drive-by last night, he could have been the one in the back of the pickup blasting away with BJ's carbine."

"Or maybe it was someone involved in one of the earlier home invasions. It looks to me like there were more than three in that crew, and they took turns doing the crimes. Harder to arrest them when they traded off. It would give each one an alibi once in a while," Gordon pointed out.

"I'd like to get more damning evidence against the guy. When he was arrested downtown, McConnell claimed that he was just defending himself, that it was me who jumped him. In a way, he could make that case," Charlie said, "though Gina could press stalking charges—which also might be hard to prove."

"Well, he violated his probation with that weapons charge, so for now he's in jail. I bet that the Geigers are going to avoid any contact with McConnell now. Ted visited the dojo, but they can't know for sure we've got visual evidence to prove it," Gordon said.

"Okay. But once we pass on what we've spotted to DuPree, it'll be something for the Rio Rancho detectives to look over," Charlie replied.

"We're almost done with the images from the parking-lot cameras. Next up, those from the camera mounted out back of the cleaners. That won't take long because there are very few images that show anyone except dojo employees, mostly Ray. None of the sensei are smokers who'd duck out back for a cigarette, so they are rarely seen. But I recall a few pictures with Frank, and at least one with someone I thought at the time was an old friend of his stopping by after hours. I wrote that one down because it took place the day after Ray's arrest and I was looking for that third member of his crew. Want me to call that date and time up first?"

"Why did you think it was an old friend?"

"We assumed that Ray was hanging around people his own age, but this guy came across as older, maybe in his fifties. I got that impression because of his bulkier build, middle-aged belly, and the way he moved—less attitude. I didn't get a look at his face, however. It was in the shadows and some distance away. And the guy was wearing a Yankees cap—with the bill facing forward. That's something you usually see among older guys who actually know what the bill on a cap is for."

"I see your point. That suggests a New Yorker like Frank, and Rio Rancho has a boatload of people who moved there from back east. Could be one of Frank's pals from his old days on the NYPD, or maybe a local cop off duty, unofficially keeping Frank up to speed on Ray's situation."

"Yeah. Their detectives have been pretty laid-back about the whole thing now that Ray's out on bail," Gordon responded. "Let's take another look at this guy."

It didn't take long to find the right data disk and call up the date and time. Gordon ran the images at normal speed first.

"When the guy knocked, Frank let him in immediately," Charlie observed. "He was expecting him. Probably called once he was within a minute or two of the dojo. Run through it frame by frame now."

After three sequences, Charlie shook his head. "You're right about the ball cap and general impression of him, but there's no way to get an ID on the guy. Too far away and too dark to catch any facial features."

Gordon nodded. "The camera image isn't good enough to clean up with software, I'm guessing."

"How about when the guy left?"

"I didn't write the time down, but we can scan ahead."

They watched the Yankee fan step out quickly, then walk into the darkness, this time in the opposite direction. "Whoa, the guy definitely knew there was a camera aimed in his direction," Gordon pointed out.

"Yeah. He arrived with his back to the camera and left the same way. So, how did he get to Bojo? Where did he park?"

"I hadn't followed up on that. Let me switch to the CD showing the parking lot on the same evening. Though I doubt he'd have parked his vehicle around front, in clear view, then walked around back, hoping to hide his face."

"He probably left his car nearby and walked over."

"But we still need to rule that out," Gordon replied, reaching for the disks from the parking-lot cameras. "Let me find the ones for the time period."

There were no vehicles that they could link to Old Yankee, as they nicknamed the man, so they decided to go over all the earlier surveillance to see if he'd come to visit during the daytime, before the Geigers had become suspects. After about a half hour they found someone in the parking lot who fit the description, including the distinctive cap.

"Bingo!" Gordon announced. "We don't know which vehicle he came in, but we know what he looks like now. Now all we have to do is add a name to that face."

"Screenshot that image, send it to our cell phones and the office computer, and also e-mail a copy to DuPree. We can show the image around here, but maybe, with the databases available to APD, we should try to trace the guy back east. If he was a cop or has a military record, or both, we should be able to get a hit," Charlie said.

"Of course, he may not have anything to do with the crimes at all, at least the ones we're worried about, Charlie."

"Agreed. But at least it's something new to rule out." He looked at his watch. "I'd better get ready to join up with the Randals. It's my turn to provide cover."

"You've been under a lot of pressure lately, bro. I'll stick with them tonight so you can get some sleep," Gordon offered. "Nobody but DuPree and the girls know where you're hiding out. Not even the Randals."

"Naw, I had a nap while you were gone, and I'm too pumped right now for any more sleep. You know it doesn't take much to wake me up anyway. Mortar fire, no; a window opening, yes. Besides, you and the girls need a break from the routine," Charlie reminded him.

"Okay, but if you change your mind, give me a call. I'm going now. I need to return Jake's SUV so he can go home."

It was 9:00 PM. Charlie was half asleep on the sofa in the living area of the Randals' home, absent-mindedly watching a baseball game, and Margaret was seated in an easy chair across the room, crocheting some afghan project. Sam, at the other end of the sofa, was messing with his tablet when his cell phone rang.

Sam grumbled, picked up the phone from where it was resting atop the end table, and looked at the display. "Private caller," he announced. He hesitated for a moment, then put the phone to his ear. "This is Sam."

Charlie was instantly alert, looking toward the back door automatically and feeling for his handgun, still at his waist. Sam had forwarded the home number to his new cell and, at least to the caller, had just created the impression that he was at home. Margaret had stopped crocheting and was now looking back and forth between him and Sam.

Sam listened for several seconds, then hung up without speaking.

"Who was it?" Margaret asked immediately.

Sam shook his head. "Some crank. He said I should watch my back, and that he wasn't done with me yet."

Charlie reached for the remote and turned off the game. "You two stay where you are for a minute," he ordered. "Margaret, turn off your lamp, please."

As she did, Charlie reached over and switched off the lamp beside him. There was a small light underneath the counter in the kitchen, so he walked in and turned that off as well. The interior of the house was now much darker, illuminated only by lights from the front porch and back patio.

He slipped over and took a look out back toward the alley, then into the bedrooms, one at a time, verifying the windows were still closed. Finally he returned to the front room, walked over beside the curtains, and looked out into the street. There was no sign of anyone in the street or along the sidewalk, and the only cars were those in the driveways, belonging to neighbors.

"Go ahead and turn the lights back on. I'm just being careful. Nancy told me that sometimes burglars will call to see if anyone's home. I know you forwarded it to your cell, Sam, but who has your home number?"

"All my employees. It's also listed in the phone directory. Whoever invaded our home and struck at my business knows my name by now from the news reports, even if they didn't before," Sam pointed out. "They could just look it up."

"Maybe we should change the number," Margaret suggested hopefully.

"They still know where we live, but maybe that'll help with the trolls. I'll set that up tomorrow," Sam replied, then turned to Charlie. "Do you think the caller was really someone connected to the home invasion and the rest? I thought that the ones who did that are . . . no longer a problem."

"Somebody has been trying to kill Charlie, Sam," Margaret reminded him. "But why would they call us?"

"Because this is where it all started, maybe?" Charlie suggested. "Other than revenge for the deaths of their friends and the arrest of Ray Geiger, what motive could there be at this point?" he added, still not convinced that they knew the real reason for the original attack.

He decided to bring that up again. "I can't figure out who was after you, Sam, not only here but at the hospital that first night. Are you sure it's not someone from your business operations or your past? Those thieves, maybe, or the electrical contractor."

Margaret looked down at her crocheting, her expression revealing anxiety—or was it fear?

"People who find themselves in trouble tend to blame those who caught them instead of accepting the responsibility, but I just don't see those people striking out at me now," Sam replied. "I've been racking my brain, wondering who else I may have offended. I know people have been stalked and killed because of some road rage incident, or even from some Internet chat room argument. But I haven't experienced anything like that. I just have no idea. I'm sorry."

Charlie noted that Sam had looked in his direction but avoided eye contact, a sign of possible deception for an otherwise honest person. Both he and his wife had lied about something in the past few days. But what, and why?

"And you didn't recognize the caller?"

Sam shook his head. "No, only that it was a male, probably younger than thirty. A normal voice, not deep or high, and if there was an accent, it was more cowboy or southern than anything else. He didn't sound distinctively ethnic. Just a local gringo-type voice."

"Okay, but if you can think of anything else, let me know," Charlie replied. "I'm going to call Nancy and tell her about this in case someone tries to sneak over here through the alley between the houses."

"Are we still safe?" Margaret asked, finally looking up.

"I'll make sure nothing happens to you or Sam. Go ahead with your normal routine, remembering what we've already talked about. Don't stand in front of any windows, and don't go out-side alone," Charlie said. "If I have to get up during the night or make any noise, I'll let you know it's me."

"Thanks, Charlie," Margaret said. This time she looked him in the eyes and smiled before she started to crochet again.

An hour later, Sam and Margaret turned in for the evening. Charlie watched the baseball game with the sound off, which was no problem because the play-by-play was sometimes more annoying than helpful. They couldn't even call a home run a home run anymore. It went into extra innings, the D-backs won with a sacrifice fly in the bottom of the twelfth, and Charlie finally turned off the set and went to sleep. For the first time in days, he woke up the next morning not remembering if he'd dreamed during the night.

When he'd gone to the Randals', Charlie had parked his blue rental van down the street in front of a house with a FOR SALE sign at the curb. This morning Sam was clearly worried, so Charlie offered to escort him to work, taking Margaret along. When Charlie pulled up across the street, Sam, with Margaret beside him, backed his car out of the garage. He'd follow the couple until they reached Firm Foundation, then leave Sam under the protection of his company security for the day and take Margaret with him to FOB Pawn, just to break up the routine.

Charlie had noted that Sam was distracted at breakfast and kept his handgun with him everywhere he went in the house. Once Sam was at his business, Charlie could begin what was hopefully going to be a routine workday.

A half hour later, Margaret seated beside him in the van, Charlie drove south, heading into Albuquerque's north valley, where FOB Pawn was located. They were barely a mile away from Firm Foundation when he noticed that Margaret was fidgeting nervously.

"Something wrong, Margaret?" he asked softly, at the same time checking the rearview mirror, wondering if she'd noticed someone following them.

She nodded. "There's something I've been keeping from Sam, you, and basically everyone. It may be nothing, but it's getting so dangerous now I need to tell someone."

He looked over and saw her hands shaking. "Does it have

something to do with those two men who stole from the company, or that electrician, Jim Eldon?"

"Yes. Jim Eldon. How did you know?" she responded, looking at him, a relieved look in her eyes.

"Every time his name came up, your face changed expression and you looked away, like you were keeping a secret. Is there something going on between you and Eldon? Do you think he could be behind all this?"

Margaret sat up straight, even more than before, and cleared her throat. "Nothing is going on between Jim and me. It's not like that, at least from my side. But the reason Sam stopped hiring him for contract jobs was because Jim had started flirting with me. I never encouraged him, but one time Sam came out of his office and overhead Jim saying something suggestive to me. Sam grabbed Jim by the collar, shoved him toward the door, and told him never to come back. If he came back or tried to get in touch with me, Sam would beat him to a pulp."

"But Jim came back?" Charlie guessed.

"No, but that confrontation scared the hell out of me. I'd never seen Sam lose it like that. He trusted me, and I've never let him down, but a few weeks ago I accidentally ran into Jim at Home Depot, and he immediately accused me of costing him all that business. *He* was the one who'd hit on *me*, but all of a sudden I was the troublemaker."

Charlie nodded. "Then what happened?"

"I just turned and walked away. Sam was over in the lumber section, and I'd been looking at hardware for the kitchen cabinets, which is why we weren't together. I hurried to the lumber counter, hoping Jim wouldn't try and catch up to me once he saw my husband. It must have worked, because I didn't see Jim after that."

"But you never told Sam about it."

Margaret shook her head. "No. I was afraid he'd go looking for the man or wait to catch him in the parking lot, and I didn't know what might happen next. I love Sam, and I didn't want him to get into a fight."

Charlie thought about it for a while, wondering if Jim Eldon had any connections with the Geigers, connections that might explain the attack on Sam Randal. Anytime personal and business issues crossed paths, trouble soon followed, but unless Jim Eldon was a psycho, the whole issue just didn't seem to make sense.

"You think Jim Eldon hired those people to attack Sam? Or am I overthinking this?" Margaret asked, her voice back to normal now.

"I doubt he's involved. It all seems too much like a soap opera script. Still, I'm going to ask the detectives to take a closer look at Eldon," Charlie decided.

"You going to tell Sam?"

"Not unless we get something more concrete to go on. But if you decide to tell Sam about the Home Depot incident, try to do that when someone else is around. We might need to calm your husband down to keep him from overreacting," he advised.

They were coming up the street toward the shop, and he took a quick glance at Margaret. "Thanks for trusting me," he said. "Things are going to work out. Don't worry about it anymore, okay?"

"Okay." She nodded, wiping away what was probably a tear.

He parked down the block in a customer slot at his friend Melissa's laundry—she'd already agreed to the arrangement—and escorted Margaret down the alley to the rear entrance to FOB Pawn.

Gordon and Jake were already there, and greeted them immediately when they stepped into the short hall next to the office and storeroom. Gordon smiled and said hello.

"Jake, this is Margaret Randal, and Margaret, this is Jake Salazar. Jake knows more about this business than Gordon and I ever will," Charlie announced, introducing their guest for the day.

"Nice to meet you, Mrs. Randal. I hope your arm is healing," Jake said, noting the bandage before gently shaking her right hand.

"Ruth will be in around ten," Gordon said. "She's taking Rene for his measles booster. But she wants to meet you, Margaret."

"Ruth and Jake have been keeping this business on an even keel, so I've heard. I'd like to help wherever I can be useful today," Margaret said, looking into the office. "Just point me in the right direction and tell me what to do."

With help from Margaret—who had years of office experience—Charlie and Gordon were able to lighten the load that Ruth and Jake had been carrying lately, and things went smoothly. Charlie managed to pull Gordon aside up front, when they were working on paperwork, and quickly filled him in on Jim Eldon. Gordon wasn't happy about being left in the dark, but he agreed that, if nothing else, it would give him someone else to watch out for.

Unfortunately, Charlie hadn't thought about getting a description of Eldon until they'd already arrived at the shop. They planned to ask for one when the opportunity arose.

It was midafternoon when Nancy came in through the front entrance, the bell above the door ringing her arrival. Charlie was completing the paperwork for a just-completed pawn transaction but looked up as she walked over. "Hi, Sergeant," he greeted cheerfully. "Have any good news?"

Automatically he glanced around the room, noting the pres-ence of a woman in her midthirties looking over some guitars with Jake. Ruth and Margaret were in the office working with the busi-ness software, and Gordon was storing away some pawn in the back.

"Anyone try to kill you today?" Nancy whispered.

"So far, so good," Charlie answered dryly.

"Then that's the good news. On the negative side, DuPree got a call from Detective Johnson at Rio Rancho, and they haven't conjured up any leads from their interviews with Ray Geiger's stu-dents and staff. And they didn't get anything new from Lori, the former instructor you and Gordon collared. But they did get cop-ies of the surveillance taken by the lady at the dry cleaners and sent official copies to APD. Their people are going to look them over as well."

"What about the guy Gordon and I spotted sneaking in the back, the Yankees fan?" Charlie asked.

Nancy shrugged. "They're adding him to their UK list. They also wanted a copy of any hits DuPree gets via NCIC or the other national databases. If the guy was a cop or a crook, or has had a background check or served in the military, we should know sometime today. Hopefully this guy isn't just an old next-door neighbor of the Geigers."

"Nancy, the way the guy came in through the back, then ducked out to avoid the camera getting a look at his face, makes me think there's something hinky going on. This meet-up took place after Ray was arrested."

"Okay. And some more bad news. There was no usable DNA from the scratch on the face of the guy we believe to be Ray Gei-ger. There was chemical or cross-contamination, probably from when Margaret was given first aid after getting shot. Disinfectant or something like that. Where is she, anyway?" Nancy looked around the front of the shop.

"In the office with Ruth, last time I went back there," Charlie answered. "Maybe she's helping Gordon in the storage room," he suggested.

"So the failure to get DNA, along with Margaret being unable to ID Ray, makes my testimony that much more important, doesn't it?" Charlie asked.

"Unless something else comes up that'll guarantee a conviction. The other two guys that were involved in the Sunday incidents are dead, according to current theory, so any connection with Ray is still only circumstantial."

Charlie looked around again, then lowered his voice. "I don't see why Margaret couldn't ID Ray. She was right next to him, within arm's reach, obviously. She didn't get a good look at his face?"

Nancy shrugged. "You'd think. DuPree and I've talked about that. All that we could come up with is that sometimes fear blocks it out, or maybe she was looking away, or had been twisted around somehow. She was trying to escape."

"Yeah. Or she's lying. Why would she not want to testify? Fear of retaliation? At first, I thought maybe, but that seems unlikely now, considering the fact that two-thirds of the home invaders are gone for good. But I might have a new suspect, based upon something Margaret confided in me this morning on our drive over here. She asked me not to tell Sam, but she realized it was time to tell the rest of us. Just in case."

"Just in case? Tell me about it now, before we're interrupted," Nancy insisted.

Charlie quickly related the incidents with Jim Eldon and Margaret's reasons for withholding the story until now.

Nancy listened closely, but when he was done, she shrugged. "I'll make sure we can determine the man's alibi, if he has one. I'm not convinced this will lead us anywhere new. All this over a tasteless comment and a few lost jobs?"

"Yeah, it seems like overkill, considering what she says happened. Unless there's a lot more she's still holding back," Charlie speculated.

"My instincts still point to Ray Geiger and the crew we've pretty much identified. This is something that could land Ray in prison, and I understand why he wouldn't want her to identify him. But I doubt he or his father was able to threaten her directly."

"What about through Sam, then? Last night he did get that mysterious phone threat," Charlie reminded her.

"I suppose. And we know, unfortunately, that there might still be someone out there who's after your hide," Nancy said. "And it's not likely to be Eldon."

"Agreed. And if that ankle bracelet, monitor, or whatever, is really working, it can't be Ray."

"How about Frank?" Nancy suggested. "The guy has the knowledge and training and isn't being tracked. But he has that bad leg and can't hide the limp."

"Then they hired it out."

"You're thinking Mr. Yankees? Maybe he's just the middleman, supplying the shooter for a price."

"Once we get an ID on the guy, we'll have more to go on, I suppose." Charlie looked past Nancy and saw that Margaret had come out of the office and was looking in their direction.

Chapter Nineteen

"What's happened? Is it Sam?" Margaret exclaimed, walking quickly up the aisle toward them.

"No, Margaret. I've just come to see how everyone is doing, and to pass along some information to Charlie," Nancy responded.

"About what? The guy he caught stalking Gina?"

"No, this has to do with the DNA testing of the scrapings from your fingernails when you scratched Ray Geiger's face."

"So he's the guy, for sure?"

"It didn't give us any answers, unfortunately. Either there wasn't enough tissue or the sample was contaminated. The only DNA that could be identified was your own, from the blood from the bullet wound. That means Charlie is going to remain a target," she added, looking directly at Margaret. "I came to remind him once more that someone is trying to kill him."

Charlie saw the woman cringe slightly, then recover. He knew Nancy was trying to elicit a reaction that might get Margaret to open up if she was keeping any more secrets.

"I never intended to put you on the spot, Charlie. You and

Gordon saved our lives. Did you tell Nancy about our talk this morning?" This time she looked straight at him, and it appeared Margaret was sincere.

Charlie nodded. "I had to, Margaret. Nancy is also in danger, and she needs to know where it might be coming from next time. As for me, I'm working hard to stay alive, and here I am among friends. Once we find out what these incidents are all about, the true motive, I think we'll have the answers we're looking for," he said. "But would you mind giving us a description of Jim Eldon anyway?"

"Sure," Margaret replied.

A few minutes later, both Charlie and Nancy had written down everything Margaret could provide, including the work clothes Eldon usually wore.

There were several awkward seconds of silence; then Margaret spoke again. "I should probably get back to helping Ruth," she said, looking back toward the office. "Thanks for everything, Nancy." She smiled, then walked away.

Nancy hung back.

"What did you think of her reaction?" Charlie asked softly, his eyes still on the paperwork. "Not about Eldon, I mean."

"She didn't seem that disappointed with the DNA news," Nancy replied. "I wonder why I hadn't picked up on her deception before. Is she that afraid of identifying Ray in court?"

"Despite her revelation concerning the incidents involving Eldon, I still don't think she's telling all she knows. When I saw Sam's reaction to that phone call, and his explanation as to what the caller said, I wondered even more. He's been lying about something too. Still, hearing her speculation that maybe Jim Eldon had something to do with this doesn't wash."

"I tend to agree with you, Charlie. When you look at all that's happened, it's clear that there is no simple explanation to what's going on," Nancy said.

"I think we should be using every database available to dig deeply into the backgrounds of everyone involved, and not just the Geigers. Sam has to be put under a microscope as well. They all came from back east, yet ended up here among a much smaller population. Coincidence, or could there be a previous connection? What if they did business together and there was a lawsuit or something? A reason for revenge, maybe?"

"I know that DuPree went pretty deep into checking up on Ray and Frank but barely scratched the surface with Sam's background. I'll get on that. Meanwhile, let's see if something turns up on that guy with the cap who visited Frank. If we can get an ID . . ."

"We know he came to the dojo, but unfortunately, we couldn't connect him with a vehicle. A license tag would have really helped," Charlie said.

"As a last resort, I may have to ask Frank who the guy was."

"Think he'd give you a straight answer?" Charlie asked.

She shook her head. "I think he'd more likely refuse to answer me at all. The very mention of the guy would just tip him off that we know or suspect something and have been going through surveillance images. I don't have any jurisdiction in Rio Rancho, and I still believe he may have a contact in that department. If the question came from them, once Frank knows about it, we may never be able to find the guy."

"Yeah. And ultimately, this may not have anything to do with the case. Maybe the guy is just one of his poker buddies," Charlie said. "If he plays poker."

*   *   *

Everything seemed normal at the moment, with no attacks or threats, just ordinary work, not only for him but for the Randals as well. Maybe the bad guys were working on a new plan, Charlie thought as he drove south toward Albuquerque on Highway 313, which became Fourth Street once he entered the city.

For the last three days he'd taken a different route into work from the motel in Bernalillo, just in case he was being followed, but tomorrow he'd have to repeat himself. He liked the old road he was on at the moment, less traveled, two lanes wide, hence easier to spot a tail. The only problem was, an ambush would be easier to set up and less public, which was why he kept his backup Beretta on the center console. It would be easier to deploy the weapon now, fortunately, because the cut on his finger was healing well.

He wasn't being complacent, and he suspected his enemies were either setting him up or rallying before their next move. The lack of activity, though, was a little nerve-wracking, and he hated having to spend his nights in a motel. Traffic around the nearby tribal casino was noisy, and their business resulted in a twenty-four-hour disturbance. He'd thought about ear plugs or drowning out the activity with music, but he couldn't afford to drown out nearby sounds. Needless to say, he hadn't slept well and had been having those godawful dreams again. Still, it beat being shot at—probably.

Ten minutes later, he parked at Melissa's laundry down the block. When he walked up the alley to the loading dock of FOB Pawn, Charlie saw that Jake's SUV was there already. Gordon was babysitting the Randals again.

Charlie knocked to signal his presence before using his key to come into the shop, even though they had a camera covering the back door with a monitor in the office, so Jake could check to see who was outside. He walked into the narrow hall, then turned to lock the door behind him.

"Morning, boss," Jake said, stepping out of the office with the cash register tray cradled in his powerful arms. "Had your second cup?"

"Hey, Jake. Not yet. Sorry if I've had a lousy attitude lately. I just haven't been able to sleep more than a few hours at a time in a strange place, and it's catching up to me. I got used to it in the service, but I'm not as young as I used to be," Charlie admitted, though Jake was twice his age and still full of energy nearly every day.

"It's even harder to sleep when punks are shooting up your bedroom and planting bombs in your kitchen, I'd imagine. How are the repairs on the house going?" Jake asked, returning to the office, coffee cup in hand.

"Nestor hired an Albuquerque handyman who's supposed to have a crew there this morning. He got an estimate on the repairs, which come to about three thousand dollars, materials and labor. The job should take about three or four days. I'm paying his insurance deductible and replacing whatever was broken."

"Lucky the heating and cooling systems weren't damaged. A gas line, water heater, or furnace could have been more than expensive to replace. Things could have gone boom!"

"I'll take bullets over explosions every time, Jake. Join me for a refill?"

"Don't mind if I do. This Italian dark roast is a winner. All it needs is a couple of sugars."

Charlie was sitting across the desk from Jake, halfway through his coffee, when he noticed movement on the split-screen monitor. Ruth had just pulled up in her white Camry. He missed being around the woman, who always seemed to get his heart beating a little faster when she was standing close. They were usually talking shop, or about her first-grade son, Rene, but it didn't matter what the topic was. He had never done or said anything untoward, of course—his parents had raised him better than that—but he often wished she no longer worked for FOB Pawn so he could ask her out.

Gordon kept insisting he make his move anyway, saying Ruth liked him back, but he didn't want to create an awkward situation, especially if her answer turned out to be no. Although Ruth had been raised in an upper-class eastern home and married a millionaire, the experience had been a nightmare for her and their son. Her abusive ex-husband was now in prison, and she was still a protected witness, having provided much of the testimony and evidence that had put him away for twenty years. Ruth didn't need any more anxiety in her life right now.

"Good morning, gentlemen," Ruth announced when she appeared at the office door. Charlie and Jake stood at the same time, both schooled in a previous generation's gesture of respect for a lady. A few minutes later, they were all seated in the small office, coffee mugs in hand.

"So, catch me up on how Rene is doing at North Bosque Academy, Ruth. You mentioned that he was more excited to attend summer school than the rest of his classmates," Charlie said, finally feeling at ease for the first time in days.

"He can't say enough about all his new friends, his soccer team, and even his teachers. Finally being able to socialize has really brought him out of his shell."

"That's great news. You had to keep him close at home and away from the public for so many years, Ruth," Jake pointed out.

Ruth hadn't wanted to send her son to any school when he came of age, fearing that her secrets would be discovered when birth certificates and other documents for him would be required. When Charlie first met her, she was still living below the radar.

"I bet playing soccer takes a lot of energy out of him. That should help him get to sleep at night," Charlie speculated.

"It does. The good thing is that soccer practice is in the morning before it gets too hot. But Rene's still worn out by dinnertime. We read together, but he's usually in bed by nine," Ruth said.

"I'm looking forward to next Saturday. We have some great conversations," Charlie said. Ruth worked every other Saturday and always brought Rene with her instead of finding a sitter. Rather than put him in front of a video game to pass the day, she made sure he divided his time between reading, schoolwork, and helping dust and clean. Of course, once in a while Charlie or Gordon would challenge the boy at an arcade game—with Ruth's permission.

She smiled. "He missed you being here last time, Charlie. But Gordon kept him occupied cataloging the toys and games."

"What's *he* doing here at this hour?" Jake interrupted, looking up at the monitor.

"Detective DuPree? I hope nothing's happened to the Randals," Ruth said.

"Not likely. He'd be dealing with that instead," Charlie said, moving to the back door.

DuPree was startled for a second when Charlie opened the door just as the detective was about to knock.

"I need to talk to you, Charlie. Outside would be better," Du-Pree suggested, sounding excited for the first time in days.

"I'll be back in a few minutes," Charlie said to Jake and Ruth, then stepped out onto the small loading dock, closing the door behind him. "How about some coffee first, Wayne?"

DuPree shook his head. "Maybe later. I need to pick your brain for any details or background Sam Randal gave about himself, or something his wife might have said that could prove useful. It turns out that the real Samuel Randal died during birth fifty-three years ago."

"We talking about the same Sam Randal, from somewhere in Connecticut?" Charlie asked.

DuPree nodded. "Yeah. I've checked and double-checked. The person we thought was Sam Randal is an imposter, living under that name. His real identity is unknown right now."

"You think he's in the Witness Protection Program, like Ruth?"

"No, and I checked. Whoever this guy really is, his whole background, at least what's in the databases, is fiction. Everything was planted, undoubtedly by someone on the inside, and very well done. But it's all fake."

"What about his fingerprints?" Charlie asked.

"There are none on record, and we never took his prints for comparison because we already knew the perps were wearing gloves so we didn't need to rule anybody out. All along Sam was the apparent victim, not some stranger with a secret identity, so we had no reason to check that deeply into his record."

"Nancy, Sergeant Medina? Does she know this?"

"Yes. Actually, she was the one who made the discovery and passed along the information to me. But listen, you're supposed to be guarding Sam the rest of today and tonight, right?"

Charlie nodded. "You want me to get his fingerprints for you?"

"Exactly. But whatever you do, don't let him suspect what's going on. I want to find out everything I can about the guy before he knows we know."

"This adds a whole new world of possibilities when it comes to a motive for the home invasion—and the kidnapping attempts. Right?"

"Correct. Until I know who Sam Randal really is, I don't want to make a move. If he's a fugitive, he may bolt if he suspects we're onto him."

"You think Margaret knows the truth?" Charlie asked. "She kept information from us before, regarding that electrical contractor, Eldon. Why not lie about Sam as well?"

"It's possible. She's a local, with ties here that can be checked out, but Sam may have kept the truth from her, at least until he came under attack."

"If he did open up to her, that's a reason for Margaret to lie about being able to identify Ray Geiger," Charlie speculated. "He might have convinced her that it's for their own protection. We've suspected for some time that there must be an underlying connection between Sam and the Geigers."

"Which is why we don't want to tip our hand. I need you to get those prints. I'd do it myself or send a tech, but I'd need a warrant, and that would tip him off. Once you get the prints, I'll have them run. We need that information and we need it fast, and I'm willing to risk getting into trouble."

"Okay, Wayne. I'll find a way to get some good prints sometime today. Worst case, tonight. I'll be escorting Sam and Margaret home and spending the night at their place. I'll pass along a bottle or glass that Sam has handled to Nancy."

"Good. So, for now, I'm going to dig deeper into anyone Ray or Frank knew from their past, back in Connecticut or wherever. If I get a hit on Sam's real identity, all the better." DuPree glanced toward his car and thumbed the key fob.

"Before you go, have you learned anything new about Jim Eldon? We have his description now."

DuPree nodded. "I got that from Medina. Looks like Eldon's not involved, at least directly. The reason why officers haven't been able to track him down until today is because he's been on a job for a friend who has a cabin near Navajo Dam, up in the Four Corners. Eldon's been out of central New Mexico for the past week, including last Sunday."

"Good to know. Meanwhile, I'll get back to work, Wayne. Okay if I tell Gordon about Sam?"

"Yeah, he can keep a secret. Just him, though."

"Of course. But once you know who he really is, you're going to tell me?"

"Yeah. After all the crap you've been through, you deserve to know the rest of it."

A half hour later, Gordon arrived at FOB Pawn, having delivered Sam and Margaret to Firm Foundation for the workday. As he entered the office, Charlie saw him through the Plexiglas window and nodded. Once he finished the paperwork on a transaction, Charlie had to tell his pal the news about the man formerly known as Sam.

Gordon was barely able to contain his anger. Charlie hadn't expected any other reaction, and although they were working, they spent every free moment during the next hour trying to recall anything that might lend a clue to Fake Sam's real background. They even tried to recall his speech patterns, vocabulary, and accent but could only confirm that, yes, he was probably from somewhere back east.

Finally Charlie had an idea. He walked over to where Gordon was standing beside the front register, waiting for a customer who'd gone back to look at something in one of the displays.

"Gordon, did the Randals have their usual wine last night with dinner?"

"Yeah, some red wine with an Italian pasta dish. The three of us finished off the bottle. What does this have to do . . . Oh, yeah. Sam opened the wine with that fancy cork remover and poured for all of us. His prints are all over the bottle."

"And now it's in the trash. Outside, hopefully?"

"Yeah. Sam took it out, but I led the way to make sure the backyard was safe. The trash, well, garbage too, is in one of those white plastic bags with the red ties. You plan on going through the smelly stuff?"

"Yep. This way I won't have to try to pick the lock or use the key Margaret gave Gina. Keeps everyone else from being put on the spot. How about I go now, before lunch, and pass the bottle along to DuPree or Nancy? We don't want the summer heat to degrade the prints."

"At least the trash container is in the shade. Go, but take along some wipes and paper towels, and hope that bottle didn't come into contact with any gooey stuff." Gordon grinned.

"How gooey? What didn't you guys eat all of last night?"

Gordon laughed. "Hey, if the bottle is all messed up, you can always use the key and go inside their house to look for something else. Just remember to turn off the alarm as soon as you get inside."

"What's the code for the keypad?"

"I have no idea, so forget that. Let's hope the bottle is clean—except for the prints, of course. Good luck."

"Yeah. And don't worry, this shouldn't take long. I'll be back," Charlie replied.

"Copy."

Gina and Nancy were both at work, but Charlie had a key to their place and let himself in through the front. He walked into the kitchen area, opened a cabinet drawer—he knew where the girls kept things—and brought out an empty paper grocery bag. He grabbed some paper towels next, then went out through the French doors onto the patio. Seconds later, he was over the wall, across the alley, and in the Randals' backyard. He opened the big plastic waste container underneath the eaves along the side of the house and found three filled plastic bags inside. He reached down and pulled out the one on top by the red ties. When he eased it down onto the concrete pavers, glass clunked, and he suspected he had the right bag.

Untying the plastic tie, he found the green Cabernet Sauvignon bottle immediately, relatively clean, cork still intact, among mostly used paper towels and an empty frozen-veggie bag. He gripped the bottle by the top of the neck and placed it into the grocery sack. After putting the trash back into the container, he returned to Nancy and Gina's kitchen, locked up, then climbed into the van. Looking around in case any neighbors might be watching, he brought out his phone and called Nancy. If she was closer, he'd hand over the bottle to her rather than DuPree, who might be downtown.

Fifteen minutes later, he met up with Nancy outside a small

New Mexican restaurant on Fourth Street and handed over the
sack containing the bottle. Then he headed back to FOB Pawn.

Around four thirty, Charlie left the shop to pick up Margaret and
Sam. He and Gordon both were frustrated that there was still no
news from DuPree or Nancy on Sam's identity. The lab people
should have gotten a hit by now if there was a set of prints on file.
Gordon was going to stay behind with Jake until closing. Ruth had
clocked out at four to pick up Rene.

He was driving up the frontage road from the south when the
sound of a siren from behind interrupted his musings. Glancing
in the side mirror, Charlie saw the flashing lights of a police vehicle and slowed, pulling to the right just as it hurtled past.

Uneasy at the thought, he glanced ahead, looking in the direction of the Firm Foundation buildings and yard. It was still a
half mile away, but there were lights flashing in that area as well.
Charlie reached over for his cell phone on the console, then realized he could probably get there before the call was answered. He
pulled back into his lane and accelerated toward the turnoff onto
August Avenue, hoping, with a trace of guilt, that it was someone
other than the Randals who'd just created a need for the cops.
Well, not so much with Sam, who was, at the very least, a fraud
and a liar.

His stomach sank when he approached and saw that one of
the emergency vehicles was a white EMT unit and that people
were clustered around the open gate. As he slowed and pulled over
to the curb, the rescue people were tending to someone on the
ground at the entrance to the yard.

Charlie parked, and as he was climbing out of the van he noted
an APD police officer looking his way, hand on the butt of her

service weapon. Thinking it might be wise, he reached down and removed his holster containing the Beretta and placed it on the floorboard of the van. Then he locked the vehicle.

"Charlie!" Sam Randal yelled, stepping away from the gathering of employees and emergency personnel. "Margaret is gone! I think she's been kidnapped! And one of my security guards was attacked."

Another police officer, a sergeant, intercepted Sam and held him back, removing him from the group. Charlie wanted to know everything, of course, but knew that a smart cop didn't compromise a witness—or have him talking to a civilian before he could be interviewed.

"Mr. Henry?" the sergeant asked.

"Yes. Charlie Henry. I'm here because I was supposed to transport the Randals back home. Detective DuPree and I spoke just this morning. He and Sergeant Nancy Medina can both vouch for me."

"The detective has been notified and should be on scene within minutes," the officer explained. "Mr. Henry, please don't speak to anyone except our officers until the detective arrives. It's procedure."

Charlie knew the drill, so he walked over to those clustered around the wounded security officer. It was a woman, not Pat, he quickly learned. People all around Sam Randal were getting hurt, and now Margaret was missing. It was time to confront the man and find out just who he was, and why his wife was in danger once again.

Chapter Twenty

Charlie realized the woman security guard was still alive when he saw her struggling to sit up. The EMTs working on her, however, coaxed her to lie back down and tell them what happened. The second guard standing there, Pat, managed a smile, then walked over to join the sergeant speaking to Sam. A second officer joined them, leading Pat away from the two.

There was the sound of squealing tires in the street, and Charlie looked over as Detective DuPree climbed quickly from his unmarked car. DuPree walked toward the people clustered around the EMTs, who were lifting the injured woman onto a gurney, then noticed Sam, the police sergeant, and Charlie, who was as close to Randal as permitted.

DuPree motioned to Charlie, a scowl on his face.

"Once I speak to my officers and learn what went down, I need to interview Sam, so keep an eye on him. It's time to confront Randal. If his wife has been kidnapped, this might be the best time to apply the pressure. Got that?" DuPree stated.

Charlie nodded. "Maybe that will lead to a motive for why all this has happened."

"I'm hoping. We may need to keep him out of jail for a while longer in order to get his wife back. My priority now is her safety. I've got to get what I can on Margaret's abduction and what happened to the woman security guard before the FBI steps in. I may have to fight them to retain custody of Sam."

DuPree walked over to Sam, spoke to him a few seconds, and then pointed toward the business office. Sam nodded, then headed toward the building.

Once Sam entered his office, Charlie waited outside, watching the door out of the corner of his eye. At the same time, he inched closer to listen as DuPree and the officers questioned the other Firm Foundation employees. Overhearing Pat, the male security guard, Charlie learned that he'd been away with Sam, who'd been called to a work site in response to some vandalism. When they returned to the yard, they were the ones who'd discovered the open gate—the lock cut off—and the unconscious woman security guard.

According to what she was able to tell them after regaining consciousness, the guard had come to the gate to see what the man wanted. But she'd been Tased, then injected with a syringe before she could draw her weapon or yell for help. Whatever she was given knocked her out in just a few seconds.

Moving closer to the fence, Charlie was able to see that the surveillance camera mounted up high to monitor gate traffic had been damaged. From a distance, it looked like the optics had been shot out. It must have been a silenced, small-caliber round, however, or someone at the yard would have heard.

The approach of a marked police car and a familiar-looking pickup got his attention. Charlie stood, watching, as Nancy climbed out of her unit and strode toward the gate. Gordon jumped down from his own vehicle and hurried to catch up with her.

Nancy passed through the taped-off area, accompanied by Gordon, who walked in her footsteps until they were clear. She continued on toward DuPree, signaling for Gordon to stay behind.

"Gordon," Charlie called and got his attention.

"Should have called, sorry," Charlie apologized as his friend approached. "DuPree sent Sam to his office, out of the way until he has a chance to grill him."

"Randal needs to start telling the truth if he hopes to get Margaret back. What went down here, anyway?" Gordon asked.

"From what I've overheard so far, the attacker apparently lured the woman guard to the gate, Tased and tranked her, then cut the lock and took Margaret from the office. He got away with her, and I don't know if anyone ID'd the vehicle."

"What about the cameras?" Gordon asked, looking at the posts.

"I think the one at the gate was put out of action by a .22 with a suppressor. Don't know about the others, not yet," Charlie explained.

"You talk to Sam?" Gordon asked.

"Just a few words before DuPree sent him inside. Wayne wants to get as much of the truth as possible from Sam before the Feds show up."

"Who do *you* think snatched Margaret? Certainly not some damned amateur. This whole thing is a lot bigger than that," Gordon replied grimly.

Charlie shrugged. "Yeah, but *we* were supposed to keep her

safe. Let's see if we can get her back. My money is still on the Geiger connection—Frank, probably. Ray is no Einstein."

"While DuPree is working things here, let's see if we can get
a lead on our own, maybe get an image of whatever the kidnapper
was driving. There's that RV storage facility at the frontage road
intersection up there, Charlie. Most of them have cameras. If
they're working and have the right angles, maybe they have a shot
of a vehicle coming and going on this street during that time
frame."

"Good idea. Now that Sam's in his office, there's no need for
me to stick around anyway. Let's go." He nodded toward Gordon's
pickup, parked alongside the road. "Your truck?"

"Yeah. You want to let DuPree know what we're doing?"

"Later, if we get lucky. Meanwhile, he can give me a call if he
needs something. Sam still has to be interrogated, and once the
FBI is called to the scene, DuPree could be tied up for hours. Let
me grab my weapon; then we can get out of here," Charlie urged.
"The longer we wait, the more lead time the kidnapper has."

Charlie picked up his pistol and holster, then walked to the
passenger side of Gordon's truck and stepped up into the cab. Instantly he realized someone was lying on the floorboards behind
the seat. He reached for his Beretta just as Gordon held up his
hand.

"Stand down, bro, it's Sam, and he's not armed," Gordon called
out softly, his eyes shifting back to the activity in the company
yard.

"I need your help in finding Margaret before she gets hurt,
guys," Sam whispered. "I'm not Sam Randal. My real name is Bill
Woods. Get me out of here so we can find those bastards."

"Okay with you?" Charlie asked Gordon.

"Yeah, but let's take this one step at a time. Start talking, Bill, or we're turning you over to the cops right now," Gordon answered, turning his pickup around in the street, then heading west away from the business and the gathering crowd.

"I know who took Margaret, or at least who's behind her kidnapping. It's Frank Geiger, no surprise, and he's been trying for days to force me to return the money he gave me to invest."

"Which you stole from him?" Charlie said.

"Yeah, he was a crooked cop, and he received over a half million from under-the-table payoffs and bribes when he was on the force. I was an investor, and he was one of my clients. He paid me a bonus to hide the transactions and keep my mouth shut. Easy money. But then his department of internal affairs caught on to his activities and started to investigate. I found out and decided to change my identity and split with the money," Sam explained. "I didn't want any enemies in the mob, and besides, what could Frank do, accuse me of stealing his bribes? I thought I'd gotten away clean."

"How'd he track you down, Sam . . . Bill?" Gordon asked.

"The guy is a bloodhound. Apparently he was able to find out that I'd come to Albuquerque, except he didn't know my new identity. At some point he moved to this area, hoping to track me down. Unfortunately, a few weeks ago the damn local paper ran my name and photo. Frank must have seen it, then decided to hire some punks to do his dirty work. Sunday, when they tried to grab me, Ray said he was there for his dad, Frank, and unless I returned his money I was as good as dead. He said to keep the cops out of it. Those were his exact words," Sam added, rising off the floorboards and sitting on the small jump seat in the extended cab.

"Margaret never overheard—that took place after she'd escaped. She still has no idea who I really am."

"So now you think Geiger wants to trade your wife for the money," Charlie concluded.

Same nodded, brushing dust off his sleeves and pant legs. "Of course. I'll do anything to get Margaret back unharmed. Once that's over, you can turn me in to Nancy or DuPree. I'll testify—do whatever they want—but first, help me find my wife."

"We'll try. But the next time we run into some cops you're going with them," Charlie replied, seeing Gordon nod.

Charlie thought about it a moment. "How did you get past me at the office, Sam? There's no back entrance."

"There's a trapdoor in the heater closet leading down into the crawl space. I got out at ground level on the opposite side of the building through an access panel and just walked out the gate. I climbed in here because your van was locked," Sam explained. "Now let's find Frank Geiger. He's got Margaret."

"That might take some time. Whoever it was that took your wife isn't going to take her to anyplace we know," Charlie responded. "But Gordon has a plan worth looking into."

It took a few minutes and a twenty-dollar bill to convince the day manager at the storage facility on the corner of August Avenue and East Frontage Road to let them look at the afternoon surveillance, but they were getting used to scanning these recordings and quickly reached today's images. Gordon sat at the table running the equipment, and Charlie stood beside him, taking a position that made sure he was between Sam and the door. Though he doubted the man would try to get away, Charlie no longer trusted him.

"We missed something, or the guy went the opposite direction, across the field, like before," Gordon said, stopping the feed. "There's your van."

"Run it back, Gordon, something didn't look right," Charlie asked.

They watched the blue van passing the camera. "Stop!" Charlie ordered as the vehicle was in full frame on the monitor.

"Yeah. I can't see anyone but the driver, and either you're low-riding or that's not you behind the wheel. And you're not wearing a ball cap."

"The timing is off by a half hour, and I didn't show up until after the cops. It's not me, it's someone shorter and bigger around, though the jacket looks like mine. So that's not my van. The bastard was posing as me. That's how he was able to get the guard to move in close," Charlie observed, bitterness in his last words.

"Close enough to take her out," Gordon said, muttering a curse. He ran the surveillance forward and caught the same van and driver coming back out onto the frontage road, past the storage facility.

"Hey, did you flash on that cap?" Charlie asked. "Run it back, and pause on the driver."

"A Yankees ball cap. That couldn't be the same guy," Gordon responded.

"The sneaky guy at Bojo meeting with Frank? That's one hell of a coincidence," Charlie added, looking over at Sam, who just looked confused.

"Which we don't believe in," Gordon said. "And check this out. According to the time record, he went east on August Avenue at 4:03 PM and came back through this intersection just, what, nine minutes later?"

"Let's get a better fix," Sam suggested, stepping closer to the screen. "How much time went by before Pat and I returned to the compound?"

Gordon nodded and manipulated the controls. "There you are, and Pat. See the truck with the Firm Foundation sign? Now let's take another look at the van leaving the area."

"No sign of a passenger, guys," Charlie observed as they viewed the images frame by frame. "Margaret was hidden in the back somewhere. It's obvious that the kidnapper has been watching me—he knows what I'm driving now. He got hold of a nearly identical model and color van and was waiting for a chance to pull this off. I bet that vandalism at your work site was a diversion to get you and Pat out of the office so he could grab your wife."

"Bastard. If he hurt her . . . ," Sam muttered.

"Don't think about it, Sam. She's no leverage if she's . . . injured," Charlie pointed out. "If he wanted to hurt her, he could have done that already, then left her behind as a final warning."

"Who is this guy anyway? You suppose Nancy ever got a hit from the dry-cleaner image? There was a facial recognition effort going on down at the station, wasn't there?" Gordon asked.

"She would have told us, right?" Charlie replied. He checked his watch, then glanced up from the monitor and saw the storage-lot attendant standing at the open door of the small office where they were gathered.

"Any luck?" the middle-aged man asked, walking over to the desk.

"I think so," Charlie answered. "We have to leave now, but please, whatever you do, don't erase this information or let anything happen to it. I'm going to call the investigating officer, and he'll probably send someone down to make a copy."

"It's set to save everything until the boss manually overwrites the stored images. I'll make sure to tell him not to do that. You have a few days left. He overwrites on Fridays," the man advised them. "I could make a copy, though, if an officer comes before my shift is over. I'm here until nine PM." He handed Charlie a business card with a phone number.

"I'll pass this along," Charlie said.

"Oh, before you guys go, did you want to take a look at what the other camera picked up?"

"Other camera?"

A few minutes later they'd discovered that the second camera covered enough of the frontage road so that they could see the rear end of the van as it drove away—that, and the plate number. Charlie quickly wrote that down, then called Nancy as soon as he climbed into the passenger side of Gordon's truck.

Nancy spoke first, her voice low and angry. "Is Sam with you? DuPree said you were supposed to keep an eye on him. Needless to say, Wayne is really pissed."

"Yeah, Sam's with us, and he's come clean. His real name is Bill Woods, and he's a former investor. He skimmed half a million of Frank Geiger's illegal bribe money, which provides the motive we've been looking for. Sam, well, Bill, wants to cut a deal with Geiger in hopes of getting Margaret back," Charlie explained.

"Don't take me back to the police. Not now!" Sam whispered.

"Tell DuPree we won't let Woods out of our sight, but we've got a lead on the blue van that was used to haul Margaret off," Gordon yelled. "We need to run with that before the trail grows cold."

"You hear that?" Charlie added, putting the phone on speaker.

"Yeah," Nancy replied. "And here's some more good news,

Charlie. I have a positive ID on the guy wearing the Yankees cap, based on facial recognition. You didn't happen to get the plate number on that van?"

"Now we're getting somewhere," Sam mumbled.

"Never been up this close to the mountains, at least on the west side," Gordon commented as he drove into the Sandia foothills on a narrow street.

"That's because you don't have any rich friends," Charlie replied. "Big lots, massive houses, high ceilings, tall windows facing west to overlook the entire valley. Ever notice the hundreds of windows flashing on this side of the city around sunset?"

"Yeah, I guess. At least the wealthy don't tamper much with the natural look. Their homes are earth shades, built right into the mountainside, surrounded by big granite boulders, junipers, and tall sagebrush and drought-tolerant shrubs. No huge lawns or tall trees of non-native species. Organic, with strict neighborhood covenants, I'd guess," Gordon said. "Like most of high-end Santa Fe."

"So this Dennis Myers we're looking for is from New York City. He has a history of arrests related to assault, attempted murder, and other violent behavior, not to mention reported mob affiliations. Doesn't the term 'affiliations' sound kind of wimpy for a gangster?" Charlie asked.

"Politically correct label for 'yeah, he's a punk-ass mobster, but we can't really get enough evidence to keep him in jail,'" Gordon joked. "So what's he doing living in an upper-class New Mexico neighborhood?"

"Crime must have paid, for him at least. I'm thinking he's retired, if any organized-crime soldier can actually leave the family,"

Charlie responded. "Nancy said he hasn't been arrested since he moved to Albuquerque ten years ago and has stayed off the radar. He's not employed, probably living off 'investments.'"

"Like a hedge fund manager or a bankster. Not hard to guess where that money came from."

"Which leads right back to here. You sure you never heard of the guy, Sam?" Gordon asked. "You invested crooked cop money, and Myers must have some ties with Frank Geiger if he's working with him now."

"I don't recall Myers, though I didn't meet all of my clients face-to-face. If I'd have known any of them were actually involved with organized crime, I would have stayed clear," Sam responded. "Dealing with a cop on the take was dangerous enough. I guess it's possible, though. I just don't recognize the name."

"Well, we're pretty sure Geiger took mob money, so he must have had contact with some of the players," Charlie said.

"Big-city crooked cops, organized crime? Like we've never heard of that before," Gordon added. He looked over at the GPS mounted on the dash. "Sunset Ridge is just ahead. Myers's house is on the outside of the next curve."

Charlie nodded. "The guy is supposed to be violent, but he's never been accused of kidnapping, and managed somehow to avoid actual prison time. Still, if he's involved with the Geigers, he might be the guy who tried to take me out at least once, beginning at the Outpost with that hopped-up Passat."

"If that's true, he'll know this pickup on sight," Gordon warned.

"Nancy suggested we do a quick drive-by unless we spot the van, which had stolen plates," Charlie responded. "Then we sit tight until DuPree and more officers arrive."

"I'm not waiting another minute, guys. If there's a chance he still has my wife, I'm going right up to his door," Sam said.

"And maybe get yourself shot? No, we've got to stay smart," Gordon responded.

"Sam is right about making a move as soon as possible, though. If we get lucky and Myers *is* there, we need to get involved immediately. If we wait around for APD and SWAT, we could end up with a hostage situation. Once that happens, any chance of making a deal to get Margaret back without putting her life on the line goes right out the window."

"Well, making a tactical entry into places and grabbing people *is* within our skill set. Let's see what we're facing, then do whatever makes sense," Gordon suggested.

"I'm in," Sam said. "Either of you have an extra pistol?"

"No way, Sam," Charlie responded. "We're the ones with the training and experience. You're our client, and you'll have to stay in the truck, out of sight."

"Margaret is my wife, and I intend to do everything I can to get her back," Sam argued.

"And you're our bargaining chip, the one who'll have to come up with the ransom money once we make contact with the kidnappers," Gordon reminded him. "We need to hold you back until the right moment."

"Here's a plan," Charlie said. "How about I hoof it in for a look, circling up among the rocks and staying in cover as much as possible? You two stay with the truck in case he decides to leave while I'm still out there."

Sam shrugged. "Whatever. But let's get to it."

Gordon stopped the pickup as far to the side of the road as

possible—there wasn't much of a shoulder here—and Charlie climbed out.

"I may text instead of call," Charlie said, looking up into the cab. "I'm going to hike up the hillside and take a look over the wall. I may need to climb, depending on the layout."

"I'll get as close as I can and still keep the truck hidden from the house."

"Don't take your eyes off the place. We may have to move quickly if he spots one of us. And keep Sam out of sight. Got that?" Charlie asked, looking at Randal.

Sam nodded.

"Copy," Gordon replied. "Be careful."

Charlie turned and looked up the rocky hillside of what was essentially the last foothill before the mountain proper began. Picking his route, he left the pavement and began the reconnaissance, his pistol still in the holster and his cell phone in his shirt pocket, set on vibrate.

This, the west side of the Sandias, was steeper in most places and much drier than the forested east side, but the enormous weathered granite boulders and shelflike outcroppings with shadowed overhangs provided decent cover, though his advance was more of a climb than a hike.

The house itself was pueblo style, with the exception of the tall windows, skylights, and a large two- or three-story-high turretlike element that reminded Charlie of a kiva, or maybe a castle keep. From up there, the inhabitants could see for miles to the west.

The closer he got, the thicker the vegetation and the better the cover, but he still had to pick his way around the enormous rocks and boulders, and he moved slowly. At this point he could no longer see Gordon or his pickup, though he knew his pal and Sam were hiding, watching the narrow driveway for vehicles coming or going.

It had occurred to him a half hour ago that there was probably a neighborhood watch program up here and a private security service. Charlie doubted he'd be spotted, but Gordon might have to explain his and Sam's presence if a patrol came along. Hopefully, if Myers had taken Margaret up here to hide her away, he was too busy dealing with her to be looking out a window right now. What the guy would have, Charlie guessed, was his own set of surveillance cameras and, maybe, motion detectors.

The entire property was surrounded by a tall adobe-style wall built into the hillside and following the terrain. It would be difficult getting over that barrier in many places, with the ground sloping away. After taking a tactical assessment, he figured best bet would be to come over the wall from uphill, and he'd already located a piñon tree close enough to climb and, hopefully, be within reach of the top of the wall.

Climbing the piñon tree proved to be tricky. He had to stick close to the trunk or risk breaking a foothold branch, and there were a lot of dried-out, dead smaller branches that poked him constantly. His cut finger ached a bit as well, and that scratch on his stomach itched where he'd rubbed up against the rough bark.

He'd forgotten about the needles themselves, and was about to give up and find his way back down the fragrant but sticky tree when he realized the wall was just a little bit taller. Charlie found a limb that looked sturdy enough to go just one foot higher, and he could probably reach up and pull himself up onto the wall, or at least have a look over into the yard below. His cell phone, which he'd switched to his back pocket to keep it from falling out, began to vibrate. Unfortunately, with his back against the trunk, there was no way he could reach it. If it was Gordon, he'd just have to wait.

Finally he pulled himself up, elbows on the rough surface of what was obviously a plastered cinder-block fake-adobe structure, and looked down into the yard. A long, wide veranda lined the back wall of the L-shaped home, and it contained a wrought-iron patio table and chairs, plus a banco that surrounded a fire pit, with one of those new-style gas heaters in the center.

A flagstone walk extended from the back door of what was probably the garage, and another to a smaller, corrugated-metal pitched-roof barn or storage building. That building was close to his location, only a half-dozen feet from the wall, and might offer the means for him to get down inside the compound. He hadn't expected such a drop-off on the inside—it was probably fifteen feet or more—and there was no sense in him breaking an ankle or risking a knee injury sliding down the wall. All he had to do now was to pull himself up onto the wall, work his way over about twenty feet, then step over onto the shed roof. Even if he slipped off, he'd be a lot closer to the ground.

Just then the French door opened beneath the veranda, and a man wearing tan slacks, a Yankees cap, and a blue short-sleeved polo shirt came out. It looked like Myers, and he was talking on a cell phone as he walked across the flagstone toward the backyard. Charlie lowered his head, hoping his silhouette would blend in with the pine branches behind him.

In the distance, sirens suddenly sounded, echoing against the mountainside and up the canyon. As the sounds grew louder, Myers lowered the phone, reached down for a pistol tucked into his tan slacks, and began searching the yard.

He spotted Charlie immediately and brought up his pistol.

Charlie ducked, then heard the thump of a slug impacting the wall, then the whine of another bullet going high overhead. Running footsteps could be heard below, and then the sound of a door opening.

He risked a look and saw Myers disappear into the shed. It was time to make a move. Logic told him that Myers was racing to check on his captive, probably stashed in the outbuilding. Or it could be a trap. Once he climbed up onto the wall, he'd be a sitting duck if Myers suddenly popped back out.

Charlie pulled himself up onto the eight-inch-high, slightly rounded top of the wall, then stepped gingerly to his right, balancing himself carefully, trying to focus on the wall, not the ground twenty feet below.

The sounds of sirens were very loud now, and he tried not to imagine what Myers might be doing inside the shed. Now, within reach of the shed, he took a deep breath and leaped over onto the top of the pitched roof, landing like a spider as much as possible, sprawled out and hugging the metal.

The roof was slippery and hot from the summer sun, burning his cheek, hands, and knees through his pants. He raised his head off the surface and decided to slide down, aiming his feet toward the ground, intending to drop down, over the edge and off the shed. His only grip on the roof came from his fingertips and the palms of his hands now, and his phone was vibrating again.

A hole appeared just inches from his left hand, accompanied by a loud boom. Myers was shooting blind, but that was too close. Charlie made fists, lost his grip, and free-fell off the roof just as two more holes appeared where his body had been a few seconds earlier.

As he toppled over the edge he looked down, trying to time himself for contact with the ground. Fortunately he missed the flagstones and landed on soft sand. He relaxed his legs upon impact, using his knees as shock absorbers. Just then there was a loud thud and the crunch of wood breaking from somewhere close by. Maintaining focus, he tumbled into a roll, relying on the training that had taught him years ago how to fall and minimize injury.

He came up into a crouch, his Beretta already in his hand, safety off, and whirled around in the direction of the noise.

"Charlie!" yelled Detective DuPree as he stumbled through the shattered wooden gate beside the garage. Right behind were Nancy and a burly officer holding a steel battering ram.

"Myers ducked inside here," Charlie replied, pointing his weapon toward the shed.

"Was he alone?" Nancy asked, her pistol directed at the shed as she advanced, in a crouch, down the side of the structure toward the back. There were no windows on the sides Charlie could see.

"Yes, at least when he went in," Charlie answered, moving around to the opposite side, checking to see if there was a window or another door. Out of the corner of his eye, he could see uniformed officers entering the house through the unlocked back door.

DuPree, also crouched low, held his weapon on the door while they examined the outside of the structure. Several seconds went by; then an officer came back out of the house. "Clear!" the officer yelled. "No sign of the victim in the main house. There's a fifty-cal sniper rifle in one of the bedrooms, however, and a small pistol with a silencer. Ammo too, and ear protection."

Nancy and Charlie came back toward the front where DuPree

was positioned, their weapons still directed at the only way in or out. "He's trapped," Nancy whispered harshly, "and he left his heavy firepower in the house."

Charlie nodded. "Where's Gordon?"

"He and Woods took off after a silver pickup that came up behind them. Sweeney told Medina that he thinks it was Frank Geiger behind the wheel," DuPree replied, still crouched, his eyes on the shed door.

"Can't say this is a big surprise. I hope it's not too late for the hostage now," Charlie said. "Anything else from Gordon?" he added, remembering the missed calls.

"I haven't heard back from him," Nancy answered, stepping back and looking at the roof. "Are those bullet holes?"

"Yeah. Myers was shooting blind when I came off the wall onto that roof," Charlie responded. "Are we going to wait for SWAT?"

DuPree nodded. "They're already on standby. I'll make the call. Cover the door, Sergeant," he told Nancy, as he stood and stepped to the side and out of the potential field of fire. He fumbled for his cell phone with his left hand, keeping his pistol, in his right, directed toward the door.

"I tried to call you about five minutes ago, Charlie," Nancy said, her eyes still on the shed. "I wanted to warn you that your backup was gone."

"Felt the vibration, but I was up a tree outside the wall. Couldn't get to my phone," Charlie replied.

"Let's see if we can do this the easy way," DuPree whispered, motioning for the three uniformed officers who were beside the veranda to position themselves where they could cover the sides and back of the shed. He stepped back, facing a front corner of the shed, and stood where he was protected by the corner post—a smart move if the kidnapper decided to shoot through the shed wall at his voice.

"Dennis Myers! Put down your weapons, release Mrs. Randal, and then come out with your hands on your head. You're surrounded, and you have no way to escape. Release your prisoner and surrender now before someone gets hurt. Once SWAT and the FBI get here, your safety will be in someone else's hands, someone with tear gas and assault weapons. What do you say?"

A few seconds went by; then Charlie heard a faint scream. "You hear that? A woman's voice. Suppose he's locked her in a trunk?"

"That's all we need," DuPree grumbled, inching closer to the wall.

Chapter Twenty-one

Nancy inched closer to the door, then lay down, her head close to the threshold. She held up her hand, pointed to DuPree, then motioned with her thumb and fingers for him to speak.

"Mrs. Randal! Are you okay?" DuPree yelled.

Charlie heard the voice again, too faint to make out the words.

Nancy rolled away from the door and stood. "She said she's okay. She thinks he's gone."

"A trap?" Charlie asked.

"She wouldn't set us up," Nancy insisted, reaching for the doorknob, looking at DuPree.

"Tactical entry," he whispered, getting into position. Charlie came up to cover him, but DuPree waved him away, then signaled the closest cop.

Four seconds later, Nancy swung open the door, covered by the officers. DuPree went in low, pistol aimed, followed by the second officer and Nancy.

"Clear!" DuPree shouted, but it sounded more like a question.

He reached over to the wall and flipped a switch. A fluorescent light fixture came on, illuminating the interior.

Charlie stepped into the shed, which was about ten by four-teen and crowded with the four of them inside. The structure had a tongue-and-groove wood-composite floor that felt solid beneath his feet. A garden tool rack mounted on the wall held three well-used shovels, a superfluous snow shovel made of hard plastic, and a couple of rakes and a hoe. A worn pick rested against a wall, and a big wheelbarrow completed the major gardening implements.

There was also a Craftsman table saw, a workbench against the back wall, and a big pegboard where various woodworking tools were hung, such as a hammer, framing square, and hand saws. On the floor, close to the wall opposite the wheelbarrow, was a small wooden table, upside down with three legs sticking up. The fourth leg was on the workbench. The leg was unfinished, clearly a replacement that had yet to be attached. On the floor in the cor-ner was a big padlock, unlocked.

"Where the hell is she?" Charlie asked.

Nancy held up her hand for silence. "Margaret! Where are you?"

"Down here! I think I'm in a cellar. I smell dirt!" came a faint reply.

Charlie got down on his knees beside the overturned table and tried to lift it up. It was stuck to the floor, but he quickly discov-ered why. "It's attached to the floor by concealed hinges along one side!"

The tabletop swiveled up, resting against two legs, and be-neath, set into the wooden floor, was a sturdy wooden trapdoor with a hefty steel hasp and a big brass grab handle, recessed into the wood and flush with the surface.

"Are you sure he's not down there with you?" Nancy yelled, gripping the handle but hesitating to pull up.

"I felt a draft, like another door opening, and I can't hear him breathing anymore," Margaret replied, her voice a lot louder. "He handcuffed me, and there's a bag over my head. I can't see."

"Open it up, but stay clear," DuPree whispered, his pistol directed at the hatch.

Nancy swung the door open in one quick motion, ducking back.

Charlie, standing at an angle so he could look down, saw two bare feet—a woman's, from the size and shape. "She's on a dirt floor, sitting in a chair," he announced, then looked around for a flashlight or lantern.

DuPree brought out his cell phone and activated a flashlight app. He aimed it down into the hole, and they saw Margaret tied to a wooden folding chair with what looked like a pillowcase over her head, fastened at the neck with duct tape.

"My arms have gone to sleep. I can't feel them anymore," Margaret said, her voice shaking. "Get me out of here."

DuPree, on his knees now, aimed the light behind the seated victim. "There's a wood-lined tunnel that leads in that direction," he said, pointing toward the back wall of the shed—and the property wall.

Turning his head, he looked up at one of the uniformed officers. "Get officers to circle the property. Myers must have a tunnel exit uphill somewhere, but look close to the wall. It can't run too far in this rocky ground. And get people out on the roads and to nearby houses and outbuildings. I want a complete search of the neighborhood. If he's on foot, we need to track him down before sundown, or he may lose us completely. Put out a BOLO on

Dennis Myers using his DMV photo." He turned to Charlie. "You see what he was wearing?"

Charlie nodded. "Blue polo shirt, tan slacks, and a blue Yankees ball cap."

The officer nodded.

"Go!" DuPree ordered the uniform. "Now, let's get down there."

There was a short ladder constructed of two-by-six boards attached to the floor joists, and Nancy went down into the tunnel first. There was a click, and a light came on below.

Charlie watched as Nancy placed her hand on Margaret's shoulder. "It's just the two of us down here, Mrs. Randal. Myers is gone. I can see a hatch at the far end of the tunnel, leading up."

Nancy holstered her pistol and examined the hood covering the woman's head. "I'll cut the tape so I can pull this thing off your head. Don't move."

Charlie glanced over at the tools, found a big bolt cutter, and pointed it out to DuPree, who was still on the phone. DuPree nodded, so Charlie grabbed the tool and stepped back to the trapdoor.

Nancy had just pulled off the hood, and Margaret looked up anxiously. "Is Dolores okay? Is she alive? She went outside to see who was at the gate. Then this man wearing a mask over his face came into the office and shot me with a Taser. I fell, he stuck something into me, and I passed out. When I woke up, I was here."

"Dolores is the security guard?" Nancy asked.

"Yes. She was conscious and talking when the EMTs helped her into the ambulance," Charlie said, handing the bolt cutters down to Nancy, who was maneuvering around behind Margaret's chair to get to the handcuffs.

"Good. Was anyone else attacked? Is Sam okay?"

"Everyone was just fine when we left to look for you," Charlie replied. It wasn't the time to mention her husband was really Bill Woods—if she didn't already know. He stepped down the short ladder. He saw that the woman's feet were taped together and to the folding chair legs, so he reached into his pocket for his knife.

There was a loud snap, then another, as Nancy cut off the handcuffs, and Margaret sighed with relief, bringing her hands around front. "Who is Myers? Is he the guy who took me?"

"Let's get you out of here first," DuPree said, still on his knees looking down at her.

A few minutes later, Margaret Randal was pacing back and forth beneath the shaded veranda of Myers's house, trying to work out the cramps from being tied to the chair.

The two officers and Charlie were waiting for the opportunity to question her further, but then DuPree's phone rang.

"What you got?" the detective asked the caller, sounding annoyed.

DuPree listened for a moment, then responded. "See if you can find footprints or anything else he might have left behind. Keep searching, but warn everyone that the subject has a record of violence and knows we're looking for him. Make sure every house and structure in this neighborhood is checked out. He may have broken in and taken a hostage. And patrol all the local streets and roads leading out of here."

"How about dogs?" Charlie asked, not really wanting to be around when DuPree confronted Margaret about her husband's real identity. He knew it would be coming soon.

"I've put in a request," DuPree responded.

"I can follow a trail," Charlie volunteered. "Maybe hurry things up a bit? It'll be dark in a few hours."

"That true what they say about Indian trackers?" Nancy asked.

"Somewhat. Most of my skills were picked up in the Boy Scouts, though," Charlie admitted.

"Go for it, but let me know if you hear anything from Sweeney," DuPree replied. "I'll tell the officers on the hillside you're coming up."

Nancy pulled Charlie aside. "You don't want to be around when it hits the fan about her husband, do you?" she whispered.

"Got that right. I'm just hoping she'll be surprised. Sam said that he's never told Margaret who he really is, but that doesn't mean she hasn't already figured it out."

"I like Margaret and would hate to have to arrest her after all she's been through," Nancy replied.

Charlie nodded. "Me too. Gotta go, bluecoat, before sign grow cold."

Nancy rolled her eyes. "Whatever."

As he hurried out the gate leading to the street, now propped open, Charlie had to chuckle at her reaction. Back when he and Al were in their elementary school years, they used to tease each other using Hollywood-stereotype Indian-talk learned from old cowboy movies that ran on Saturday and Sunday afternoon TV. They also played their own game, Indians and Indians, working together and always ambushing the cavalry. Playing Cowboys and Indians didn't make much sense in a part of the country where many, if not most, of the Navajos were also cowboys.

He was making good time climbing to where the hidden exit was located. There was no longer any need to stay in cover or keep silent, and the officers who'd gone uphill left an easy trail to

follow. Hopefully, the officers hadn't also walked all over Myers's tracks. Charlie recalled the man was wearing some kind of
cross-trainers or athletic shoes, so he should be able to distin-
guish between those tracks and the street shoes the uniforms
wore—if they were still there.

His phone began to vibrate, and he slowed his climb to bring
it out of his pocket. Seeing it was Gordon, he stopped to answer
the call. "Hey, bro, we've recovered Margaret, and she's safe,"
Charlie quickly said, starting his climb again.

"Excellent, I'll tell Sam. What about her kidnapper, Myers?"
Gordon replied.

"He got away through a hidden tunnel and is now on foot.
APD is searching the neighborhood. There are a lot of places to
hide, and it's going to be dark soon. They're going to be bringing
in the dogs, but I'm hoping to pick up his trail before that. I'm hik-
ing up to where his tracks begin. Where you at, Gordon?"

"I lost the pickup around Louisiana Boulevard. At least we
know where Frank lives and can send over the troops. I'm coming
back up Montgomery Avenue and should be in your area within
minutes. Give me a call next time you reach a street and I'll catch
up to you," he suggested.

"Copy!" Charlie said, picking up the pace and putting away
the phone now that he'd spotted two officers standing several feet
from the outside wall of the Myers place. Charlie recognized one
of them as a sergeant he'd seen before with DuPree.

"Mr. Henry," the sergeant said, nodding as Charlie came
up. "Here's the exit to that tunnel." He pointed to what looked
like an overturned boulder, and beneath it a squared-off, stained
wooden-framed support structure with a short ladder leading
down into the tunnel.

"The old hollow fake boulder trick," Charlie muttered, wondering if he'd have recognized the fraud if he'd only gone a few more steps earlier. The tunnel exit was just a short distance uphill from the tree he'd climbed.

"I've seen these placed over septic tank openings," the sergeant said. "This one blends perfectly with the other boulders around here. I think it was painted to match. And it's well placed so runoff won't flood down into the tunnel. Here are the tracks. We've made sure not to mix them with our own."

Charlie nodded. "The next street is atop that ridge, isn't it?" He pointed.

"Yes sir. About a hundred fifty yards, give or take. Two officers are already headed in the general direction of the tracks, but they're moving slow, checking every potential hiding place," the sergeant replied. "They're circling uphill, I think."

"I'll follow the tracks directly. Detective DuPree sent for a K-9 unit, but I'm not sure how long it'll take to get them here."

"Want some backup?"

Charlie shook his head. "I'll probably meet up with the two officers before long. But you might want to look around for other fake boulders."

"To cover another hidey-hole? Hadn't thought of that," the sergeant admitted. "This Myers guy is pretty smart. He could be twenty feet from us right now, waiting for us to leave, then popping back up."

"Just a thought," Charlie said, finding the athletic-shoe pattern he'd already decided must belong to Myers, then looking for the next footprints. "Be careful, this guy is dangerous."

Despite the rough, rocky ground, consisting of a blend of coarse granite sand, rocks, plant debris, and sediment, Charlie had no trouble following Myers's footprints. Before long, he reached a path taken by small animals—probably rabbits and prairie dogs or squirrels—and crossed a gently sloped canyon, rising toward a rounded ridge that, even from a distance, Charlie could tell contained one of the narrow streets. There were several large homes visible in the almost rural neighborhood, but the tracks led away from all of them.

As he approached the crest of the ridge with the road, still paralleling Myers's tracks, he stopped and looked back. The two officers, in their dark blue APD uniforms, were higher up the canyon, apparently hoping to spot Myers from their vantage point. One of them had binoculars and, after a few seconds, waved in recognition. Charlie nodded, then topped the slope, which was steepest at the upper edge.

He spotted the athletic-shoe pattern, revealing that Myers had stepped up onto the dark blue-black asphalt, leaving evidence from the lighter, dusty sand on his shoes. He knew that very soon the dusty outline would fade and he'd lose the trail.

But the tracks led out onto the asphalt only about fifteen feet, made a ninety-degree turn, proceeded, getting fainter, another six feet, then stopped, as if Myers had suddenly been lifted straight up. Doubting it was divine rapture that had taken him skyward, Charlie got down on the hot asphalt and lay nearly flat, checking in front of the shoe prints. Sure enough, there was the distinct impression of tire tracks, pressed slightly into the heat-softened tar-gravel mix.

Myers had climbed into a vehicle here, then driven away. Either he'd happened to get a ride at exactly the right time— unlikely—or he'd had an escape vehicle parked here uphill from his home, just in case. If he was lucky, not just smart, Myers might have been able to drive out of the neighborhood before the road-blocks were in place. The bastard could be miles away by now.

Charlie made a quick call to Nancy, passing along the theory that Myers had entered a vehicle, type and color unknown, and driven away. She reported, in return, that the blue van used in the kidnapping was in the garage at the Myers home, along with an older-model silver Volkswagen Passat. But she concluded with good news. Gordon had just dropped off Bill Woods and would probably be joining Charlie soon.

Charlie crouched down again, this time taking a close-up photo. He checked to make sure the tread pattern was clear, then stood and looked up and down the street. He was standing at a sharp curve in the road, which led toward a boxy two-story house slightly uphill and straight ahead, maybe two hundred yards away, and a Frank Lloyd Wright-ish structure a little lower than his current location, across the street and closer, to his left. A small sign almost overhead told him this was a different street than the one Myers's house was on, but it looked like they inter-sected downhill.

Deciding to stick close to the road rather than hike cross-country again, he chose to go left. It was downhill, he was hot and tired, and the sun was low in the sky.

Gordon's pickup came up the street only a few minutes later, just as Charlie reached the home that, to his untrained eye, re-minded him of those Prairie-Style Revival houses he'd read about in some dentist's waiting room. The broad, gentle roofs, big low chimneys, and long horizontal lines were all there, along with the natural wood colors. Even the mailbox was in the same style and shades. He'd seen very few houses like this, even in Albuquerque, and would have enjoyed looking around inside.

Gordon pulled up beside him. "Nice house, Charlie. Thinking of buying it?"

"Yeah. FOB Pawn is making money like there's no tomorrow." He walked over to look at the mailbox.

"Well, at least you've saved Margaret's tomorrow. Too bad about Sam's. You done searching the neighborhood?" Gordon asked.

"Just getting started." Charlie looked down at the buff-colored concrete driveway that led up to the low wooden gate and, beyond, a three-car garage. "How about that?" he commented.

"How about what?" Gordon looked down at the ground.

"The tire tread in the sand dusting this driveway matches the one from the vehicle Myers climbed into once he reached the road." He brought out his camera, looked at the photo he'd taken earlier, then scrunched down low to capture this tire print.

"And where was this car or truck parked?"

Charlie pointed. "The outside of the curve over there."

"That's, like, a hundred yards. Why park there, then escape by driving here, a short walk away, then drive into the garage?"

"Doesn't make sense, does it? It must be just the same make of tire. Lots of Mercedes up here." Charlie handed Gordon the phone, and his pal swiped back and forth between images.

"They look the same. More like an SUV, though. Too wide for a sedan."

"You think the officers searching the 'hood checked out this place already?"

"Should have. I see two sets of fresh shoe prints, not his. But I'm going to give it a second look anyway."

"Let me pull over and I'll go with you. I need to stretch my legs," Gordon said.

A minute later they approached the big gate, then saw another, nearly concealed much smaller gate, clearly for foot traffic.

Charlie discovered a call button set into a wood post and pressed it. They waited a minute; then he pressed it again. "Looks like nobody's home."

"Or they're being held hostage," Gordon said.

"Not again. Let's at least go check to make sure there hasn't been a break-in."

Gordon pointed to a camera mounted beneath one of the long, low eaves. "Smile, we're on camera."

"I'll risk it." He reached over the gate and flipped the latch. The gate opened, and they stepped inside the yard, which was tastefully xeriscaped with desert plants. Placed underneath the eaves on a raised wooden deck was a long stone-topped counter, the kind used for outdoor cookouts.

"No grill or smoker?" Gordon commented softly as they walked past a small bistro table and two iron stools. "Not even a bar. How primitive."

Charlie looked down at the sidewalk. "Oh crap, I recognize that new set of shoe prints." He reached for his pistol.

Chapter Twenty-two

"Hands away from the weapon!" came a man's voice from his left.

Charlie and Gordon turned, finding an Anglo man wearing a tan shirt and pants and a cap—some kind of tribal police uniform. It wasn't for the Navajo Tribe; Charlie knew their insignia. He was aiming an autoloading shotgun at them.

They froze.

"Where's your Yankee cap?" Charlie asked.

"So you're Dennis Myers," Gordon said. "Since when are you Native American?"

"Shut up, Sweeney. Hands on your heads, both of you. Slowly, so I won't have to spray your guts all over the patio."

Charlie nodded, and he and Gordon complied.

"Now, shorty, you first. Reach over with your left hand, take out your handgun with index finger and thumb, and then place it on the counter."

"You talking to me?" Gordon asked.

"Do it."

Gordon did as he was told.

"Now you, Charlie. And don't try that flatten-and-roll crap. I'm not driving a car this time."

Charlie did as he asked. So Myers *was* the guy who tried to kill him outside the bar. At least this time he hadn't already shot him and Gordon. That meant they still had a chance.

A few minutes later, their cell phones, pocketknives, and keys were on the counter, and Myers was marching them into the big garage through a side entrance. Inside was an SUV, plus a Sandia Pueblo police car—or at least a very good copy. It was a white Chevy Impala with SANDIA emblazoned on it in big red letters. Blue and red accents framed the red police label, and a blue and gold Sandia emblem the shape of a baseball diamond was positioned on the back side behind the rear tire. There were no emergency lights on top, just a black spotlight on the driver's side by the mirror.

"Good disguise if you want to get out of the city in a hurry," Charlie guessed.

"Know your enemy, right?" Myers replied cheerfully. "Sweeney, assume the position, arms up and out, feet spread, just like on TV," he ordered, pointing the gun at Charlie. "Or you'll have to drag your big pal's body."

Gordon cursed under his breath, then leaned against the vehicle as ordered.

Myers brought out a set of handcuffs from his back pocket. "These were supposed to be for the wife's legs. Don't you hate women with fat ankles?"

Charlie eyed the man, wondering if he could grab the barrel. He took a step toward Myers, but the guy dropped the cuffs onto the garage floor and stepped back, both hands on the shotgun again. "Not a good idea, Charlie. Pick them up, then put them to use on your friend, his hands behind his back. If you want to stay alive."

"Sorry, bro," Charlie replied, putting the cuffs on Gordon, keeping them as loose as possible.

As he started to turn, Charlie saw movement, but it was too late. Myers whacked him on the back of the head with the gun butt, and as he fell to the floor, Charlie blacked out.

"Hey, naptime's over," Gordon whispered, poking him in the back. Charlie opened his eyes, his head aching. It was hot, dark, and cramped, and he could smell car exhaust.

"We're in the damned trunk, aren't we?" he muttered weakly. His arms were numb, asleep, and behind his back. "Bastard cold-cocked me, then tied me up. Feels like zip ties. "

"Yeah, they're heavy-duty, too. At least he busted a gut trying to put you in the trunk. If he had any brains, he would have had me put the cuffs on you, then made you climb in while still conscious."

"If he had any brains, he wouldn't have messed with us."

"Yeah, Charlie. Look at the position we've got him in now."

Charlie started to laugh. "Ow, my head hurts. No more jokes. We're clearly on the move. Any idea where we're headed?"

"We went downhill for a while, then rode straight for several minutes, then climbed up and really accelerated into traffic. I think we went up a ramp and are now on the interstate. From the inertia of the turn, I'm guessing we're headed to the right rather than the left, which means to the north."

"In the direction of Sandia Pueblo. That puts us exactly where you might expect to find a Sandia Pueblo police car. This guy is smart. He's established an alternate hiding place—complete with patio—then an escape strategy out of the city, just in case," Charlie pointed out. "The car and uniform would get him through any roadblock not manned by a Sandia Pueblo cop."

"Fitting for a guy with mob connections, having a Plan B. He must have known Frank Geiger back in one of the other News, York or Jersey," Gordon suggested. "Maybe Myers was his mob contact."

"Yeah. Hopefully we'll get all the answers, but right now we've got to get out of this alive," Charlie reminded him, "and step one is getting our hands free."

"You can't work on my cuffs without some kind of wire or tool," Gordon replied, "but maybe we can find a sharp edge on the trunk lid or interior somewhere and I can cut through the plastic zip tie around your wrists. My belt buckle has got sharp edges—well, kinda sharp—if we can't find anything better. The problem is finding a rough edge that you can place behind your back without slicing your wrists," Gordon said.

"Then let's work fast. We don't know how much time we have," Charlie whispered.

After about five minutes of feeling around in the dark, Charlie finally gave up. "Let's try that belt buckle. Spoon me, Gordon."

"Okay, but if you start to grope me I'm going to scream." Gordon chuckled.

"I'll be gentle."

"We never, ever, tell anyone about this," Gordon replied. Just then, the car slowed, turned, and rolled to a stop. "Crap. Out of time. Do we go for it now?" Gordon asked.

"Yeah. Otherwise, we may have just arrived at our burial site," Charlie answered, twisting around, trying to maneuver so his feet were toward the trunk opening. "When he starts to open the trunk, we kick the top—when I say *now*. Maybe we can knock him out, or at least down onto the ground."

"Then what, jump out, tackling, kicking, and head-butting?" Gordon whispered.

"And stomping. Don't forget stomping."

"Ready?" Gordon asked.

"Ready," Charlie replied, his heart beating through his chest.

They waited, feeling the weight shift as Myers got out of the car. There was a short pause, and then the car door closed. Footsteps sounded, but they grew fainter, then faded away.

"He's going somewhere," Gordon whispered. "Now's our chance to try and kick this lid open."

"Wait just a few more seconds. Just listen. I don't hear traffic or other noises," Charlie said.

He heard a different car door open, then close again. An engine revved up; then a vehicle started moving, tires crunching on gravel. As Charlie listened, the sound faded away to nothing.

"He met someone, and they've driven off," Charlie decided.

"It should be dark outside by now, or nearly so. Let's kick ourselves out of this tin can," Gordon replied. "But be ready to run."

"At the count of three. One, two, three!" Charlie yelled. He and Gordon kicked the trunk lid as hard as they could.

Something snapped, and the trunk flew open. Outside it was twilight—the sun had set.

Gordon, who was closest to the back of the car, tried to sit up, sticking his legs over the rear of the car. He groaned, then rolled over onto the ground.

Charlie tried to sit up, too, but his legs ached like hell. He stayed where he was for a moment and looked around. Turning his head, he saw the Sandia Mountains to the southeast and realized they were just north of the town of Bernalillo, on some side road. I-25 was miles to the east, with vehicle headlights revealing its location just below the foothills. There was a small housing development about a quarter mile away, but otherwise, they were in a rural setting, mostly brush and cottonwoods, part of the bosque.

He climbed clumsily out of the trunk, his hands behind his back, his arms aching, and his legs so stiff he could hardly stand. "I feel like crap, but, hey, we're alive."

"And obviously kicking. Wonder who he met up with? Frank and Ray Geiger?"

"That would be my guess," Charlie replied. "Let's see if we can get our hands free. Anyone who spots us now will think we're escaped prisoners, and wonder why we're beside this police car. With so many people packing weapons these days . . ."

"A sharp rock first, maybe, for that zip tie?" Gordon suggested, looking around.

"Or a piece of glass." Charlie turned and looked at the rear taillight.

"Naw, that's plastic. But this is New Mexico, and we're beside a road."

"Which means there's got to be a broken beer bottle close by. Glass is much better," Charlie replied. "Let's be careful trying to pick it up, though, and try not to slit my wrist too much."

With darkness falling, the search took more time than they thought it would, and they had to settle for an aluminum Coke can. It was quickly stomped flat, then worked back and forth until it split into two pieces. The sharp aluminum edge at the tear was like a knife, and in moments Charlie was free.

A few minutes and a piece of rusty wire from a downed fence later, Charlie was able to free his pal from first one, then the second handcuff. The road they stood beside was more rural than urban, and during the time he was freeing Gordon only one vehicle, a shiny blue pickup, had flown past. The driver was a young woman with a child, and she wasn't eager to even slow down, much less stop, despite their waving. Maybe it was the handcuffs.

As they tried to decide which house was the closest, they saw a police car approaching and knew they'd be able to get help in a hurry now. As it turned out, the woman in the pickup had called the police to report two strangers, one handcuffed, beside a police car. After an unpleasant few minutes, their story was confirmed, and more officers were on the way.

The next vehicle to arrive looked familiar. As it pulled up, Charlie saw that it was Nancy driving her APD unit. Beside her sat Detective DuPree. "Get in, you two," DuPree yelled from the passenger side. "We've got a good lead on Myers's possible destination."

Charlie climbed into the backseat of the four-door sedan behind DuPree, and Gordon circled around and got in behind Nancy. "Where we headed?" Charlie asked while fastening his seat belt.

"Drive, Medina," DuPree growled. "We need to catch up to these bastards."

"Copy!" Nancy hit the gas, spun the car around in the loose ground, then raced back toward the main highway.

"Dennis Myers is a licensed pilot. He leases a single-engine airplane parked at Coronado Airport just off tribal land, which is our next stop. Units are on their way now, and the airport staff has been instructed to delay any takeoff," DuPree responded.

"Unless he puts a gun to their head," Gordon replied.

"There's that," DuPree admitted. "He's the one who got the drop on you two, right?"

"Yeah, that was my bad," Charlie admitted. "I was complacent, just going through the motions. I never suspected he had a second house that close."

"We found out that the Sandia Pueblo police car Myers drove through the checkpoint on Tramway was a fake. He was wearing a passable uniform as well, apparently. The officer just waved him through without a closer look," Nancy said.

"He'd already changed into that outfit when he got the drop on us," Charlie confirmed. "Even put on some boots."

"The tech geeks downtown tracked your cell phones, boys," DuPree said. "They were in the garage of the second house. Myers leased it under a corporate name. They're in that evidence box on the floor—along with your handguns. Grab them, we might need the extra firepower."

As Charlie and Gordon retrieved their stuff, a call came in over the vehicle's radio from Dispatch. Charlie was used to radio calls, and since the cryptic style wasn't too far from military jargon, he understood the message.

"Ray Geiger cut off his ankle bracelet, but it's been tracked to Coronado Airport? That's where we're headed."

DuPree looked his way, frowned, and began tapping his cell phone. He motioned for them to be silent as he worked with the device. Charlie looked anxiously toward the east, trying to gauge how many minutes it would take to get to the facility.

"You think the Geigers are trying to lure us there while they drive off in the opposite direction?" Gordon whispered to Charlie. "Why cut the tracking device off, then take it with him? Ray is no genius, but he can't be *that* stupid."

"Maybe he tried, but just couldn't get it off completely without the right tools. What if they're already airborne and we're too late?" Charlie replied.

"Got it!" DuPree announced, still looking at his cell phone.

"What?" Gordon. "Not got *them?*"

"I think he's uploaded the ankle bracelet frequency and code for Ray," Nancy said, reaching the frontage road and turning a hard left, sending them all leaning to the side.

"Yeah, and the bracelet is moving again, this time away from the airport," DuPree responded. "What the hell is going on?"

Just then another call came in from the police radio.

Nancy and DuPree cursed, almost in unison. She braked hard and pulled over to the shoulder.

"According to the airfield office, the staff there turned out the lights and locked up, so nobody boarded any airplane or took off. So what's their twenty now?" she asked DuPree.

DuPree was studying the cell phone display. "Looks like they're on I-25, heading . . . south! At least that's where the tracker is going."

"If it's still with them, then they're going to be jammed in with early evening traffic. Hang on!" she yelled, flipping on the emergency lights. "Our closest access to the freeway is Tramway."

"No, turn around, then catch the Alameda ramp further south," DuPree ordered. "Use the siren to clear the way."

"First we're kidnapped, now we're in a car chase. What's for dessert?" Gordon joked. "A shootout?"

Nobody laughed, though even DuPree smiled just a little.

"Where are they now?" Charlie asked.

DuPree checked the tracking app on his phone, then looked over at the vehicle's GPS. "Hell, it looks like they're almost even with us, over on the interstate."

Charlie and Gordon looked automatically to their right toward the freeway, which was barely fifty yards away, parallel to their travel. It was pointless, of course; the southbound lanes were past the concrete median, and all they could see were the tall trucks and eighteen-wheelers.

"I guess it's too much to hope for a traffic-stopping accident," Gordon speculated.

"That's cold," Nancy said.

"Oh, not with anyone injured. Just enough to bring everything to a crawl. Like a jackknifed load of watermelons spread across four lanes," Gordon responded.

"Only problem is we couldn't move either, bro," Charlie reminded him.

They quickly reached the on-ramp, and Nancy merged into traffic. Charlie, not behind the wheel, cringed every time it seemed like a collision was imminent. Gordon just chuckled. Vehicles were moving slowly, everyone on the way home mixing it up with long-haulers in semis, and Nancy had to cut speed, swerve, then accelerate time after time.

"Kill the sirens and the emergency lights," DuPree ordered, watching his cell phone display. "The vehicle is less than a half mile away now, and we're gaining on them, even doing fifty. We don't know what vehicle they're in—the airport staff only saw taillights—so I want to creep up on them until we know. If they spot a patrol unit in active pursuit outside the city limits, it'll spook them."

"I just hope they didn't throw that ankle bracelet into the back of some airport mechanic's pickup and we're on a joyride to nowhere," Gordon commented. "Not that the roller-coaster ride hasn't been fun, Sergeant," he added.

"We could have left you by the side of the road, Gordon," Nancy retorted.

"You still have roadblocks in place, Detective?" Charlie asked.

"Those have been taken down, but the state police, both county sheriff's departments, and the Rio Rancho cops have a BOLO out for Myers and the Geigers. All known residences, the dojo, and the train and bus stations are under observation, as well as the Sunport and private airstrips and TV station helicopters. After all the violence already, I don't want to risk a shooting incident where other civilians might be injured or taken hostage. When we catch up to these perps, I want to take them down clean," DuPree said.

"Who's got jurisdiction?"

"We do this time. We're in pursuit for crimes that began on our own turf," Nancy said. "If we lose them, however, we might have to step back," she added, glancing at DuPree.

"Which is why we're tracking that ankle bracelet as long as we can," DuPree said. "Now let me see what I can set up ahead of us. I doubt these guys are heading to Mexico, but they *are* going in that direction, and it's a rural route most of the way. There are a lot of places to get lost if they leave the interstate, however. Los Lunas is the next town down the line, and if they get off I-25 before we have visual confirmation, they could go in any direction and it could be hard setting up a roadblock. Let's try to ID the vehicle before that happens." The detective picked up the radio mike.

After less than two minutes of conversation, DuPree had summarized the situation and arranged for aerial support from a state police helicopter. "Switch over to the state police frequency, Medina," he ordered. "Once we know which vehicle's the target, we can pass that along to the flight crew, and they should be able to follow."

"Copy," Nancy replied, reaching for the control on the vehicle radio.

Traffic began to thin as they left the Albuquerque metro area. DuPree, keeping close watch on the app on his cell phone, finally narrowed the likely vehicles to an older-model dark blue pickup and a white SUV that were apart from other vehicles heading south. Both were picking up speed and still in the left, passing lane of I-25, which was now down to two lanes southbound. The pickup was several car lengths behind the SUV. Nancy had closed the distance and remained in the right-hand, slower lane, not wanting to attract attention.

"Wish I had my binoculars," Charlie commented, watching the vehicles from the backseat. "If I could read the plate, we might be able to rule out that pickup. Ray owns a red truck, and Frank drives a silver one, but clearly they've switched vehicles. Hopefully one of them will take one of the Los Lunas exits and we'll get a break."

"I can almost make it out," Nancy replied. "It's a New Mexico plate, at least. The old yellow version."

"Inch up a little closer, Nancy," DuPree urged. "Then back off while we run a check."

She picked up the pace, and they closed to about a hundred yards. "Got it! BDG-465."

Nancy took her foot off the gas, and the following distance increased as she slowed to fifty-five miles per hour.

DuPree entered the tag information into the mobile data terminal to his left, beneath the dashboard and at the front of the center console.

"First Los Lunas exit coming up," Gordon observed as they passed the big sign on the right. "Maybe we won't need the ID."

Suddenly the pickup accelerated, passed the SUV, then cut in front of the vehicle and hurtled to the right, down the exit ramp. To the east of the interstate lay most of the small city of Los Lunas.

"Crap!" DuPree exclaimed, then looked down at the cell phone. "There they go!"

"Hang on, boys," Nancy announced, flipping on the emergency lights and siren as she accelerated toward the exit.

Chapter Twenty-three

They raced down the freeway ramp. Ahead at the intersection, the traffic light was red. The pickup braked hard, then skidded into a left-hand turn, intending to run the light and pass under the interstate into the city of Los Lunas.

"Oh crap!" Nancy yelled, slamming on the brakes.

A green sedan coming from Los Lunas suddenly appeared, heading straight for the fleeing pickup. Both vehicles braked and swerved, trying to avoid the collision. The car clipped the pickup's driver's-side front bumper, then went into a sideways slide to the west, nearly rolling as it laid down an inch of tire rubber onto the pavement with a horrible screech. The pickup spun around in a complete one-eighty, coming to a stop facing west, straddling the center line.

"Gotcha!" DuPree yelled as Nancy slid to a stop barely five feet from the passenger side of the pickup.

Ray Geiger was staring right at them, his expression a perfect human imitation of a deer caught in the headlights. He was still cringing, his eyes now shut, when he was slammed back against the seat as the pickup suddenly accelerated west.

Nancy cussed loudly, glanced left, then cut sharply to the right as she raced into the intersection, making such a tight turn that she barely missed sideswiping the car that had clipped the pickup and was now facing east. As they whipped past the vehicle, the woman driver's eyes seemed twice normal size.

Nancy raced west down the road after the pickup.

"Yahoo!" Gordon yelled. "Do it again."

"Shut up!" DuPree grumbled, his hands pressed tightly against the passenger-side dash.

"Okay," Charlie observed, reading a sign as they flew past it. "We're now on Highway 9. Where does this go?"

Nancy took a deep breath, then looked over at the GPS. "Eventually, Laguna Pueblo."

"Yeah, but by then the highway connects with I-40. That won't happen for thirty miles, give or take," DuPree added, relaxing just a little.

"That's mostly empty desert, right?" Charlie observed.

"Their escape plan is shot to hell now. Looks like they've been forced into an unplanned direction," Gordon said. "We should be able to box them in."

DuPree grabbed the radio mike and contacted the state police dispatcher, passing along the new information to the helicopter crew. In exchange, he learned that the chopper had already picked up the signal from the ankle bracelet and, when they reached the area, would coordinate with DuPree and Laguna Pueblo officers, who would block access to I-40.

"Myers and company will be cut off," DuPree announced as he racked the mike.

"There's something that's still got me puzzled, though," Charlie said.

"Yeah. Why hang on to the ankle bracelet?" Nancy asked. "Even if they think it's been disabled."

"You think Frank and Myers now have no choice but to set up a Butch Cassidy and Sundance Kid dying-with-your-boots-on shootout?" Gordon offered. "Or maybe suck us into an ambush. He left that sniper rifle behind, but we don't know what other weapons Dennis Myers has with him."

"If you're trying to get me riled up about this, Sweeney, you're not helping. Myers was a mob soldier, reportedly a hit man," Du-Pree reminded him. "I'm not looking forward to what's coming."

"But he could have killed us earlier and passed up the chance," Charlie countered, "and before, getting rid of me was near the top of their agenda. This time, Myers got cold feet. He doesn't need more heat to come down. He wants to survive, to escape one more time."

"But what if Gordon is right? Now they know they'll either have to give up or take us on," Nancy countered. "Their airplane flight to Mexico or wherever didn't quite work out."

"None of this makes any sense now," Charlie admitted. "That monitor is still with them, and they can't get away as long as it's sending a signal."

"Let's think way outside the box for a moment. What if Ray *wants* us to catch up to them so he can surrender?" Gordon suggested. "I'm guessing it was his dad who pressured him into the home invasion that started all this, intending on kidnapping Sam and forcing him to give up the money. With that bum leg, Frank knew he couldn't pull it off himself, and maybe he's getting low on cash. Believe me, I know how controlling an old man can be."

Charlie nodded. Gordon had hated his late father, who'd been abusive to his entire family, especially to Gordon's mom. The man met his demise when one night he had fallen down some stairs and broken his neck.

"Whatever the case, we have to operate under the possibility that we'll be confronting three potentially well-armed men—at least two of them very familiar with firearms," DuPree said. "You two need to stay under cover and defend yourself only if attacked. The responsibility for taking these perps down belongs to Sergeant Medina and myself, plus whatever law enforcement is on scene when it goes down. Got that?"

"Wayne, you know by now that Charlie and Gordon are going to react to the situation and take action whether we want them to or not," Nancy observed, not taking her eyes off the road. They were traveling close to ninety miles an hour.

"Okay, but just for the record, I advised otherwise."

"This started with us, guys, and I'm in it till the end," Charlie stated, not bothering to remind the officers that he and Gordon had been trained to maneuver and fight at night, and had much more experience with firefights than either of the cops

"I'm with Charlie on this," Gordon added.

"We take all of them alive, if possible," DuPree replied.

Charlie nodded, knowing that such an outcome was in the hands of their targets. Five minutes later, in the middle of nowhere, the speeding pickup suddenly slowed, braked hard, then slid off the road, nearly tipping as it entered a dirt road leading toward a closed gate and cattle guard in the fence line. A cloud of dust erupted, hiding the pickup.

"Now what?" DuPree exclaimed. "I didn't see any signs of life at all around here."

Nancy braked, slowed, then made the turn at a much more reasonable pace, fishtailing only slightly. Ahead, the metal gate had been smashed open and part of the wire fence thrown aside. A trail of dust churned up by the fleeing pickup quickly revealed its general direction of travel, though its running lights had been turned off.

Nancy drove the squad car slowly over the raised cattle guard with a rumble of tires. "Where are they going now? Some abandoned ranch house?" She continued slowly down the primitive road, following the one set of tire tracks.

"Who knows? The only fresh tracks leading in right now are from the pickup, so it's not like there's any regular traffic. Follow, but whatever you do, don't get stuck in the sand. Everyone keep watch," DuPree said, reaching for the radio mike. "I'm calling this in."

"We're being set up for an ambush," Gordon suggested, looking at Charlie. "They turned off their lights and probably believe this is the only road back out to the highway."

"I agree. They want to catch us in a trap before help arrives. With this squad car in their hands they still might have a chance to make their escape back through Los Lunas," Charlie replied, trying to see beyond the headlights. "It's what I'd do."

Nancy turned her head toward Charlie. "Then I'm turning out our headlights. We'll become invisible, like them." There was no moon out at this hour, and at this location, away from city lights, it was very dark.

"Yeah," DuPree agreed, putting back the radio mike. "Let's stop, get out, and take cover while we develop a plan. It might be better just to set up a roadblock and wait for backup. Time is on our side, and once the helicopter is here they can drop a flare or two and light up the desert for miles."

They climbed out of the car in a hurry, dome light off, and

Nancy grabbed a shotgun from the rack between the seats. Du-Pree took a flashlight before Nancy locked the doors. Charlie motioned for them to meet behind the car; then they remained silent for a while.

Except for the sound of crickets and the ticking of the cooling car engine, it was very quiet. After several seconds, DuPree spoke. "No engine noise, which means they've stopped as well, or gotten stuck in the sand. If that's happened, they'll have to take this car to get out. You may be right about an ambush, Gordon."

"They can't afford to wait," Nancy whispered. "They're either going to launch a quick attack on us, or they've already headed for the highway on foot."

"They can bypass us and try to hijack some vehicle along the road—which would be risky, considering they have to know backup is headed this direction. They might, however, make a move on us," Gordon said. "I doubt that Ray could see all four of us in the headlight glare a while ago. They might not know they're already outnumbered."

"If they attack, what's their strategy, best guess?" DuPree asked, looking down the dirt track where the pickup had gone.

"They'll send Ray or Frank at us directly, up the road in the pickup with the high beams on to try and blind us, while the other two circle on foot and take us in the flanks. Ray has less experience with a handgun, so I'm guessing he'll be the one in the pickup. If we try to use the vehicle for cover and protection from the frontal threat, we'll be vulnerable from the sides and rear," Charlie added.

"How about we ambush their ambush? I've got a plan," Gordon offered. "It's risky, but that's what makes it viable."

DuPree groaned. "Let's hear it."

• • •

Nancy jumped into the car, turned on the engine and revved it loudly for several seconds, then turned off the engine again and got back out. In the meantime, Charlie, Gordon, and DuPree had grabbed some dried brush and placed it around the rear tires.

"Okay, they'll think we're stuck, hopefully, and that we're out gathering more brush to put around the tires for traction," Gordon whispered. "Now let's hope they buy it."

Suddenly they heard the sound of the pickup, and distant headlights probed from the direction their prey had fled.

"Here comes the diversion," Charlie whispered. "Let's get into position *now!*"

They moved quickly, Charlie and Nancy taking the right flank—the passenger side of the car—and Gordon and DuPree the left. They had to move fast, then hide where the oncoming head-lights wouldn't pick them up out of the low brush and scattered clusters of juniper. They also had to get outside the likely distance their attackers would maintain in their hasty attempt at a flank-ing operation.

"What if they just rush past the car and make for the high-way?" Nancy whispered, crouched low behind a pungent juniper, shotgun ready.

"Then we shoot out their tires and pin them down. But why try that move here and now? They could have done this back on the highway where they didn't have to risk getting stuck in the sand."

Nancy nodded. "You're right. It's safer to assume two of them are on foot, sneaking around in the dark. Let's just be sneakier."

They could see the front of the truck now, less than a hun-dred yards away and closing, bouncing wildly and fishtailing across the sandy ground. Several seconds later it came to a sliding stop in a cloud of dust about twenty feet from the police car.

Charlie had been watching out of the corner of his eye, not wanting to lose his night vision from the headlight glare. "Keep an eye on the truck," he whispered. "I'll hunt down whoever is on foot."

Crouching, he moved silently, picking his way slowly from cover to cover in a wide circle back in the direction the pickup had come from. After a minute, he saw movement to his left. Charlie froze, listening, his pistol up and ready. Eyes searching, his breath silent and under control, he heard something crunch—a branch or plant debris being stepped on. There was a shape there, behind a wide sage about three feet tall.

After a moment, he saw an odd shape, then realized it was the head of a man wearing a baseball cap. Charlie knew who it was.

Slowly, carefully, Charlie moved forward, his eyes on his opponent, who was watching the police car. If he deduced that no one was underneath or around the vehicle, Myers would start a careful sweep, moving either deeper into the brush or toward Nancy, to Charlie's left.

He couldn't risk letting Myers get past him and spot her first.

There was a juniper about five feet high just to Myers's right. Charlie began moving in that direction, intending to approach from an unexpected direction, behind Myers.

Having developed some serious hunting skills and stealthy habits in the extremely dry deserts of the Middle East, Charlie was right at home here in the Southwest. He'd also learned, while growing up, how to move without making a sound—something he doubted Myers could do outside an urban environment with no streets, sidewalks, or stairs.

A shout and a single gunshot came from beyond the police car and made Charlie flinch. Myers, who was wearing overalls now, started to stand, then squatted back down again, probably reconsidering his options. Charlie kept moving, now behind and to the man's right side, barely twenty feet away.

To his left, ahead and silhouetted by the glow of the headlights, Charlie saw more movement. Either it was Nancy or something had gone wrong. Myers stood.

"I'm a cop, Myers." Nancy yelled, menace in her tone. "Don't move or I'll blow you away!"

The perp's head turned slowly toward Nancy, his pistol hand coming up.

"She means it!" Charlie added, trying to get a clear line of sight as he worked his way around the juniper. He didn't want to miss and hit Nancy.

"Shit!" Myers cursed, moving his head only slightly this time. "Okay. You win. This time. Setting my weapon on the ground. Don't shoot." The man bent his knees, stooping to place what looked like a .45 auto on the ground with his right hand.

But his left hand was busy at his ankle. "Gun!" Charlie yelled.

Myers brought up a small backup pistol, shooting at Nancy, who flinched as her shotgun roared and flashed with fire.

Charlie shot through the branches, hoping for a hit, then rushed forward for a clear shot.

Myers was backing away and snapped off two quick rounds. The bullets whistled over Charlie's head as he dropped to one knee. He brought his pistol up, but Myers had fled, leaving only the thump of footsteps and the crash of brush as he ran away.

"Nancy!" Charlie yelled, seeing his friend staggering.

"Took one in the vest," she gasped.

"You sure?" Charlie responded.

"I'm okay, just out of breath," Nancy managed, trying to keep her balance. "I'll call DuPree. Keep watch."

"No, I'm going after him. You stay ready in case he circles back or the guy driving the truck makes a move." Charlie turned and moved in the direction Myers had fled, knowing that Gordon and DuPree were probably handling their part of this takedown, dealing with the kid and/or the gimp. He just had to make sure he didn't walk into an ambush.

Charlie advanced silently, then, after a few minutes, stopped to listen. He heard the sounds of movement—brush and branches being crushed by footsteps—then silence. Myers hadn't been running in panic; he was also hunting, and he'd also stopped to listen.

Charlie knew approximately where the man was hiding, at least in what direction, and could tell from the sound level that he was pretty close, probably less than fifty feet away. There was one old Hollywood Western trick that was almost always successful among those who weren't tactically schooled. He'd try it.

Charlie waited for a moment, then bent down, selected a chunk of sandstone about the size of a slice of bread, and threw it in the direction of the footsteps.

There was a thud, then the sound of movement, just a few footsteps, but that was enough. Myers had shifted, turning around in the direction of the sandstone impacting on the sand instead of just looking. Charlie was betting that the man would hunker down to set up an ambush rather than run.

There was silence for almost a minute; then Charlie heard the sound of a helicopter approaching from the northeast. Once the chopper was overhead, there would be a flare or searchlight that would give away Myers's position. Unfortunately, it would also give away his own location.

The helicopter crew wouldn't know who was who from overhead. Charlie was in civilian clothes—like Myers. If they spotted him first, he might be forced to give up his weapon, making himself vulnerable to Myers for a short interval. If he was lucky, it would be the other way around. Charlie didn't believe in luck, but he had another plan, a risky, half-assed plan. And it just might work.

Chapter Twenty-four

He tried to get inside Dennis Myers's head for a moment. The guy was supposedly a mob soldier, a hit man possibly, and he knew the ways of the city—but maybe not so much the desert. He was armed, dangerous, and desperate enough to shoot a cop in order to avoid capture. His only reasonable hope to escape was to get transportation, but to do that, he had to avoid immediate capture—get away from the incoming chopper's almost unlimited visual capabilities and overwhelming speed.

The only two vehicles in the area were too dangerous to approach, which meant Myers had to continue toward the highway. Once he was there, he'd have to take the risk and try to carjack someone. But he'd have to do that before law enforcement shut down the highway to civilian traffic. It might already be too late for Myers.

Charlie listened, and, sure enough, he heard Myers heading south in a hurry. The chase was on. If he could move fast enough, he could cut Myers off.

He raced toward the highway, less than a quarter mile away,

trying to move fast enough to get ahead of the man, then lie in wait for his approach. All Charlie had to do was get there first, unseen and unheard.

The sound of the helicopter would drown out his footsteps, but hopefully not capture him in a searchlight or flares. Charlie tried to gauge how fast the fleeing middle-aged man could run— and go a little faster. He knew he was younger, probably in better shape, and longer-legged. Unless Myers was the Road Runner himself, Charlie would win this race.

Five minutes later, Charlie reached the fence line barely fifty feet from the highway. To the east, he recalled, there was an arroyo that ran beneath the road. It would be a good place for someone to hide, someone like Myers, hoping to pop out and stop a car when the opportunity came. Charlie ran along the fence line, keeping an eye to his left—north—not knowing exactly where his opponent was at the moment.

He moved slowly as he approached the arroyo, discovering that it was deeper than he'd guessed. His prey might have dropped down into it farther north and already be inside, close by.

Charlie realized he was breathing hard, despite being in pretty good shape. It would be the same, maybe more so, for Myers. Charlie crouched down low beside a cluster of sagebrush and listened. The helicopter was to the northwest, deploying a powerful searchlight and circling in the area of the cars, probably looking for him and Myers. Hopefully it would stay far enough away long enough for him to locate his target.

Then he saw headlights approaching on the highway from the direction of Los Lunas to the east. The absence of emergency lights or sirens, and its normal speed, suggested it was a civilian vehicle.

Whatever the situation, apparently the road hadn't been blocked yet—unless this vehicle had already passed the site or came from one of the homes or businesses this side of the barrier.

Charlie crouched low, watched, and continued to listen as the vehicle approached. Then he heard someone moving close by. Suddenly a figure rose up from the arroyo, on the opposite side. It was Myers, silhouetted in the oncoming lights. He'd been down in there, just below ground level, waiting. Now it was clear he intended to catch a ride, one way or the other.

Myers turned to look in his direction, and Charlie ducked down. Myers didn't react, instead turning back toward the oncoming headlights.

There was a twenty-foot gap between them, and Charlie's only hope of stopping the guy before he could interact with the approaching vehicle was convincing him to surrender, or shooting him.

Just as Charlie raised his Beretta, Myers turned his head and fired in his direction—a snap shot. Charlie ducked, shifted right, and then rose up to return fire. Myers jumped back down into the arroyo before Charlie could take the shot.

Instead of dropping down into the erosion channel and presenting an easy target at point-blank range, Charlie leaped out, trying to land against the far bank, hitting the vertical bank slightly above and behind where he calculated Myers must be crouched, pistol aimed up. He might even land on the guy.

Instead, Charlie crashed onto a pile of windblown tumbleweeds, losing his pistol in the process. Trying to ignore the scratches on his hands and neck, he turned anxiously, trying to locate the man. Luckily, Myers had disappeared.

Charlie found his weapon quickly, then lunged to his feet off the dried, scratchy weeds. To his left was a culvert running beneath the road. That was where Myers must have gone.

He ducked down, feeling with his fingers as he pointed the barrel at the ground, trying to make sure his weapon was free of debris. At the same time, he took a quick look inside the four-foot-high concrete pipe. He jumped back, seeing movement inside. Two bullets whizzed by him, accompanied by loud booms amplified by the enclosure.

Better you than me, Charlie thought, knowing that the sound created by firing from an enclosure was deafening, even with the smaller-caliber weapon Myers was carrying.

Charlie fired one round in return, without a target but knowing from the angle that a ricochet was certain. He might get lucky, and unless Myers had a spare clip for that .380 or .32 backup gun, he was almost out of ammo, having expended six out of a potential seven-to-ten-round magazine. Charlie's old Beretta 92 predated 1994 and was serviced by a prerestriction fifteen-round mag.

Whatever the case, he also knew that it only took one well-aimed or lucky shot.

Charlie heard running footsteps, and then the sound changed from hard to soft. He probably hadn't hit the man, but the shot had driven Myers out of the culvert. He was in the sandy bottom of the arroyo, running south.

Charlie gave chase, running through the low concrete tunnel in an awkward duck walk while trying to look ahead. Once there was a quick way to climb out of the arroyo, Myers might go for it, and he couldn't risk losing him again. Fortunately, the oversized tracks on the sandy bottom were dead giveaways, and running in dry, loose sand was exhausting. Charlie would be able to run the man down as long as he stayed in the arroyo, but he had to close in and wait for his shot.

Somewhere behind him, along the highway, Charlie heard shouts of police officers yelling back and forth, then saw a spotlight beam probing in his direction, the bright rays flashing on either side of the arroyo. The car Myers had hoped to carjack was apparently an unmarked police car. That could have been interesting if the fugitive had run up to a window waving his gun. There was the wail of sirens now, and the slap of helicopter rotors closing in but still some distance away.

Trusting, hoping, that DuPree or Nancy had already communicated the news that he was pursuing Myers and was not the target, Charlie kept after his prey. The arroyo was widening, and the walls lowering, which was natural, considering the fact that it was downslope at this location and the terrain was nearly flat. He caught a glimpse of the running man less than fifty feet ahead, and it looked like Myers was staggering from exhaustion. The man stopped, turned, and saw him.

Charlie zigzagged right to left, then back just as Myers took a shot. The bullet went by so close he felt a tug on his shirt. Charlie hated to shoot on the run but returned fire with two more rounds. Myers flinched, dropped his pistol, then groped for something in his pocket. Charlie closed in, his pistol directed at the center body mass. Myers brought out a pocketknife, saw the pistol directed at his chest, and let the knife fall to the ground. He slowly raised his hands into the air. "Don't shoot," he gasped, his chest heaving, "I'm hit."

Charlie remained still, his pistol aimed at Myers's torso, and saw blood near the man's left kidney. "Face down on the ground, arms out, away from your sides," he yelled. He stepped closer, slowly, then stopped as Myers complied, groaning in agony.

He could hear running footsteps behind him, closing in. The helicopter flashed by overhead.

"I'm Charlie Henry, a civilian traveling with Detective DuPree and Sergeant Medina," he yelled, hoping to be heard over the sound of the aircraft. "The shooter is wounded, on the ground, and under my control. I am armed. Approach slowly, then please take over the scene."

After all the crap that had gone down today, he didn't want to be shot by some nervous volunteer deputy.

Charlie caught a ride at the highway with a newly arrived Valencia County deputy five minutes later, and not long afterward he stepped out of the unit into the midst of law enforcement vehicles from at least three jurisdictions, including the state police. He spotted Nancy sitting on the tailgate of a Los Lunas police pickup truck, talking with Gordon. The EMTs had already checked her out and were moving to treat Myers, who'd received first aid at the highway and was being guarded by at least three officers.

After filling them in on what happened with Myers, Charlie had some questions of his own for Gordon. "I heard that you and DuPree had no problem dealing with the Geigers. Tell me how it went down."

"Crushed it. Frank had a hard time keeping quiet with that bad leg of his, and we got the drop on him while he was following our tracks in the dark. Dumb-ass then tried to run. DuPree shouted and fired a warning shot. The guy tripped trying to dodge a bullet that was going into the air, and took a face plant, dropping his shotgun. DuPree cuffed him, and then we heard the gunshot coming from your direction. DuPree said to check it out. I found

Nancy, aching and pissed, still watching the vehicles. By then, you were tracking Myers, I guess."

Charlie nodded. "Ray was the one driving the pickup, right?"

"Yeah, and he didn't do jack. When Nancy and I ventured over to join DuPree and his prisoner, Ray was sitting on the ground, his hands zip-tied behind his back. He'd surrendered to DuPree, who'd come to put Frank in the squad car and found Ray standing there, wanting to surrender. The guy was unarmed. His pistol was still in the pickup—unloaded."

There was a lot of activity still going on around them, and Charlie watched as Frank Geiger was transferred from Nancy's unit into a state police car, joined by DuPree. The detective waved to them before climbing in the front passenger side. He'd already told Nancy he was going to accompany two officers and their prisoner back to APD headquarters. Ray, guarded by another officer, was quickly loaded into the backseat of Nancy's cruiser.

"DuPree wants to keep the Geigers apart," Nancy said, standing. "You two ready to roll? We're going to be busy with interviews and paperwork for hours, so we might as well head back to APD downtown and get started."

Before long, they were heading east toward Los Lunas and the I-25 ramp that would take them back to Albuquerque. Nancy was driving, and Charlie was seated beside her, up front, holding on to Gordon's weapon as well as his own. Gordon was in the backseat next to Ray, who was handcuffed, his hands on his lap.

They'd been en route for only a few minutes before Ray spoke. "Take me to the district attorney, or whoever I need to meet to make a deal. All this kidnapping crap and the rest was my dad's idea. I need to get away from him. He's trashing what's left of my life."

"You've already been read your rights, Ray," Nancy reminded. "You can talk all you want."

"But you'll let them know I want to cut a deal, right?"

"Of course. But you'll also want to tell your attorney."

"Screw that cockroach. Dad hired him, not me. Give me a public defender, anyone else," Ray added.

"I'll pass that along," Nancy replied, looking over at Charlie, eyebrows raised.

"So then, let me get this out of my system before my pop gets the chance to screw things up," Ray added. "Ask me anything you want, and I'll answer as truthfully as I can."

"Okay, Ray. First, tonight. The ankle bracelet was found in your gym bag in the back of the pickup," Nancy pointed out, glancing at him in the rearview mirror. "It was still active even after you cut it off. Did you know we were still tracking you? It uses a satellite link-up; there's no range limit."

"That's what I was hoping. I'd cut it off my ankle but brought it along in my gym bag. Dad didn't know. He thought it was just a change of clothes in there. This was the only way I could make sure you'd be following us," Ray confessed.

"You wanted to get caught?" Charlie asked.

"Hey, I had to do something to get my life back. I never really hurt anyone, except for that woman, and that was by accident, a lucky shot. Unlucky, actually. All I wanted to do was scare her back into the house. Dad has the bad leg, so he told me to hire BJ and Tony to rob the place and help me grab Sam Randal. His real name is Bill Woods. Dad said the guy ripped him off years ago when Dad was still a cop. Then, after Tony got himself killed, BJ freaked out, screaming about getting his revenge on Charlie."

"By then, you'd been arrested and had that ankle monitor," DuPree said. "But then what happened?"

Ray continued. "Dad used a burner phone to communicate back and forth. He kept them amped up, hoping they'd take care of Charlie 'cause he could ID me. He also called up Myers, some gangster he'd met back in Jersey when he was still with the NYPD. When we moved out west, I thought we were done with all that. I worked to get my shit together, but not Dad. Turns out the reason he brought us to New Mexico was to track down Woods. He guessed that Woods had come here after digging through the guy's trash and finding a tourist flyer for Albuquerque. It was a long shot, but Dad never let go of anyone. Ever since I could walk, he's been on my back, dogging me about something, always calling me a loser. I'm not about to go down with them. I'll testify for the state if I can cut a deal."

"Frank discovered that Sam Randal was really Bill Woods after they ran Sam's photo in the local paper, right?" Nancy asked.

"Yeah. Then Dad used his contacts on the Rio Rancho police force to find out where Sam lived. Once he had that address, he pressured me into making the kidnapping look like a home invasion," Ray responded. "Dad said that once we had Sam, his wife would have to pay us off to get him back, and no cops would ever know. Sam couldn't rat us out without being arrested."

"Myers was paid to shoot up that crane?" Charlie asked.

"Yeah, to scare Randal so he'd hand over some of the money. Sam knew Dad was behind all this. Then, after BJ ended up getting killed in that drive-by at your house, Dad decided to take the wife. He paid Myers all the money we had left to grab Randal's old lady. You know the rest," Ray concluded.

"Who dumped BJ's body behind our pawnshop?" Gordon asked.

"Myers, I think. He was with him when they shot up your house. I couldn't take part because of the ankle bracelet—thank God for that," Ray answered.

The questions and answers continued for the remaining half hour it took to return to APD headquarters. Once there, Charlie and Gordon were escorted to Detective DuPree's desk and told to wait. DuPree and Nancy still had procedures to follow before they could get together again for more interviews and paperwork.

Tired and dusty, Charlie and Gordon sat in chairs silently for a while, picking stickers and plant debris out of their socks, pants, and, for Charlie, sleeves and shirt collar.

"Looks like you've gone organic, Charlie. What'd you do, roll among the native plants to cover your scent?" Gordon teased.

"Just the tumbleweeds, and not exactly on purpose. Right now, I need a fifteen-minute shower just to get rid of the stickers and pollen," Charlie said, knowing that brushing off the little spines was hopeless. They would have to be picked out one at a time.

They sat there a little longer before Gordon spoke again. "I heard from DuPree that Sam, well, Bill Woods is upstairs in a cell. The department is awaiting the arrival of some Feds from back east."

"Sam played us all, including Margaret, I guess, if you can believe her."

"I don't think she knew, not until yesterday. They were actually in love, Charlie, and he wanted the protection for her, not him. As it turns out, the company is in her name. Sam insisted that Margaret didn't know about that either. Maybe it was done to protect the assets and her financial situation if the Feds ever caught up to him. Wonder what she's going to do now?"

"You mean, will she stick with him?"

"Yeah. What would you do?" Gordon pressed, "If your wife turned out to be an imposter—and a criminal."

"May I never have to answer that question, Gordo." Charlie shrugged. "Knowing you'd been betrayed, at one level, would certainly generate other questions that you might not like answered. One thing for sure, she'd have to be worth the risk."

"I hear you."

Charlie heard footsteps, then saw DuPree and Nancy entering the squad room. Both looked exhausted, but he knew they'd probably all be there until daylight—at least.

It didn't take that long, as it turned out. After learning that Margaret was spending the night at Gina's, Gordon was able to get his pickup from APD impound. Instead of driving Charlie all the way to his motel room in Bernalillo, they went to Gordon's place, not far from FOB Pawn, and Charlie crashed on his friend's couch. He was asleep in minutes.

Charlie was geared up, taking part in a dawn recon on the same street where his company had come under heavy mortar fire three days ago. The Taliban had either fled the village or repositioned for another attack, but today's mission was to provoke them into giving away their positions—if any remained in the area. "Live bait," Gordon called it.

There was trash, rubble, and debris on the streets, and the ever-present dust, mingling with foul odors. The most offensive scents came from those who'd been killed recently, mostly Afghani civilians who'd been in their homes or had carelessly stepped outside to watch the Americans pass through one last time. Some of the dead had been left in place despite religious and cultural beliefs because it was still too dangerous to dig for those who were beyond help with the area still under enemy observation.

The mortar rounds hadn't discriminated between women and children and the older men. As for the younger males, they were armed, dangerous, and out there somewhere. Just whose side they were on wasn't clear, which made "trust" a flexible term around the Afghan military and their police.

He recognized the dwelling he was approaching, or what was left of it, but something in the remnants of the roof looked odd. If someone was hanging a butchered goat to cure in the sun, why put it there?

As he got closer he could see into the shadows and instantly knew what was dangling from the roof beam.

The woman's head was dotted with flies, but he recognized her face. She was the same teenage girl he thought he'd saved during the mortar attack by pulling her over the wall. Now she was dangling from a noose, lynched in the wreckage of what had been her home. He had to look away, bile forming in his throat.

"What's up?" Gordon called from behind. His buddy stood there, his M-4 aimed loosely toward the wrecked building. "Oh, shit!" Gordon mumbled. "Is that the . . ."

"Yeah. Remember how upset the old men were that I'd pulled her over the wall, seen her face uncovered? You don't suppose . . ."

"Hey, bro," Gordon responded. "It probably had nothing to do with you."

"Yeah. But let's cut her down anyway," Charlie mumbled, reaching for his knife. As he stepped through a gap in the crumbled wall, he *forced himself to take another look at the woman's face. It was now Margaret Randal.*

Charlie sat up, his heart pounding through his chest and sweat pouring off his brow. Gordon was standing in the doorway, watching him, and Charlie finally realized where and when he was.

"Easy, Charlie. Welcome back to reality. One of those dreams, huh?" Gordon asked softly.

"Sorry to wake you," Charlie replied, relieved that it was over for the moment, and that it hadn't been real, at least not the face at the end.

"Wanna talk about it?"

Charlie's head began to clear, and he thought about it for a while. "Yeah," he finally mumbled. "I think that's the only way to get my thinking straight again and lose this particular nightmare for good."

Charlie stood at the grill in Nancy and Gina's backyard, flipping the burgers as he recalled what had happened last time he'd been standing here. He looked over at the picnic table, where Nancy, Gina, Gordon, and Margaret were chatting as they piled red onions, sliced tomatoes, and Hatch green chiles on the oversized homemade buns.

The conversation was light, he noticed, concerning the possibility of rain, the heat from the supposedly mild chiles, and the benefits of lemon slices in the iced tea. Anything but what had happened over the past two weeks. It was Sunday, the day of rest, but there was a big elephant on the patio, and he wondered when someone would bring up the subject of Sam . . . Bill. Charlie was betting it would be Gordon.

"Stand by for a platter full of burgers, cooked to perfection by the Beef Master," Charlie announced, placing the last of the batch atop the Santa Fe–style stoneware.

"Shouldn't that be Chuck?" Nancy teased, taking the heavy plate with two hands and setting it in the center of the checkered tablecloth. "That's a beefy term."

"You still hate being called Chuck?" Gina asked him, a grin on her face. "You did back in high school. You'd only answer to Charles or Charlie."

"He was called Chuckie by some of the guys in our platoon during our first deployment," Gordon offered. "Like the big doll with the bigger knife in those movies."

Charlie laughed. "Better than Chuckles the Clown. Or Upchuck."

"He got airsick the first time we were in a helicopter," Gordon explained. "We're about to eat, so I'll skip the details."

Margaret laughed for the first time today, spearing a hamburger with a fork and placing it atop a bun slathered with mustard. "Thanks for small favors, Gordon."

She took a long sip of iced tea, then clinked the glass with her spoon to get their attention again. "I appreciate the invitation today, and the friendship you've all shown, even before our rescue, what, two Sundays ago? You all put your lives on the line for my husband and me more than once, and you looked over us like we were your children.

"Now it's time for me to be up front with you," Margaret added. "I hope I haven't lost your trust in me, and I'm guessing you're curious to know what I'm going to do now. Especially when you're my attorney." She nodded toward Gina.

Charlie looked at Gina, who shrugged.

"Sam—well, I suppose I need to start calling him Bill—is going to be in the hands of federal and Connecticut authorities for several days at least, probably more, as the investigation into his past crimes is completed. He's answering all their questions and describing his previous activities in detail. He told me, during our only telephone conversation—they wouldn't let me be there in person—that he never stole any funds from investors he thought to be honest."

"Wouldn't that be hard to know?" Gordon asked.

"He admitted that. But with people like Frank Geiger, who had much more cash coming in than their salary provided, he had an idea it was illegally obtained. Those individuals apparently gave themselves away by requiring secrecy, overseas accounts, fake names, and such," Margaret explained.

"So he can identify several of the criminals he worked with," Nancy said. "That suggests that he has even more enemies who might be interested in finding him."

Margaret nodded. "I'm worried about his safety, of course. He's been assigned a security detail and isn't being kept in a local jail. Some military brig, so I gather, but that location hasn't been given out, not even to me."

"Hopefully he'll be able to cut a deal, identifying those criminals in exchange for reduced charges," Gina said.

"He mentioned that possibility to me," Margaret replied. "I'll just have to wait and see how it turns out."

She stopped, looked down at her plate, then took a bite of hamburger.

They all started to eat, not speaking for a while, passing around the big bowl of potato salad and buttered corn on the cob.

"Okay, I've waited long enough. What *are* your plans, Margaret?" Gordon asked.

"I'm not legally married, am I?" Margaret asked Gina.

"That's what I'm trying to sort out. With so much business conducted with the Randal name, it's taking time to determine who owns what," Gina replied.

"Okay, so it's sufficiently vague at the moment," Margaret said. "Gordon, I'm going to arrange for Jeff Candelaria to take over day-to-day operations unless a court order comes in to shut down the company. As for me, I'm still trying to decide what to do with my life. I love Sam—sorry, Bill—but I'm not sure who he really is, and what is true about him anymore."

"He loves you, *that's* the truth," Nancy suggested.

"Yeah, and that's what sucks. If I didn't love him back, I'd just walk away and start all over," Margaret managed, tears in her eyes.

"But you're going to try to work things out," Charlie concluded, thinking of his sister, Jayne, who had a boyfriend she was still trying to save from himself.

Margaret nodded. "You're exactly right. Now let's eat, people, before these wonderful burgers get cold."